2ND GEN

Andrea and William Vaughan

This is a work of fiction. Names, characters, places, and incidents either are the product of the authors' imagination or are used fictitiously. Any resemblance to actual persons, living or dead, events, or locales is entirely coincidental.

Published by:
Hickory Nut Publishing
Clermont, FL

ISBN: 978-0-69209-369-6

Cover design by William Vaughan

Cover Illustration by Fred Gambino | fredgambino.co.uk

Title Logotype Design by Aaron Belyea | alphabetarm.com

Interior Illustrations by Eric Geusz | ericgeusz.com

Book design and production by Gary A. Rosenberg | thebookcouple.com

Editing by Carol Killman Rosenberg | carolkillmanrosenberg.com

The ultimate test of man's conscience may be his willingness to sacrifice something today for future generations whose words of thanks will not be heard.

—Gaylord Nelson

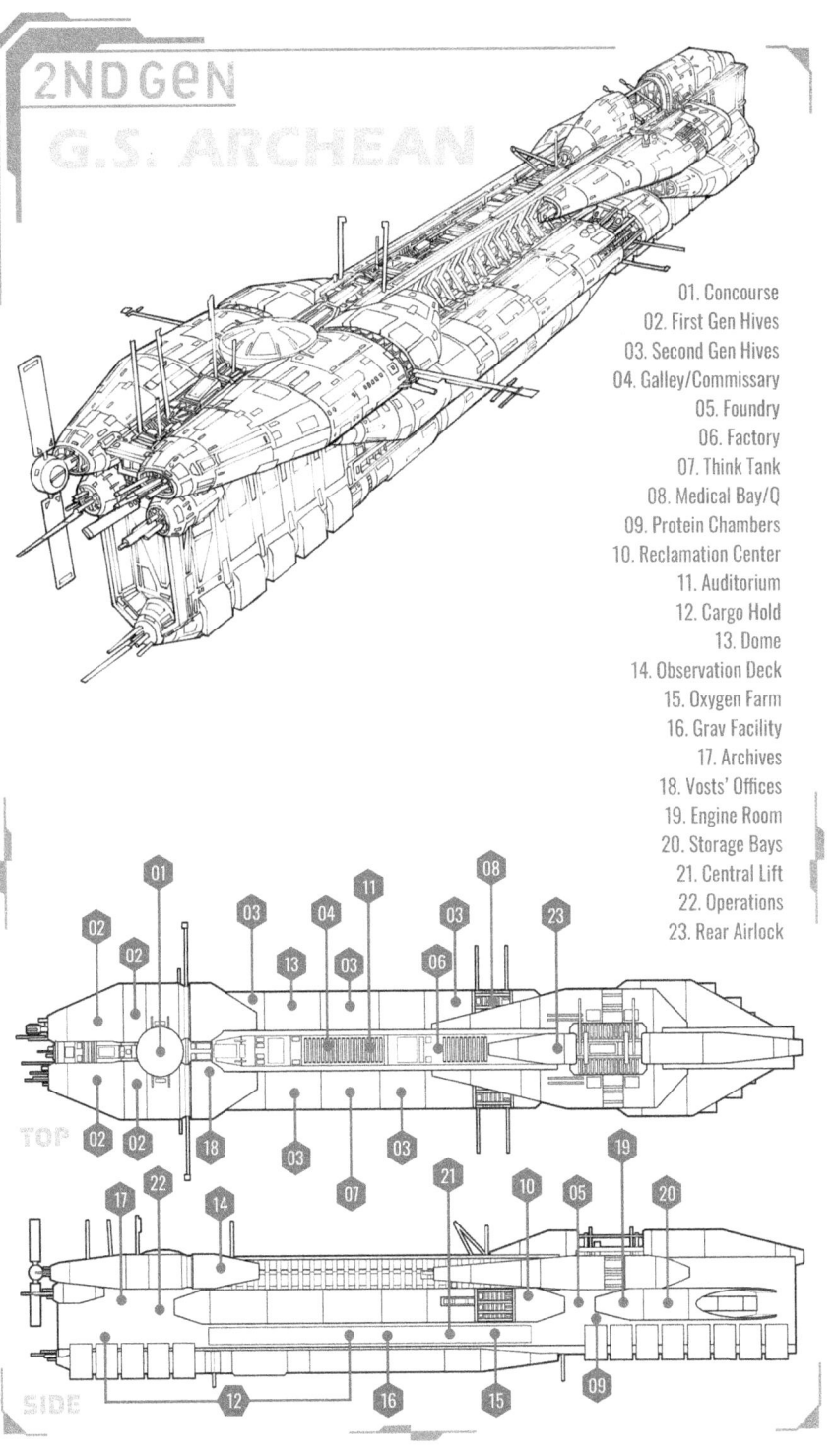

2NDGEN
G.S. ARCHEAN

01. Concourse
02. First Gen Hives
03. Second Gen Hives
04. Galley/Commissary
05. Foundry
06. Factory
07. Think Tank
08. Medical Bay/Q
09. Protein Chambers
10. Reclamation Center
11. Auditorium
12. Cargo Hold
13. Dome
14. Observation Deck
15. Oxygen Farm
16. Grav Facility
17. Archives
18. Vosts' Offices
19. Engine Room
20. Storage Bays
21. Central Lift
22. Operations
23. Rear Airlock

TOP

SIDE

STAGE ONE

CHAPTER 01

"There's got to be a place to hide!"

The spinning red lights bounced off the cold, gray metallic skin of the exposed pipes and framework of the corridor. The deafening wail of the sirens drowned out the loud bursts of steam from the pipes that ran the length of the ceiling. At the far end of the corridor, Fisher clumsily skidded around the corner, slamming into his thin shadow on the wall. He dashed through every narrow hallway, searching right and left for an open door—any open door. Sweating and breathless, he spied the storage room to his left and let out a sigh of relief. He pushed on the entry plate. Nothing.

Relief was quickly replaced with dread. He hammered the entry plate with his fist, praying the door would open. In the middle of his fifth strike, he froze. Silence. No red lights. No blaring sirens. Dead silence. Game over.

You gotta be kidding me. Years of Grayson forgetting to lock up, and today he remembers?!

The knot in Fisher's stomach tightened as he realized his time had run out. A wave of defeat and self-pity washed over him as he slumped heavily to the grated floor.

Down the corridor, Fisher heard muffled voices, and the sound of distant footsteps grew increasingly closer.

A faint rattling across the corridor drew Fisher's attention. There, the exhaust through a vent caused the metal frame to rhythmically tap against the wall, loosening one of the latches.

Instinctively, Fisher dove across the corridor and grabbed the secure latch, attempting to open the vent. His sweaty hands made it difficult to get a good grip, but he finally managed to slide the latch up and quietly lower the vent to the floor.

Easing his way into the enclosed air shaft, Fisher quickly wiggled his thin frame into the damp space. He pulled the vent behind him and attempted to secure the latch from the inside. What was he thinking? There were no latches on the inside of the vent. How was he going to secure it back in place? The footsteps grew louder, and he knew he had little time to waste figuring this out.

Using his fingertips, he gripped the steel slats in the vent, willing himself to hold it in place. Sweat from his palms now dripped everywhere, and he frantically wiped his left hand on one of the legs of his gray coveralls, holding tight to the vent with his right. He quickly switched and relieved the sweat from his right hand. The pounding footsteps sounded as though they were just outside the vent. He closed his eyes and tried to quiet his racing heartbeat, waiting for the inevitable. Surely they had seen him enter, or at the very least heard him climb into the shaft. He didn't want to hide in here, but his time had run out. He had no other options.

To his surprise and intense relief, the footsteps ran right past him and made their way down the corridor. Fisher's shoulders relaxed, and he loosened his grip on the vent just slightly. An itch on his nose drew his right hand toward it, and the fingertips of his left hand suddenly lost hold. He watched in horror as the vent fell forward.

A corner of the vent bounced angrily on the grated floor. Then each vent corner took turns clanging against the floor and wall. Fisher squeezed his eyes shut, hoping that by blinding himself, his chasers would somehow magically be too far in the distance to hear that clatter.

Those faint, running footsteps squealed to a stop and promptly reversed direction. Fisher heard one set of the steps charging closer to him, while a second, heavier set fell behind.

Maybe they didn't hear it. Maybe they just want to check out a different side of the ship.

Who was he kidding? He knew he was busted. He just wanted to keep his eyes closed a few final moments and pretend he was safe.

When he heard the second set of footsteps catch up to the first, Fisher knew he had to peer out of the vent. Two voices whispered, and the feet were walking slowly now. Fisher saw shadows inch closer to the mouth of the air shaft. He briefly looked up and then hung his head in defeat.

"Really, Fish?" teased Helena. A glint of excitement danced in her eyes.

"Yeah, really, Fish?" repeated Echo.

"Come on, Fish," Helena instructed, "I'm going for a record today. Let's go find the others."

Fisher stuck one long leg out of the shaft, unfolding himself to his full height. Echo smirked at him.

"Ghosts in the Graveyard! Second ghost found!" Helena bellowed with pride, starting down the corridor. "We're coming for you, ghosts! It won't be long 'til you're all mine!"

CHAPTER 02

"You should have seen the look on his face," joked Helena, looking up from her journal, which she had been writing in. "Fish looked shocked that we found him in Grayson's favorite hiding spot."

"Seriously, Fish?" asked Echo with a chuckle before he broke off a piece of his protein bar and popped it in his mouth.

"What? It's a great spot!" Fisher argued.

Fisher, Helena, and Echo had joined a few of the other members of Hive 3 sitting around one of the prep tables in the spacious galley. They liked to meet here following Ghosts in the Graveyard to have a late meal now that Dom had been assigned to food prep. Everyone else ate their meals out in the commissary, but this group had been joining Dom back in the galley for "gang preservation," as Helena would call it.

The spacious room provided them a private area to hang out and allowed Dom to join them. Most of the lights in the galley were disabled when the group would meet in the afternoon except the back corner where Dom was assigned to work. This area was well lit with overhead lights that illuminated a series of metal tables used for prepping the meals, as well as a cluster of food printers lining the wall closest to the prep table the crew gathered around. These printers produced most of the handheld items that made up the crew's diet and was Dom's focus when working in the galley.

Although the printers could produce a wide variety of types of food ranging from bagels to bacon, Dom and his friends were usually satisfied with protein bars. Their parents said the bars were similar in taste to candy bars back on Earth but with the nutritional value of a full meal. Dom happily made protein bars, as they required little to no prep work and even less time with clean up.

"It's a great spot a couple of times, dude. Four times makes it a superior bonehead choice," taunted Zach, as he brushed a few crumbs off the sleeve of his coveralls.

"Four times?" asked Avery, amusement flickering in her brown eyes. "How exactly can you forget that Grayson has hidden in there multiple times?"

"How am I supposed to keep track of everyone's past hiding spots?" asked Fisher.

"Did you actually forget, or were you just hoping Sam would be in there waiting for you?" joked Grayson.

"Screw you, Grayson," huffed Fisher, tossing a nugget at Grayson's head.

Grayson laughed. "Not my type, dude, sorry to break your heart." He grabbed the nugget midair and chucked it back at Fisher.

"Shut up, Grayson!" scoffed Sam.

"Guys, seriously, enough with the alarms!" whined Dom. "I don't know why our parents even let you guys continue to use them every game." He wiped his hands on the white apron protecting his coveralls from the protein paste. "It's bad enough I'm stuck in here making all of you your meals." He gestured to one of the food printers that was finishing a batch of protein bars. "I don't even get the chance to hide in the same spot four times."

Fisher looked at Dom and laughed. Dom was likeable, even though he seemed to have a new complaint every day. He was assigned to agriculture and food prep and was stuck in either the galley or the protein chamber raking the three large pools most of the time. Dom often reminded the others that unlike their assignments, food prep didn't offer the same downtime. Most people found it hard to find fault with Dom, but sometimes it was tough to tell if they liked him or felt sorry for him. If something were to go wrong, it would go wrong for Dom. If bad luck were a personality, Dom would own it.

Fisher had always thought Dom's appearance didn't quite match his personality. Dom was a rather short, muscular nineteen-year-old, just a few months younger than Fisher, with short dirty blond hair and a quick smile. He looked as though he should have a tough-guy attitude, but instead, Dom had a tendency to defer to others. Fisher realized one of his favorite things about Dom was his ability to turn a bad day around by discussing bodily functions at just the right moment. His heart was kind, his words were honest, and his mind was dirty.

Helena inhaled slowly, got up from the table, and walked over to the counter next to Dom, putting a sympathetic arm around his shoulder. Fisher caught Sam's eyes following Helena's movements closely. When Sam noticed Fisher looking her way, her eyes darted toward the floor and a blush spread across her cheeks.

"You're right, Dom," Helena said softly. "It's not fair that you have to work all the time."

"Dom, why can't you remember this?" huffed Zach. "Let me

break it down for you one more time. Alarms sound, we run and hide. Alarms stop, it's go time. It's really very simple. Without those alarms stopping, we have no idea when the ghost hunter starts the chase. Now that all the Arc is fair game, we can't just yell, 'Ready or not, here I come!' Besides, we're not five anymore. And I'm sorry, but it's not our fault that your OCP was food prep."

"Ahem, my occupational career pathway is agriculture and food preparation, Zachary," clarified Dom, mimicking his parents in a way that made even Zach smile.

"Don't listen to him, Dom," Helena gently intoned, returning to the table. Everyone knew Dom hated being shortchanged out of as much credit as he deserved.

Fisher was always impressed with Helena's ability to show compassion to just about anybody. He remembered the time they had all been studying for their assessment exam. Everybody had been exhausted from staying up most of the night cramming. They'd all known just how much would be riding on the outcome of the test. The morning of the exam, Avery had shown up bleary-eyed and disheveled. She started to melt down as their teacher walked toward her, about to hand her the exam questions. Helena leaned over and whispered into Avery's ear. Avery's anxiety seemed to melt away, and a relieved little smile appeared on her face. Helena glanced at Fisher, gave a quick wink, and started her exam.

Fisher was also amazed at how grounded Helena remained. Not only was she the reigning Ghosts in the Graveyard champion, but she also happened to be the subject of all the guys'—and at least one of the girls'—first crushes. Some girls on the Arc would haughtily flaunt their assets in front of every guy down every corridor. Not Helena; she seemed oblivious to all the crushes directed her way. It was as if she were this walking mirror, reflecting the good qualities of other people right back at them.

She could always manage to put a positive spin on any situation that was posed to her, too. She was a good fit for the medical bay. Helena could lift someone out of the depths of depression with a kind smile and simple phrase or story. The others gravitated to her in both times of stress and celebration. And although she would sometimes boast about her countless Graveyard victories, everyone knew she was humble to her core and would relinquish her victor status in a heartbeat if it meant more to someone else.

Dom glared at Zach for a moment and then eyed everyone at the table.

"Guys, this is a kids' game. It's dumb. Aren't you slightly embarrassed to be playing it after all this time?"

"What do you know? You haven't joined in since your OCP draft," asserted Sam. "You're just jealous that you can't play anymore."

Fisher grinned as Sam called Dom out in classic Sam-style. This was just another reason why Sam was Fisher's best friend; if people needed honest feedback, they went to Sam.

Sam was considered one of the guys. Unlike the rest of the crew, she wore the top part of her coveralls hanging down with the sleeves tied around her waist, revealing a white T-shirt that she personalized with a hand-drawn pi symbol. Against her mother's constant pleading, Sam wore her black hair short like Dom's, but her long bangs swooped over to one side, covering her left eye. Despite her I-don't-give-a-shit look, she was the brightest of the second generation on the ship. From an early age, Sam often helped the first gen with some of their more vexing mathematical problems. She was well suited for the think tank and loved working alongside Echo's mom.

"All I know is that it's a dumb, useless game that ends the minute someone gets found," said Dom. "Oh, sign me up for that, please! Yeah, I want to melt my ass off in a nasty, old ventilation shaft. And seriously, guys, the Arc isn't that big. Haven't you run out of hiding spots after all these years?"

With that, Dom nodded, appearing as though he knew it was one of his better arguments in the past few months. He turned back toward the protein printer before he could be interrupted by more talk of what he obviously considered a stupid game. He removed the finished bars from the printer bed, tossed one to Sam, and placed the others on a serving tray.

Everyone at the table exchanged looks and laughed. Same old dance with Dom. They would finish a Graveyard game, come back to talk about it, and Dom would protest the ridiculousness of the charade. Now that he never had time to play, the whole thing just seemed pointless to him.

"Come on Dom, You know that's not how the game is played," Zach said with a smile.

"Actually, Dom is sort of right. We're not even playing it correctly."

Everyone's eyes turned to Fisher.

"What are you talking about, Fish?" blurted Grayson.

"Fish, you've been playing Graveyard for what, twelve years now, and you still don't got it right?" exclaimed Avery. "No wonder you get caught every time."

"Seriously, the original game includes only one ghost hiding, and once the ghost is found, everyone runs back to home base."

"Get outta here," said Avery.

Helena put her hands on the table. "No way!"

"Fish, if what you say is true, how could we be playing it wrong the whole time?" asked Sam.

"Dunno," answered Fisher, pulling on his left earlobe. "I guess rules just got lost in translation over the years, and we didn't know any better. We just trusted that we were playing the right way or the right version of the game."

A huge grin spread across Dom's face. "So, let me get this straight. You bozos have been running around like rug rats all these years, and you're playing it wrong? That's awesome!"

"Dude, why didn't you tell us this sooner?" asked Grayson.

Fisher paused to consider the question. Why hadn't he shared this tidbit with the group? He couldn't even recall when he first learned about the discrepancy in the rules. All he knew was that one day, he'd learned that there was an original Ghosts in the Graveyard that looked different from how they played it, and it just fell off his radar of importance. Really, what difference did it make?

"Yeah, Fish, why would you keep something like this to yourself? You think we can't handle the truth?" asked Helena playfully.

"No, it's not that. I don't know why I never said anything. Hell, I can't even remember how I found out about the real rules. Sorry, guys. I wasn't trying to keep anything from you. It just didn't seem important."

"So, we should stop playing then," said Alec sharply.

Fisher spun around and gave Alec an incredulous look. Alec would often spout theories and ideas that were vastly different from the others, but Graveyard was one of this group's sole staples of entertainment.

"What are you talking about?" asked Avery. "Why stop playing?"

"What's the point in playing something wrong?" scoffed Alec. "All this time, and we never even played it right. What does that say about us? Dom's right. We're just a bunch of kids who can't even play a game right."

Dom grinned and poured liquid protein into one of the printer's reservoir.

Fisher paused for a moment. To be fair, Alec's concern had actually been simmering in Fisher's thoughts for a while now. He admittedly felt a bit silly playing a hide-and-seek game at this age. Even the other second generation hives had stopped playing years ago. He could name about six other games for them all to play right now, such as chess or the various card games their parents played. The simple fact was he kept playing Graveyard for two reasons: Helena and Echo.

Helena was the clear champion and mastermind of Graveyard. Consistently the last "ghost" to be found, this title had almost become a part of Helena's identity. She was always so generous in lifting up everyone else, and Fisher just enjoyed seeing her beam with pride in each victory. He couldn't bear to take that away from her.

Echo was a different story completely. Poor Echo. As his earned nickname indicated, he hadn't quite found his stride in life. The only championship Echo could win would possibly be the Arc's Greatest Follower. He followed people, ideas, words, and orders. He had so little self-confidence that he acted like Helena's shadow each time she was chosen to be ghost hunter. Fisher felt bad for the guy, and he knew that Echo's one sense of community and belonging occurred during the game. Fisher couldn't bear to take that away from him, either.

"You guys would actually stop playing Graveyard just because of some technicality?" challenged Fisher. "Come on, who cares? It's the only thing we have on the ship to blow off some steam. Pretty soon you know we're not going to have time for this anyway, right? Let it go. This is what we do. It's who we are."

Everyone's attention was suddenly drawn to the other side of the room as the door to the commissary swung open.

"Hey, Lance!" greeted Dom with a cheerful motion for him to join the others.

"You ladies still going on about your kiddie game again?" crowed Lance approaching the table.

"We were waiting until the *queen* herself graced us with her uplifting presence," countered Sam, stabbing the tall, handsome boy with an icy glare.

"Don't you have some equations you need to solve?" Lance snapped.

Sam rolled her eyes as she bit off the end of her protein bar.

Fisher sank down in his chair a bit, and his mood sank right along with his posture. It seemed like every time they were enjoying themselves, Lance came along and ruined it. It's not like they had fun that often, either. Once a month, they would run around the Arc in a frenzy, forgetting the stresses and realities of their trapped lives. Since the parents had determined Graveyard to be a somewhat disruptive game taking place throughout the ship, they limited it to a monthly activity. Part of the tradition included gathering around the galley afterward and laughing at each other, pointing out why one person's hiding place was worse than the next. And each time, Lance would saunter in and manage to flatten the rare, joyful mood of the entire room in an instant.

Fisher could never understand what Lance's problem was. He had it made—the job, the girl, the looks. What more did he want? Nearly twenty-two years old, Lance was the firstborn male on the ship, a title of which he proudly reminded the others on a regular basis. Tall and strong, Lance walked with an air of bravado that lingered even after he left the room. The hottest girl on the ship was clearly smitten with him, and he also derived great satisfaction alerting the others of the "Helena effect" he exuded. His OCP was outrigger, a member of the crew responsible for maintaining the ship's mechanical external functions. This important position inflated Lance's already swollen ego to a height Fisher dreamed of deflating.

The only thing that kept Lance's feet on the ground was the shock that his father had chosen Fisher over him to work in the foundry on the geodetic rings. Lance had erroneously assumed that working with his dad was a done deal. He'd bragged about his assumed future OCP since age four. Lance and Fisher had been pretty tight friends growing up, but the moment Lance's dad recommended that Fisher be assigned to the foundry, an irreparable rift was born between the two young men.

Lance turned to Helena and snatched the pen from her hand. The move caught her by surprise, as she was recording the latest Graveyard events in her journal.

"Hey, gorgeous," Lance said, "you documenting your mad hiding skills?"

"Babe, I told you that this month was my turn as ghost hunter. I was the final ghost in the last game as usual, so today I was the hunter. Honestly, you're worse than Dom sometimes. Why don't you play with us next time? Just once? You'll remember that it's still really fun. Or are you just afraid you wouldn't find me?" she added with a sly glance.

"Why don't we just go back to my pod and play a different kind of hide and seek?"

"*Niiiice,*" said Dom, a giant smile plastered to his face.

Sam's disgusted grunt was audible, and Fisher poked her in the ribs.

Helena giggled and grabbed her pen back from Lance.

"You, Lance, are a hopeless case."

"I second that," chimed Zach.

"Third," said Echo.

Lance glanced around the table and said, "Honestly, guys, don't you have more pressing things you could be thinking about than ring-around-the-rosy? The Pairing is three months away, and the next ring deployment is less than two months from now. We have so much work waiting for us. What are you doing wasting all your time on this stupid game?"

The *Pairing Ceremony.* Every time the event was mentioned, spirits sank.

"Anyone up for a round of First Things?" Sam asked, changing the subject.

Fisher knew this subject was a major sore spot for his friend.

"I don't know why you guys always play this," moaned Lance. "I am going to do exactly what I said I'm going to do when we get to Uelara the past one hundred times we've played this idiotic game."

"First thing I'm doing is peeing on a tree!" declared Dom.

"Gross," said Avery.

"What? It's galactically understood that it's marking your territory!" Dom replied as he sat to join the others.

"And this is the guy who prepares our meals," snorted Sam.

"I'm running as fast as I can and diving straight into the ocean," dreamed Fisher.

"I'm rolling down a giant grassy hill," said Avery.

"We're going to be in our fifties, Avery. I don't think hill-rolling is going to be on the top of our list at that age," chimed in Zach.

"Speak for yourself. I'm going to be a young fifty," she proudly predicted.

"Ooh, I'm in," said Sam, as she clinked her cup with Avery's.

"I'm staring at the star so long that it burns my retinas," said Grayson.

"I'm walking ten miles anywhere without my boots on," said Zach.

"I'm walking eleven miles anywhere without my boots on," said Echo.

"What about you, Helena, any new firsts for you?" asked Sam.

Helena looked up from her journal, smiled softly, and said, "*Everything*. I'm going to do everything, all at once."

"I'm getting as far away from the Arc as possible and never looking back," mused Alec.

"I'm gonna be the first one to put down a flag," said Lance importantly.

Sam followed with, "You *always* say that. Why don't you want to do anything fun?"

"'Cause then everyone will know that I have singlehandedly saved the entire human race from extinction," he replied matter-of-factly.

"Oh, so we can all just kick back since *you* have everything covered, right?" joked Fisher. "I mean, between you and your dad, I'm sure you guys can handle the work of the one hundred–plus crew. Remind me again why they thought they needed so many people for this mission?"

"Come on," said Lance. "Everyone knows Captain Matsuo is going to hand over his role of captain to me and that my father and I are the critical players in this mission. None of this would be possible without us. So go back to your juvenile dreamland and chase games. That's more your speed anyway."

"Speaking of your dad," said Fisher, "he told me to let you know he can't tuck you in, so you're on your own tonight."

Everyone at the table laughed.

"Burn," whispered Zach.

Lance smirked, knocked Fisher's cup over, then tugged at Helena's ponytail, planting a sloppy kiss on her mouth. Helena wiped her mouth and gave Lance a light shove.

"Get out of here, you dork," she said, returning to her journal.

Giving Fisher one last glare over his shoulder, Lance made his exit.

Sam turned to Helena. "You know, as hard as I have tried, I have yet to find a glimmer of insight into what exactly you see in him."

"Have you seen his abs?" joked Avery.

"Now who's gross?" said Dom.

Helena continued writing in her journal without looking up.

"What could you possibly be writing in that thing?" asked Dom, leaning across the table and pretending to peek.

Helena placed her silver pen gently in the center of the journal, carefully closed the pages together, and looked up at Dom. "I told you, I am documenting our journey. At some point, there are going to be a heck of a lot of people interested in what life was like on the *Archean*. We are the only people in history to make this insane journey, and I want to record every moment, every decision that determines the future of humanity."

Dom pushed himself out of his chair and hopped up. With

a mischievous look, he took off in a run toward a clear counter. In a single motion, he deftly leaped into the air and landed both feet on top of the counter, arms outstretched like an announcer. "Dear Diary: Day twenty-seven. I woke up. I went to work. I ate. I went to bed. Day 162. I woke up. I went to work. I ate. I went to bed. Day 535. I woke up. I went to work. I ate. Wait for it . . . I went to bed."

Helena rolled her eyes at him, and Dom turned around, shaking his butt at his audience.

"Keep it to yourself, man," Alec told his younger brother, but with mock authority.

Squatting down, Dom launched off the counter into a back-flip, but landed too close to Grayson and fell in his lap.

"What the—" cried Grayson, as his chair slid backward with the force of Dom's flailing body.

Everyone roared with laughter. Helena tried to keep a stern face, but the corners of her mouth started to bend, and soon she was laughing along with the rest of them.

CHAPTER 03

People of the Earth,

Yet another game of Ghosts in the Graveyard has come to an end, and as predicted, I hit record timing finding all the ghosts. While the words in this entry could never truly describe Fish's expression when I discovered him today, I'll do my best.

I found Fish hiding in the same air shaft that Grayson hid in just two months ago. I don't think Fish has found an original hiding spot in about four years. When he looked up at me from the opening of the air shaft, he was covered in sweat and looked as if he were going to be ejected from an airlock. He always seems so nervous when we play, but boy, does he love this game.

I'm not quite sure why Fish gets so anxious playing Graveyard, but it really becomes an ordeal for him. He's always been a bit nervous, now that I think about it. Hmm, maybe not nervous as much as lacking confidence. I wish Fish could see himself the way I see him. He's a great guy, he really is. I actually had a bit of a crush on him when I was younger. He's just this sweet guy who wants to keep the peace most of the time. He's kind of cute, too, in this understated sort of way. He's got these warm, hazel eyes that light up when he laughs. But as I've grown older, I've started looking for different qualities in a man. More on that in a minute. Back to Graveyard talk.

I must admit that I'm feeling a bit mature to continue our old, classic childhood game. I mean, I'm twenty-two years old. When my mom was this age, she was preparing for space travel! I just don't think I could let Fish down. It seems like it's one of the only things that makes him smile, and he really believes it defines us. Maybe I should retire my crown soon and pass it on to someone else. Is it fair that I keep on robbing the others of the experience of being the last ghost found? I don't think I can give up my new hiding spot, though. It's too good! We'll see . . .

After recapping the highlights of the game, we played another round of "First Things." It's my favorite thing to do with the group, but I don't know how many more firsts I can come up with after so many years of playing. Dom continues to dream up new things to urinate on, Fish seems fixated on his beach scenarios, and Echo . . . well, Echo still hasn't come up with an original first.

It's strange that I have to continue explaining why I choose to write in this journal. Frankly, I'm not sure why the others aren't logging their escapades. What a precious relief this journal has been for me. So many pent-up concerns and emotions come pouring out of me with such ease. Could an inanimate object such as a journal be considered a friend? If so, then this journal certainly is a great one! It's always here for me, ready to lend an ear (or blank page, I should say), and I usually emerge as a calmer person once our "chat" is through.

I know I should probably maintain my entry writing within the space of my pod. However, I often become more inspired following lively interactions or evening walks throughout the Arc. The pods are simply not designed to be used for much more than sleeping. Sure, my pod is large enough for me to sit and write, but the confined space doesn't provide room for me to move around and allow my thoughts to flow. Of course, Lance would argue that the pods can sleep two comfortably, but the motivation behind this assertion is pretty obvious.

Although it's heavily frowned upon by the first gen, walking the corridors of the Arc at night when it's in reduced power mode and the entire crew is asleep in their pods almost feels like I'm somewhere else. With room to explore and no eyes upon me, it's the one time I feel like I can be myself. My journal entries following these isolated strolls tend to reflect my truer, deeper sentiments. I am painfully aware that many of the second gen look to me for encouragement and optimism. Truth is, being happy and positive all the time can be exhausting. Sometimes I wish I could be more like Avery. She almost wears her misery with pride. As taxing as it can be spending time with her, I respect that she has the courage to be so open and honest. I bet she sleeps better than anyone. She's probably one of the most authentic people on the Arc.

I know I should be thankful for this amazing opportunity I've been born into, but I'm tired of waiting for this promised life off the ship. Maybe my parents have done too good of a job with their descriptions of what life on Uelara will be like. They've planted a seed that has sprouted and grown roots in my mind, making me long for life outside the Arc. Sometimes I wish we'd never been told about Uelara. Maybe then I wouldn't know anything other than life on the ship, and I could be blissfully ignorant to what I'm missing.

Envisioning life after the Arc has been a saving grace for me time and again. I cannot even begin to fathom what it really will feel like setting foot on an actual planet. Uelara sounds amazing.

The beauty, all the unknowns—it's too much to take in for me sometimes. I want to experience everything!

Now for the man talk. Sam was on me again today about Lance. She keeps asking me why I'm with him. Honestly, it's getting a bit annoying. She's such a beautiful friend, and yet her lingering jealousy is getting a bit weary. I wish she could become interested in someone else and move on.

Unfortunately, Sam's not the only one who questions my judgment about Lance. I am so tired of justifying my feelings for him to the others. I mean, I get it; Lance has a rough exterior. I get that he can rub people the wrong way. Yeah, he doesn't make much of an attempt to listen or make other people comfortable. Yes, he has a temper . . . and yes, *that* is getting a bit annoying. Sure, we've been fighting a lot lately, but with his increased responsibilities and pressure that accompany the outrigger OCP, it's understandable that it would take its toll on our relationship.

The bottom line is he's a strong, confident, decisive guy, and he loves me. Oh, I just wish everyone would see the sweeter Lance that I see. The Lance that swept me off my feet the moment I turned nineteen. The Lance that leaves me notes in my pod that paint stories of our lives together once we arrive at Uelara. Lance is a good guy, and I really believe he's the best match for me. I just hope the Pairing council comes to the same conclusion.

CHAPTER 04

Fisher was having a better morning than usual. He was ahead of schedule with his assigned tasks in the foundry, and he had something new to look forward to as well. Today he was on "Quint" duty.

The Quints were a set of red-headed, freckle-faced, five-year-old quintuplets. Fisher was convinced that there was nothing natural about five identical children, and he often joked that they had obviously been created in the medical bay by Sam's parents. Of course, everyone else knew this to be incorrect since they'd watched Sam's mom carry the children for almost seven months before giving birth to them. What was universally agreed upon was that the Quints' birth was not a "scheduled event." Fisher's parents referred to them as a "happy accident."

The second generation of the crew had all been born within a three-year time period. So, when the Quints came along fourteen years after Echo and Dom, the youngest of the second generation, they had come as quite the surprise to everyone, their parents included.

Fisher felt the Quints were . . . creepy. Maybe it was that they were the only children on board, and Fisher simply had no point of reference. Perhaps it was the way they all moved and spoke in unison at times. They seemed to have their own language. Something about the Quints made everyone else on the ship feel like outsiders. Whatever the reason, Fisher felt they were . . . creepy.

Fisher had been tasked with aiding in teaching the Quints the history of the *Archean's* mission. The first gen thought it would be a good way to slowly integrate the Quints into the second gen crew. So today's history lesson had been passed on to him, and if the transition was a success, more of the second gen'ers would begin taking on the task of teaching the Quints their lessons.

With his father's assistance, Fisher had been preparing for his session with the Quints for a few weeks and believed he was ready for them. He looked at the digital display on the wall and realized it was time to leave the foundry. He packed his notes, grabbed the media cube he'd loaded with a collection of images, and headed to the rec room outside of Hive 3.

Fisher entered the rec room that had been converted into makeshift living quarters shortly after the Quints' arrival. It had all the comforts of the sleeping pods Fisher and his friends had always used, with none of their privacy.

When the Quints turned four years old, it was recommended by Dr. Fiona, one of the ship's psychologists, that it was best for the Quints to be placed close to Sam so that they could begin to slowly integrate with the second generation. Fisher and the rest of Hive 3 had instantly and inadvertently been recruited to read bedtime stories and chaperone late-night trips to the lavatory.

In the far left corner where several treadmills had once lived sat a small set of desks, an interactive whiteboard, and other teaching paraphernalia. The setup reminded Fisher of his time in school with the other second gen'ers, before occupational pathway courses began when they all hit their late teen years.

Fisher placed the media cube on the table, activated it, and dimmed the lights in the room. He used the digital display on the top of the cube to navigate to the directory of images he'd prepared and put the media cube into projector mode. Colored lights projected from the front of the cube, and an image of the Earth from orbit appeared on the wall. It was odd, but in a way, Fisher felt like it was *his* home, even though he'd never been there and never would.

After a few minutes, the door to the room slid open, and the Quints filed in one by one, followed by their mother, Margot. It truly was an odd site to see five identical kids, and the creepy vibe meter was off the charts this morning, as they all had the same eerie smile on their faces and all seemed to mimic each other's motions.

"How are you doing today, Fisher?" asked Margot before raising her portable oxygen concentrator to her mouth and taking in a deep breath. "Ready for the boys?"

Even though the oxygen farm generated purified air through the Arc, the first generation had become reliant upon the pulse delivery portable oxygen concentrators, or POCs as they were commonly dubbed, over the past few years. The poor quality of the air on Earth had caused irrevocable damage to their lungs. Although they were receiving top-notch treatment, the POCs provided extra assistance with their sometimes-labored breathing. It was difficult witnessing the first generation's health deteriorate over the years and was a constant reminder of the importance of the mission.

"I think I'm all set if they are."

"Okay, boys, now remember, give Fisher your undivided attention today. He has very important information to teach you, and I want you on your best behavior. If I get a good report back from him, I'll give all of you extra time in the Dome later today."

"Dome! Dome! Dome! Dome!" chanted the Quints.

"I'll leave you to it, Fisher," said Margot as she left the room. "Swing them by the Dome when you're done."

"What are you going to teach us today, Mr. Fish?" asked one of the Quints.

"Oh, no, you can just can call me Fisher."

"Okay, Fish."

"No . . . Fisher. Today we are going to learn about the Earth and our new home planet Uelara"—he pronounced the word slowly, *yoooh-lahr-ra*—"and our important role as the crew of the *Archean*."

"The Arc?" yelled one of the brothers.

"Yes, the Arc . . . the *Archean*," answered Fisher. "As you know, all of the parents grew up on the Earth. It was a beautiful planet, but the population just grew too large. The people used up most of the Earth's natural resources. During the second half of the twenty-first century, the Earth had become unsustainable for human life."

"Unstainable?" asked a Quint.

"I know!" shouted another. "Mom always says that when I spill food on my coveralls. She wishes we had unstainable clothes."

Fisher repressed a smile. "Oh, umm, no, unSUStainable. It means upsetting the ecological balance by depleting natural resources."

The Quints blinked a few times and stared at Fisher.

"It means that human life was going to end on the Earth unless people figured out another solution."

More blinks and stares.

This is going to be a long day, Fisher thought.

Fisher brought up the next slide, and it showed a group of scientists, telescopes, and star charts.

"Now, no one wanted to see humanity come to an end, of course. The best and brightest scientists from around the globe had exhausted all solutions to the Earth's problems and started looking to the stars for answers. These scientists studied the possibility to terraform Mars and other neighboring planets so that the environment could be habitable by people from the Earth. Although they had the technology to alter the climate of some of these planets, the long timescales and economic resources needed posed too many obstacles. Then they discovered several planets that could support human life! The problem was that the distance needed to travel to any of them was way too far out of reach."

"Oh no!" the Quints all exclaimed in unison.

Good, Fisher thought, *they're still with me. I better beef it up a little.*

"Right! That's what everyone else on the Earth thought, too. 'Oh nooooo!' But guess what? Those smart scientists came up with a plan that would allow them to travel to the closest planet, which was sixty years away." Fisher clicked to the next slide. "They constructed the *G. S. Archean,* a ship that would be crewed by the Earth's bravest volunteers."

"Mom and Dad!"

"Yup! All our moms and dads were considered heroes. They volunteered to walk away from life on the Earth to ensure that humanity would continue. Now, can anyone tell me why we call our parents *first gens?*" Fisher asked, clicking to the next slide.

Two of the Quints shot their hands up quickly. Fisher smiled and pointed to the one on the right. "What's the reason?" One Quint after another began spouting their guesses, questions, and comical logic.

"Gens stands for *generals*. They're the leaders, like generals. Everybody knows that."

"Yeah, Mom always says, 'Listen to the generals.'"

"But they're not really generals, are they Fish?"

"First gens . . . first gentlemen on the Arc!"

"No, stupid, there's ladies on here, too!"

"They're all called gentlemen. The girls don't mind."

"Generation," whispered one of the Quints.

"What was that, umm?" asked Fisher, motioning to the Quint who had given the correct response.

"That's Sean," answered a Quint, pointing to his brother.

"Sorry. Sean, what did you say?"

"Generation," answered Sean. "We call them the *first gen* because they were the first generation to run the Arc."

Now, if Sean had provided that answer the way the rest of the Quints had responded, it wouldn't have felt as odd as it felt right now. But Sean looked Fisher square in the eyes and spoke his answer in a hypnotic whisper. Fisher felt a shiver down his spine.

About a month earlier, Sean's behavior had started changing. He became quieter than his brothers. He also developed this way of staring at Fisher at the weirdest times. He just . . . stared. Fisher had interacted with Sean many times in the past. Whether it was while helping Sam babysit her brothers or sitting near him in the auditorium, Fisher never had any strange encounters with him. But lately, Sean always seemed to watch Fisher speak and move as though he were judging him. It was unnerving.

"That's . . . right, Sean. Our parents were the first generation on this mission to save the human race. Now, part of the mission's plan included the first gen having children on the *Archean*," continued Fisher, as he clicked to the next slide. "Does anyone know what these children are called?"

"Second gen!" they all cheered.

"You got it!" Fisher was enjoying the lesson now and regaining hope that he'd get through all seventeen prepared slides with few casualties. "As you may have seen, the first gen has been training the second gen how to do all sorts of jobs around the Arc. Part of the mission that we—"

"I have the most important job on the ship," exclaimed a Quint.

"Oh, you do?" Fisher asked with a smile. "And what might that be?"

"Mom says that I have to make sure none of my brothers fall out of the ship."

"She never said that, you're lying!" yelled another.

"Did too!"

"When did she tell you that's your job?" asked a brother.

"A looooong time ago. And she said I'm the best and have saved all your lives by not letting you fall out of the ship."

"None of us are gonna fall out of the ship, silly," said the Quint on the right.

"You're welcome!" exclaimed the self-proclaimed hero, beaming with pride.

Note to self: just keep talking, Fisher thought. "Now, it's really important that everyone works together on the Arc, because there's an awful lot of work that needs to be done keeping the ship running and focusing on the mission."

"I know what the mission is!" said a Quint.

Not missing a beat, Fisher clicked to the next slide. "Remember how I told you that Uelara was really far away from the Earth? Well, the scientists created this cool technology called geodetic rings." Fisher braced himself for the onslaught of questions on this one.

"Just like us!" squealed three Quints in unison.

Fisher knew better, but he couldn't resist. "You guys are like geodetic rings?"

"Yeah! We're geodentical twins!"

With a slight inhale and pause, Fisher smiled and continued to the next slide. "During the Arc's long journey, we release these special rings into space! Without the rings, it takes us sixty years to reach Uelara. Guess how long it will take to get there with the rings."

"A million years."

"Ten million years!"

"Infinity years!"

Fisher laughed. "You're going the wrong way, guys! It will only take fifteen hours!"

"Wowwww!" they all exclaimed.

"Now you're getting it!" Fisher said.

"But how do the rings work?"

"That's an excellent question!" Fisher picked up a book to use as a visual aid. "The geodetic rings are like bookmarks that help with traveling from the Earth to Uelara."

Fisher fanned the book open and held the cover with his left hand. "This cover represents the entrance gate back in the Earth's orbit." Fisher then grabbed the back cover of the book with his right hand. "And this represents the exit gate that we will build once we reach Uelara. Now, the Earth doesn't have the technology to travel from the entrance gate to the exit gate over such a long distance, so they'll be using the geodetic rings that we have strategically placed along the way."

Fisher began placing bookmarks throughout the book. "Once we have power supplied to both the entrance and exit gates, the rings will essentially fold spacetime, reducing the distance the Earth's transport ships will need to travel to get to Uelara."

As Fisher explained this, he closed the book and picked up a small metal rod. He pushed the rod through the ends of the bookmarks until it poked through the final bookmark and came out the other side. At the sight of the rod poking through, the Quints' eyes widened, and they let out a collective "Ooooohhhhh."

"When the *Archean* left the Earth thirty years ago, the scientists were already busy building the transport ships that would shuttle the people to Uelara. With all the rings in place, we will be able to transport the Earth's population to our new home on Uelara within a few years of our arrival."

"Where do the rings come from?" asked one of the boys.

"We build them right here on the Arc. And only the coolest crew members get to build them. Any guesses who I may be talking about?"

"Lance!"

"Lance?!" cried Fisher. "No, not Lance. Guess again."

"Grayson?"

"Nope. One more try."

"That tall girl from Hive 5. She's taller than Dad. She's pretty cool."

"You."

Without moving his eyes, Fisher knew Sean was speaking again. "That's . . . right, Sean. I was assigned to help build the geodetic rings with Lance's dad. We work with Narine from Hive 2 and a few others in the foundry. Once a ring is completed, we hand it off to the outriggers who are responsible for deploying it into space when we reach the designated coordinates. Anybody remember the deployment celebration we had last year? Sean, do you remember that?"

Sean didn't respond. He simply sat in his chair and watched Fisher with a blank expression. Fisher studied him for a moment, rubbing the back of his neck to get rid of the chill that was returning.

Fisher skipped the details of how their parents wouldn't live to reach Uelara. Although thirty years remained in the mission, it was probable that the first generation had only ten to twenty years before losing the battle with their respiratory illnesses. Details like that were left for when the Quints were older and would understand, just as it was when he learned those kinds of details as he got older. He understood that there was an appropriate time for a child to be given information like that.

Fisher noticed that two of the Quints were starting to nod off, a third brother was staring at the ceiling, and another appeared to need a trip to the lavatory. Sean was sitting still, watching Fisher.

"Okay, guys, I think this is a good place to stop for today. I heard that tomorrow you'll be learning about the different jobs we have on the Arc and how every crew member plays a really important role in our mission. Before we go, I want you each to tell me one thing you learned from our lesson today."

"I learned that Mom and Dad are heroes."

"That's right, good!" praised Fisher. Pointing to another boy, Fisher asked, "What about you?"

"You make geodentical rings."

"Geod—never mind, you're right, good job."

Another Quint chimed in. "I learned that my brother's a liar."

Fisher covered his eyes with his hands and rubbed his forehead. They had been doing so well. He called on the fourth brother.

"Any pearls of wisdom from you?"

"The generals grew babies to work on the ship."

"And on that note, this lesson is officially done," groaned Fisher.

"What about Sean?" asked three Quints.

"Yeah, you didn't call on Sean."

Fisher was quite content in bypassing Sean on this one. He had no desire to hear another robotic answer from that clone. He asked anyway, "How did I miss Sean? Sorry, buddy. Is there anything you learned today?"

Sean's four siblings turned to him, waiting for his answer. It felt as though time stood still, and Fisher had to remind himself to breathe. How was it that a five-year-old could create this kind of tension?

"The Earth was dying. Scientists discovered Uelara and made a giant ship to carry the first generation on a mission. The first generation had children on the ship, and everyone worked together to keep the mission going. You make the geodetic rings and other people put them in space. Then the human race gets to fly through the rings and land on Uelara."

Fisher's jaw dropped open. "I should have had you teach the lesson for me, Sean!"

The other Quints cheered and tried to high-five Sean, but he remained still and straight-faced, looking at Fisher.

As Fisher escorted the Quints down the corridor toward the Dome, Fisher realized that despite the chaos, silliness, and even creepiness of this lesson, there was something also very uplifting about it all. In finding the right verbiage to explain the history of the *Archean's* mission to five-year-olds, Fisher had found a renewed sense of purpose and optimism. It was easy to fall into a rut on the ship. Dom had nailed it; each day was a replica of the day before and a forecast of the day to follow. Explaining to the Quints the importance of the mission reminded Fisher of the true honor that had been bestowed upon him.

Fisher's reflective thoughts were interrupted by arguing voices. As he and the Quints reached a quad junction in the corridor, the voices grew louder.

It was Lance barking at Helena, a more frequent occurrence these days. Before Fisher had cleared the junction, Lance looked his way and gave Fisher a nasty look. Fisher quickly herded the Quints forward and tried to create as much distance between them and the scene as possible. One of the Quints craned his neck to see what the commotion was about, but Fisher ushered him around the corner and led them all toward the Dome.

Fisher hadn't been to the Dome in several months, and the sight of it brought back fond memories of the times he'd spent there as a child with his mother. The Dome was a large circular room six meters in diameter that could fit several young adults comfortably. Vivid 180- by 360-degree videos were projected onto the dome-shaped ceiling. The imagery displayed on the ceiling surrounded the viewer with a variety of locations on Earth.

As children, Fisher and the rest of the second generation had spent quite a lot of time with their parents in the Dome. More recently, they were only allowed access through time allotments doled out by the Vosts, the Arc's clinical psychologists, who explained that the first generation had a greater need of Dome time and the benefits it offered.

The Dome provided the closest experience to being in nature, which the Vosts believed lowered levels of the stress hormone cortisol, reducing tension and stress. The artificial excursions boosted mental and physical well-being and increased the participants' ability to focus and enhanced their performance with creative problem solving.

The limited time Fisher was afforded in the Dome was always spent in the Ka'anapali Beach setting because it was an escape from the cold, gray confines of the ship. Fisher didn't always agree with the Vosts, but he did always feel less stressed following his Dome time. His self-esteem and mood often seemed lifted as well. Getting time in the Dome was always worth the price of time with the Vosts, something most avoided if possible.

As Fisher and the Quints entered the Dome, Margot greeted them with a warm smile.

"They're all yours, Margot," said Fisher.

"Thanks, Fisher. How did it go?" she asked.

"Dome! Dome! Dome! Dome!" chanted the Quints.

Fisher laughed. "Allllll yours."

CHAPTER 05

Fisher made his way into the concourse, which was the central hub that connected to the first generation's hives. The first gen primarily used this area as a meeting place at the start and end of each day before retiring to their respective pods at night to sleep. It reminded Fisher of how he and his friends gathered in the galley and the observation deck sometimes. The concourse was also a place they could relax when the ship operated on autopilot and was placed in reduced power mode until the next morning. As the first gen's health diminished and many lacked the energy they once had, they spent more time in the concourse than previous years. Being isolated from the rest of the ship, the concourse gave the parents a private location that the second generation rarely visited.

The high, arched ceiling of the concourse provided a nice change of environment from the claustrophobic low ceilings that made up ninety percent of the Arc. The room's acoustics also played with Fisher's senses, as the voices and sounds of footsteps came at him from all directions.

Fisher remembered the concourse being an empty shell when he was a child. Like many areas of the Arc, the concourse had been constructed long after the mission had started so as not to delay the launch. Fisher's mother often joked that Arc was an acronym for *always requiring construction.* To this day, portions of the Arc were still being constructed. However, many tasks on the ship were becoming automated, requiring less involvement from everyone. By the time the second generation would take full control of the mission, the *Archean* could continue to operate with only half the current crew requirement.

As Fisher scoped out the concourse, he recalled being separated from his parents and moving into a different hive when he was eight. This transition marked the beginning of two important junctures in his life: his independence and the deterioration of his relationship with his father. While there was no bad blood between them, he simply could no longer feel any real connection with his dad. Fisher always treated his dad with respect, and his dad maintained a civil attitude with Fisher. But there was no closeness, no tenderness like what he observed within other families on the ship. Now that he thought about it, he wondered if they had ever really had a deep bond.

His early memories mainly centered on his mom, reading science books together, listening to her stories of being a child on Earth, and watching her run the archives with precision and confidence. Fisher's only experiences with his father involved learning about the *Archean's* mission.

"Remember, son, this mission is not about you or me or anyone on the *Archean.* We never waver from the mission. Regardless of the confusion that will no doubt visit you in the future, you must always remember that there are times in a man's life when self-sacrifice is a small price to pay for the needs of the many."

Fisher had heard various versions of this speech countless times. He was pretty sure the message was imprinted onto his DNA by now.

Fisher sometimes considered the scenario of his parents continuing their lives on Earth, never volunteering to join the Arc crew. Would they have chosen to have a baby, knowing life expectancy would be as grim as it had become? Had his father really ever wanted a child? If the mission hadn't required sixty children to continue on the Arc's journey, Fisher questioned whether he would have been born.

Shaking off his thoughts, Fisher scanned the concourse for a few minutes, searching for his parents. He spotted the Martins sitting together near the center of the room with several other couples. Fisher walked over to them and noticed they were deep into one of their typical lively debates. Not wanting to interrupt, Fisher quickened his pace. Mrs. Martin abruptly halted their banter and beamed with pleasure at seeing one of the second gen in the concourse.

"Oh hi, Fisher!" she bubbled. "How did your lesson go with the Quints today?"

"Did they give you a chance to speak, or did they barrel over ya?" asked Mr. Martin, with a hearty belly laugh.

"I think it was a good learning experience for all of us," replied Fisher.

"Oh, boy," said Mrs. Martin. "I know how that goes. You just make sure that your dad knows how hard you worked to teach them, you hear me? You deserve extra Dome time for that one."

"Yeah, five minutes with those kids and I'd be signing up for the next spacewalk, let me tell you," said Mr. Martin.

Fisher laughed, hugged Mrs. Martin, and received an enthusiastic high five from Mr. Martin that would most likely leave Fisher's hand bright red for about an hour. It never failed; time spent with the Martins always resulted in feeling lifted and loved.

Fisher continued walking toward the far end of the concourse. As he navigated through some of the first gen enjoying the end of another long day, he caught a glimpse of the ship's chief engineer, Thomas, eyes closed, mouth open, snoring away in one of the reading chairs. Fisher was relieved that Thomas was sound asleep. As much as he hated to admit it, Fisher was more intimidated by the hulking man than any other member of the first generation. He was grateful that it was Grayson who was stuck spending all of his working hours bearing the brunt of Thomas's wrath in the engine room. It made Fisher's appreciation of his foundry OCP that much greater.

Fisher slinked past Thomas and saw Echo's father, Andrew, the senior galley director, surrounded by some of the crew. Clearly, he was weaving yet another tall tale of adventures from his youth. Unlike Thomas, Andrew was someone who always made Fisher feel at ease. Endless stories and terrible jokes were Andrew's trademark. It was pretty much a given that no one liked Andrew's jokes, yet everyone appreciated his efforts.

Just beyond Andrew and his audience, Fisher found his parents playing another intense round of chess.

Fisher missed his carefree days when he had time to play chess and other games. With most of the first gen's responsibilities being handed over to the second gen and new tasks being assigned each week, he found he had little time to do much else but sleep after each long day in the foundry. Fisher wasn't upset with his parents for his lack of recreational time, as he knew he was only being asked to do what they had done for the past thirty years.

"Hey, guys," he called out as he approached.

Fisher's dad held his index finger and thumb on the head of the bishop he was about to move and looked toward Fisher. "We were just talking about you."

"How'd it go with the Quints today?" added his mother.

"Good, I think. I was able to cover just about everything on the outline."

Fisher's dad looked down at the board with his fingers, still squeezing the head of the chess piece. "The boys give you any trouble?"

"Define *trouble*," said Fisher.

His father looked up from his game with a stern expression, the same look Fisher had grown accustomed to anytime he made a joke.

Lighten up, Dad, Fisher thought. "I'm kidding. They were fine. Lots of questions, lots of . . . interesting interpretations. But I think they got some of the basics today. I wasn't sure if I was going to be able to hold their attention, but they seemed to really enjoy the lesson."

Fisher's mother smiled. "Good, good. Must have been their teacher!"

His dad slid the bishop three spaces, his fingers not yet removed from the chess piece. A hint of a smile appeared on his mother's face and then quickly vanished. Fisher had seen this many a time. His dad was about to take a beating.

"So . . . today's lesson got me thinking," Fisher said, searching for the right words.

"Oh, yeah? About what?" asked his mother.

Fisher looked at the floor. "Well, it's about the mission."

Fisher's parents exchanged a quick glance, their faces momentarily clouded by uneasiness, and then looked back at Fisher.

"What's that, son?" asked his dad.

"So, I was explaining to the Quints about the distance from the Earth to Uelara and, like you instructed, I didn't mention anything about the first generation not living to complete the mission."

"Just as we discussed," said Fisher's dad, returning his focus to the game board. "We'll share details like that when they're older."

"Right . . . but . . ."

"What is it, Fisher?" asked his mother.

"Aren't you scared? I mean . . . you're going to die before we make it to Uelara. Doesn't that scare you?"

"Everyone fears their own mortality," said Fisher's dad in a flat tone, scratching his chin. A wheezing cough interrupted his words, and he inhaled a cleansing breath from his POC, then continued. "In that sense, sure, the thought of dying scares me. But whether we are on this ship or back on Earth, death is inevitable."

"But don't you feel robbed in some way that you, Mom, and the others have worked so hard the last thirty years and you won't get to see—"

"Son, some things are bigger than you or me," interrupted his dad. "We've talked about this."

Can't he just call me Fisher? he thought.

"Honey, the sacrifices your father and I are making are for you . . . you and all the other generations that this mission will be saving."

"Remember," added his dad, "life on Earth is coming to an end."

"I know, but—"

"What kind of parents would we be if we didn't do whatever was necessary to make a better life for you?"

"Someday you'll see how everything changes, once you have kids of your own," added his mother.

"You're not listening to me," argued Fisher.

"Now there you go again. I don't know why you question our intentions or doubt this mission," his father rasped.

"I'm not—"

"It's concerning that you can lose focus of something so important. We've been at this a hell of a lot longer than you kids. You need to accept that we knew what we were getting into and are proud as hell to pass the torch on to you and the rest of the second generation. Now, I appreciate your concern, but trust me when I say that everything is working according to plan, and your mother and I are exactly where we want to be."

Fisher's heart rate was increasing and he could feel the blood rising in his cheeks. His father had a supreme knack for completely missing the point. He watched as his dad was overcome by a long, wheezing coughing fit. His mother gently rubbed his father's back and reminded him to slow down his breathing. This was clearly not the time to try and win and argument—for either of them.

"Sorry, Dad. I really do understand."

"Not fully . . . but you will," said his father, returning his attention to the game as his cough subsided. "Always remember, your mother and I would happily make the same choices again if given the chance."

"It'll be weird making a new home on Uelara without you guys," said Fisher, locking his ankles together.

Fisher's dad looked up from the chessboard, glanced around the room, and looked down again. "Now don't go racing us into our graves so fast, son. We've still got plenty of years ahead of us, and we'll be enjoying retirement soon, don't forget."

"Your father's right, Fisher. Whether its back on Earth, here on the Arc, or on Uelara, we're just happy we get to be with you and our friends."

"Thanks, guys," responded Fisher, tugging at the cuff of his right sleeve. "I'll leave you to your game. I'm going to meet up with Sam and the rest of the hive for dinner."

"Tell Sam hello for me," said his mom. "I hope she's enjoying her work in the think tank."

"And tell Alec to get some rest," added his dad. "I don't need him nodding off again tomorrow so close to the structural 3D printers."

Fisher gave his dad a thumb's up and started walking toward the exit as his parents returned to their game.

How did their conversations always, inevitably, twist into misunderstandings and frustrations? And why was Fisher continually surprised by the failed communication? Every time he tried to connect with his father, it would go miserably awry. He had hoped that by assuming the role of teacher for the Quints, their interaction would improve. When no real shift appeared, Fisher attempted to connect with his father by voicing his assumptions of what his parents must be feeling. That backfired as well. Fisher shook his head. Maybe one day he'd find the magical equation that would finally get his father to utter the words Fisher longed to hear for so many years. He sighed and turned back to look at his parents, overhearing their final exchange of the match.

Making his final move, his dad boasted, "How do you like them apples?"

"Check . . . mate," said his mom.

CHAPTER 06

Sam stood in front of a large interactive whiteboard in the center breakout hub of the think tank. The clattering of keys from the keyboards vibrated as a team of engineers sat working at their personal terminals, which surrounded the hub in a radial array.

While the think tank was commonly referred to as simply the Tank, many of the first gen called it the Cave due to its lack of lighting. The overhead lights were always off in the Tank, except for the central hub light above where Sam stood, and the glow from the terminals lit the faces of their operators. No walls or dividers separated each work area, but the falloff from the pools of light emitting from the terminals provided a sense of isolation that Sam and the others liked.

Sam placed her hand on her chin, hyperfocused on the wall of equations. Fuel calculations and trajectories crunched in her head, as her eyes darted to different spots on the whiteboard. Unlike some of the others working in the Tank, she could calculate numbers all day. Sam loved their black-and-white nature. No gray areas. Numbers didn't lie, and they were uncomplicated. Simple. If only people could be the same.

She paused on a pair of numbers three-quarters of the way

down on the board, and her eyes widened. "Found the issue!" she exclaimed, pushing her bangs away from her eye.

"What?" responded Debra in disbelief. "You've only been at it for two minutes."

"Not sure what to tell you, Debra. It's a simple mistake. Someone has the horizontal and vertical positions swapped for the second stage of the ring's trajectory."

Debra stepped next to Sam, pushed her reading glasses to the tip of her nose, and peered over the frames at the equation. "Well, look at that. I've had the whole team reviewing it for the last two days, and you come along and solve the issue in no time. Impressive."

Sam smiled and walked back to her own equation, which she had been working through at her station, trying to downplay her excitement for the quick win. While she had learned a great deal from the other first gen crew in the Tank over the last few years, she enjoyed working with Debra, Echo's mother, most of all. Debra was a brilliant engineer who had worked for a research and development center on Earth that focused on the construction and operation of planetary robotic spacecraft, before she and her husband, Andrew, had volunteered to be part of the crew of the *Archean*.

Debra was tall and thin and carried herself with an unmatched grace. She hated the use of profanity, something Sam couldn't relate to but was always mindful of when around her. Debra brimmed with decisiveness and confidence, yet she didn't show the displays of arrogance that Sam had seen in some of the other parents on the ship. Debra was patient and an excellent mentor to Sam and the others. While she had a forgiving spirit, she was short on compliments. Anytime Debra gave a compliment in the Tank, everyone knew she meant it.

Sam kept a mental scorecard of the positive feedback she and the others received from Debra, and she was always in the lead. Zach was Sam's only threat, and while they each pretended to not keep tabs, both were well aware of the current score.

Sam had mixed feelings about Zach. She could relate to his obsession with all things math and found that, many times, he was the only one who could keep up with her when discussing the work they were tasked with in the Tank. He clearly had one of the sharpest minds on the Arc. It was unfortunate that his looks lacked the same appeal. Pudgy and nearsighted were the descriptors that came to Sam's mind, and he obviously spent more time behind his terminal than in front of a mirror.

Zach could rub Sam the wrong way at times. He had a tendency to talk about himself, and often she felt like she was being talked at rather than having a conversation. She knew that, at his core, Zach was kind, but sometimes she found it hard to reach that side of him.

"Nice work, Sam," goaded Zach as he walked over to Sam's desk.

"Thanks," said Sam, crossing her arms over her chest, bracing herself for whatever backhanded compliment was about to be delivered.

"I can't believe none of the others saw such an obvious mistake. I was curious if you'd find the flaw. I spotted it yesterday," he boasted.

Gimme a break. If you spotted it yesterday, you would have been announcing it to the entire crew in about four seconds, she thought.

Zach barraged Sam with his unsolicited feedback about how he would have tackled the problem, which pretty much translated to, "I'm brilliant, I'm the best, me, me, me." As usual, Sam pretended to listen as she plotted a way to escape the conversation.

Over Zach's shoulder, Sam watched as Dr. Gage and Helena entered the workspace, followed by Samar, a second gen'er from Hive 4.

"Zachary . . ." Dr. Gage announced with a flat tone.

Free at last, Sam thought.

Startled, Zach looked over his shoulder.

"Uh, yes sir?"

"Time for the Q," said Helena softly, looking down at her tablet.

Zach looked back at Sam as if he were just given a death sentence and mumbled, "See you in a week."

Sam could easily poke at Zach with plenty of cruel comments for what lay ahead of him but decided to lighten the tension in the room. "It'll be over before you know it, Zach."

Zach shuffled toward Dr. Gage as Samar tightened her lips and scowled at Zach. As the group left the workspace and headed down the corridor, Zach looked back at Sam like a child who had just been scolded by his parents.

As much as Zach could be a thorn in her side, Sam felt bad for anyone who had to do another stint in quarantine, especially if he were Q'd with someone he didn't like.

Dr. Gage and the other first gen'ers had decided it was better to select partners for Q'd crew members to make time in the Q more digestible. Sam and Fisher, as well as a few others who had been Q'd together, grew close relationships as a result. However, Zach and Samar had not been so fortunate. Poor Zach loathed Samar. For some reason, the two were like oil and water. After their second time in the Q, it was painful to see the two interact.

Samar was a striking young lady with curly jet-black hair and a brilliant smile. Of course, any casual observer would be shocked to learn that a smile existed in Samar's repertoire of facial expressions when she was within two meters of Zach. Many of Zach's friends repeatedly told him that he lucked out sharing Q time with her, but Zach could not be convinced. Similarly, Samar's friends from her hive knew how much she was drawn to the smart, nerdy type. Everyone believed this should be an easy win—everyone except Zach and Samar. Sam guessed that the odds just weren't in their favor.

Each stay in the Q was challenging. Sam and Fisher had spent five weeks of isolation when they were thirteen, and the experience had left a permanent mental scar for Sam. She still found herself having nightmares about it. Five weeks was too long to be cut off from everyone. Sure, Fisher had been there with her, and they had grown to be best friends over the years, but after a few days, Sam had started feeling caged in, and Fisher had taken the brunt of her anxiety.

The Q played a vital role in the success of the crew's preparations for life on Uelara. The *Archean* was a giant clean room where no natural viruses or bacteria developed. Since birth, Sam and the others had been inundated with colds, viruses, and more in the Q. Without time in the Q, where the second generation was introduced to the collection of pathogens supplied by the Global Center for Disease Control and Prevention, the young crew's immune system would gradually atrophy in the ship's environment.

Dom would always refer to the latest visit to the Q as "one more serving of the suck." It was hard enough to spend time with the same person in such a small space. Add to it that one spent the entire time in the Q either puking, scratching, dripping, or crapping. The fact that Fisher could still stand to be around Sam after years of time in the Q either showed that he was a true friend or that he was simply an alien, as others had joked.

Is Fish an alien? Many signs point to yes, she thought, and smiled.

CHAPTER 07

Helena's Log, Y22 D132

People of the Earth,

I would like to discuss the topic of proximity today. People and proximity, to be more precise. When born on a spaceship alongside sixty other children and raised together in one confined space, life can become rather challenging. My parents have shared many stories with me, and if I understand correctly, people on the Earth rarely stay in one place for very long. They even move to other lands away from their friends and families. While I love the crew of the *Archean*, this concept does have me feeling a little envious. I'll try to explain.

Today, Avery stopped by the medical bay on her way to the factory. She always seems to be obsessing about something, and today she was revisiting the discussion of time on the Arc. She isn't sure she can take thirty more years of life on the ship. Avery can't stop dreaming of Uelara, and I can't say that I blame her. While she waited for me to package up her weekly supply of nutritional supplements, I did my best to ease her anxiety by playing a couple rounds of First Things with her. That usually does the trick with Avery, and today's distraction didn't disappoint. I also gave her some more beauty tips—she loves when we discuss her hair! I showed her how her face can look fuller if she lets her auburn hair down to frame her face. When she saw her reflection, her cute little reaction made my day. While I realize it's only temporary, I think these diversions should hold her over until her next appointment with the Vosts.

No more than ten minutes later, I got caught up in a depressing conversation with Zach and Samar, who were obviously looking for a distraction of their own from the Q. I usually cut most people in the Q some slack, as the misery that comes with being isolated and sick is a guaranteed setup for negativity. However, Zach was pushing all my buttons with his take on a better way to boost their immune systems rather than time in the Q. Don't get me wrong. Zach's a smart guy, but I think Dr. Gage and the crew of the medical bay might have a bit more experience than Zach and his baseless theories. While he never came close to convincing me, it did take some time to persuade Samar that Zach was a bit clueless. What makes debates like these so irritating is that we seem to have them every time this duo is in the Q.

Sometimes I feel like I've heard every conversation I'm going to hear for the rest of my life. I feel like I know what everyone is going to say or do, and how they'll respond. Dom's going to pee on something, Avery's going to cry about something, Sam's going to solve all the Tank's math problems, and the tedious list continues. Though I struggle with admitting it, I'm starting to agree with Dom: nothing really changes—including people.

This thought leads me to my next realization: Not only could I possibly have run out of new conversations, I haven't met a single new person—ever! I know everyone I will ever know until the transport ships arrive on Uelara.

All this time I have been fixated upon the idea that, in thirty more years, I'll be able to interact with thousands of people from the Earth. And I do not use the term "fixated" lightly. Here's an example: Each member of the crew wears an *Archean* mission patch on their clothes. Nothing fancy, just a simple reminder patch of what we are trying to accomplish during this long journey. Well, when I turned eight, I decided to create a unique Uelara patch of my very own. Every morning when I get dressed, I am reminded by that simple piece of fabric of our end goal. All these opportunities are waiting for me at the other end of this journey. I tell myself each day that I will finally get to greet the weary, Earth-born travelers, and my patch will be a symbol for them of the new lives they are about to create.

But in reality, who knows how long it will take before the transport ships actually arrive? I know all the time estimates the Tank has spouted, but honestly, I think there are so many uncertainties with too many variables to know for sure. And what will the people be like at that point? What if life on the Earth has drastically changed decades after the Arc's launch? We would never know. We haven't had communication with the Earth in more than twenty years! My father used to talk about how difficult it was for the first generation when they reached that point in the mission where they knew communication was ending. They were aware that at a certain distance, the Arc would no longer be capable of sending or receiving transmissions. I can only imagine how painful it must have been to know when their final message would be made to their loved ones back home. It's different for my friends and me—we have no point of reference. The one thing we all have in common, however, is lack of insight into Earth-born people today, much less in the next thirty years.

This brings me to a slightly different topic—a much more painful one that my friends and I have all been avoiding. But I want to address this because no matter how much I avoid talking about it with them, I can't seem to escape the pain, and I find no relief except through the pages of this journal. So here I go:

I cannot imagine life without my parents on this ship. I can't envision life without any of the first generation! They've all raised us, in a way. They've sacrificed so much so that we can have a future. The first gen'ers have taught us everything we know—about this ship, about the mission, how to interact with each other. Have they taught us how to carry on without them?

I really don't know why I'm worrying about this right now. We've got a good ten to twenty years left with them. Yeah, I'm being a bit silly, aren't I? I guess it's just a reminder for me of how grateful I am for their influence on our unusual lives.

Sometimes I wonder if Earth-born kids could ever imagine the life we live on the Arc. From all the stories I've heard, life on the Earth, at least before it had become so toxic, sounded pretty sweet. Those kids could leave the confines of their homes and venture off into nature by simply walking through a door. Mr. Martin has shared stories of how when he was a child, his family would travel hundreds of kilometers from their home and do this thing called camping where they actually got to sleep, outside, under the stars!

Mrs. Martin explained to me how she got to choose what she wanted to study, what occupational path she wanted to pursue, and she even got to choose Mr. Martin as her partner. So much freedom. The more I think about it, the more I wonder how different my life would have been if I had been born on the Earth.

I do realize there are obvious tradeoffs. I mean, there are some amazing benefits to living on the Arc rather than plodding through life on the Earth. I know that I'll have food to eat, the air I'm breathing isn't going to poison me, and no war is going to break out on the ship. Most importantly, my future is certain.

I'm going to land on Uelara and help prepare this new world for the inhabitants of the Earth. This is the thought I hold on to when things get me down. This is the vision I try to share when attempting to lift up the others on the Arc. Sometimes it's the only thing keeping me going, but I will never let the others see that. They need to stay focused, and I think I've found my purpose on the ship through this vision. As long as I can motivate the others that our time on this ship is limited and we are paving the way for generations to come, I can hold on another day and help my friends do the same.

CHAPTER 08

Lance, Toby, and Kayla descended the ladder into the archives. For most of Lance's life, the archive room had been off-limits to the second generation. He had only become aware of its existence five years ago, and six months into his OCP he was given access.

The archives housed both the ship's physical and digital records. Lance didn't understand why they had created so many physical copies of things to be stored, as he thought it was a waste of space. His father explained to him that if any of the systems on the ship went down, it was always good to have offline material. But as far back as Lance could remember, the Arc had never had any systems malfunction. Most of the crew's day-to-day operations ensured that everything continued to run.

All *Archean*-related data could be found in the archives. The outriggers could access blueprints of any portion of the Arc to aid in the external maintenance runs they would perform. The room was lined with shelving and cabinets from floor to ceiling, and an array of rack-mounted drives hummed in a closed-off portion of the room. This digital storage area required lower temperatures to prevent the drives from overheating, and although it was sealed off from the main portion of the room, the overall temperature of the archives was still much colder than most areas of the Arc that Lance frequented.

Lance could see that Deuce, Mia, and the other outriggers were already gathering around the large, circular display table in the center of the room. Fisher's mother looked up from the table over toward the trio, and everyone followed her gaze.

"Nice of you to join us," she said.

"If it wasn't for—"

Lance knew better than to make excuses for being late. He raised his hand, interrupting Kayla. "So sorry, Maggie. It won't happen again."

Maggie's long, dark hair had become locks of gray over the past few years, and she wore them with an air of pride, as if she had earned every silver strand. There were two sides to Maggie: the warm, motherly figure Lance remembered as a child, and the stern, no-nonsense woman who stood before him. She took her role on the Arc seriously and expected everyone else to follow suit. While working in the archives, Maggie's verbal bite could sting if someone stepped out of line. But off duty, she transformed into a softer person who could ease troubles and calm worried minds with her caring touch and gentle smile.

Lance had a close bond with Maggie and held the utmost respect for her. She was the closest thing to a mother he had ever known. Lance's mother had died while giving birth, something that weighed on Lance even to this day.

Lance had heard the story multiple times, and yet he never could seem to come to terms with her death. Dr. Gage had explained that once settled on the Arc, Lance's mother began having issues with her kidneys. She was advised that childbirth was too great a health risk. Confirming her reputation as both selfless and stubborn, she was determined to contribute to the success of the mission, which of course meant having a child. The pregnancy put too much strain on her kidneys, and Lance's mother went into labor fourteen weeks early. An emergency Cesarean section was performed, and Lance was born. While the technology and medication aboard the ship saved Lance's young life, his mother's kidneys were never able to withstand the trauma of surgery and delivery. She passed away holding Lance in her arms.

After the death of his wife, Lance's father spent little time outside of the foundry, so many of the first generation on the Arc had played a role in raising Lance. It was Maggie, though, who filled the void most of all.

During the first two years of his life, Lance had had Maggie's love and attention all to himself. He was just a toddler when Fisher was born, and although Lance had no memories of that timeframe, he knew that he had been replaced in Maggie's eyes. How could he not? Nothing could change the fact that he was not really Maggie's son—Fisher was. Lance was reminded of this every time he looked at Fisher.

Maggie reached down and tapped a few times on the table's display. Pale blue light illuminated the group as large blueprints appeared on the table's surface. "Although we are years away from initiating the project, we're going to start discussing the plans for constructing the build site for the exit gate," explained Maggie.

"Are these the schematics for the first gen hives?" asked Mia, pointing at the table's display.

Other than Kayla, Mia was the only other female outrigger. She was the shortest in the group, but her size didn't interfere with her becoming a crew shift leader just like Lance. In fact, he trained with Mia prior to being assigned to Stringer's outrigger crew. He admired her strong spirit and had always thought that if Helena weren't in the picture, he would surely have hooked up with Mia.

"Very good, Mia. As you know, many aspects of the *Archean's* design were built with the idea of repurposing as many components as possible." Maggie placed her index and middle finger of each hand on the table and slid them away from each other. The schematics enlarged, zooming in on the concourse area of the blueprints. "The concourse was designed as a build site for the exit gate. Unlike the geodetic rings, the exit gate will be too large to deploy from the back of the Arc."

Pointing at the display, Kayla asked, "If it's too large to release the gate from the back of the ship, how will we—?"

Maggie swiped at the schematic with her right hand, double tapped on a small thumbnail image, and it filled the display. "This portion of the Arc was purposely built on the top deck, isolated from the rest of the ship. As you can see here, the upper hull of this portion of the Arc is retractable, and these four entry ways can be sealed off from the rest of the ship, making the whole area one giant airlock."

"Whoa, never noticed that," marveled Deuce.

Deuce was the spitting image of his father, Jack. They were both tall and stocky with thick, bushy eyebrows. It was common for the two to be mistaken for each other when seen from a distance. Deuce's real name was Jack as well, but he quickly received his nickname from the first generation, something Lance had only recently learned during one of their spacewalks. Deuce was extremely reliable, and Lance felt safe during their time outside the ship knowing that Deuce was watching his back.

"But why have a build site so close to the hives?" asked Toby.

"It's actually quite brilliant," replied Maggie. "The engineers designed the hives based on many of the same components as the entrance and exit gates. Sixty percent of the first gen hive's components can be reclaimed to construct the exit gate. So, the majority of the gate components will already be right next to the build site."

"Where's the other forty percent?" asked Lance.

"Twenty percent is stored in the Hold, and the remaining twenty percent will need to be manufactured by the factory crew," she answered.

Lance was always impressed with Maggie's rapid-fire responses.

"So, we'll be dismantling the first gen's hives?" asked Kayla, raising her hand.

"Yes, but not until . . ." Maggie paused, searching for the right words. "They're no longer in use."

The group at the table went quiet.

"But won't we need those pods for when the third generation is born?" inquired Mia.

"No. Remember, there will be a period when all three generations will be on the ship at one time. That should put the entire crew count at roughly 235, so the first gen will still be housed in their pods, and the third gen will need pods of their own." Maggie covered her mouth as a lengthy cough interrupted her explanation. The group waited patiently for her to continue.

Once she was able to speak clearly, Maggie added, "I'm working with the other team to construct additional hives over the next decade for the third gen."

Toby raised his hand. "Doesn't seem very efficient. Wouldn't it make more sense for us to wait to have kids until you guys have . . . umm."

"You wouldn't know where to begin raising a kid, Toby," teased Kayla, attempting to help dig Toby out of the hole he just dug himself. Everyone around the table laughed.

"Kayla does have a point, Toby," added Maggie with a smile. "Remember, while the first generation *is* slowly handing over the core responsibilities of the mission to all of you and the ship is becoming more autonomous, we'll still be here to guide you along the way. This includes helping raise your kids, our grandchildren."

"And if they're anything like Lance or Toby, we'll need all the help we can get," joked Kayla.

Laughter filled the room. Maggie joined in and let out a small laugh.

"You would be so lucky to have a kid as good-looking as me," boasted Lance.

"Let's not get too far off course here," said Maggie. "We have quite a bit to cover if we're going to get through everything today."

"What's our focus today?" asked Lance, attempting to help steer the conversation back on track.

"Today we're going to take a close look at the pod schematics, particularly the components we plan to reclaim for the construction of the exit gate."

When Lance was younger, he had found most of his lessons boring, but now he really enjoyed this kind of stuff. He loved understanding the mechanics of the ship and believed it was this passion that landed him the OCP of outrigger.

"As you can see here," said Maggie as she pointed down at the display, "each pod consists of intake and outtake components. When the first gen hives are vacant and the doors to the area have been sealed, these components will become inactive and serve no purpose. These filtration systems will be used to cool the coils that make up the interior drives that keep the gate functioning."

As Maggie continued sharing her lesson with the younger crew, Lance grew excited learning about the intricacies of the concourse. He felt less and less like a child and more like someone the first gen could count on. And the plans for the exit gate left Lance with a sense of adventure and focus that had been waning lately. He was actually going to be building the exit gate, which also meant one day they were actually getting off this ship. What an important reminder this was for him at times. He could feel his motivation rise as he thought about it. He also couldn't help but feel somewhat humbled at the sheer brilliance of the construction of the *Archean*. There was still much to learn about the inner workings of his home.

Twenty-two years on the Arc, and there are still things to discover about this bucket of bolts, he thought.

CHAPTER 09

Two weeks had passed since Fisher and his friends had recapped the last game of Graveyard. Fisher had barely made it halfway through the month, and he was already craving a break. While he was losing interest in the game and found it quite stressful at times, it did break up the monotony of non-stop work.

Exhausted from the day, Fisher replaced all the tools into their proper homes, something he wished others working in the foundry had remembered to do. He slid a small tube of epoxy into the front pocket of his coveralls and killed the overhead lights in the workroom.

First in, last out, Fisher thought.

Every fiber in his body whispered to head straight to the hive so he could get some much-needed sleep, but Fisher had one more item on his to-do list that had been nagging him for the past few days. *Better take care of it now, or I'll keep putting it off,* he thought.

Fisher entered the factory, and the racket from the army of machines overpowered his hearing. He squinted his eyes as they adjusted to the thermal engine high bay lights recessed in the ceilings that illuminated the room. It usually took Fisher a few minutes to acclimate to such a drastic change in the environment.

Most of the crew didn't care to spend time here, but there was something about the intense white lighting and rhythmic hum of the machines that made his heart race. The factory was one of Fisher's favorite areas on the Arc, and he often wished he would have been assigned cross-training here instead of the medical bay.

His father ran the factory, and for years, Fisher had assumed he would be working alongside him. It was common for most of the second gen'ers to presume that they would be drafted to work with their parents. Many were surprised when an announcement declared that an assessment exam would be given to determine OCP placement. Despite the second gen's pleas, the council held firm to the belief that the ship would be better run with crew members whose affinity and abilities matched the task, not the genetic similarity to the first generation. In addition, it was also suggested that fewer conflicts would arise if they were obeying orders from someone other than their own parents. So, Fisher landed in the foundry with Lance's father, and Alec followed the guidance of Fisher's dad in the factory.

All the components that were manufactured on the ship were created here, and it was the largest open area on the Arc, aside from the Hold. Rows of large machines lined both sides of the facility from bow to stern, with workbenches running down the center of the room. Oversized spools of a variety of materials ranging from plastics, metals, and fabrics sat between the machines. Fisher stopped in front of one of the 3D printers and watched as four high-powered lasers warmed areas in the resin tank, creating one layer of a part at a time. The factory had several types of 3D printers, knitting machines, and other technology to produce parts, but Fisher most loved watching parts being grown in the 3D printers.

Something about watching the printers produce these layers of complicated components relaxed him. It was hard to say exactly what this printer was producing. According to the digital display, this part was only fifteen percent completed, and so many of the components that were used on the ship looked similar. Fisher was always amazed at just how many things around the ship were created from these units.

"Traveling by way of the moon," Fisher's dad had always said.

With the Earth's natural resources depleted, engineers had created mining operations on the surface of the moon. The lunar surface had been stripped of large quantities of engineering metals such as iron, aluminum, magnesium, titanium, and silicon during the construction of the *Archean*. Most of the ship's core structure had been built by feeding these metals into giant 3D printers. These large ship components had then been constructed in the Earth's orbit, and smaller components were created for production on the *Archean* during the mission using similar 3D printing technology.

The lunar metals continued to be the source of much of the raw material used in production on the *Archean* and took up a considerable portion of the space in the cargo hold in the belly of the ship. These raw components made up most of the source material for the parts printed in the factory. Something about this fact always put a smile on Fisher's face. "Traveling by way of the moon" had a fantastical sound to it that reminded him just how amazing this journey was.

He looked past the rows of printers and saw Alec at one of the workbenches.

Alec was Dom's older brother by a year, something he loved to hold over Dom when things got heated between the two of them. Fisher and the others always questioned whether Alec and Dom were truly related, as the two couldn't be any more different. In addition to their contrasting physical appearance, they held opposing personality styles as well. Where Dom was the ship clown, Alec was more on the introspective, serious side. Alec could be found in his pod reading, while Dom could be seen racing down the corridors just to make it in time to watch the outriggers leaving the locker room in their extravehicular maneuvering units. Dom was the poster child for extroverts, and Alec was probably the most introverted of the second generation.

Fisher had become intrigued by Alec through the years. He had watched Alec evolve from a shy kid into this young adult who, although reserved, would still draw many others to him. Fisher wasn't clear how Alec did it. Maybe it was his no-nonsense, logical manner that the other second gen'ers respected. Alec was constantly in his head, analyzing and studying the people and situations that formed their isolated world. He was pensive and purposeful in his words and actions. Fisher sometimes wished he shared more of these qualities.

When they were younger, Fisher and Alec had been much closer than they were now. Prior to their respective OCP assignments, Fisher had spent every waking day surrounded by Alec and the other members in his hive. Now they were just two years into their OCPs, and Fisher could feel their friendship becoming strained. Since they were all assigned to different departments on the ship, the daily routines had changed, and their experiences were changing, too. Fisher noticed that Alec was someone he no longer knew as well as he had in the past.

As Fisher approached, he noticed Alec staring up at the ceiling, deep in thought. Fisher knew that look, and for a minute he considered doing an about-face and heading straight for the hive.

"What's up, Alec?"

Alec jolted in his chair, caught off guard. "Whoa, dude! Give a guy a heads up before you sneak into a room."

"Sorry," replied Fisher. "I didn't realize you couldn't hear me come in. What's got you working late tonight?"

Alec rose from his chair and walked to another workbench. "To be honest, I'm not really accomplishing much tonight. I've just been thinking about things and must have lost track of time."

"Everything okay?" asked Fisher tentatively, not really wanting to dive into this again with him.

"That's just it," sighed Alec, "I think everything *is* okay, but I, well . . . I should be happy, right? I mean, I landed a sweet gig when I was assigned the exact OCP I was gunning for, unlike Dom, who had his heart set on being an outrigger and got galley duty instead."

"Yeah, Dom talked about that since he was four," said Fisher. "He always wanted to be the first to piss in space."

"True," agreed Alec with a chuckle. The smile on his face quickly vanished. He paused, looked around to see if anyone else was nearby, and then lowered his voice. "With the Pairing Ceremony coming up in less than three months, it's really got me thinking about everything we are doing."

"We're all nervous about the Pairing, Alec, you're not the only one," shared Fisher. "Hell, I do everything I can each day to hide the fact that I'm terrified half the time just thinking about it."

"But that's just it. I'm not nervous about the Pairing. It's just part of all of it. Look, I get it. I'm part of a rare crew that will change the future of humanity, but I can't shake the thought that . . . I have no choice."

"No choice?" questioned Fisher.

"Yeah, with any of it. All of it. I mean, as exciting as it is, would you have signed up for any of this if you had a choice?"

Fisher was at a loss for how to respond.

"Think about it," Alec said before Fisher could find an answer. "None of us were ever given a choice. We were born into this. I can't help but think what my life . . . our lives . . . would have been like if we grew up on the Earth."

"The Earth is a hellhole, you know this," argued Fisher. "If you were born on the Earth, who knows what your life would have been like? Our parents only lived on the Earth for twenty years or so, and they have permanent lung damage. It's why we're headed to Uelara. It's why our parents signed up for all of this."

"Fish!" interrupted Alec. "I get it. I know. But that's kinda my point. Our parents volunteered for this. *We* didn't! Here lately I can't help but think about how my life isn't mine. Like I'm watching someone else go through life, and I'm just a spectator. I mean, I've never made a single decision . . . about . . . anything."

"What are you talking about?" Fisher asked. He noticed a bit of a wild look in Alec's eyes that was unfamiliar.

"Think about it," asserted Alec. "Have you ever chosen a meal? You definitely didn't choose your occupation. None of us did! The grand ol' OCP chose it for us. Hell, we won't even be deciding who we will be partnering with or whether or not to have kids, thanks to the Pairing."

Fisher had an aversion to thinking about the Pairing but hesitated to cut Alec off. He crossed his arms, looked toward the doorway and allowed Alec to proceed with his rant.

"Would you and I even be friends back on the Earth? Would we even know each other?" continued Alec.

"Why wouldn't we?" asked Fisher, surprised by the question.

"Fish, we're only friends because we were assigned to the same hive," grumbled Alec. "How many friends do you have from the other hives on the ship?"

Fisher didn't answer.

"Exactly! Don't get me wrong, Fish. I like you, I *do* consider you a friend. But I've been feeling like even my friendships have been assigned, no different from my occupation or my soon-to-be-wife. I can guarantee they wouldn't be assigning us wives on the Earth!"

Fisher counted to ten before responding again. Alec went through this existential crisis on a regular basis—every year or so. And somehow, the recurring struggle always seemed like it was presenting itself to him for the first time. Fisher consistently countered Alec's concerns with the same logic and reasoning, and he would always manage to talk Alec off the ledge. This time, Fisher could sense Alec's angst was building to a level that would be tougher to assuage. Fisher realized that the growing stress for Alec made sense; the more time passed, the more difficult the lack of control over his life would become.

"I understand," said Fisher, "I do. But I think you're forgetting the big picture here. This is all just temporary . . . small sacrifices. Remember that once we complete the trip to Uelara and finish setting up the exit gate, our mission will come to an end. We will be free to do *anything* we want. We'll be set for life."

"But we won't make it there for another thirty years. Half of our lives will have passed by," argued Alec. "That's a massive sacrifice that has been forced on us."

"I won't argue the size of our sacrifice, but we'll be free of this ship and get to live the rest of our lives as we please. And just like our parents, we'll be remembered by all of humanity for the sacrifices we have made. Would you rather make sacrifices now and eventually have a better life than you ever imagined, or live on the Earth where everything is absolute shit, but you're free to decide?"

Alec was quiet for a moment and let out a long sigh. "Maybe you have a point. I'm probably just tired and need some shut-eye. Sorry to be a downer."

Fisher felt sorry for Alec's grim outlook and was exhausting his list of consoling words and logical arguments. He asked, "Have you talked with the Vosts lately?"

"I'm supposed to meet with Dr. Ben this week. Lot of good that'll do, huh?"

"Eh, they're not that bad. They have their moments. Helped me a time or two, actually," offered Fisher.

Alec nodded, then asked, "What did you swing in here for?"

"Almost forgot! Was hoping you had my nameplate for my pod."

"The printer finished that days ago. It's over there on the shelf. I still don't get why you keep replacing it, Fish. You know Lance is just going to screw with it again. How many replacements does this one make?"

"I think this one is creeping into the twenties at this point," Fisher said with a smile, "but as long as he keeps breaking them, I'll keep replacing them. Otherwise, he wins."

"Ah, that's how you see it," said Alec. "Well regardless, be sure to give the old one to Echo so he can recycle it."

"Will do. I'm beat. Heading to the hive. Want to go with me? You could probably use the sleep as much as I could."

"Good idea. Give me a minute to shut everything down."

Alec straightened up his workspace, shut off the light at his workbench, and the two young men headed for the hive. On the way out, Fisher started laughing.

"What's so funny?" asked Alec.

"You do realize that regardless of whether or not you were able to make choices in your life, Dom would still be your brother."

Alec groaned. "Don't remind me!"

CHAPTER 10

Fisher stared at the hexagonal tiling of the pods back at the hive. *Home sweet home,* he thought. He looked up at the old nameplate above his pod where Lance had snapped the right end off, leaving only the first four characters of his name: F-I-S-H.

He reached up and, using his index and middle fingers, slid the damaged nameplate from the grooves that held it in place and shoved it in the lower left pocket of his coveralls. He removed the new plate from his lower right pocket and slid it into the grooves. As Alec crawled into his pod, he whispered over to Fisher, "Pointless, Fish . . . absolutely pointless."

Fisher shook his head, reached into his front pocket and pulled out the small tube of epoxy he had taken from the foundry. He squeezed a small trail of glue along the track that held the nameplate and smiled.

"Good luck this time, Lance," he whispered. He shoved the tube back into his pocket and retreated into his pod.

Once in, the door to his pod slid shut, and Fisher released a long sigh. He knew he'd be asleep in minutes. He activated the white noise machine built into the ceiling of the pod, which provided a degree of isolation by producing a variety of soothing sounds. Fisher had become dependent on this sleep-aid to be able to get a good night's rest. These subtle audible waves masked distractions, such as Dom "exploring himself" in the middle of the night, something that had become somewhat of a ritual with Dom these past few months.

Sam once explained to Fisher that the pods' hexagonal tiling construction was the most efficient way to divide the hive's twelve sleeping pods in such a small space. Efficient or not, it was far from ideal when it came to privacy. The inner walls of the pods were constructed out of thin sheets of molded ABS plastic. Multiple panels held in place by recessed screws ran along the walls of the pod and gave the maintenance crews easy access to the air-filtration system. While it had great aesthetic qualities and strength to last several generations, it did little for soundproofing.

The white noise machine provided multiple options, but Fisher preferred the ocean waves setting. Being born on the ship, Fisher had never experienced a real beach, but his mother had shared fond memories of her trips to the beaches from when she was a girl. From her descriptions, Fisher's memories were as if he had been there with her, with sand between his toes and the salty air blowing against his skin.

Fisher set his alarm, rolled onto his side and looked at the wall where he had hung a faded picture of Ka'anapali Beach that his mother had given him. This photo was the only item that personalized Fisher's pod, and it was the imagery that came to mind anytime he thought about what Uelara would be like. As sounds of waves crashed onto the shore, Fisher closed his eyes and quickly drifted off to sleep.

He found himself lying on the sand a few yards away from crashing waves. He sat up and could feel sand brush against his skin, as wind danced across the beach. Fisher sunk his hand into the pale yellowish-brown sand beneath him and lifted a handful of it up in front of his eyes. He slowly loosened his grip and watched, as a stream of tiny granules poured from his hand. Fisher looked out at the sky above the ocean and marveled at the intense pinks, lavenders, and blues that blended together. The waves mirrored the colored sky as the sun appeared to recede into the distant horizon.

Fisher got to his feet, took in a deep breath and exhaled, taking in his surroundings with all his senses. He scrunched his toes and could feel millions of particles caressing his feet. In the distance he could hear people laughing, but a quick survey around him failed to locate the source of the crowd.

"Fisher," whispered a voice.

Fisher spun around but couldn't see where the voice came from. He started walking away from the beach toward a patch of trees where he could still hear the faint sound of laughter. As he walked closer, he could hear rustling coming from within the dense growth of trees and shrubs. Moments later, Sam emerged, laughing.

"Fisher, it's even better than we imagined!"

"What is?"

"Uelara. Come see what we found!"

Sam reached out, grabbed Fisher's hand, and pulled him into the thicket. As they raced along, Fisher could hear a faint ringing coming from all directions. The volume of the sound increased, drowning out the sounds of the distant waves coming from the beach.

As Fisher's eyes slowly opened, he found himself staring at the ceiling of his pod. He reached over without looking and activated the snooze function on his alarm. He shut his eyes with the hope that he could return to Uelara and catch a glimpse of what the others had found.

CHAPTER 11

Lance stood on the exterior hull of the ship, wearing his extra-vehicular mobility unit. No matter how many spacewalks he'd logged, he was always impressed with the size of the *Archean*. Even though he had seen portions of the ship from various observation windows throughout his life, nothing compared to walking in space and staring back at his gigantic home.

The *Archean* was just under 2,000 meters long, and some areas of the exterior looked almost unfinished, revealing the underlying manifolds and struts. Looking toward the back of the craft, Lance could see a dim blue light emitting from the cluster of engines that propelled the ship toward Uelara. He marveled at how something so gargantuan could be moved through space so effortlessly.

Individually, the components that made up the exterior of the Arc seemed no different from what could be found in the oxygen farm, engine room, and other facilities inside the ship. Looking to his left, Lance gazed at what appeared to be an endless construction of smooth, interlocking metal plating, as well as modules that reminded him of the images of giant cities found on the Earth that his father had shown him as a child. It amazed Lance to think that the first generation had played a role in the ship's construction and that he had been given the opportunity to maintain such a complex structure.

"Lance, what's the hold up?" barked Stringer through the earbuds in Lance's communication carrier assembly. Stringer was notably the most well-respected first generation senior outrigger. Lance was aware of his good fortune being assigned to Stringer's team.

Lance spoke into the boom microphone that ran from the right ear area of the CCA to his mouth. "Just catching my breath, sir."

"You'll have plenty of time for that down below," said Stringer. "We're burning oxygen. Need to wrap this up soon."

Lance turned around and could see Stringer, Kayla, Toby, and Deuce four meters up ahead. Lance started making his way to the rest of the group. Each step he took was slow and methodical. Although he had several months experience in the EMU, both inside the Arc and during actual spacewalks, Lance still found that movement in the suit took an incredible amount of effort. He was drenched in sweat.

Every time Lance raised a foot, the magnetic boots resisted, requiring much more force than a normal step. As each foot came close to making contact with the hull, the magnetic force of the boots snapped down with a jolt, locking it to the metal surface of the Arc. While it took a great deal of force to move, it was a constant reminder that he wouldn't simply float away from the ship, a reminder that Lance welcomed.

"Operations reported a leak of 275 pascals per day coming from one of these," said Stringer, pointing at rows of condensers. "That corresponds to a daily loss of about a quarter of a percent of the factory's normal air pressure."

"What should we be looking for?" asked Deuce.

"Look for any unusual wear and tear, and if no visible signs jump out at you, try using the ultrasonic leak detector unit located in your left arm display," replied Stringer.

Lance and the others surveyed the condensers.

"I think I found the culprit," said Kayla, looking at a display on her suit and pointing to the condenser closest to her. "I've got an erratic frequency showing on my wireless sensors."

Lance joined Kayla and took a closer look at the unit.

Kayla was one of two female outriggers from the second generation. When Kayla had first been assigned to Stringer's crew, Lance had thought she wouldn't be able to handle the work, but it wasn't long before he realized he couldn't have been more wrong. The two quickly became friends, and she was Lance's first real connection with a second gen outside of his hive.

"I think it may be the vacuum jumper that equalizes the pressure across the unit," he said.

"Good work," said Stringer. "Let's see if we can patch it or if we need to replace the jumper."

Lance held the jumper in place as Kayla removed a patch kit from one of the pouches on the side of her suit. With what looked like little effort, Kayla had the vacuum jumper sealed tight.

Lance overheard voices communicating through his CCA.

"Operations, this is Stringer. We think we've rectified the problem. Can you confirm?"

"Operations here, we're tracking a temperature increase. Give us a moment to confirm that the leak has dissipated."

Lance and the others continued to survey the area for any additional issues that may have been overlooked.

The voice returned over the CCA. "Stringer, this is Operations. All signs indicate the leak has been resolved. Thanks for the assist."

"Copy that," replied Stringer. "We'll continue surveying the area and will be down soon."

"I've logged the unit into the system, sir," said Toby, keying a few characters into his portable terminal.

"Good. We'll check back in a few days to make sure the patch holds," said Stringer. "Okay, we've got about twelve more minutes. Let's check the ventilation pipes that run along this paneling on our way back."

Lance looked over at Kayla and gave her a thumbs-up. "Nice work, partner!"

"Thanks . . . you too," said Kayla with a smile.

As the crew made their way to the airlock, Lance stole one last look over his shoulder, taking in the blanket of stars surrounding him. It was as if they were within his reach.

"I wish Helena could see this."

CHAPTER 12

Dom stood with his forehead pressed against one of the observation windows, staring off into space. He'd just spent the last two hours watching Lance and the rest of the outriggers survey the exterior of the ship and repair what looked like one of the condensers.

Dom understood that, in theory, the tasks they were performing were really no different from his Ag duties or even the general maintenance that Echo was tasked with. Even with that knowledge, he couldn't help but be dismayed that he would never get to experience life outside the Arc until they set down on Uelara. And even then, it would be too late to experience a spacewalk.

Ever since he could remember, Dom had wanted to wear an EMU and spend time outside the ship. He had been convinced that he would be assigned to the outriggers, but wanting something badly enough apparently held no weight with the OCP council. Dom felt robbed.

Amber lights began to flash, and sirens wailed as the inner airlock slid open. Dom watched as the outrigger team emerged from the decompression chamber.

Lance looked at Dom and smiled. "What's up, Dom?"

"That was AWESOME!" exclaimed Dom. "Tell me all about it!"

Dom had always looked up to Lance. Before the OCP assignments, Dom had spent a lot of time hanging out with him. Most of Dom's life skills, knowledge of the female anatomy, and overall cool factor were attributed, in Dom's mind, to spending so much of his time with Lance. When Lance was assigned to the outriggers, Dom decided he'd have to settle with living vicariously through Lance, and Lance seemed more than happy to oblige.

Lance's smile grew twice the size as normal. "You in a rush today?"

"I have the next hour free before I have to be back at the pools," answered Dom. "How about you?"

"Cool, I have a surprise for you that I think you'll dig," said Lance as he motioned to Dom to follow him behind the rest of the outriggers.

"Break down the EMUs and go get some R and R. You guys did well out there today," said Stringer as he entered the locker room.

Pointing to his suit and rocking his helmet between his forearm and waist, Lance said, "Dom, let me ditch this kit and we can go. Wait here for a minute."

Lance followed the others into the locker room of the middeck and motioned for Dom to wait outside. His mind raced with ideas of what Lance had in store for him. Stringer emerged from the locker room and looked over at Dom.

"How's Andrew treatin' you guys in the galley?" asked Stringer.

"Not bad, sir."

Stringer smiled. "Tell him I said go easy on the fructose. My crew was letting them rip all afternoon."

Dom laughed. "You got it, sir. Actually, can I ask you a question about Andrew?"

"Shoot."

"What was he like when you first met him?"

"What do you mean?"

"I don't know. Did he always talk so much back then?"

Stringer laughed and put his arm around Dom. "Dom, Dom, Dom . . . you have no idea. That man could out-talk all five of the Quints any day of the week. When he was your age, the only thing that would shut him up was when Debra entered the room. I have him to thank for my hearing loss in my right ear!"

Dom let out a laugh but set a mental note to stand back a little next time Andrew was shouting orders in the galley.

Stringer gave Dom a wink, turned, and walked down the corridor. "And tell him he should spend more time getting creative with the meals and less time staring in the mirror."

"I don't think he'll be doing that anytime soon!" shouted Dom. Dom could hear Stringer's laugh fade down the corridor.

One by one the outriggers left the locker room, each giving nods to Dom. After a few minutes, Lance stuck his head out of the room and whispered, "Quick, get in here!"

Dom's eyes widened, and his trademark Cheshire grin crept onto his face as he dashed into the locker room.

"I could get into a lot of trouble for doing this, so we gotta make it quick," whispered Lance as his eyes motioned to the EMU he had just crawled out of.

"No. Way." Dom gasped. "Seriously?"

Lance smiled. "It's pretty ripe in there, so enter at your own risk."

Dom stepped into the lower portion of the EMU as Lance lowered the upper hard torso assembly and connected it to the lower part of the kit. After a small adjustment, Dom heard a loud *click*. Lance placed the communication carrier assembly on Dom's head and adjusted the microphone in front of Dom's mouth. Lance grabbed his helmet and secured it onto the upper torso, twisting it into place.

Lance wasn't kidding, thought Dom, as his eyes started to tear up and burn from the odors coming from within the suit. Lance's remaining sweat dripped from the CCA onto Dom's head and down the sides of his face. After a few minutes, Dom was decked out head to toe in Lance's EMU.

"Almost a perfect fit," joked Lance, seeing it was clearly two sizes too big.

Electricity fired through every nerve in Dom's body. He had never been so elated, and it took everything for him to try to remain calm. "Sooo, can I take it for a spin?"

Dom attempted to stand up but wasn't prepared for the weight of the suit. He fell back onto the bench with a thud.

"Whoa! Are you crazy? Stringer would have my head if he knew you were even in the locker room, bud! I'm taking a major risk here, Dom."

"Sorry, man. But I had to ask. You know this, right?"

Lance laughed. "Of course, I get it." He pointed to the display on the left forearm of the suit. "We used the ultrasonic leak detector in this display unit to find the leak in the vacuum jumper today."

"Sweet!" squealed Dom.

A noise from outside the locker room drew Lance's attention toward the door. Dom held his breath and could see Lance do the same. After a few moments of silence, both exhaled with relief.

"Okay, time's up. Let's get you out of there before the cleaners arrive."

Dom pouted. "Awww, man!"

As Lance helped Dom work his way out of the suit, Dom fired off question after question about Lance's experiences of being an outrigger. This was the norm whenever he was with Lance, and like the big-brother surrogate he was, Lance always made time for him.

Dom stood behind as Lance peered out of the locker room, looking down the corridor both ways. Like two kids sneaking treats out of the galley after midnight, they quickly crept out of the room.

"Thanks, Lance, that was really cool of you," said Dom, smiling up at his friend.

Lance nodded and lightly punched him in the arm. "No problem."

Dom coughed. "Dude, you reek. Is that really what I smell like right now?"

"I warned you!"

CHAPTER 13

A few days after Zach had left for the Q, Sam started to realize just how much more productive she was when she wasn't constantly defending every word that came out of her mouth. She had already finished the flight path simulation coordinates and condenser algorithm updates she'd been assigned and was waiting for the next batch of tasks to come her way. This gave her time to work on a personal project she had been working on for the past several months.

Sam was obsessed with finding the optimal solution to any problem, even problems that had already been solved. She had been reviewing the location of every geodetic ring they had released since the start of the mission and believed she'd discovered that they could increase the distance between the rings if they released them nine hours later than they normally did. While nine hours could appear to be a trivial amount of time considering the length of the mission, over the course of a couple of decades, this could save them from releasing one, possibly two rings by mission's end. Fewer rings translated to shortened travel time for the transport ships' journey to Uelara.

She hadn't mentioned her discovery to anyone yet, especially Debra, as she wanted to be positive her theory was solid. If correct, her proposal would change everything.

"Thought I'd find you here," said Fisher as he entered the room.

Sam looked over at Fisher in confusion. "Shouldn't you be working?"

"Our shifts ended three hours ago. You missed dinner . . . again."

Sam looked at the time on her terminal and was surprised to see how quickly the last few hours had passed. "Wow, time really did sneak by me today."

"Man, Debra must really be keeping you busy."

"Actually, I've been working on something outside of my assignments. I haven't shown anyone but have been dying to get this in front of someone with a fresh pair of eyes. Got a minute?"

"Of course, but first, take these." Fisher reached into his front pocket and pulled out two protein bars. "Courtesy of Dom. Shame, really. Dinner wasn't half bad. You would have been surprised."

Sam grabbed the bars and placed them next to her terminal. "I'd probably starve to death if it weren't for you guys. Thanks for looking out for me." Sam grabbed the virtual reality headset that was connected to her system and handed it to Fisher. "Put this on and get comfortable while I queue up the simulation."

"Cool, been a while since I used one of these bad boys," said Fisher with a grin. "What are we going to play?"

Sam sat in her chair and slid toward her terminal. She initiated her simulation. "It's not a game, Fish. It's better."

"Alright . . . now you have my attention," said Fisher, tightening the strap on the back of the headset.

Sam pressed a series of keys, and the headset began to hum. Inside the headset, it was as if Fisher stood in open space. Several amber rings began to appear, followed by a neon blue ribbon that connected them.

"Whoa!" he exclaimed.

"Okay . . . see those rings? Those represent all of the geodetic rings that have been deployed from the *Archean* since the start of the mission."

"And the ribbon represents the path the *Archean* has traveled up until now?" asked Fisher, raising his hand and pointing.

"Correct!" she answered. Sam pressed a few more keys, and then a series of purple dots appeared offset from the amber rings along the blue ribbon. As each purple dot appeared, it grew farther from the next amber ring.

"What are the purple dots?"

"Those dots represent my proposed location of the rings using calculations I've been working on."

Sam hit a few more keys on the keyboard. In the top right portion of Fisher's display, purple and amber digital zeroes appeared, stacking vertically. Moments later, a red tetrahedron appeared at the start of the blue ribbon.

"The red tetrahedron represents one of the transport ships that will travel from the Earth through the rings. But I want you to keep an eye on the digital counters in the top right of your display."

She pressed a key on the keyboard, and the tetrahedron traveled the length of the ribbon. As it moved, the digital numbers increased. The purple numbers increased at a faster rate than the amber ones. The tetrahedron reached the end of the ribbon, and the digital counters stopped. The purple counter's value was higher than the amber counter by over three thousand.

"Okay, so what does this mean exactly?" asked Fisher.

"Isn't it obvious?" Sam jumped out of her chair and rushed to Fisher, placing her hands on his shoulders. "By these calculations, we could have reduced the number of rings by three, which in turn would have shaved a few hours of travel time for the transport ships. The first gen'ers must have miscalculated the distance the geo-rings need to be from each other to cover the distance to Uelara!"

Fisher shook his head in wonder. "How could they have been so off?"

"I've been thinking about that," she replied. "Without the exact data recorded from the trip so far, it's possible they were working with insufficient information. We are constantly updating the flight plan, and there is a two-hour window for all three stages of the ring deployment. Half of what we do here in the Tank is reevaluate the schedule based on new numbers. It's why we are always reworking the flight plan and timing of ring deployment. But honestly, it's possible they just needed a fresh perspective on this."

"So, what does Debra think about all this?" asked Fisher.

"She hasn't seen it. I mean, I really want to make sure my calculations are accurate before showing her. I know it's too late to do anything about the existing rings, but it isn't too late for the remaining rings that would be placed over the next three decades. This means we could cease production of new geo-rings a few years before arriving at Uelara. This is BIG, Fish!"

Fisher removed the headset, rubbed his eyes with his index finger and thumb, and looked at Sam quizzically. "So why not get Debra involved?"

"Debra isn't the type of person you present every theory and idea you have. I want—no, I need to have all my data air-tight before getting her involved. I still need to run my simulation on the remaining portion of the ship's path to confirm my theory, and then I'll write up a full report and present it to her."

"This is big. Like, really big, Sam."

"I know! And get this. I think we could be ready to implement the changes for the release of the next ring."

"What can I do to help?"

"If you're up for it, you could hop on Zach's terminal and help feed the remaining flight-plan data into the sim while I plot the ring deployment locations based on my new algorithm," she said smiling, downplaying how boring data entry was.

"I gotcha covered!" said Fisher as he walked toward Zach's terminal. "Wait until everybody hears about this!"

"Whoa, you can't tell anyone about this until I've talked with Debra, got it?" she commanded. "Last thing I want is false hope spreading throughout the ship. If it turns out I'm wrong, everyone would be furious with me."

"Understood," he replied, and with a wink added, "But, Sam, when was the last time you were wrong about . . . anything?"

CHAPTER 14

Helena's Log, Y22 D140

People of the Earth,

I haven't logged experiences about my role on the Arc recently and thought today I'd share my day in the Bay. I spent the morning tending to Zach and Samar in the Q. Today marks day eight of their time in quarantine, and they are in the middle of their bout of influenza, a contagious respiratory illness. It's hard to say whether they were struggling more with their aching muscles and runny noses or each other. I do have to say that they haven't been at odds with each other as much the last few days.

I did my best to address all their needs and to remind them how important it was that they experience the virus now. Dr. Gage explained that certain viruses could lead to longer recovery times and could even be fatal with older adults, a factoid that Zach made clear didn't help the diarrhea he was experiencing today.

Samar appeared to pity Zach's excessive trips to the lav. Maybe their time in the Q this round is bringing them closer together. It wouldn't be the first time that happened to guests of the Q. It was my time with Lance in the Q that sparked our connection with each other. It's where the real Lance was revealed to me, the kind Lance that opened up about the loss of his mother and his unending desire to make his dad proud of him. If Lance would only show others this side of himself, they would see what I see.

My afternoon was overwhelming. Dr. Gage had me operate the volume spectral computed tomography scanner, which takes a series of pictures using x-rays as it rotates around the patients while they lie on a table. Once the scanning process is completed, the data is computed and generates a volumetric model that allows us to view detailed cross sections of their bodies. This three-dimensional imaging is amazing. It allows us to obtain high-resolution images of blood vessels, soft tissue, organs, and bones. We're able to detect the smallest of lesions, and it helps us diagnose diseases with more confidence.

Although my parents talked about the damage the Earth's environment had done to their bodies, seeing the scans of the first generation today was still shocking. Abnormal masses could be seen in the lungs of every single person we scanned today. I'm not sure how I could possibly minimize the effects of their diseases when we see them breathing through their POCs every day, but apparently, I was in some sort of denial.

Dr. Gage explained that those masses are carcinoid tumors, and that they could be found in all the Earth-born crew. None of them seemed fazed when he explained to them that the tumors are continuing to grow and spread. It was as if he had told them that they had a headache that would pass in a few hours.

These tumors are at the core of why the first generation's lifespan is going to be much shorter than the second generation's. It's also a reminder of just how lucky I am that I was born on the *Archean*. The air we will breathe on Uelara won't contain the poisonous gases that caused these tumors. We will have a fair shot at living out full, healthy lives.

What an emotionally draining experience this was. Dr. Gage explained that the treatments the first generation receive help to slow the growth of the tumors considerably, but let's face it, the parents just aren't going to live as long as we all would like. I've known for several years that the first gen wouldn't be joining the second gen on Uelara, but seeing the scans today made it all that much more real for me. I spoke with Dr. Gage about it, and he said that as a doctor I must learn to live with the inevitable fact that some patients die. He explained that he wasn't immune to grief, but it was this grief that made him more aware of just how important his role was in relieving others of their suffering.

To be honest, today has me questioning whether I'm cut out to work in the medical bay. Kaman from Hive 4 has been working with me in the Bay for about two years now, and she just seems much more prepared to handle these kinds of stressors than I will ever be. I'm not sure if she realizes how much I admire her. She has this presence that remains calm, positive, and reassuring, no matter what chaos surrounds her. I may be fooling the others, but only I know the inner turmoil that is my near-constant companion. Maybe I'll just pretend to be more like Kaman, and someday my psyche will begin to believe the changes.

I don't know if I'll ever be as hardened as Dr. Gage. Will I be prepared for the deaths of all our parents? My friends? I don't know, maybe Dr. Gage is right. Death is inevitable, and if I can help ease someone's suffering, maybe working in the Bay will be worthwhile. And who knows, maybe it will prepare me for the losses to come.

CHAPTER 15

Lance entered the small waiting room outside the Vost's offices. He looked over and saw Kaman with her nose in an over-sized book with the title *Clinical Handbook of Internal Medicine* embossed with silver foil on the spine.

She worked with Helena in the medical bay a couple of days each week, and Lance would see her when visiting Helena on her breaks. Kaman was from Hive 4, and until the second generation had been assigned their OCPs, he really didn't have much interaction with her. Her mother was from a place called Hong Kong, and English was her second language. While Kaman's accent wasn't as thick as her mother's, she would sometimes mispronounce English vowel sounds and consonants. Lance found the way Kaman spoke intriguing but secretly felt nervous when she was around. Something about her gave off a superior air, yet he could never pinpoint what exactly created it. She seemed humble enough, and yet Kaman was knowledgeable, it seemed, on virtually every topic. She could usually be found studying after dinner, eager to learn as much new information as she could absorb. It was tough for Lance to understand how someone could be that studious by choice. He respected her but couldn't relate.

"Doing some light reading, Kaman?"

Kaman looked up at Lance and giggled. "Hey, Lance! What'd you do this time?"

"You know me, straight and narrow!"

Kaman smiled. "Sure."

Toby, also from Hive 4, was one of the other outriggers in Lance's crew, and he had a thing for Kaman. He talked about her all the time. Lance couldn't understand why Toby didn't simply put the moves on her. It had worked for Lance with Helena.

"So, you here to see Dr. Fiona?" asked Lance, taking a seat next to Kaman on the couch.

"Yeah. She's mentoring me as part of my OCP cross-training."

"Wait, you're not going to become one of these head-knockers, are you?"

"Sure, I find it interesting. Don't you?"

"Are you kidding me? It's just a bunch of psychobabble," said Lance, twirling his index finger by his right temple.

Kaman laughed. "You're so bad."

"That's what everyone keeps telling me," Lance said with a smirk.

The door to Dr. Fiona's office slid open and Avery walked out, her eyes red and puffy. She glanced toward Kaman and Lance and quickly dropped her gaze to the floor. The color crept up into her cheeks, and she quickened her pace toward the exit. Through her sniffling, she said, "Oh, hey, guys. I gotta run, but I'll catch up with you later."

Before Kaman or Lance could respond, Avery was gone.

Dr. Fiona stood at the doorway. "Why hello, Lance. Good to see you again! It's been a while."

"Yeah, Stringer has us pretty busy these days."

"Have you been waiting long? I'm sure Dr. Ben will be ready for you shortly."

"Just got here. No rush."

"Come on in, Kaman. I've got some fascinating things to share with you today."

Kaman walked toward Dr. Fiona's office and looked back at Lance over her shoulder. "Don't give Dr. Ben too hard of a time in there, Lance."

"Who, me?"

Kaman and Dr. Fiona retreated into the office and slid the door closed. Moments later, Dr. Ben's office door slid open, and Alec walked out.

"What's up, Alec?"

"Hey, Lance. Dr. Ben asked me to send you in on my way out. Good luck. He's feeling *extra* helpful today," said Alec with a smile.

"Thanks for the heads up. I owe you one."

Lance stood up and made his way into the office, sliding the door behind him. The room was dimly lit, and three of the walls were lined with shelves overstuffed with books. Additional books were stacked into several piles on the floor, and on the fourth wall hung four ornate masks that Dr. Ben had collected from his time back on Earth. The masks always made Lance feel uneasy, as if they were eavesdropping on his conversations with Dr. Ben. One of the masks wore a hideous smile that had haunted Lance as a child, and to this day he still felt uncomfortable at the site of it. Dr. Ben also played a digital audio file of trickling water that was supposed to be soothing but usually just made Lance feel like he needed a trip to the lavatory.

Before joining the crew of the *Archean*, the Vosts had made a name for themselves in a country called England. They were most known for their research of long-duration expeditionary missions where they theorized about the psychological and sociological effects of life on a generation ship. The first gen always talked about how lucky the crew of the Arc was for having the Vosts on board, as they were the ideal candidates for the ship's psychologists. Lance disagreed and believed they could easily have found better options.

"Ah, good to see you, Lance," said Dr. Ben, sitting behind his large, black desk. "Grab a seat."

Lance loathed his time in this office. Over the years, his disdain toward the Vosts had grown like an incurable infection.

At one point, the Vosts' accents had made Lance think they were smarter than the rest of the first generation. But for the last few years, their voices reminded him of the whine of the metal casings being dropped in the cooling baths. That sound could travel the length of the ship all the way from the engine room.

It wasn't just the tone of their voices that made Lance want to jump out of the ship. Dr. Ben would take long, drawn out pauses before talking. When he would manage to speak, there was an exaggerated delay in uttering each word. Lance fondly referred to this mind-numbing speech pattern as "sedation speak."

"It's been a while, Lance," said Dr. Ben as he stood from his desk and walked toward a pair of chairs. "Have a seat. Catch me up on how things are going."

Dr. Ben sat in one of the chairs and motioned to Lance to sit in the open seat. Lance grabbed the back of the chair, pulled it about a meter away from where Dr. Ben was sitting, and slumped into it.

"Not much to report, Doc. Stringer keeps us busy throughout the week, and I squeeze in as much time with Helena as I can."

Dr. Ben opened his mouth to speak and paused for a beat. "And . . . how are things with Helena?"

"Couldn't be better," said Lance, looking at the floor.

Dr. Ben sat silent for a moment, but Lance could see that he wasn't finished. Lance turned these long pauses into a game. He started counting in his head, *One Archean, two Archean, three Archean* . . . The record was twenty-four *Archeans*.

"So . . . do you know why I've asked you here today?"

"Nope."

Dr. Ben flipped through his files in his lap, and then looked up at Lance. "Anything happen yesterday that you'd like to discuss?"

"Nope."

"Well . . . I'd like to discuss the altercation you had with one of the young men from Hive 2."

Lance looked at Dr. Ben and then back at the floor. He ran his fingers through his wavy, dark hair and then dropped his muscular arms to his sides as if they were lead weights. "That? That was nothing, just goofing around."

"Interesting," said Dr. Ben, looking back at his files. "Says here the other fellow left the medical bay after you two were 'goofing around' with a split lip and bruised retina."

"We were just playing around, and he accidently stepped into my elbow," said Lance with an annoyed tone. "You can ask him. He'll tell you the same thing."

"I'm sure he will," replied Dr. Ben. "I'm not challenging your . . . story."

"Sure feels like it," grumbled Lance, tensing up.

Dr. Ben looked down at Lance's fists tightening and then looked at Lance. Lance caught the look and relaxed his fists.

"So . . . have you been using those techniques we discussed?" asked Dr. Ben.

"Sure, I guess. I mean, why is this all on me? I can't help it if people provoke me."

Dr. Ben sat silent.

"Everyone thinks I have an anger issue, but did anyone consider that the problem might not be me?"

Ben paused and slightly opened his mouth.

One Archean, two Archean, counted Lance to himself.

"Lance, everyone gets angry. Your anger is normal. It's a healthy emotion, but it's important to deal with it in a positive way." Dr. Ben reached over and pulled the POC from his desk, inhaling slowly. After a brief moment, he continued. "Your impulse control could definitely benefit from a little attention as well. I fear that one of these days your knee-jerk reactions are going to be too severe and will lead you to a point of no return."

"I tried your techniques. Those little mental timeouts only increase my frustration with people."

"What about the Tai Chi practice?"

"That Kung Fu garbage that Sam does? Nah, I'm good. I'd rather spend my allotted exercise time working out instead of dancing and waving my arms around and calling it martial arts."

"It's not garbage, Lance. There are countless studies that indicate Tai Chi can enhance your mood and decrease levels of depression, anxiety, and stress."

"You saying I'm depressed, Doc? Do you see me walking around here, bawling my eyes out like Avery? You know, for someone with all your credentials, you'd think you would be a little more observant."

Dr. Ben sighed. "All I'm suggesting is that you give it a try. Your displays of anger and impulsivity are doing you no favors on this ship, and one would imagine that you would want to be perceived to be in top physical and emotional form as we approach the next ring deployment."

Lance turned his head away and looked at the artificial plant sitting on the bookcase. *Damn him,* he thought. Dr. Ben was right. He hated when Dr. Ben was right. If he kept getting into these altercations, as Dr. Ben called them, the first gen would strip him of his OCP and have him sorting bins with Echo. There was too much riding on the ring deployments to have someone who was considered a loose cannon out there.

"Well, it sounds like we need to try something new. Outbursts won't fix anything and will only make things worse," said Dr. Ben.

"Seems to work for others on the ship. Have you talked with anyone who works with Thomas in the engine room? Or do your beliefs about anger management only apply to us young folks?" Lance asked.

"We're not here to talk about Thomas or Avery or anyone else. We're here to talk about what you can do to control your anger before it takes a toll on your relationships and your health."

"My relationships are fine, and I'm the healthiest person on this ship."

Dr. Ben flipped through his notes, looked at Lance and paused.

One Archean, two Archean, three Archean . . .

"Look, Lance, I only want to help you."

"We've been at this for how many years, Doc? Maybe you're the wrong person to help. Ever think about that?"

"Would you like to start meeting with Dr. Fiona?"

"Is that an option?" Lance didn't want to spend any time with the Vosts, but if meeting with Dr. Fiona would mean he could be finished with Dr. Ben and his bullshit, he was willing to try anything.

"If you're willing to come back with an open mind and listen to what Dr. Fiona has to say, I think we can arrange it."

"Sign me up."

"I only ask that in the meantime, you continue to try some of the techniques we've discussed the next time you start becoming angry."

"You got it, Doc."

"Perfect. I'll speak with Dr. Fiona, and she'll be in touch when she can meet with you. I'd also like to schedule you some time in the Dome."

As convinced as he was that Dr. Ben had nothing useful to offer him, Lance couldn't argue with the idea of extra Dome time. He'd be a fool to reject that prescription. Plus, he could sneak Helena in with him to really relieve some stress. Now Dr. Ben was speaking his language.

"So . . . are we done?"

"We still have a few minutes left in our session. Let's . . ." Dr. Ben paused.

One Archean, two Archean, three Archean, four Archean . . .

CHAPTER 16

Fisher gritted his teeth in annoyance as he entered the auditorium. Arriving late on a theater night reduced the chance he'd get to sit with his friends, and he was really looking forward to catching up with Sam.

Years ago, the first gen'ers had suggested that it could be fun to perform hacked-together plays to entertain the crew. What had begun as a temporary effort to distract the kids quickly evolved into an all-out *Archean* favorite tradition. The entire crew would eagerly anticipate each performance, regardless of how silly, implausible, or just plain bad the plots or acting were. In the last few years, some of the second generation had started participating as well, making it that much more entertaining for Fisher and his friends.

Tonight was a continuation from last month's show, which had ended with a cliffhanger, and everyone was excited to see how tonight's saga would end. As he entered the auditorium, Fisher scanned the seats looking for Sam and the others.

"Yo, Fish!" shouted Dom as he stood up on his seat and waved his arms.

Fisher saw Dom, Alec, and Sam sitting in the far back corner of the auditorium. On the way to his friends, Fisher saw the Quints sitting with their parents in the front row. They were all talking, pointing, and looking around the room, but as he passed by, Sean stared at Fisher with a slight smile on his face. Not a "hey-there's-my-buddy-Fisher" type smile. It looked more like a "I-know-where-you-sleep" type smile. A familiar chill ran down Fisher's spine.

"What's with that kid?" Fisher muttered to himself. He quickly bolted up the stairs toward his friends and tried to shake the eerie feeling.

"Dude, we thought you'd forgotten about the show!" said Dom.

"Are you kidding me? And miss out on Dr. Ben making a fool out of himself in front of everyone? Never." Fisher looked over at Sam who appeared to be deep in thought, a look he recognized well. "Trying to solve an equation?" he asked, nudging her as he took the empty seat beside her.

"Huh? Nah, just thinking about my conversation with Debra today," she answered absently.

Fisher's eyes brightened. "Oh, yeah. I was curious how that went. What'd she say?"

The lights in the auditorium dimmed. Conversations in the room continued but softened into whispers. Sam looked toward the stage. "One sec. Here comes my mother."

Margot walked on stage, and the audience grew quiet. "We will be starting the show in just a few minutes. Please find your seats, and we'll begin shortly."

Fisher's attention was pulled to the front row. Peering over the back of his chair sat Sean, staring at Fisher with the same, creepy smile.

Why the hell is he staring at me like that? thought Fisher.

Sam leaned closer and tapped Fisher's arm. "I'm still processing my conversation with Debra, but I'm a bit perplexed."

"Perplexed?" questioned Fisher, still looking down at Sean.

"Yeah, I mean, I expected her to either show some sort of excitement of even the slightest possibility that I had something viable or to quickly dismiss it as rubbish."

"Well, what did she say?" asked Fisher, turning fully toward Sam.

"That's where I'm confused. She didn't say much." Sam bit her lower lip.

"How'd you guys leave it then?"

"She said that it was worth a closer look, and that if I was correct, she'd discuss it with Lance's dad."

"That sounds promising to me. What am I missing here?"

"That's just it, I'm not sure there's anything to miss. It's just . . . I know Debra. And I've never seen her react the way she did today. It's not so much what she said as what she didn't say."

The lights in the auditorium dimmed lower and the stage lights lit up. Sam's mom walked on stage again, and the audience quickly quieted down. "Last time we met, our hero's ship was disabled, and two of his crew members were being mind-controlled. We now return to the Caverns of Regula."

"So, what's your—?" asked Fisher, but Alec cut him off.

"Guys, the show is starting. Keep it down."

"Let's chat after the show," said Sam.

Fisher nodded.

A loud roar erupted in the audience as Andrew made his grand entrance from the left side of the stage, followed by three of the second gen'ers, one of which was Zach.

"Kick some alien ass, Zach!" yelled Dom.

The audience laughed.

"You're gonna have to do your own dirty work now. Do you hear me? Do you?" yelled Andrew, speaking into a small box in his hand.

The lights on the right side of the stage brightened. Dr. Ben was sitting in a chair next to a desk with an old terminal on the other side of a partition that separated the left and right side of the stage.

"You're still alive . . . my old friend," said Dr. Ben.

"Still, 'old friend.' You've managed to kill just about everyone else, but like a poor marksman, you keep missing the target," taunted Andrew.

"Perhaps I no longer need to try, Admiral," said Dr. Ben.

Margot walked to the edge and looked toward center stage. Mia and Kaman ran to the center of the stage, grabbed hold of a cart bearing a crate resting on top, and dramatically pushed the cart to the opposite side of the stage into the shadows.

"Using the Reliant's teleporter, the Genesis is beamed away from the cavern," announced Margot.

"Nooooo!" shouted Zach falling to his knees. "He can't take the Genesis!"

Several gasps came from the audience.

"Give it back!" shouted one of the Quints.

"You have Genesis, but you don't have me!" rasped Andrew, speaking into his hand. "You were going to kill me. You're going to have to come down here! You're going to have to come down here!"

The auditorium fell completely silent.

"I've done far worse than kill you, I've hurt you," said Dr. Ben. "And I wish to go on . . . hurting you. I shall leave you as you left me. As you left her. Marooned for all eternity in the center of a dead planet, buried alive. Buried alive!"

Andrew fell to his knees, dropped his arms, and screamed at the top of his lungs. "KHAAAAAAAAAAAAN!"

The stage lights went dark and the room exploded with applause.

CHAPTER 17

People of the Earth,

Today will be a day that will live on in the *Archean* history books for years to come. Today, I will be retiring from Ghosts in the Graveyard after I successfully win yet another round. That's right, today is my final game. It's a bit anticlimactic, since we all kind of see the game coming to an end soon anyway, but I like the idea of it being on my terms.

To be honest, it really hasn't been the same the last few months, but I haven't had the heart to throw in the towel, since I know the others really look forward to playing. Who am I kidding? I'm sure it will only be a footnote in the history for the *Archean* journey. Still, I like the idea of going out as "The" ghost, the undeniable reigning champion.

Lance will finally have one less thing to complain about, and soon my responsibilities in the Bay will kill any free time for sure. Dr. Gage has really been putting pressure on me to invest more time in my studies. Although he hasn't made any official announcements, it's become very clear that he's going to have me assume his role when he retires. I don't get what the rush is. We still have plenty of time before that happens, and he's pretty much got me running the Bay already.

That said, there are a few tasks that Dr. Gage doesn't seem to trust me with. I think sometimes he forgets that he was only a few years older than I am now when the Arc launched. I'm sure it's challenging for the first gen to change their perspectives about the second gen, but we're no longer children. It feels like they will always see us as helpless kids who can't take care of themselves. Of course, some of us still play Graveyard every month, which probably isn't helping our image all that much.

Lance and I have been talking about the Pairing Ceremony, which is coming up in a few months. We're both convinced we'll be paired. Not only are we the two oldest of the second generation, but we've also been in a serious relationship for almost three years now. I just can't imagine our parents ripping us apart and pairing us with someone else.

Although Lance doesn't like to discuss children, I'm extremely excited thinking about bringing a new life into the universe. Actually, I'm hoping for twins. One boy and one girl. I can just imagine my daughter having curly blond hair and bright blue eyes. My son, of course, would look just like Lance, with dark, wavy hair and the same cute dimples, and he'd be the strongest of all the third gen. I must confess that I envision our little family often. We would be one of the first families to set foot on Uelara and pave the way for thousands of other families. I'm sure Lance will eventually come around and enjoy talking about having kids together. They say that boys mature much more slowly than girls, and THIS I believe. I am surrounded on the ship by evidence of this fact.

Okay, I'm heading out to play my last round of Graveyard. I'll report back later with the details of my final victory!

CHAPTER 18

Helena closed her journal and smiled. Soon this journal would be full, and it would join the others in storage. She had so much material to pull for the book she was going to write once settled on Uelara. She already knew she'd make it into the Earth's history for the role she was playing in the Arc's mission, but that wasn't enough for her. She wanted to be *the* crew member with the *official* story of what life was like on the *Archean*. Who better to tell the story than the first born on the Arc? When they set down on Uelara, she would be the oldest, most experienced crew member.

Helena always saw herself playing an important role as an ambassador of sorts who would welcome the travelers from the Earth to their new home. She was certain the Earth-born would be eager to hear details of the Arc's journey and all its crew.

She dropped down from her pod and headed to the auditorium. As she walked, Helena rehearsed what she planned to say to her unsuspecting friends after her victory today. She wanted her retirement to be memorable, and she wanted to be prepared when they tried to convince her to continue the game next month.

When she arrived in the auditorium, most of the crew were already there.

"And here comes the reigning champion who will lose her title today!" shouted Sam.

Helena bowed toward Sam and gave her a smile.

"I'm gun'n for you, Helena," continued Sam. "I'm on to where you've been hiding, and you're as good as found."

Helena didn't skip a beat. "Well then, today should be very interesting, shouldn't it?"

The last of the players joined the group.

"Okay, everyone is here, so let's get this party started," said Alec. "Sam, you were the final ghost to be found last month, so head to the upper deck and fire off the alarm."

Sam ran toward the spiral staircase as everyone bolted toward the exits of the auditorium. As the last few players scattered out of the room, Helena stood at one of the exits, blew Sam a kiss, then turned and sprinted down the corridor.

As Helena made her way down the corridor, she heard Sam yell, "Better find a good spot, ghosts! I'm coming for you!"

Helena smiled and sprinted toward the engine room. While areas of the ship like the engine room and cargo hold were off limits for the game, the storage bays near the engine room were fair play, and many others had hidden there before.

Several weeks ago, Helena had discovered that the empty power cell casings placed on the far back wall of the east storage bay hadn't been removed for quite some time. The outer shell of the casings were made up of collapsible panels that, when slid open, gave access to the inner workings of the cell. After being recycled several times, the casings themselves became too fragile to reuse, and the guts of the cell were repurposed into newer casings.

The spent casings were scheduled to be melted down and repurposed for the construction of the exterior panels for the geodetic rings, but there were always more casings waiting to be recycled than what the foundry needed, and over the past several weeks, they had started to pile up more than usual.

Helena found that she was small enough to fit into one of these spent casings, and with the aid of a simple Allen wrench, she could slide the panel shut from the inside.

But Helena took it one step further. She found two casings that were positioned just right so that she could climb into the first one and shut the panel, open the back panel of the one she was in, and then open the front panel of the casing that was behind the first casing.

If anyone was smart enough to look in any of the power cells in the front row, they would find nothing. She worked out this perfect spot after hiding in the front row casings a few times. Alec could have found her if he hadn't given up after only opening the first three along the wall. One more, and she would have been found.

When two rows of casings had formed over time, she had come up with this foolproof plan. And foolproof it was. Helena had heard Alec open all the casings in the front row during the last game.

Helena now sat snug in the casing with only small streaks of light piercing through the panel seams of her hiding spot. Two hours had passed, and she was so close to victory she could taste it.

Suddenly, she heard footsteps approaching from the engine room, accompanied by whispering voices. She did her best to peer out of a small break in the panel seam, and she could see two figures heading straight toward her. She couldn't tell who they were, but she was sure they were walking directly toward the casings.

Had the casing moved when she shifted her weight? Was some of her hair sticking out of the casing? Maybe Sam really had worked out her hiding spot. Had she let Helena sit there for two hours to give her a false sense of victory? Helena held her breath and waited for Sam and the others to discover her for the first time in years.

CHAPTER 19

Dom poured the protein mix into the reservoir on the side of one of the food printers, screwed the cap back on, and keyed in a seven-digit code on the keypad before pressing enter.

The printer's gears rocked back and forth a couple of times, and then the printhead moved to the far left corner of the print bed. The head of the printer started releasing a thick paste onto the printer bed in a circular pattern every stroke. Once the first layer was created, the printhead lifted a little and started a second pass, releasing the paste onto the first layer.

Fisher was mesmerized by the printing extravaganza unfolding before his eyes. Why was it that all this wonder was wasted on crew members who couldn't appreciate the brilliance of this technology? Fisher would have given anything to spend his days printing hull struts, replacement parts, or hell, even coverall buttons. Meanwhile, Dom would be content peeing on a printer just to see what would happen.

"And that's how we make the doughnuts. And, well . . . just about everything else around here," Dom said with a grin.

"What about the sausages?" asked Echo, licking his lips with anticipation of breakfast.

Dom smiled. "Same."

"And the bacon? Clearly bacon isn't made like this," said Sam. "Same."

"Sometimes I think it's better not knowing," mumbled Fisher.

"Then you definitely don't want to see how we process the artificial tofu," said Dom, pretending to retch.

"I think now would be a good time to end the cooking lesson for the day," proposed Zach.

"Well, I know you guys are going to ramble on about it anyway, so let's hear it. How'd Graveyard go today?" asked Dom.

"It was something to see," marveled Fisher. "I think Sam could have beaten the record today if we had found Helena. Sam ran a mean crew, and we found everyone within the first hour."

Dom turned from the printer and faced Fisher. "Wait . . . so you had over two hours with everyone looking and you still couldn't find Helena? You guys are weak," he teased.

"I think we're just overlooking the obvious," added Alec.

"Yeah . . . that OBVIOUSLY you guys suck at this game," said Dom.

Everyone around the table laughed except Alec, who shot Dom an irritated look. Dom straightened his posture, proud of his quick comeback.

"Where's Helena anyway? Shouldn't she be here by now?" asked Avery.

Leaning back in his chair, Zach added, "Yeah, I would have thought she'd have raced here to rub it in our faces."

"Maybe she and Lance decided to celebrate her victory with a quickie," said Dom.

"Nice!" added Grayson.

"Gross, Dom!" cringed Sam. "Anyway, no way would Helena pass up on the chance to gloat about yet another win."

"Yeah, no way!" said Echo, still eyeing his breakfast being printed.

"Which one of you was it?" yelled Lance as he charged in through the galley door.

Everyone fell silent and turned toward the door, startled by the sudden intrusion.

"What did you guys say to Helena?" demanded Lance.

"Whoa! What are you talking about?" asked Fisher.

"I wanna know right now which one of you pieces of shit upset Helena!" shouted Lance. "So speak up. I can't hear you!"

Dom held up both hands in an attempt to calm Lance's tirade. "Hold on, Lance. What did she say?"

"She said there was no point in being together anymore, that everything was a lie. What the hell does that mean? You guys were the last to be with her. One of you must have put these crazy thoughts in her head."

Sam walked up to Lance, stood toe to toe with him, hands on her hips, and looked up at him. "What are you talking about, Lance? We haven't seen Helena since the start of the game. No one talked to her before she took off to hide."

"Bullshit!" spat Lance. "One of you said something to upset her, and I want to know who did it. NOW!"

Lance took a step back from Sam, but she moved toward him, closing the gap between them again. "Now you listen here, Lance. None of us said a thing to her. Did you ever think that maybe she just came to her senses and realized you're not the right one for her. Everybody else can see that. Why is it that the losers are always the last to see the obvious?"

The sound of the moving printhead echoed off the walls of the galley. Nobody seemed to be breathing. Fisher was stunned. He had seen Lance angry before, but never like this. He had also never seen Sam confront anyone in such a biting, mean-spirited manner. What was she thinking? Lance was already out of control. How could she possibly think this could help?

Fisher watched as Lance's lips tensed. His nostrils began to flare and his face distorted into an enraged sneer. He grabbed Sam by the shoulders, shoved her to the floor, and stormed out of the room.

"You okay, Sam?" asked Zach, extending his arm to help her up.

Dazed, Sam accepted Zach's hand and said, "I'll be fine."

Zach pulled Sam up, and she brushed the sides of her coveralls.

"Someone should go defuse the bomb that's about to go off in Lance's head," suggested Fisher. "He's on the war path."

"I'll talk with Lance!" said Dom eagerly, running out of the room.

Fisher couldn't understand what just occurred. He realized that Helena could be the one to make sense of all this madness. He looked at his friends and said, "I think we should find Helena and see if she can shed some light onto what's going on."

"Good idea. Let's go check on her," agreed Avery.

"Yeah, let's go," said Echo.

"Guess that rules out Dom's quickie theory," said Grayson.

"Asshole!" chided Alec.

"What?" replied Grayson.

Everyone started heading toward the door as Grayson continued to eat his breakfast. "Wait . . . what did I say?"

CHAPTER 20

As the others split up and began searching for Helena, Sam went straight to her hive. She had a pretty good feeling she'd find Helena in her pod.

Sam felt she knew her better than anyone. Before Helena and Lance had hooked up, she and Sam had been inseparable. Sam had had a crush on Helena for as long as she could remember but always felt Helena was focused on the boys in the hive. And then the unimaginable happened: to Sam's joyful surprise, Helena disclosed that she had feelings for her. Their relationship became romantic for a brief moment in time. Sam clung to every word, look, and caress, hoping in her heart that it wouldn't be short-lived.

But it was. It was barely a month after Helena's confession when she was placed in the Q with Lance. And the rest was history. Sam bravely accepted the breakup to preserve her friendship with Helena, but to this day, her heart never felt quite whole. Truth was, she was still holding out for some sign that Helena would have a change of heart.

Sam knew that any time Helena was having an off day or was upset with something Lance had done or said, she would always retreat to her pod in the hive. She would pretend she was fine and tell people she simply needed time to write in her journal.

Sam arrived at their hive and could see Helena's silhouette in her pod. She gathered her thoughts and tapped on the door using the secret code they used to use when sneaking out of the hive late at night to make out in the Dome.

Sam could see movement in the pod, but Helena did not respond.

"Helena, it's me," whispered Sam. "What's going on?"

Silence.

Sam struggled to find words. She knew that Helena probably just needed space. When she was ready to talk, she would. "Just know that I'm here for you. When you're ready to talk, come find me."

Sam waited for a response. Any response. Even a simple "Leave me the hell alone!" would have been a relief. *She would never say 'hell,'* Sam thought.

Sam reached out, placed her hand on the frosted glass that separated them, and closed her eyes. The glass was only a few millimeters thick, yet Helena felt kilometers away. She hated that she couldn't talk with her friend. It pained her to know that Helena was upset, and she was unable to help.

Sam pulled her hand away from the pod's door, turned, and left the hive. Making her way down the corridor, Sam began searching for the others to inform them that she had found Helena. Up ahead, she could see Lance barreling toward her.

"Is she in there?" barked Lance when they came close. "Is she in her pod?"

Sam stopped. "Yeah, but she needs to be left alone."

"Did she say that?"

"No, but you're not going in there." Sam widened her stance and raised her hand.

"Come again?" growled Lance.

"Helena needs time alone. I'm not letting you in there."

"Oh, so you're Helena's keeper now?"

"No, but neither are you. Just give her some space, Lance. She doesn't need you yelling at her right now."

Lance huffed and attempted to shove past Sam. Ready this time, Sam twisted her upper body out of the way and swung her left open palm into the side of Lance's head just behind his right ear. She wasn't going to allow Lance to get the better of her again, and she knew he would attempt to shove her rather than hit her.

"Bitch, I'm going to—!"

Sam moved fast and wrapped her right arm around Lance's neck from behind, making sure her elbow was under his chin. She placed her left hand behind his head and squeezed her bicep and forearm closed, pushing his head forward.

Lance tried to shake her off, but Sam didn't budge. His body gradually went limp and collapsed to the floor. Sam slowly released him and sat next to him, catching her breath.

Adrenaline raced through her body. What had she just done? She'd gotten so caught up in the moment and hadn't stopped to think about what would happen when Lance woke up. Sam knew she couldn't keep him away from Helena forever, but maybe he would be calmer with Helena when he awoke.

Sam got to her feet, stood over Lance, and turned back toward the hive. She decided that it was better for her to stand guard in case Lance came to with a vengeance. She wasn't sure she could take on Lance in a fair fight, but she would do everything she could to keep him away from Helena until he had cooled off and her friend was ready to come out of her pod.

"Sleep tight, asshole."

CHAPTER 21

The foundry was buzzing with activity the next evening. Narine and Lance's father, Jeremy, were working on the outer shell of the geodetic ring that was nearing the end of its construction. Fisher unloaded the four remaining exterior panels Echo had delivered earlier in the day and placed them down at the base of the ring.

"Ah, perfect timing, Fisher," said Jeremy as he grabbed one of the panels. He lined up the holes on the four corners of the panel to the threaded rods on the ring's framework and slid the panel in place. "Narine, help secure the top two bolts, and I'll finish the lower two," instructed Jeremy.

Narine started threading the bolts into place as Jeremy removed two bolts from his pocket.

Fisher got along with Narine and always thought that if they would have been from the same hive, they probably would have been good friends. Narine was a year older than Fisher and was quick to master any task Jeremy and the others threw at her. She spoke with a watered-down accent that she had adopted from her parents who were from a place called Russia. Her parents worked in the factory with Fisher's dad and Alec.

Both Echo and Alec had shown romantic interest in Narine in recent years, but she showed no sign of interest in either of them. This hadn't stopped Echo from trying to strike up a conversation with her every time he made a delivery to the foundry. It was painful to watch Echo stumble over his words, trying to play it cool when talking with her. Unlike Alec, Echo never picked up on any of Narine's social cues. Narine knew the score but was always kind to Echo, something Fisher appreciated but worried would only prolong Echo's infatuation with her.

During the first couple of months working with her, Fisher thought Narine didn't have an interest in anyone on the ship, and he began to wonder if she had more in common with Sam than others realized. But that theory soon faded when Ashin from the Hold started swinging by to chat with her. Fisher would watch from his workbench as Narine's body language transformed the moment Ashin entered the room.

Fisher always thought it was interesting that such a small distance of separation could determine how close the connections between the crew members could become. Narine and Ashin's hive was just on the other side of the commissary from his own, and yet Fisher only really interacted with them once he was assigned to the foundry. Dr. Ben explained that, according to Clines' Social Development Theory, it was important for children to have opportunities to meet new people and have new social encounters as they matured. Separating the second generation into five hives and limiting their interactions until the OCP draft insured that they could have at least somewhat of a healthy social development.

"Start on the left panel, Fisher," said Jeremy. "Remember, guys, don't fully tighten any of the bolts just yet. We may need to remove the panels if the test run on the internal drives produces any anomalies."

Fisher placed the panel over the rods and headed over to the back wall to collect the bolts. On his way, he saw Sam and Debra entering the foundry.

"Jeremy, I have the latest figures," said Debra as she walked toward Jeremy's office.

"Excellent," said Jeremy. "Narine, you and Fisher finish the panels. I'll return soon."

Jeremy joined Debra in his office and slid the door closed.

"Hey, Fish," said Sam.

"What's up, Sam? How's Helena today?" Fisher asked, as he pulled a small drawer open in search of bolts.

"Still hasn't come out of her pod," she answered. "I went by the medical bay earlier and told Dr. Gage that she needed to take the day off. No reason for her spotless record to be tarnished." Sam tightened the loose knot of her coverall sleeves around her waist. "I was also afraid Lance was going to make things even worse for Helena, so I asked him to give her some space."

"And he listened to you?"

"Let's just say I was able to reason with him," Sam replied with a grin. "I just don't get it," she continued, as her grin faded quickly. "I've never seen her like this. I keep waiting for her to break out of this funk. Not that I've ever really seen her this low before. But come on, this is Helena. She's always the one cheering us up, you know?"

"I know. I don't think I've even seen Alec or Avery retreat for this long, and you know how depressed they get at times," he said.

"It has to be something Lance did to her," she insisted.

"Look, I don't like Lance, either, but I don't think I can agree with you on this one. Have you forgotten how Lance freaked out about Helena after the game?"

While Fisher and Lance's relationship had splintered in recent years, he felt like he could still be objective, unlike Sam. She was always targeting Lance, looking for weak spots to attack and hoping Helena would find them as well. Fisher knew Sam still had feelings for Helena, and he believed her judgment was clouded. Fisher pulled open a large drawer and pushed a few parts around, still searching for the bolts.

"True, but he could have easily just forgotten some stupid shit he said to upset her," Sam argued.

"This has to be more than just Lance's insensitivity toward Helena. She is pretty much impervious to that side of him by now."

"Well, whatever it is, it's got me concerned. I can't get her to come out of her pod. Twenty-four hours?" Sam shook her head. "She's never stayed in her pod this long. She won't even talk to me."

"She's not talking to anyone, Sam. You can't take this personally. I think we have reached a place where we need to go to the Vosts, or her parents at least."

"You're probably right. If she's still in her pod tomorrow morning, we'll fill them in."

"Sounds like a plan." Fisher initially thought it was odd that Helena was isolating herself to this extent. Now, after discussing all this with Sam, his concern was growing. He knew that if he were feeling this uneasy, Sam must really be feeling bewildered.

Fisher enjoyed being Sam's close confidante. He could think of nothing that would make him betray the trust she bestowed upon him. Sam's feelings for Helena ran so deep, and Fisher felt fairly ineffective when trying to console Sam over her repeatedly broken heart. It was painful to watch Sam suffer while Helena moved on with Lance as though she and Sam had never exchanged so much as a handshake.

What he didn't enjoy was a strange feeling of envy. Fisher couldn't quite identify the source of his jealousy. Was it the fact that Sam had such a boundless capacity to love? Fisher had no experience with emotional intensity of that magnitude. One would imagine that Sam's tears should have been enough of a deterrent for him to wish for love and all the drama and pain it carried. However, he still longed for a beautiful, life-shattering connection to someone. The only person he felt even a fraction of that type of connection with was . . . Sam. And well, it was pointless to allow his thoughts to proceed down that path.

Sensing she was still very much on edge, Fisher placed his hand on Sam's shoulder.

"Don't worry. Helena is strong, and she'll get through whatever this is."

"We're ready for you, Sam," called out Debra, standing in the doorway of Jeremy's office.

"Catch you at dinner," said Sam as she walked toward the office.

Fisher nodded and returned to his search for the bolts.

"Fish, you hand-crafting the bolts over there or what?" yelled Narine.

CHAPTER 22

Echo sifted through the large processing bin, separating the various items and placing them into a collection of smaller bins. He loved working in the reclamation center. He understood that he played an important role maintaining the upkeep of the Arc, and he took pride in his work. Alec and Dom's father, McHail, ran the Center and told Echo he hadn't seen anyone more dedicated. Echo proudly shared with his friends McHail's glowing recommendation, but they never seemed all that impressed with the accolade. Didn't matter. Echo's boss was pleased with him, and that was enough.

Every recycled item helped sustain both life on the ship and the success of the mission. He'd seen overused printer components melted down and turned into external braces in the construction of the new hives being built for the future third generation. Used power cell casings also played a vital role in geodetic ring construction.

Echo loved giving purpose to each and every discarded item he collected and sorted and was quick to correct the others if he saw them discarding items in the wrong bins.

"Have you done your rounds today?" asked Finn as he approached Echo's work area.

"Earlier today. Why?"

"Good to hear. Some of the others are running behind, and I have to drop off my reports to McHail before the end of the day. I appreciate you staying on top of things. It's one less task to track down. If I don't see you on your way out, have a good one."

"Thanks. You, too."

Finn moved over to Vlad's work area, and Echo resumed sorting the contents of the bin. Being separated by hives, Echo hadn't really gotten to know Finn all that well until the two of them were assigned to the reclamation center. Finn was from Hive 2 and was quick to pick up the duties assigned to the crew in the Center. He had helped Echo when he struggled during the first couple of years. Finn was a nice guy, yet Echo couldn't help but pity him a bit. Finn was considered by the rest of the second gen to be at a huge disadvantage, simply by virtue of his being the sole offspring of Ben and Fiona Vost.

Echo couldn't understand why so many people disliked the Vosts. Dr. Ben and Dr. Fiona were always so nice to him. He loved his visits with Dr. Ben. Unlike many others on the ship, Dr. Ben took his time speaking with Echo, something Echo appreciated greatly. He didn't have to rush his thoughts or answers. He could really listen and absorb the wise advice Dr. Ben would offer. Sometimes Echo would even try to share Dr. Ben's advice with his friends, but it just didn't seem to have the same effect on them.

Echo grabbed the last item from the bin and placed it in a small container labeled COPPER. He collapsed the larger bin and placed it on the completed stack.

That makes nine! he thought.

"Looking good, Echo," said McHail as he approached Echo's work area. "How do you get so much done so quickly?"

Echo turned around and said, "Like you always say, 'The best way to get things done is to begin!'"

"True, true," said McHail. "I have something important that I need my top guy on. You up for the task?"

Echo dropped the item he was pulling from the bin, turned to McHail, and smiled. "Absolutely."

"Perfect. As you know, we've been receiving fewer power cell casings over the past few weeks. It appears Thomas and the crew in the engine room have found a way to get more life out of them. Looks like we're going to need to up the quantity of raw aluminum. The Hold can only afford one of their guys to deliver it, but it's a two-person job. They said their guys can pull the order if we can help deliver it. I know it's late, but it would really help if you were up for it."

"No worries, sir. You can count on me."

"I know I can. I'll buzz the guys and let them know you're on the way."

McHail walked back toward his office as Echo straightened up his work area. Echo loved that, of all the people working in the reclamation center, *he* had been handpicked for this important task.

As he walked to the central lift, Echo spotted Narine heading toward him in the corridor. He lengthened his stride and greeted her with a wide smile and big wave, even though she was less than a meter in front of him now. He always made sure Narine knew he was happy to see her.

"Hi, Narine! How's it going today?"

Narine paused for a moment, her gaze elsewhere. A slight smile appeared on her face, and she gave Echo a light, friendly hug.

"Hey, Echo. Good to see you. I'm late for a . . . thing in the foundry. Catch you later?"

"Oh sure. Don't want to make you late. Maybe I'll catch you tonight?"

Narine smiled and quickened her pace. "Umm, Maybe. See ya!"

Echo reached the central lift and saw that it was shuttling its way upward. He waited patiently and passed the time thinking about Narine. She was fun to think about. She was always too busy to meet up with Echo after work, but he knew that one day she'd get some free time. Maybe the two of them could have dinner together, or he could talk her into playing Graveyard. Time would tell, and Echo knew his patience would pay off eventually.

The lift was taking extra long today. Time to shift his thoughts while waiting. His mind drifted to Helena, and Echo wondered what could have upset her so much that she felt her relationship with Lance was over. Not that he would argue. Echo didn't like Lance; he couldn't recall a time when Lance had ever been kind to him. Echo had learned at an early age to avoid him at all costs, especially if Lance were in one of his moods. Helena, on the other hand, was one of the kindest people on the Arc. Echo recalled countless times when Helena had made him feel special, like he mattered. A new vision entered Echo's mind. Maybe if Helena and Lance broke up, Helena would give Echo a chance in the relationship department. As he considered this exciting prospect, his thoughts circled back to Narine and decided that he had put in too many months waiting on Narine to quit now. Helena would just have to find someone else.

At last the lift reached the top, jolted to a stop, and the slated guard raised up. Andrew and a few other first gen'ers stepped out of the lift.

"Hey, Echo, heading down?" asked Andrew through chattering teeth.

"Yeah, I have a delivery to pick up for the reclamation center."

"It's extra cold today. Don't forget to gear up on the way down," advised Andrew, fiercely rubbing his arms, trying to warm up.

"Yes, Dad," said Echo with a smile, rubbing his hands together, preparing for the temperature drop that was about to take place. He pulled the slated guard down and pushed the fourth button on the right labeled CARGO. He reached for one of the jackets hanging on the back wall.

As the lift lowered, Echo could hear his dad's voice trail off down the corridor, "I still can't feel my face," followed by the group's laughter.

CHAPTER 23

Sleep was going to prove to be elusive to Sam tonight. No matter how hard she tried, she couldn't come up with a single reason for why Helena would continue to be this upset. And if she didn't get some sleep soon, Sam was going to end up as messed up as Helena. She tried the technique Dr. Fiona had taught her of counting down from one hundred, and, for the first time, she made it all the way to zero without even the suggestion of a yawn.

Sam tried her best to think of anything but Helena. She thought about her brothers and what her life was like at their age, busy discovering the wonders of the Arc rather than dealing with the challenges that her life now presented. Even Avery had been carefree until her teen years.

With her mind on the simple lives of her brothers, she finally drifted off to sleep. Unfortunately, her rest was short-lived. Sam jolted awake. How long had she slept? She looked at the digital display on the pod's wall.

Forty minutes? Have I really only been asleep for forty minutes? she thought.

Sam closed her eyes again, hoping to catch a few more hours of sleep before her day began, but all she could think about was Helena. Surrendering to the fight, she decided it made more sense to get an early start on the day. Perhaps keeping busy in the Tank would keep her mind occupied. She could always take a short nap at her workstation if necessary, and she had a feeling that Debra would understand.

Sam quietly slid out of her pod, not wanting to wake anyone else. Stretching her arms above her head and letting out a silent yawn, she scanned the pods, and it looked like everyone was still asleep.

Perfect! she thought. *No lines for the lav.*

Sam looked up at Helena's pod and was surprised to finally see it empty. She was there when Sam had entered her own pod last night. This was a good sign. Maybe Helena was starting to feel better. No need now to go to her parents or the Vosts.

"Wow, you're up early," yawned Dom, coming out of the hive's locker room, scratching himself.

"Couldn't sleep. You?"

"I wish. Nah, I'm off to get things going in the galley. Andrew is always on our backs about showing up to work on time." Imitating Andrew, Dom straightened his posture and raised his index finger on his right hand. "Breakfast isn't going to make itself, you know."

Sam smiled. "Hey, did you see Helena this morning? She's not in her pod."

"Nah. Happy to know she's out, though."

"Same here. If you see her, tell her I'm looking for her, will ya?"

"Sure. See you at breakfast?"

"Yeah, see you in a few."

As Dom left for the galley, Sam headed into the hive's locker room and grabbed a towel and washcloth from the shelf. She walked over to one of the showers and placed them on the bench outside the stall. As she undressed, she tried to remember the last time she showered without having to wait in line. She placed her clothes in a pile on the bench, grabbed the washcloth, and caught a glimpse of herself in the mirror.

Even though she was fairly comfortable with her body, Sam realized she never spent much time looking at herself. Aside from the fact that the hive locker room was usually crowded, she couldn't stand when the other girls stared at themselves in the mirror, complaining about the size of their thighs.

Why the hell do they care about the size of their thighs? she always wondered. Sam had made a vow with herself years ago that she wouldn't be caught dead checking herself out like that.

Now, embracing the solitude of the moment, she stole a quick glance. Sam then turned to face her reflection straight on, letting her eyes settle on her feet and then slowly looked upward. Her body had changed. Her legs were stronger. She noticed that the seven-year-old scar on her ribcage had grown fainter. Her breasts were a bit fuller than she recalled. Her hips had a curve to them now that, for some reason, evoked this strange sense of strength and power. As she surveyed her body, her thoughts drifted back to Helena. A visual of Helena's natural beauty made Sam catch her breath, and she remembered Helena's gentle hands touching her in ways foreign, new, and exhilarating.

She shook herself out of her splendid daydream and stepped into the shower stall, reached over, and pulled down on a lever. She watched it slowly retract and then looked up. Water began collecting into a reservoir above her. She closed her eyes and tilted her head down. Moments later warm, soapy water slowly trickled down from the stall's ceiling, and Sam ran her fingers through her hair, lathering her scalp. A few seconds later the water stopped. Sam continued to lather as the soapy water dripped onto the floor.

There was something different about her shower this morning. Sam couldn't help but feel that she was washing away the stress from the past two days, ready for normal Arc life to return.

With her eyes closed, Sam reached out and pulled the lever down again. As the water collected in the ceiling's reservoir, Sam wished she could stay in this moment for the rest of the day. Warm water began trickling down from the ceiling, rinsing the suds from her body. Seconds later, the water stopped. Sam always felt like she was cheated out of the full two minutes of rinsing with the second stage of the shower. It never felt long enough.

Sam stepped out of the stall feeling refreshed and optimistic. Helena was out of her pod, and the possibility of talking to her gave Sam's spirits a lift. Maybe she would get the opportunity later today to follow up with Debra about her simulation. It was a new day, and Sam thought she was ready for whatever that day would hand her.

CHAPTER 24

"Dom, you can piss on as many trees as you'd like, but I'm—"
Alec went silent as Fisher interrupted him. "Enough, guys. It's not helping!"

"Fisher's right. We need to focus on Helena," added Avery.

Fisher could sense that Dom was worried about Helena and was merely attempting to ease the tension in the room. Unfortunately, Dom's attempted distraction had the opposite effect.

Dom looked down at the floor. "Sorry, guys. I was only—"

"Don't worry, Dom, we all know you were trying to help," said Avery.

"I just hate seeing everyone so upset. Are you sure I can't make anything else for you guys? You barely ate this morning, and none of you have touched your lunch," said Dom.

"No, thanks, I don't really feel like eating right now," said Fisher.

"Same here," added Echo.

Fisher felt almost dizzy. He couldn't recall the last time he had experienced so many emotions in such a short period of time. Excitement led the day with breakfast reports from Sam and Dom that Helena had left her pod. Everyone was reveling in the anticipation of life returning to normal. When Helena failed to join the others at breakfast, confusion set in. Fisher was certain he would at least see her during his shift in the medical bay. Again, no Helena. When Helena's seat remained vacant at lunch, panic dominated the room.

"I hope Sam gets here soon. I need to head back to the Bay in a few minutes. Without Helena there, Kaman and I are swamped," said Fisher.

"And no one in the Bay has seen or heard from her today?" asked Zach.

"No one. Kaman didn't seem concerned, and I haven't had a chance to speak to Dr. Gage yet," said Fisher.

"Can anyone tell me why we haven't gone to any of our parents?" asked Zach.

"What are we, children?" replied Alec.

"Uh, yeah!" confirmed Avery.

"Kinda true, Alec," added Dom.

Fisher realized that Zach had a point. As much as he and the others tried to be independent, they always had their parents as a safety net—a safety net that received a lot of use, even to this day.

The door to the galley swung open, and Sam walked in. "Still no Helena?" she asked.

"No. We were hoping you had some news," said Fisher.

Sam looked disheartened. Fisher couldn't remember a time that he had ever seen Sam like this. She was always so tough, so driven. Now Sam seemed like a lost little girl.

"I've been looking since I left you guys at breakfast this morning," said Sam.

"Did you run into Lance?" asked Fisher.

"No, but I—"

"I did," interrupted Grayson.

Everyone in the room looked at Grayson.

"Why didn't you mention this earlier?" asked Fisher.

"No one asked," huffed Grayson.

The group sat silent, waiting for Grayson to continue.

"Dude, what did Lance say?" blurted Dom.

"Huh? Oh. He asked if I had seen Helena," replied Grayson.

"That's it?" asked Alec, slamming his fist on the table.

"Yeah. Why?"

The group simultaneously shook their heads.

"Did he look concerned?" asked Sam.

Grayson shrugged his shoulders. "Concerned. Pissed. Maybe a little of both."

"Guys, let's walk through this again," suggested Fisher, trying to refocus the group. "We know Helena was in her pod last night."

"That's right," said Alec. "I was the first back to the hive last night, and I saw her in her pod before I went into mine."

"And Dom and Sam noticed she was missing early this morning, right?" asked Fisher.

"Yeah," confirmed Dom.

"I think we need to get the first gen involved," suggested Zach.

"I agree with Zach," said Sam.

"Okay," said Fisher, "so it sounds like the plan is that we need to talk to our parents. I need to head to the Bay. I'll speak with Dr. Gage as soon as I get there. The rest of you should inform the seniors of your departments. Sam, go fill your mom in on what's going on. Avery, try to find Helena's parents and make sure they know she's missing. Dom, ask every person who enters the commissary if they've seen Helena. Talk with Andrew, too. See if he has any idea."

Dom began gathering the group's trays of uneaten meals, and everyone started to leave the galley. As Fisher walked to the medical bay, he began to play out the conversation he was about to have with Dr. Gage. How was it possible that a week ago his greatest stressor involved a nameplate, and today his friend was missing.

He found himself longing for lame rounds of First Things.

CHAPTER 25

Fisher was really hoping to find Helena in the Bay when he returned from lunch. His concern for her increased when he arrived and she wasn't there. Dr. Gage was in the room nearest the medical bay's entrance, pointing to a volumetric rendering displayed on a monitor. Mr. Martin stood next to Dr. Gage as the two conversed.

"Hey, Fish," said Kaman, walking out of Quarantine B wearing a surgical mask and gloves and carrying a biological hazard waste bag. "Just in time to help disinfect the room."

Fisher sighed. "Lucky me. Let me gear up."

Fisher walked over to the storage room and grabbed a pair of gloves and a surgical mask from the shelves. It was times like this he wished he'd been assigned anywhere else for his cross-training. Fortunately, he had been so caught up in the discussion at lunch that he hadn't eaten. The smell of disinfectant and a full stomach hadn't worked out well for him the last time. Fisher placed the mask over his face and pulled the gloves on his hands. "Everything already in the room?"

Kaman grinned. "Everything but you and some elbow grease. You can only delay this for so long, you know!"

As Fisher walked toward Quarantine B, he looked to see if Dr. Gage and Mr. Martin had wrapped up their conversation.

The two were still talking and from the looks of it, they were going to be a while.

"Hey, Kaman. You didn't happen to run into Helena during lunch, did you?"

"No. Weren't you going to look for her?"

"Yeah, several of us did, but we still couldn't find her."

"Did anyone check in with Dr. Fiona? If she is as depressed as you mentioned this morning, she could be with one of the Vosts."

"That's worth checking into. Mind if I swing by—?"

Kaman raised her hand and gave Fisher a cold stare. "Whoa, you're not bailing on me now. Help me finish this room, and then you can go."

"Right," groaned Fisher. He dropped to his knees and started scrubbing the floor.

"I don't want to sound mean, but your hive is flooded with drama," said Kaman as she sprayed disinfectant on the floor panels in front of Fisher.

"Huh?"

"There is so much drama that takes place in your hive. The other second gen hives don't even come close. Everyone talks about it, you know."

"Uh, no, I didn't know that." Confused, Fisher asked, "What's there to talk about?"

"Are you serious? You don't see it?" asked Kaman, looking puzzled.

"Apparently not."

"You've got the Lance and Helena fiery romance, the Dom and Lance Bromance, you crushing on Sam even though that's never going to happen, now Helena is missing—"

"Wait, what?" said Fisher as he stopped wiping down the floor and looked up at Kaman.

"Helena. She's—"

"No, what do you mean about Sam and me?"

"Fish, it's obvious that you have a thing for her."

"Sam's my friend. My best friend. That's all."

"Okay, if you say so," said Kaman, rolling her eyes.

"Plus, Sam isn't interested in guys."

"Tragic, right? Unrequited love. It must suck being you."

"No, I mean—"

"Oh, give it up, Fisher. You can try to fool yourself, but you won't fool me and the others."

Fisher was speechless. Who did Kaman think she was? Fisher didn't have a crush on Sam. Just because he spent any free time he had with her didn't mean anything. Did he think Sam was attractive? Well, sure, but anyone would think that. The bottom line was that Sam was attracted to girls. Crushing on her was not an option.

"You missed a spot," ribbed Kaman, pointing down at the floor. "Finish the floor, and we'll call this one done."

Kaman picked up the soiled rags, grabbed the bottle of disinfectant, and walked to the storage room. Fisher wiped down the remaining panels on the floor, stood up, and left the room.

He hadn't realized just how strong the odor from the disinfectant was until he made it outside of the Q. He pulled off his gloves and pulled down the surgical mask. He took in a deep breath of clean air and exhaled. He was probably going to smell like disinfectant for days.

"I'll see you in a few weeks," called out Mr. Martin, making his way out of the medical bay.

"Tell your better half I said hi," replied Dr. Gage.

"Will do!" said Mr. Martin, already around the corner.

Dr. Gage started walking toward his office. Fisher wanted to catch him before he got caught up with something else.

"Dr. Gage, you have a minute?" asked Fisher.

Dr. Gage looked over at the digital display on the wall and then back at Fisher. "Sure. My next appointment isn't for another few minutes. Everything okay?" Dr. Gage walked over to a set of filing cabinets, opened the middle drawer, and slid a file folder into place.

"Not sure. It's about Helena."

"Is she still resting? Sam said—"

"No. The thing is, no one knows where she is."

Dr. Gage looked up from the drawer of files. "What do you mean?" he asked, sounding concerned.

"Several of us have been looking for her most of the day."

"And how long has she been missing?" asked Dr. Gage.

"Since early this morning."

"This isn't part of that hiding game you play?" asked Dr. Gage, raising a brow.

"No. She's just . . . missing." Fisher was surprised at how anxious his voice sounded.

Dr. Gage raised his hand. "I understand. I'm sure she's fine, but let's play it safe. I'll reach out to a few people."

"Thanks. We're all worried about her."

"I'm sure she will be happy to hear that when you see her," said Dr. Gage. "If you can finish preparing room three, I'd appreciate it. We'll need it ready later this afternoon."

"No problem. I'll have it fully prepped within the hour," said Fisher, shuffling toward the room.

"Fisher," said Dr. Gage.

Fisher turned to look at him. "Yes, sir?"

"Don't worry. I'll make this my top priority."

Fisher nodded and smiled. Although it was a brief exchange, Fisher felt relieved that the first gen was now involved.

Dr. Gage walked into his office, entered a three-digit code on the call box, and pressed the large red button.

"Operations," a voice answered on the call box.

"This is Dr. Gage. I need to speak with the captain."

CHAPTER 26

The next morning, everyone filed into the auditorium. Sam surveyed the room, hoping to join Fisher and her other friends. The makeshift props from the play still sat on the stage behind some of the first gen, all of whom were whispering to each other. Sam wished this gathering was for a different matter. Helena's parents looked restless as they talked with the Vosts, and Sam spotted Lance sitting with his outrigger crew in the front row.

"Sam, over here!" yelled Fisher.

Sam saw Fisher sitting with Alec, Dom, and Echo and headed over to join them.

"Any updates about Helena?" asked Alec.

Sam shook her head. "Nothing. Not a damn thing. My mother told me they are going to be forming search parties after they fill everyone in on the details."

"Where are your brothers?" asked Fisher.

"With my mom in the rec room. I just left them. They don't need to hear any of this."

"This is crazy. I just don't get how anyone could go missing on the Arc," whispered Alec.

Instead of the usual anticipation for theater night, the auditorium was filled with puzzled expressions and whispers of concern. After several minutes, Helena's mother took center stage with her husband by her side.

"If I could get everyone's attention, please," announced Helena's mother.

Everyone quickly took their seats.

"As I'm sure everyone is aware by now, my daughter, Helena, from Hive 3 is missing." She hesitated, looked down, and then continued. "Helena was last seen in her pod two nights ago by her hive members. No one has seen her since."

Helena's mother tried to fight off the tears and struggled to get any words out. Helena's father pulled her tight to his chest, whispered something to her, and then addressed the gathering.

"I'm sure you can all imagine our concern. We've assembled everyone here in an effort to expedite our search for Helena. I'm going to hand the floor over to Captain Matsuo, who will be organizing the search."

Captain Matsuo stepped forward and clasped his hands behind his back. His presence in any room commanded respect and attention. Matsuo was a small but muscular man with sharp features and perfect posture. The left side of his face was lined with a thick scar, and he wore it like a badge of honor. Any quiet conversations that had been taking place while Helena's parents were talking ceased the moment he started walking forward.

"Thank you," said Matsuo in a gravelly voice. "Rest assured, we will find Helena."

Helena's parents stepped off to the side, where the Vosts met them with consoling hugs.

Matsuo turned to the crew and continued. "We'll be splitting into groups according to your OCPs. Each department's senior has already been briefed on how we will be conducting the search. I expect each of you to do whatever you're asked to help make this search successful. All other duties and scheduled events are postponed until further notice."

Avery stood up and cleared her throat. "Do you think something bad has happened to Helena?"

"We have no reason to believe that Helena is hurt, and I have every bit of confidence that she will be just fine once we locate her. Now please hold further questions for your department seniors. I don't want to delay the search any more than we already have. Meet in your departments within the next thirty minutes. I appreciate your support in this matter."

Matsuo turned to Helena's parents and escorted them to one of the exits.

"Do you think Helena realizes how much shit she's going to be in when they find her?" asked Dom.

"What makes you think she's not hurt or trapped somewhere on the ship?" Sam chided.

"But you heard Matsuo. He said—"

"Sam's right, Dom," added Fisher. "Remember that time Echo locked himself in the storage room, and it was hours before anyone heard him pounding on the door?"

"I'd like to forget that day," said Echo.

"Helena and Lance probably got into another fight, and she's trying to make a statement to get back at him. We've seen this before," said Dom,

"Giving your boyfriend the silent treatment for a few hours is very different from vanishing for two days," said Sam. "Plus, we've been up and down the ship calling out to her and have heard nothing."

"Don't worry, Sam, with everyone searching I'm sure we'll find her within the hour," said Fisher, placing his hand on her shoulder.

"Um, shouldn't we be heading to our departments?" asked Alec.

"Yeah, we should get going," added Echo.

Fisher and his friends started walking toward the exit doors. Sam broke off from the group down the west corridor to head to the Tank. As she turned a corner, she noticed Lance and a few of the outriggers up ahead.

Sam had been feeling a bit remorseful about the choke hold. Did Lance deserve it? Absolutely. Maybe *remorseful* wasn't quite the right word. Perhaps it was more a feeling of concern. Would shutting him out like this really help find Helena? The whole "keep your enemies closer" idea started swirling through her mind.

"Hey, Lance!" shouted Sam.

Lance looked back over his shoulder and saw Sam running toward him. He stopped, mumbled something to the group he was traveling with, and then turned toward her. "I didn't do anything to her."

"Whoa . . . I didn't say that."

"Yeah, but I know that's what you're thinking."

"Actually, I just wanted to check in with you and see how you were holding up. Look . . . I'm not going to pretend we suddenly like each other. But as much as it turns my stomach, I know you and Helena are close. I just wanted to make sure you're okay."

"Okay?" snarled Lance. "My girlfriend has been missing for two days. How okay do you think I am?"

"So glad I asked."

Softening his voice, he said, "Look, just help me find her. Helena's smart . . . I don't buy what the others are saying, that she accidentally locked herself in a storage unit or something."

"Well, for once you and I can agree on something. There's just no way it's something as simple as that. That's what's got me worried. I'll let you get back to your group. I need to head to the Tank as well."

Sam started walking away when Lance called out, "Hey, Sam."

"Yeah?" Sam asked, looking back at him.

"Thanks for not telling anyone about the choke hold," he whispered. "I was a real ass. I wasn't thinking straight."

"No one needs to know about that. I was only trying to do the right thing for Helena."

"I know. But I wanted to let you know it was cool of you. I can't say I would have kept it from everyone if I were in your shoes. So . . . thanks."

"Just help find Helena. That's all that matters now."

Lance gave Sam a nod before heading off down the corridor.

Wow, Lance was actually capable of civil conversation, she thought.

Sam made her way to the Tank where the engineers were already assembled. Debra was making a list on the interactive whiteboard of the locations they would be searching and assigning them to teams.

"So, what's the plan?"

CHAPTER 27

"Why is Stringer having us check the Grav? Do you really believe Helena could be in here?" asked Kayla as Lance entered the security code above the door's entry plate.

"I'm up for checking every square inch of the ship if it helps us find her."

"Yeah but . . . only a handful of people have access to this place. Hell, you and Deuce are the only two from our crew who have even been inside."

"Look, I agree. The chances of Helena being in here are slim to none. But let's do a quick sweep just in case. I've already searched every place I could think to find her before the meeting was called, and we've been searching for most of the day. As far as we know, she could be anywhere, including here."

Kayla nodded. "Understood."

She had never seen Lance look so distraught. Kayla had heard others whispering rumors of Lance playing some role in Helena's disappearance, but she just couldn't see it. When she had first started working with Lance, she'd thought he was an asshole, but over time she grew to see that, while he lacked tact in many situations, he was a good guy. She liked that Lance was straightforward and spoke his mind, even if it meant upsetting someone. That kind of honesty was rare on the Arc, and she respected him for it.

Kayla had no doubt about Lance's feelings toward Helena. He always spoke about her with genuine respect, and a smile often appeared on his face after saying her name. As far as Kayla was concerned, Lance was innocent, and she wanted to do anything she could to help find her.

Lance kicked off his boots and started to remove his coveralls. "Lose your gear. It's safer for us if we aren't wearing anything metal," he explained.

Kayla removed her boots and coveralls. Being seen in only her underwear was something she had grown accustomed to doing in front of the male members of her outrigger crew.

Wanting to distract Lance a bit from the stress of the search, Kayla decided to keep him busy answering questions. "What happens if we're wearing metal?" asked Kayla.

"According to Stringer, there is an extremely low possibility of an electric arc jumping from the artificial gravity generators that feed the gravity plating that line the interior deck plates."

"So why can we wear metal on other parts of the ship?"

"You're only in danger of an electric arc when you're close to the generators."

"Good to know."

The two entered the facility. After taking a few steps inside, Kayla stopped and stood in awe. In the center of the room, three concentric rings were suspended in the air spinning rapidly, creating an intense whirring sound. She had never seen anything like it. "What . . . is . . . that?"

"Pretty cool right? That's the GEM."

"GEM?"

"Gravitoelectromagnetism superconductor. It's the main source of gravity on the Arc. As the rings spin, they produce a powerful gravitomagnetic field."

"So that's what allows us to walk around on the ship. Can't believe I never asked about it before. What do the artificial gravity generators do?"

Lance pointed to six large units that sat along the back wall behind the rings.

"Those are the generators. They feed the gravity plating but don't generate a strong enough field for the entire ship. They're really just auxiliary units."

"Reserve units?" asked Kayla.

"In a sense, yeah. You can never have too many backups when gravity is involved in the depths of space," explained Lance. "Just a heads up, the closer you get to the GEM, the lighter you're going to feel. Don't worry though, you'll stay grounded."

Kayla followed Lance past the GEM and just as Lance had explained, she began to feel as if she were floating.

"Should we split up to search more quickly?" she asked.

"Good idea." Lance pointed to several large modules to his left. "I'll check behind all these compensators. Why don't you take a closer look near the generators?"

Kayla nodded and walked around the GEM toward the first generator. As she did, it felt as if she were hovering above the floor. The closer she got to the generators, the heavier she felt. Kayla surveyed the areas around each generator, but as she suspected, Helena was nowhere in sight. After a thorough search, she met back up with Lance at the entrance to the facility.

"Where to now?" asked Kayla as she slid into her coveralls.

Lance pulled his boots on. "Let's check back in with Stringer and see if any of the others found her."

He had answered her with no eye contact. Kayla knew this was Lance's indicator that he was having a tough time.

"You okay?" she asked.

No reply.

Kayla tugged at the zipper pull on her coveralls. "Someone has had to have found her by now, don't you think?"

"With the entire ship looking? I have to believe so," answered Lance, still averting his eyes. "Why don't I meet you there? I'll check in with Helena's parents on the way."

Kayla could tell he needed some space. The two started walking in different directions down the corridor. Kayla stopped and turned toward Lance.

"Hey, Lance. Don't worry. Helena is going to be okay."

Lance turned to Kayla and said, "She has to be."

CHAPTER 28

With the entire crew searching for Helena, Fisher couldn't help but compare it to a large scale version of Ghosts in the Graveyard. He only wished it were an elaborate game rather than reality.

After yesterday's full day of searching, the parties grew smaller as most of the crew needed to return to their departments to keep the *Archean* operational. Fisher wanted to continue searching with the last remaining group, but the urgent need to finish the current geodetic ring they were constructing took his attention elsewhere.

Having lost a few days of production, Fisher had little choice but to return to work in the foundry. He walked over to the bins and discovered there were no copper wire spools to be found.

"You got any copper over there?" asked Fisher, calling over to Narine and the others.

"I think we're out," Narine answered.

Fisher took a quick survey of the bins and noticed they were running low on many of the components. He went to the terminal on the far wall and pulled up the inventory spreadsheet. It appeared that things matched.

He closed the spreadsheet and called up the delivery logs. As he suspected, Tuesday's delivery had never arrived. Fisher reached over to the call box on the wall and pressed 311, followed by the large red call button.

"This is Bart in the Hold" answered a voice on the call box.

"Hey, Bart, this is Fisher in the foundry. I wanted to check in and see when we could expect our next delivery. Running thin here."

"Things have been a bit backed up, as you can imagine. Most of my team were out yesterday, and half of them are still searching the ship. Let's have a look and see where you guys fall in line."

Fisher could hear the sound of Bart rapidly typing on a keyboard. After a few minutes and a long sigh, Bart said, "Hate to say it, buddy, but I don't think you'll be seeing us until after the weekend. My guys are currently pulling a huge order for Ag, and that will take the rest of the day, and after that—"

"I understand, but is there any way we can squeeze in a partial delivery today? I'm in a bind here with hitting my deadline," interrupted Fisher.

"You're not the first to tell me that, Fish. I really would love to help, but unless you want to come pull the order yourself, there's not—"

"On my way down," said Fisher.

Bart coughed. "Really?"

"See you in ten!"

Fisher pressed a few keys on the keyboard and printed the latest order. He folded the printed sheet twice and slid it into his left pocket as he headed toward the foundry exit. "Back in a few, guys. Heading to the Hold," he said over his shoulder.

"While you're down there, grab me some low noise block converters!" shouted Narine. "And if you see Ashin, tell him I said hi," she added with a smile.

Fisher made his way to the central lift, stepped in, and pulled the slated guard down. He pushed the fourth button on the right labeled CARGO.

The lift jolted, catching Fisher off guard, and then slowly started to descend. He stepped closer to the large jackets hanging on hooks on the back wall of the lift, grabbed one, and put it on. He then took a hard hat from a small shelf, placed it on his head, and twisted a small knob on the helmet's strap until it was snug.

As the lift lowered, Fisher could feel the temperature around him drop and could start to see his breath with each exhale. His knuckles started to burn. He grabbed a pair of safety goggles from a small bin on the back-wall shelf and slid them on, followed by a pair of gloves. Even with the heavy gear, Fisher was freezing. His teeth started to chatter and his eyes watered.

The lift came to a stop with another jolt, and Fisher raised the door. As he stepped off the lift, ice crystals cracked under his feet. He started toward the office but paused to take in the sheer size of the place. The cargo hold was gigantic. Fisher had only been down here a handful of times, but each time, he was taken aback by the enormous area. The Hold measured almost the entire length of the ship. Fisher could see the hull of the Arc's sides but couldn't see the front or back of the ship. It appeared endless.

The blue lights that dimly lit the Hold made it seem that much colder. He understood the reasoning behind not wasting energy heating a space solely used for storage of the ship's resources. However, he wondered why the engineers couldn't have used a yellow lighting source to at least give the illusion of some warmth.

As he walked to the office, he could hear a lot of commotion from the crew pulling orders. He also heard several scissor lifts ascending and descending, as well as the annoying beeping of cargo carts backing up.

As Fisher swung open the office door, a blast of dry heat swept across his face.

"Cold as shit, right?" Bart asked, laughing.

Bart was a second gen'er from Hive 2. Fisher had seen him over the years at group events but had never really made much of a connection with him. He was small with olive complexion and long hair pulled back into a ponytail.

"I can't feel my feet," said Fisher between chattering teeth. "How . . . how do you guys stand it down here?"

Bart laughed. "You get used to it, but I have it lucky, man. I get to spend most of my time in here processing orders. I guess it's one good thing about being small and lacking any upper body strength."

"Very true!" said Fisher. He could start to feel the warmth of the office as the feeling crept back into his feet and face.

"You sure you want to pull this order yourself?" asked Bart.

"Yeah, I know you guys are short staffed and have enough work on your plate. I don't want to interfere."

Bart shrugged his shoulders. "Okay. Just grab a cart, load up, and come grab me when you're ready."

"Perfect," said Fisher.

Bart's expression changed to a more serious one. "Crazy they still haven't found Helena, huh?"

"Yeah, it just doesn't make any sense. I mean, where could she be?" Fisher lowered his head and felt his chest tighten.

"Well," said Bart, "they've gotta find her soon. The Arc is only so big." Changing the subject, Bart reached down into his desk, pulled out a small unit, and asked, "Ever use one of these?"

"No, but I was down here six months ago, and I saw it being used," said Fisher.

Bart waved Fisher over with his left hand. "Come take a look. It's pretty easy."

Fisher walked over as Bart continued.

"Hold the unit up to the Bartcode and press this button," he said, pointing to one of the long rectangular buttons on the keypad. "Then enter the number of units you're taking, followed by the enter key."

"Bartcode?"

Bart grinned. "I like to pretend I invented this shit."

Fisher laughed and nodded along with his instructions.

"Do that for everything you pull, and when you've got your order completed, press this button," he said, pointing to a pill-shaped button on the unit. "You may find that you need to scratch ice off the barcodes for the reader to get a clean scan. I've found it helpful to get up close and breathe on them a few times before wiping. The heat of your breath is usually enough to do the trick."

"Tricks of the trade?" asked Fisher.

"Yeah. You pick up things quickly when your balls are frozen like ice cubes and you want to fill an order as fast as possible."

Fisher laughed and then said, "I don't know how you guys do this every day."

"Not much of a choice really, I guess. I just remind myself that this is all just temporary. Once we get to Uelara, I'll never have to set foot in the Hold again. Thoughts of my life on Uelara keep me warm and motivated."

"I'll keep that in mind when I'm out there," Fisher said with a smile.

"You'll also want to take this with you to find your way around," said Bart, pulling a small catalog from his front pocket. "Make sure you get that one back to me. I've got a couple of years of notations in that, and it would suck if I lost it."

"No problem," said Fisher.

Fisher walked toward the door and hesitated before opening it.

Bart laughed. "Waiting's only going to make it worse."

Fisher took in a long breath and opened the door. A cold blast hit him in the face as he stepped out from the office. Fisher let out a loud cry in pain. "You gotta be kidding me!"

As the door closed behind him, he could hear Bart laughing.

Fisher walked over to one of the carts, unplugged the charging cable, and sat behind the wheel. He pressed the green button on the dash, and the cart started to hum. He looked at the first item on his list, cross referenced it in the catalog, and drove off toward his first pickup.

As Fisher approached the copper spools, he tried to imagine the crazy logistics that must have been involved getting the vast amount of resources into the cargo hold. Even with the strict rationing that had taken place throughout his entire life, Fisher had trouble comprehending just how many supplies were needed for a mission like this. The huge amount of inventory for the ring construction alone was difficult to take in.

Over an hour had passed, and Fisher's body ached. Every inch of him was frozen to the bone, and he was happy he found himself back at the office.

Fisher opened the door and welcomed the dry heat as it hugged him like a warm blanket.

"Who ordered the frozen Fish?" joked Bart.

Now that's a new one, thought Fisher.

"That kids' game? Not really," grunted Vlad.

"Come on. It'll help pass the time."

Vlad rolled his eyes and sighed, "Okay, let's hear it."

"First thing I'm going to do is roll down a big hill!" exclaimed Echo.

"The first thing you're going to do when we get to Uelara after spending your entire life on this ship is roll down a hill?" scoffed Vlad. "Wow, Echo, way to dream big!"

"Thanks!"

The two approached a utility room door just outside the protein chamber, and Vlad struck the entry plate with his fist. The door slid open, and an overhead light flickered on.

"Surprise, surprise. No Helena. Do we really need to keep checking the utility rooms? I find it a bit ridiculous that anyone would think she would be in one," said Vlad.

"But McHail said we need to check all of them," replied Echo, dragging a stylus across the surface of his tablet to cross out their current location.

"And we wouldn't want to skip any, and just say we looked in all of them, of course."

"That's right," said Echo. "Good news! We're down to the last four."

"Yay, us."

Echo and Vlad continued down the corridor toward the next utility room.

"So, what about you? What are you going to do?" asked Echo.

"Huh?"

"What's the first thing you're going to do when we get there?"

"Oh. I thought we were done with that," replied Vlad. "I guess I'll do a whole lotta nothin'."

"What do you mean?"

"All we do is work. For the next thirty years, we have nothing but the same labor to look forward to, so I'll be happy being away from the ship doing nothing."

"Won't that be boring?"

"Not as boring as sorting garbage in the Center day after day."

"I like working in the—"

"I know you do, Echo," interrupted Vlad. "How about we play a new game."

"Sure, what do you want to play?"

"It's my favorite. It's called the silence game."

"Oh, everyone in my hive loves this game!" effused Echo.

"I bet they do."

CHAPTER 30

Grayson slid his heat-resistant synthetic fiber jacket on and fastened the three industrial latches on the left side to close it. He pulled a pair of aluminized gloves from the side pocket and grabbed his helmet from the assembly table.

Sweat dripped from his brow. *How'd I end up working in the engine room, of all places?* Grayson wondered.

He sluggishly walked over to one of the power cell compartments on the east wall of the engine room. He put on his helmet and gloves, lowered the face shield on the helmet, and let out a deep sigh.

He couldn't believe that now, after three days of searching, there was still no sign of Helena. Grayson wanted to continue helping the crew locate her, but Thomas, the senior engineer and his direct supervisor, insisted that he return to the engine room. Grayson disagreed that his mundane tasks were more important than Helena's well-being. As usual, second generation opinions held no weight.

Grayson opened the hatch to the compartment, revealing a power cell, and wheeled a cooling bath to the exposed unit. He pulled a lever down, tilting the power cell out of the framing that held it in place. The power cell slid into the cooling bath.

An explosion of steam erupted from the bath as the metal released a high-pitched screech. After the steam cleared, Grayson wheeled the bath to the side and walked over to a power cell deployment lift. He pushed it in front of the open compartment and powered it up.

He entered a three-digit code onto the lift's keypad, and the unit rejected him with a loud buzz. Grayson paused and thought for a moment, *Why was six afraid of seven?*

He grinned and entered a new three-digit code. The lift jolted to life, raising the fresh cell up to the opening. Grayson pressed the release button on the unit, and the power cell slid into place inside the box. He lowered the lift and moved it off to the side.

With the new power cell in place, Grayson raised the lever on the compartment and closed the hatch. He wheeled the cooling bath over to an assembly table on the far east wall of the engine room, strapped the swing arm around the power cell, and hoisted it onto the table.

Grayson removed his helmet and gloves, followed by his jacket. His coveralls were soaked with sweat. He slid the collapsible doors on the cell casing open to gain access to the bolts holding the rechargeable cell to the outer casing and reached for a wrench. As he loosened the top bolt, he surveyed the inner cell.

"This is going to take the entire day to clean," he whined.

"Grayson!"

Grayson spun around, startled. Thomas was directly behind him. Thomas stood over two meters tall. His forearms looked to be the same circumference as Grayson's thighs, and he had a thick handlebar mustache that compensated for the lack of hair on his head.

"Why do you think I'm standing here in front of you sweating in the engine room, instead of relaxing in my temperature-controlled office?" growled Thomas.

Grayson knew there wasn't an answer that was going to change whatever had Thomas on edge. He'd seen him like this many times before. Actually, Grayson had come to realize this was Thomas's default state.

Thomas wasn't an easy man to work with. When things were good, Thomas was still hounding Grayson and the others about something. Thomas had a permanent stick up his ass, and from as far as Grayson could tell, Thomas must have thought Grayson put it there.

"You got nothing, huh? What a surprise," scoffed Thomas.

Grayson began to speak, but he still wasn't sure what would come out of his mouth. He just knew he needed to respond.

"Let me ask you an easier question," continued Thomas, muffling a cough. "What are your plans with that spent casing you got there?"

Grayson started to feel a little less tense. He knew this one. "I'm going to remove the power cell from it and place it in the storage bay to be recycled . . . sir."

"Okay, and when do the recycling elves come and collect the cell casings for recycling?"

Grayson scratched the back of his head and looked down. As he opened his mouth to ask what recycling elves were, he realized where this was going. He'd been putting off delivering the spent casings for weeks. "Sir, I'm aware that the casings are piling up in the east storage bay, but I thought I'd wait 'til I—"

"Son, since when have you been tasked with thinking? There should never be more than four casings in the storage bay at any given time. I count twelve. Yep, twelve. For the last thirty years, we've had this system in place. To date, you're the only fitter who can't seem to follow basic instructions and keep in line with the system."

Grayson knew there was no good reason that he hadn't transferred the casings to the reclamation center. He simply didn't want to do it. He hated his job. He spent the majority of his time in the engine room concocting new ways to get out of working. After he got away with skipping delivery of the empty casings for the first couple of weeks, he figured it wasn't a big deal and kept skipping every third casing, week after week.

He knew better than to speak at this point. He'd let the old man bark at him for however long was necessary and then deal with whatever shit detail got thrown his way.

"I'm giving you until the end of the day to clean up this mess you've created," continued Thomas. "If the storage bay isn't clear of all those casings by the time I finish my shift, I'll have you transferred to filtering moondust in the Hold . . . permanently. Are we clear?"

"Yes, sir," replied Grayson.

Thomas marched off toward two of the other fitters and began shouting about schedules and deadlines. Grayson felt like Thomas had gone easy on him this time, but looking at the digital display on the wall above the assembly desk, he knew he didn't have time to celebrate.

As bad as he felt he had it in the engine room, the last place he wanted to be was in the Hold. Those guys always looked miserable. His friend from Hive 2 could never seem to get warm, even hours after he'd been on the upper decks of the ship.

Grayson headed to the storage bay and, one by one, tilted the empty casings on their bottom edge, rolling them over to a pallet.

Next time I'll leave them in the west storage near someone else's area, and Thomas won't know it was me, he thought.

Grayson went to tilt one of the remaining three casings that stood up against the wall, but it did not give.

"What the—? Who put a live power cell back here?"

Grayson bent down and pulled back one of the collapsible panels to confirm that the casing did, in fact, still contain the cell. He wondered if the cell itself was damaged and no longer viable.

As the panel retracted, a high-pitched scream rattled his eardrums. A moment later, he realized the scream had come from his own mouth. He found himself staring at a Uelara patch and long strands of blond hair.

"What the hell, Helena? I almost shit myself!" gasped Grayson. "Everyone's been looking for you! What are you doing in there?"

Helena didn't respond. The hairs on Grayson's neck stood up, and a cold streak ran down his back. "You . . . you okay?"

Grayson tapped her on the arm. Helena didn't move. He grabbed her arm—it was cold and stiff.

CHAPTER 31

Sam stood deep in the forest surrounded by blooming magnolia trees. White and pink flowers engulfed the canopy above her, and she could hear the wind whistling through the branches that stretched out in a thousand directions.

Tears formed in her eyes, and she fought to keep them from falling. She needed to fend off this sadness, so she could think straight. After a visit with Dr. Fiona, she was granted some time in the Dome to help ease her distress. Desperate to find Helena, Sam had chosen her friend's favorite Dome program today, hoping it would spark an idea of where Helena could be. After more than an hour, she was still without answers.

The magnolia blooms made Sam's pulse quicken. It was visuals like this one in the Dome that reminded Sam of just how gray her day-to day surroundings really were.

Sam jolted, as everything around her suddenly went dark. Slowly, lights on the Dome's curved ceiling began to increase in intensity, and she found herself standing in the stark, white, lifeless room once again.

"What's going on?" she muttered. Sam had asked for the Dome's playback to be set for two hours. Had it really been that long?

The door to the Dome slid open, spilling in bright yellow light from the outer room. Sam's mother stepped into the Dome and slid the door closed behind her.

"Honey, you okay?" asked Sam's mother in a soft voice.

Sam bit her lower lip as tears welled up in her eyes again. "Not really, Mom."

Sam's mother raced over and embraced her with a hug only a mother could provide. Sam no longer felt like a young adult. She was instantly transported to her childhood when her mother would hold her in her arms.

"I'm scared, Mom. I'm really worried about Helena."

"I know, honey, that's why I'm here. Grayson found her."

Sam pulled away from her mother's arms, wide-eyed. "Helena's been found?"

"Yes, and—"

"Where was she? Is she okay?"

Sam's mother paused. She seemed to be searching for the right words.

"What is it? Is she hurt?"

"She . . . she's dead, Sam."

Sam's mother tried to pull her close again, but Sam resisted.

"What are you talking about? What do you mean she's dead?" cried Sam, struggling to get the words past the lump in her throat.

"I'm so sorry, Sam. I know how close the two of you were."

"Were?!" Sam collapsed to the floor, releasing sobs that tore at her throat. Her mother knelt next to her as Sam's body began to tremor.

"I'm sorry, Sam. I'm so very sorry."

CHAPTER 32

Alec entered the protein chamber looking for Dom. Alec wasn't a fan of the Chamber, as he never really got used to the stench of the room. The Chamber contained three huge pools in the center of the room, which were constantly lit by large, bright UV lights that hung down over the pools from the ceiling. Although the pools were housed behind thick glass walls, the odor permeated the entire Chamber, and it was unlike anything Alec had smelled on the Arc. It was extremely unpleasant and turned his stomach.

Alec could see two people in hooded white suits pulling long metal rods across the surface of the liquid. Dom called it "raking the pools." The warmth from the lights along with nutrient-tainted water fed strains of high-protein algae that were developed at a worldwide scale on Earth as a food replacement when the climate changes devastated traditional agriculture.

Alec could tell that neither of the two rakers were Dom based on their heights. Several large, barrel-shaped containers sat outside the glass walls, and smaller containers were shelved along the walls of the room. Alec walked through the Chamber and saw Dom by one of the larger containers.

"Dom!" shouted Alec.

Dom looked over at Alec. "What's up?"

Dom slid the top of the protein container to the side and pulled a large syringe from his belt. He lowered the syringe into the container and squeezed the end to collect a sample of the fluid inside.

"Did you hear they found Helena?" asked Alec.

Dom's shoulders appeared to tense up. "Yeah. I heard from Avery that Grayson found her in the storage bay. Man, I can't believe she's dead."

"I know," agreed Alec.

"Do you think whoever did this is going to do it again?" asked Dom, as he squeezed the protein liquid into the open reservoir connected to a small unit on a cart next to him. "I'm actually still at a loss for who would do this . . . that anyone on the ship would do this . . . to anyone," continued Dom, as he studied the graph on the unit's display.

"You know, is it really that hard to believe that someone finally lost it? I mean, people weren't designed to live a caged existence like this. Maybe one of the first gen snapped. If I knew I weren't making it to Uelara and had to finish my life on this miserable ship, I'm pretty sure I'd—"

"Hold on a sec, I think I may have solved this," interrupted Dom.

"Dom, focus!"

"I am, but I've also been trying to nail this amino acid sequence for weeks now and I—"

"Dude, Helena's dead!" Alec yelled, raising both hands high in the air. "Someone killed her, and you wanna talk about enzymes? What the hell is wrong with you?"

"Alec, calm down! I know Helena is dead. I understand that we don't know what happened to her. But going on about it isn't going to solve anything, and if I don't get this worked out,

Andrew will limit my work detail to the galley. As exciting as working a food printer looks—"

"You're being selfish, Dom," snapped Alec. "You should be more concerned with your friend's death."

Dom dropped the syringe, crossed his arms, and stared at Alec. "I thought you knew me better, Alec," said Dom. "My stomach's in knots, I haven't eaten in more than a day, and all I want to do is scream at the top of my lungs. So, screw you and your concern."

Dom pushed Alec aside and started walking away.

Oh, so he's going to resort to Lance's tactics now? Alec thought. He grabbed Dom's arm and spun him around.

Dom's eyes were filled with tears. "I can't deal with this right now. I just want to stay busy and keep my mind on work. You handle this madness however you see fit. Me . . . I'm going to keep myself busy and just try and make it through the day."

Stay busy and just make it through the day. Alec heard these words and realized they summed up every second gen'ers existence. Clearly Dom was going to continue life as usual on the Arc and blindly follow orders like Fisher and the others. Regardless of how Dom explained his behavior, Alec couldn't imagine dismissing a death as tragic as this one for any reason.

"Alright, I can see you're busy. Catch you later," said Alec.

As Alec turned to leave, Dom asked, "How did Lance take the news?"

CHAPTER 33

Large pistons pounded in the engine room as a crimson spatter streaked across one of the metal panels on the floor.

"I swear it wasn't me!" cried Grayson, as Lance slammed his fist into Grayson's jaw.

"Bullshit!"

Lance sat on top of Grayson, pinning him to the floor of the engine room wearing a ravenous expression. Lance swung his fists repeatedly as Grayson attempted to block his attack. Grayson's face was already starting to swell from previous blows.

"You killed her and tried to cover your tracks! And now you're going to die, you piece of shit!" growled Lance in a nearly unrecognizable voice.

Sounds from the fight were muffled by the loud hammering of the pistons. Grayson's arms fell limp as Lance continued to pound on him.

Lance felt something grab him from behind, and before he could tell what was happening, he could feel himself being lifted off Grayson. His arms were pinned at his sides, and his feet weren't touching the ground. Looking down, he could see a pair of large forearms wrapped around his chest, and an immense pressure made it difficult for Lance to breathe.

"That's enough, Lance!" shouted Thomas.

"Let me go!"

"Calm down, and I'll consider it."

"This piece of shit killed Helena, and he's going to pay for it!"

Thomas tightened his arms around Lance's chest. "And what has you so convinced of this?"

"Isn't it obvious? No one on the ship could find her, and out of the blue he does? I don't buy it!"

"If he killed Helena, why would he tell anyone where her body was? Why would he hide her in his work area?"

"It's a perfect way to look innocent!"

"Son, you're giving Grayson way more credit than you should. You also didn't see him after he found her. I did. He was near catatonic."

Lance found it difficult to breathe, and he felt all his energy draining from his body. "He was . . . faking it," said Lance in a shallow voice.

"No way was he faking it. That boy was terrified by the discovery. Hell, he hasn't been the same since. Now, I understand you're upset, but this is not your problem to solve. The captain and the others will get to the bottom of this. In the meantime, I think you need to cool off."

"I'm fine. But someone is going to pay for what happened to Helena!"

Thomas loosened his hold on Lance. "Now this is something we can agree on. Whoever did this will definitely face the consequences."

Thomas lowered Lance to the ground, and Lance could finally feel the floor with his feet.

"Now, I'm letting you go, but you're going to help me get Grayson to the medical bay. If I think for one second you're going to try anything, I'll snap you in two, you hear me?"

Lance nodded his head. He was still filled with rage, but he wasn't stupid. Thomas was twice his size, and Lance knew Thomas could deliver on his words without even breaking a sweat.

"Wheel that empty cooling bath over here. We'll use it to get him to the Bay," instructed Thomas, bending down to check on Grayson. "You really did a number on him. You better hope he's okay."

At this point, several fitters had approached, drawn in by the commotion.

Thomas looked at the onlookers. "What the hell are you looking at? Did I tell anyone to stop working?"

Everyone quickly scattered from the scene. Lance pushed the cooling bath over, as Thomas lifted Grayson up. Incoherent groans and whimpering came from Grayson. His eyes were swollen shut, and a pool of blood stained the floor where he once lay.

Thomas lowered Grayson's limp body into the bath, walked over to the handle on the cooling bath, and started to push him toward the exit. "Run ahead and let Dr. Gage know we're coming, and when I get there I better find you sitting quietly out of the way or Grayson here is going to have some long-term company in the Bay. Do I make myself clear?"

"Yes, sir," said Lance in a soft voice before running toward the exit.

As he neared the medical bay, Lance's rage-filled haze slowly began to dissipate. Thomas' words about Grayson's innocence were becoming hard to ignore. After all, Lance never stopped to think . . . what possible reason would Grayson have to murder Helena? He looked down at his red, swollen hands and thought, *What have I done?*

CHAPTER 34

"**S**uit up," instructed Stringer, standing in the doorway of the locker room as Kayla, Deuce, and Toby laid out their gear. "You three are going solo today."

"You're not joining us?" asked Toby.

"I'll be in operations today covering for Helena's father. But I'll be right there with you communicating over your CCAs," replied Stringer. "We've got a simple survey walk, so you should only be out there for about an hour today."

"What about Lance?" asked Deuce.

"Lance is sitting this one out," explained Stringer. "I just need you to survey the jumper we patched and the exterior compensator we replaced. The three of you should be able to handle it without him."

"Is Lance okay?" asked Kayla.

"Lance is fine," answered Stringer. "I need you guys in the airlock in fifteen, so get to it."

The three junior outriggers stood tall and replied, "Yes, sir!"

Stringer gave the crew a nod and exited the room.

"You heard him," Kayla asserted, stepping into the lower portion of her EMU. "Airlock in fifteen."

Kayla was excited to hear that Stringer felt confident in her and the others enough to let them go out on their own today, but she wished Lance would be joining them. He was probably so heartbroken about the news of Helena's death that he needed some time to himself.

She tried to imagine what Lance must be feeling right now. How could he go on, knowing Helena would never again be by his side? He had spent so many days talking about his future, a future that had always included Helena. He was certainly going to be left with a hopelessness that made Kayla consider something even deeper.

As tragic as this loss was for Lance, perhaps it would also create a common bond between his father and him. After all, Lance's dad had lost his wife. He had been coping with the loss for twenty-two years. Surely, he would have some valuable wisdom he could pass on to Lance about finding new meaning in broken dreams. Everyone was fairly aware of the distance between Lance and his father, and maybe after some time passed, Lance could get a little emotional support from the one person who could relate to losing a life partner. Kayla knew that no matter how she tried, she could not be that resource for Lance. She just couldn't relate.

Now that she thought about it, the closest thing to a partner Kayla could envision for herself was Lance. There had never been anything romantic between the two of them; she'd held the utmost respect for his relationship with Helena. But Lance was her favorite person on the Arc. He made her daily job fun. He was there for her when she got frustrated with her hive. She trusted him, and he trusted her as well. She always felt a special pride when he would share his plans for surprising Helena with some sweet gesture. And was he funny! He would sometimes make up stories about the first gen that made her laugh so loud that Stringer would usually end up yelling at her to stop using up all her oxygen on their spacewalks. Kayla could list a dozen more reasons why she would be devastated losing Lance. And he wasn't even her boyfriend.

"Where's Lance?" asked Toby.

"Not sure, but did you hear what he did to Grayson?" whispered Deuce.

Toby leaned toward Deuce as he pulled his left glove on. "No, what?"

"One of the fitters in the engine room said Lance beat Grayson half to death last night. Said there was blood everywhere."

"Really?" asked Toby. "Did it have something to do with Helena?"

Deuce stood up and grabbed his helmet from the upper shelf. "He said Lance believes Grayson killed her."

Toby spoke in a hushed tone, "Kaman heard Lance had something to do with Helena's death."

"I can believe it," said Deuce. "I heard he—"

"Enough!" shouted Kayla, angry with the flying accusations. "You two sound like Mia and Samar swapping rumors about who kissed who at the last deployment celebration."

"What? I'm just filling him in on what I heard," explained Deuce.

"Lance is one of our crew. He deserves better," asserted Kayla. "The last thing I thought I'd have to do is defend Lance to you guys."

Toby raised his hand. "Calm down, Kayla. We were just—"

"You were just insinuating that Lance played a role in Helena's death," said Kayla. "Both of you should know better. How many years have you worked alongside Lance? How could you possibly believe that—?"

"Okay, okay, sorry I said anything," apologized Deuce.

Kayla could tell Deuce was being sincere, but she was also surprised at how easily he and Toby could turn on Lance. She had defended Lance to several of the crew throughout the day, but most of them hadn't really spent much time with him. How could anyone who got to know Lance really believe such a thing?

"So, do you think Grayson really killed Helena?" Toby asked Kayla.

"No idea. But I'm sure the captain and the others will find out what happened to her," said Kayla, picking up her helmet from the bench. "But just to be clear, if I hear either of you talk any more nonsense about Lance having something to do with it, you'll be joining Grayson in the Bay. Got it?"

Both Toby and Deuce looked at the floor.

"Yes," Deuce murmured.

"Toby?" she demanded.

Toby's shoulders dropped. "Yeah."

"Good, now let's get moving. We have a job to do."

As Kayla reached the locker room door, she looked back at Lance's EMU hanging on the wall. No amount of logic or arguments could convince her that Lance had anything to do with Helena's death. Kayla was eager for the true culprit to be determined so her good friend's name could be cleared. She knew in time that normal life would resume and Lance could join her in another spacewalk.

CHAPTER 35

"She's gone, and I'll never see her again," Sam wept softly.

Dr. Fiona pulled two tissues from the container sitting on the side table and handed them to Sam, who sat next to her on the couch in Dr. Fiona's office. "It can be hard to miss someone and know you won't see them again. What do you think you'll miss most about Helena?"

Sam still couldn't believe the word "miss" could be associated with Helena. How could she be gone? How could Sam decide what she would miss most when she was still in shock that she was gone forever?

What would she miss? It was so hard to identify a thing, or a quality. Helena was almost a part of Sam—at least that's how Sam felt. They'd spent nearly every day together since Sam could walk.

"I don't know. I just know that I miss her so much," cried Sam.

"I know you do, honey." Dr. Fiona paused for a moment. "Do you remember the time when she made origami cherry blossom flowers for all of you?"

Using the tissues, Sam wiped the tears from her eyes and glumly said, "Yeah. I still have the one she made me. She spent half a day teaching me how to make my own, but I never quite got it looking as good as hers."

"What if you made blossoms for everyone? That might be a nice way for you to help everyone remember Helena."

A hint of a smile graced Sam's face. "That would be nice. But what if they're not perfect?"

"I'd like the most flawed blossom you create."

"Why?"

"*Wabi-sabi.*"

"Wabi-sabi?"

"It's Japanese, meaning 'beauty of things imperfect,'" explained Dr. Fiona.

Sam smiled. "I like that."

Dr. Fiona put her arm around Sam and said, "The beauty of life is in its imperfections. The blossoms you create can be a reminder of our own flaws and vulnerabilities and what makes us unique. If we learn to accept these imperfections, we can open larger spaces for love. Love of others and for ourselves."

Sam marveled once again at Dr. Fiona's ability to find just the right perspective to help make her burdens feel lighter. When Helena and Sam had broken up, Dr. Fiona provided just the right words and suggestions to regain hope that she could somehow carry on.

"I have an idea that I think you'll like," Dr. Fiona said. "Do you remember the journals Helena wrote in?"

"Yeah. She wrote in her journal every day. I tried doing the same but always struggled with what to write."

Dr. Fiona stood up, walked over to her desk, and pulled one of the drawers open. "I have a fresh, new journal somewhere in here that Helena requested a week ago. I think you should use the pages from it to create the blossoms." Dr. Fiona held up a journal that looked like the ones Helena wrote in. "But first, I think you should write something you remember about Helena on every page. The things that made her unique, the things that you loved about her."

"I don't know," she said doubtfully. "That could take a while."

"There's no rush, Sam. I'd suggest you take your time and enjoy the process. Give each page some thought and write something special about Helena or about a specific time with her you remember."

Sam smiled. "Like the time she helped me play a practical joke on Alec and Dom?"

Dr. Fiona sat next to Sam and handed her the journal. "Exactly. See? You will have no problem flooding the pages of this journal with all the wonderful memories Helena has left you with. I want you to focus on those memories. It's the best way for you to honor your friend."

Sam closed her eyes, pulled the journal to her chest, and said, "So, you were going to give this to Helena?"

"Yes, and now it's yours. I have a feeling Helena would have wanted you to have it."

"Really?"

"Without a doubt. Helena loved you. Why don't we write your first few entries together? Would that be okay with you?"

"Sure."

Dr. Fiona pulled a pen from her pocket and passed it to Sam. "So, what's the first thing you'd like to remember about Helena?"

Sam opened the journal to the first page and stared down at it. She had so many wonderful memories of Helena, but she wanted this first entry to be special. She closed her eyes and was instantly flooded with wonderful moments she shared with

Helena. Sam looked at Dr. Fiona and said, "I think I have a good one."

Dr. Fiona smiled at Sam and said, "I'm sure this will be the first of many. And when you run out of pages in this one, I'll have another journal waiting for you."

Sam began to write in the journal with lovely thoughts of Helena dancing in her head.

CHAPTER 36

Fisher stood outside room four of the Bay, looking at Grayson through the door's portal window. It was hard to imagine that under all the swelling and bandages was Fisher's friend. Kaman sat next to Grayson's bed, talking to him and caressing his hand. She'd been there for most of the day, but Grayson hadn't woken up.

Fisher turned around and walked toward the quarantine bays. Through a glass door, he could see Lance pacing back and forth. The first gen decided that until things calmed down, it was best that Lance be locked in quarantine and separated from the rest of the crew.

Earlier that morning Grayson's parents had come by to check on him but spent most of their time berating Lance. Fisher couldn't remember a time where he'd seen any of the parents so upset. If it weren't for Dr. Gage intervening, Grayson's parents might still be on the rampage.

He looked toward room three where Helena's autopsy had been performed, but he wouldn't approach it. Fisher was relieved that he had not been asked to assist in the procedure. How could he have possibly witnessed poor Helena's body being opened up like that? Fisher shuddered at the thought that his good friend was just on the other side of the wall, but he would never get to speak with her again.

Dr. Gage entered the Bay from the east corridor, followed by Helena's parents.

"Fisher, could you bring a pitcher of water and some glasses to my office?" asked Dr. Gage.

Fisher went to the counter on the back wall, grabbed a large carafe, and filled it with water. He grabbed a set of smaller beakers and walked them to Dr. Gage's office, setting them down on the corner of the desk nearest to Helena's parents.

"Can I get anything else?" asked Fisher in a soft voice, avoiding eye contact with the grieving couple.

"That'll be all, Fisher, thanks," said Dr. Gage. "Could you shut the door on your way out?"

"Sure," said Fisher, sliding the door closed behind him.

Fisher knew it wasn't the right thing to do, but his curiosity outweighed his ability to respect their privacy. He stepped into the storage closet adjacent to Dr. Gage's office, closed the door, and dropped to the floor. He put his ear close to the small vent on the wall that bordered the two rooms and slowed his breathing. The voices were muffled, but he could still hear what was being said.

"Suicide?" questioned Helena's mother. "Our daughter would never kill herself!"

"I know this is hard to take in," Dr. Gage replied, "but the autopsy report shows large amounts of morphine in her system. The MDS also—"

"MDS?" interrupted Helena's father.

"Forgive me . . . the medication dispensary system we use to track all medications we process in the Bay. It shows Helena's access number was used to remove the pills just days ago."

"How could you not know the drugs were missing until now?" Helena's mother asked incredulously.

"You know that we run inventory checks weekly," explained Dr. Gage. "This wouldn't have come up until Friday, and even then, it might not have been flagged. While this is a strong painkiller, it's also commonly prescribed to the crew when they have been injured."

Morphine? Why would Helena take morphine? Fisher wondered.

Dr. Gage continued. "Some of her friends also reported that she displayed several signs that commonly lead up to suicide. She was depressed, spent days in her pod—"

"It still doesn't explain who put Helena in the power-cell casing," said Helena's father.

"My best guess is that Helena went to the engine room, took the pills, and—"

"We've heard enough!" cried Helena's mother.

"I know this is hard to hear, but—"

"Do you? Do you know?" she snapped. "Is your daughter's body lying on the table in there?"

Helena's father sighed, "Honey, that's not fair."

"Is anything about this fair? Our daughter is . . ." she sobbed, unable to finish.

"I'm sorry, you're right." Dr. Gage conceded. "I couldn't possibly know what you're going through. Just know I'm here. The whole crew is here for you."

"Thank you. I appreciate all that you've done . . . for all of us," said Helena's father.

Helena's mother added, "I'm sorry. I know you're just trying to help. I don't mean to take this out on you. I just . . . our baby is gone."

"Tell you what. Why don't the two of you spend some time in the Dome? Take as long as you need. I know it won't change anything right now, but it's certainly a calmer setting than this."

"No room change is going to bring my—"

"I think he's right, honey. Let's head to the Dome."

"Come on. I'll walk with you," said Dr. Gage.

Fisher could hear chairs sliding across the floor. He jumped to his feet, brushed off the front of his coveralls, and bolted out of the storage room and into room one of the Bay. He could hear Dr. Gage and Helena's parents walking toward the exit.

Fisher went to the doorway and peered at the room Lance was in. Lance was standing at the door, glaring at him. How long had he been watching? Did he watch Fisher go into the storage room? Did he see him race out in a panic? The look on Lance's face indicated he had.

Lance pushed a button on the call box in the room. "Start talking!"

CHAPTER 37

Earlier in the day, Alec asked Dom if he would be interested in visiting the storage bay where Grayson had discovered Helena's body. He was initially taken aback by the idea, but as the day progressed, morbid curiosity crept in, and Dom couldn't let the idea go. Now, standing in front of the casings, Dom felt an uneasy sensation run through him.

"Why would someone put Helena's body in one of these?" asked Alec, staring down at the empty power cell casing.

"I'm still at a loss for why anyone would kill her," replied Dom, scratching the back of his head.

Alec shrugged his shoulders. "Dad says thousands murder people every day back on the Earth."

Dom couldn't even begin to follow his brother's logic. "The Earth is a mess. The Arc has always been a safe place. You can't compare the two."

"Well, there is one major variable that exists on both, though," Alec reasoned.

"What's that?"

"People."

"What does that mean?" asked Dom.

"People can be unpredictable," explained Alec. "Like I said the other day, maybe caging up a hundred-plus people on a single ship for decades is starting to take its toll, and someone finally snapped. This is why the sooner we get to Uelara, the better. You know that sometimes even I get to a point where I feel like I'm going to lose it on this damn mission."

"I don't know . . . sounds a bit extreme if you ask me."

"And yet, here we are, with one of our friends having been found murdered," replied Alec.

Dom still couldn't accept that anyone on the ship could be so cold as to kill another crew member. But Alec had a point. Whether Dom could understand it or not, Helena had been found murdered in the very spot he now stood.

Although he agreed with Alec, he was sensing a troubling change within his brother. Alec's reactions to Helena's death seemed to be transforming somehow from despair into something less tragic and more impersonal. His prior sentiments of concern and compassion were now being replaced with statements of wonder and curiosity. Even Alec's facial expressions appeared different. His once warm eyes were now rather emotionless.

Alec sat on the edge of one of the casings and looked up at Dom. "I know you and Lance are friends, but . . ." Alec looked at the floor and paused. "All signs point to Lance."

With this theory, Dom became agitated. Alec wasn't the first to suggest Lance's involvement. "I know everyone thinks that, but the Lance I know would never kill anyone."

"You sure about that? Have you seen Grayson? And do you remember how hard he pushed Sam in the galley?"

"That's different, and you know it," argued Dom. "Hell, you and I have had some knockdown, drag-out fights in the past. Does that mean one of us could kill someone?"

"That's completely different. How can you compare—?"

"Hey, guys! I've been looking all over for you."

Dom turned to see Echo standing just outside the storage bay. "What's going on, Echo?"

Echo glanced over to the casings and then quickly averted his eyes and stared at the floor. "Fish wants all of us to meet him in the west observation deck at the top of the hour."

"Do you know why he wants to meet?" asked Alec.

"He said he wanted to fill us in on what's going on. Sounded important."

"Thanks for the heads-up. We'll meet you there," said Dom.

"See you there, Echo," added Alec.

"Okay, guys, I'm going to go let the others know," said Echo as he dashed away.

Dom turned back toward Alec. "What do you think Fish wants to talk about?"

Alec stood up from the casing. "My guess is it has something to do with Helena. He was supposed to work in the Bay today, and Mom said Dr. Gage was going to be performing an autopsy on her."

"Autopsy?" asked Dom.

"Yeah, to determine what happened to her," replied Alec.

"Think they found clues as to who killed her?" Dom asked, and then shook his head. "Never mind. I don't think I really want to know."

Dom looked down at the casing again, and his eyes filled with tears. Poor Helena. No matter what happened to her or how it happened, no one deserved a fate like that.

CHAPTER 38

Fisher entered the west observation deck and waited for his eyes to adjust to the dark area. The observation decks on the Arc were always dimly lit to prevent the interior lights from reflecting onto the windows that overlooked the exterior of the ship and out into space. He looked toward the windows and could see the *Archean's* exterior lights flooding the observation deck, framing Sam's silhouette sitting alone on the bench closest to the center window.

"I thought the others would have beaten me here," said Fisher, walking toward Sam.

Sam wiped away a tear as she turned toward him. "Nope . . . just me."

"Whatcha thinking?" Fisher asked.

Sam looked back out over the deck and sniffled. "I was remembering the time I was here with Helena and told her the sappiest thing."

Fisher smiled and let her continue, knowing better than to stop her train of thought.

"She was just so . . . I don't know. She just looked so beautiful sitting here on this bench, with the blackness of space surrounding her blond hair. I was just caught up in the moment, I guess, and so I just sort of blurted it out."

Fisher waited.

"Aren't you going to ask me what I said?" Sam asked.

"I'm not sure if you want to risk having it thrown in your face for the next thirty years."

Sam smiled.

Fisher said, "Ok I'll bite. What did you say?"

"I told her that she could outshine even the brightest of stars. Go ahead, laugh, I don't care."

Fisher grinned and gave Sam a hug. He felt her squeeze his shoulders tight, and he rubbed her back. "Your secret's safe with me. It was a sweet thing to say."

Sam looked at Fisher with grateful eyes.

Fisher was almost sorry he had asked Sam what she was thinking. How was he going to make the transition from sappy love quotes to suicide? He didn't have the faintest idea how to buffer the upcoming news, but he had a feeling it would help to inform Sam before the others arrived. Fisher pulled away from their embrace.

"So I have some news about Helena that I think you should hear before I tell everyone else."

"It sounded important when you called earlier."

"I don't know any easy way to say this, Sam. She . . . she wasn't murdered."

Sam's eyes widened. "What do you mean?"

"Helena took her own life." Fisher's words came out like a steel weight. "She overdosed on pills she took from the Bay."

Sam shook her head as if to brush off Fisher's inconceivable words. "Impossible," she said firmly. "The Helena I knew would *never* do that. *Never.*"

"Do what?" asked Avery, as she entered the room.

186

Both Fisher and Sam turned toward Avery. Fisher looked at Sam and then back at Avery. "I've got news about Helena," he said.

"What's the news?"

"Let's wait until the others arrive. I do not have it in me to repeat this multiple times."

"Repeat what?" asked Echo, joining them on the deck.

Fisher sighed. "Exactly."

Fisher still couldn't wrap his head around the fact that Helena was gone, never mind that she had killed herself. How many times had the gang gathered together like this through the years? Every single meeting he could recall included Helena at the helm. Whether they were bantering back and forth about whose OCP was more important, which Graveyard hiding spot was the best, or worst possible Pairing selections, Helena was a constant. And now she was just . . . gone.

One by one, the group on the deck grew larger. Dom and Alec were the last to arrive.

"Looks like everyone who is going to show is here," said Avery. "So, what's going on?"

"I overheard news about Helena this afternoon," said Fisher in a whisper that caught him by surprise.

"You know who killed her?" asked Dom.

"Was it Lance?" added Alec.

Fisher raised his hand. "Guys, no one killed Helena. She did it to herself."

A collective stillness fell upon the group. After a few moments, Avery broke the silence, snapping, "No way. You don't really expect any of us to believe that, do you?"

"You weren't there after the autopsy. Dr. Gage said it . . ." Fisher paused and panned the room, looking everyone in the eyes. "Okay, just know you can't repeat this. No one is aware that I know this."

"Fish, alright already. You know this won't leave the group," said Alec.

Fisher stepped in closer. "I overheard Dr. Gage talking with Helena's parents. Helena stole pills from the Bay and overdosed on them."

"Wait, what?" asked Zach. "So now she's a thief, and she killed herself? Who are we talking about again?"

"Look, I understand that this doesn't fit the Helena we know. But neither did the Helena that isolated herself in her pod," offered Fisher.

"Okay, so can anyone explain how she ended up in the power cell casing?" asked Avery.

"Yeah, who put her there?" demanded Dom.

"Dr. Gage believes that Helena hid there after taking the pills."

"Am I the only one having trouble buying this story?" asked Sam. "I have to believe that Lance played some role in this. Maybe he forced her to take the pills against her will."

"Did you see what Lance did to Grayson, thinking he killed Helena?" asked Fisher.

"Maybe Lance discovered Helena and Grayson hooked up or something, and Lance found out. Decided to kill them both," Alec challenged.

"When I told him about her suicide, Lance was destroyed. He was inconsolable," explained Fisher.

Glaring at Fisher, Alec asked, "Wait. You told Lance before us?"

Fisher was wishing everyone would let him complete his thoughts before throwing questions at him. "Look, he was right there in the room across from me when I found out. What does it matter? He deserves to know the truth like the rest of us."

"And you believe that asshole's reaction was real?" asked Sam.

"I don't know what I believe right now," said Fisher. "But if I'm being honest, I'd have to say that Lance's reaction was genuine. Nobody could fake what I just witnessed. I think Dr. Gage's theory adds up."

"That's bullshit, and you know it!" spat Sam. "I'm not listening to another word of this!" She let out a frustrated grunt, and everyone watched in silence as Sam stormed out of the room.

"Should I go check on her?" asked Avery.

"Let's give her some space," suggested Fisher. "I'm sure none of this is easy for any of us to digest."

"What's there to digest?" Alec asked coldly. "Helena got fed up with her predetermined life on the Arc and killed herself."

"Alec, enough!" yelled Dom.

"You're right, little brother. I've had enough. Enough of all of your childish theories. I've got better things to do." Alec strolled out of the observation deck, leaving his friends speechless.

"What the hell is wrong with Alec?" fumed Dom.

Fisher knew this was going to be a rough conversation for everyone, but he wasn't prepared for such extreme reactions. He wondered what he could say right now to ease the tension in the room, but he was at a loss for words.

"I bet Alec just misses Helena like the rest of us," said Echo.

Fisher could easily argue with his friend's assumption, but Echo had just spoken the most compassionate words of the evening. Fisher thought it was best to end the meeting with the same kind of positivity.

"Maybe Echo's right. We don't know what anyone is think-ing right now. Let's call it a night, and we can talk tomorrow and help each other through this."

As the group dispersed, Fisher sat alone in the observation deck. He took stock in the intensity of the day and realized how exhausted he was. Fisher knew it would be best for him to head straight to his pod, but he wasn't sure if his racing mind could settle enough to welcome sleep. As he stared out the window, his thoughts drifted to Sam, wondering how she was going to find any peace tonight.

CHAPTER 39

With tears running down her cheeks, Sam stood in front of the pods in her hive, staring up at Helena's nameplate. After Fisher had unloaded the news of Helena's suicide, everything had become hazy. Sam felt as if she couldn't connect with her environment and had trouble focusing on the others around her. She just wanted to escape the pain she was feeling, and Helena's pod was the only place she wanted to be.

Sam cycled through the hundreds of conversations she'd had with Helena and struggled to find a single moment that could explain Helena taking her own life. Suicide just didn't fit. Sam was convinced that either Fisher had misunderstood what he'd heard, or Dr. Gage was wrong. Helena had had more life in her than anyone on the Arc. How could Fisher and the others believe such an unlikely story?

Sam felt she knew Helena better than anyone on the ship and believed she would have seen warning signs. She knew Helena had been upset the past few days, but Sam had assumed it was due to yet another tiff with Lance. Everyone had expected her to shake it off like all the other times. Even if Sam had somehow missed a big red flag, surely Dr. Fiona would have been able to see this coming. She had insight into this sort of thing.

Sam's thoughts quickly switched to Lance. It was easy for Sam to believe that he was behind Helena's death, especially with his recent behavior. According to Kaman, it looked like Grayson was going to pull through, but for several hours, it was touch and go. If Lance were capable of inflicting that kind of brutality on someone he rarely interacted with, why would it be so far-fetched to think he could do the same to Helena? He'd clearly crossed the line when he'd shoved Sam to the floor in the galley. Maybe everyone should have taken his actions more seriously. Sam questioned whether she should have reported the incident to her parents. If she had, would Helena still be alive? Sam began to compile a mental list of things she might have done that could have helped avoid Helena's death.

She crawled up to Helena's pod, opened the door, and slid in. Rolling onto her back, Sam shut the door and closed herself off from the rest of the ship. She shut her eyes and inhaled Helena's scent deeply through her nose, and then let out a long, slow breath through her mouth.

Memories of her time with Helena danced in her thoughts. She feared that, over time, these memories would be lost. Sam rolled on to her side and looked at the photos that hung on the wall of the pod. She looked at a picture of Helena and Avery making goofy faces, and it made Sam smile. Helena was always able to find the light in the darkest of days. She had been a beacon that had guided everyone through tough times over the years, including Sam. Her eyes moved to the next photo of Helena and Lance. Sam reached out, grabbed the photo, and crumpled it into her fist.

"Asshole."

Lance could easily be at the bottom of all of this. Everyone knew he had an anger issue and that he was verbally abusive to

Helena at times. He could have asked Helena to take the pills. Helena would have done anything for Lance. Sam could easily connect the dots and create a scenario where Lance was completely to blame for all of this.

She turned her head and spotted a photo of Helena and herself. Sam was instantly transported to the moment the image was captured. It was the night the crew had celebrated the successful deployment of one of the geodetic rings. Sam and Helena had left the celebration early to sit alone in the west observation deck. They'd talked about what life on Uelara would be like, along with their hopes and dreams for the future. It was also the first time they kissed.

It was Sam's first real kiss. She remembered every micro-detail of that moment. Her heart had raced as Helena brushed the hair away from Sam's eyes and pulled her head close until their lips met. Helena's lips parted, and the tip of her tongue met Sam's. It was the first time Sam noticed the light blue specks in Helena's eyes. While the kiss had only lasted a moment, it had felt like a beautiful eternity to Sam.

She wanted to stay lost in that moment forever. She pulled the photo from the wall, held it to her chest, and closed her eyes.

Sam heard a small pop come from the wall. She opened her eyes to see a corner of the panel that had been covered by the photo was missing the recessed screw that held it in place. She also noticed that the edges of the panel around the corner looked worn.

Sam pulled at the corner with her index finger and released it. The panel rattled as it swayed back and forth. She pulled at it again and peered inside. Light spilled into the dark pocket of space behind the panel, shining on something metallic.

Sam slid her hand inside, grabbed hold of a smooth, cylindrical item, and pulled it from behind the panel. It was Helena's silver journal pen.

Why would she keep her journal pen in there? thought Sam.

She reached behind the panel again and felt something else. Sam knew instantly what it was. Her pulse quickened. She pulled out the journal and brushed her hands across the cover. She paused for a moment, bit her lower lip, and then opened it. She flipped through the pages slowly until they were blank. Sam flipped back a few pages until she found the last entry in the journal. Her eyes scanned across the pages. As she read the entry, her eyes widened, and she gasped.

"What . . . the . . . fuck?"

CHAPTER 40

Fisher found himself walking aimlessly throughout the ship. As he wandered, he couldn't help but feel that the Arc had a different energy. He saw fewer people moving about, and when he did pass some of the crew, he was met with only nods or faint hellos. News of Helena's suicide had spread quickly among the crew, and everyone appeared to have trouble finding a way to talk about it.

Fisher couldn't understand what could bring Helena to the point where she believed her only option was to end her life. His memories of her involved optimism and inspiration; he couldn't recall a time when Helena was negative about anything. Was it simply a mask she'd worn? Was he that clueless? What signs had he missed? If he'd only noticed her struggling, maybe he could have said or done something.

"Hey, Fish, got a sec?"

Fisher turned to see Dom walking toward him. "Oh, hey, Dom. Sure."

Fisher had never seen Dom look so weary.

"I just wanted to catch you before you headed to your pod. You doing okay?"

"Yeah. I mean, as okay as any of us can be, I guess. I'm headed to the foundry. Thought it might be a good idea to focus my mind on work a little before trying to sleep."

"Good idea. I was going to check in on Lance before heading to bed. I think it's going to be a rough night for everyone," said Dom. "I just wanted to make sure you're doing okay. After Sam stormed off and Alec made those bizarre remarks, everyone just kind of . . . left."

"Yeah, that was weird, right?"

"It was!" agreed Dom. "I can understand Sam's reaction, but what the hell is going on with Alec?"

Fisher shook his head and leaned against the corridor wall. He was relieved to hear that someone else recognized that Alec's viewpoints and reactions were straying more and more from what Fisher was accustomed to.

"I don't know, Dom. Alec's always had this different way of thinking and feeling about the mission. Lately, I just don't feel like he's the same guy we've all grown up with."

"I know! Shit comes out of his mouth lately, and I don't even know what to say. Do you think he's . . . okay?"

Fisher put his arm around Dom's shoulder. "Yeah, he's okay. I think there has been so much stress this past week, and now finding out about Helena . . . I guess everyone is just going to handle it in different ways."

Fisher could see that Dom was fired up and wasn't slowing down anytime soon.

"I can't believe Helena killed herself. I mean, how could she do that to us?" Dom asked, his voice rising.

"Do what to us?" Fisher asked.

"Leave without saying anything! Give us a chance to talk her out of it . . . help her! Aren't you the slightest bit angry right now?"

Fisher wondered if the day would ever return where he wouldn't have to answer a single question. "Of course I'm upset, but I'm not angry with Helena. I'm angry with myself."

"But you didn't do anything," Dom pointed out.

"Right. I didn't do *anything* to stop her. I didn't even recognize that she was struggling."

"Fish, none of us did. You can't take on that responsibility."

"I know. To be honest, right now I think I'd rather not talk about it."

"Yeah, I gotcha."

"I appreciate you coming to check in, I really do, but—"

Dom's eyes darted past Fisher and widened. Fisher looked back over his shoulder and saw Sam sprinting toward them.

"Guys!" said Sam, breathing heavily.

"Sam, are you okay? What's wrong?" asked Fisher. He had never seen anyone move that fast.

Sam came to a stop, took in a couple of short breaths, and raised Helena's journal up with her right hand. "I know why she killed herself!"

CHAPTER 41

Six days earlier . . .

As the two figures moved closer to the empty casing she was hiding in, Helena did her best to control her breathing. Maybe they would only check a few of the casings and move on. She heard a soft voice whispering.

"I'm telling you . . . it's only a matter of time before Sam works it out."

Helena knew that voice. It belonged to Debra. What was she doing in the storage bay right now? First gen'ers were never around when Graveyard was being played.

"Then it's your job to convince her that she made a mistake in—"

"She doesn't make mistakes, Captain," scoffed Debra. "You heard about the other day. She didn't buy Jeremy's story of how her calculations won't work with the subsystem routines he implemented to the geodetic rings. Heck, Jeremy would have trouble convincing anyone in my department with that nonsense."

"Get creative. Can't you drag it out? Can't you—?"

"For ten years? Do you hear yourself?" interrupted Debra. "I told you, Sam's not like the other kids. When she starts something, she can't let it go. That's one of the reasons I fought to get her in the Tank."

"You need to keep her busy with other things. Maybe it's time we go with my first suggestion and transfer her to the foundry with Jeremy."

"First, I'm not letting Sam leave the Tank. She's the obvious choice to replace me in the years to come. Second, if you think transferring her is going to keep her from—"

"Okay, okay, I get it," said Captain Matsuo.

Why was Debra so concerned? What was Sam going to figure out? Helena was baffled.

"Plus, have you talked with the Vosts lately?" asked Debra.

"If you're talking about their reports of the second gen growing despondent and showing signs of apathy, we all knew that was going to rear up again at some point."

"This isn't like a few years ago, Captain, and you know it. That was classic, textbook teen angst. Fiona was telling me this runs much deeper in some of the kids. If they discover the truth—"

"Then it's our job to make sure they don't, not until they have kids of their own. Once they have children, all of this become moot. You know that."

"Look, is it possible to distract Sam for a year? Sure. Two? Possibly, but there is no way I see any plan working longer than that . . . definitely not an entire decade. Sam's smart. She's smarter than anyone on the Arc. To be honest, I'd trust her work over my own," said Debra.

"Then they need to have children now."

"Wait . . . what?" asked Debra.

"Think about it. If they find out the truth before they have children, there will be mass chaos. They cannot know until they have kids that they're not going to make it to Uelara in their lifetimes."

Helena's heart skipped a beat, and she couldn't find her breath for a moment. Did she just hear that right?

We're not making it to Uelara? Are they talking about all of the second gen? How is that possible? We're arriving in thirty years. That's what they have told us all along. Helena's mind was racing with questions.

"This is why I was against lying to them from the beginning," insisted Debra.

"You and the others made yourselves perfectly clear when the mission began. Your beliefs on this matter didn't change the council's decision then, and it's too late to change it now. If you're telling me that Sam is close to working this out, then an easy solution is for them to have children early."

"But the plan has always been to—"

"And you're telling me the plan is about to become obsolete," clipped Matsuo. "It's only a matter of time before she shares her findings with others. We simply have to change one variable to our plan to get us back on track. They'll be so preoccupied with having and raising children that they won't have time to think about any of this. And by the time they do, we will have told them the truth."

Helena covered her mouth with her hands, trying to muffle a horrified gasp.

"Look, I get it. Once they have kids, it will no longer be just about them. They'll be locked in and feel the need to complete the mission for their children. Once again, I want to go on record that I don't agree with any of this."

"Noted," acknowledged the captain.

"Do you think the council will agree to adjusting the timeline?"

"Well, do you believe we can't wait to tell them the truth?" Matsuo asked.

Debra paused. "How would this affect the overall time table? I mean shifting the birth of the third generation early by almost ten years—"

"Is irrelevant. The third generation will still be able to complete the journey. It would just mean less time for them on Uelara."

"We should get the others in on this discussion," suggested Debra. "This affects everyone."

"Of course. We start by shifting the Pairing Ceremony a few weeks early and then removing the birth control from their vitamin regimen. We'll have children on the way before year's end."

"This could work," yielded Debra.

"This *will* work," asserted Matsuo. "We'll have to rework the pill distribution spreadsheets for the second gen. I'll start up a conversation with the council."

"Who else should we bring in on this?"

"For now, no one," the captain instructed. "We'll let the council decide how we roll this out."

"Fine. I'll head to the Bay now."

"Good, good. Let's reconvene tonight back at the concourse."

Helena could hear them walking toward the engine room as their voices faded. She released a long exhale and then began breathing rapidly. She felt as if the casing were being crushed and all the air was being sucked out of it.

Everything was a lie. Her hopes, her dreams, the mission . . . all lies.

Helena pulled herself out of her hiding spot. All her joints ached. The room banked from side to side. Still finding it hard to breathe, Helena felt her throat close up, and a sharp pain pierced her stomach. She was going to be sick.

CHAPTER 42

Fisher closed Helena's journal, looked at the cover, and sat silently across from Dom in the think tank next to Sam's terminal, as Sam hunched over her keyboard, feverishly typing.

"Do you think all the parents are in on this?" asked Dom.

"Not sure," replied Fisher. "We know that Debra, Captain Matsuo, and the other council members are."

"Aren't your parents on the council?" asked Dom.

Fisher looked at the floor. "Yeah, along with Lance's dad and a few others."

"Do you think my parents know?"

Fisher looked at Dom. "There's only one way to know for sure. We'll have to ask them."

"So, they weren't going to tell us we'd never make it to Uelara?" asked Dom.

"Not until we had children of our own. Sounds like they didn't think we could handle knowing the truth," replied Fisher. He thought of his lesson with the Quints. "Similar to how they held off on telling us the first generation wouldn't make it to Uelara. Remember the meltdown many of us had when they dropped that bomb on us?"

"But this is different!" Dom protested.

"What was the name of the NASA robot Debra's grandfather worked on that was used on Mars?" asked Sam.

"Sojourner?" replied Dom with little confidence in his answer.

"Was it the Opportunity?" asked Fisher.

"Started with a C, I think," said Sam.

"Curiosity?" asked Fisher.

"That's the one," said Sam as she keyed the name into her terminal. "Damn, that's not it."

"What are you doing?" asked Dom.

"Quiet, you'll see."

"So, we're going to die on this ship," said Dom looking down at the panels that lined the floor of the Tank. "We're never leaving the ship."

Fisher felt betrayed. He found it nearly impossible to comprehend how his parents could justify deceiving him on such a grand scale. Couldn't they have come up with a better way to explain such a devastating blow?

"Guys, What's the name of that famous American astronomer that Debra always quotes?"

"Kepler?" asked Dom.

"Jansky? No, he was a physicist. Is it Cannon? She mentions her from time to time," guessed Fisher.

"Not them. The guy that assembled the universal messages on the Voyager's Golden Record," said Sam as she continued to type.

"Bob Seger?" guessed Dom.

"Carl Sagan?" asked Fisher.

"That's the one," said Sam as she tapped on the keyboard. "And . . . we're in."

"In what?" asked Dom.

"Debra's personal drive," answered Sam.

"Whoa . . . what are you doing? You can't access her files!" warned Fisher. "If she finds out, she'll have you booted from the Tank without question."

"First, she isn't going to find out," said Sam. "Second, if all of this is true, do you really think I give a shit about what will happen to me if I get busted?" Sam continued to rapidly type long strings of characters into the terminal.

"So, you believe what Helena wrote? You think our parents have been lying to us all this time?" asked Dom.

"Absolutely. Why else would Helena write that? Why else would she have . . . ?" Sam stopped herself. She didn't want to finish her question.

"If Helena believed this to be true, why wouldn't she tell one of us . . . all of us?" asked Dom.

Sam looked up from her terminal and said, "Dom, Helena made it pretty clear in her last entry. She didn't want to rob any of us of our ignorance."

"She thought we'd be happier not knowing," added Fisher.

Sam grabbed her headset and handed it to Dom. "Hold this. Fish, go grab Zach's headset. I'll jack both of you into my system."

Fisher walked over to Zach's work area and disconnected the headset from his terminal.

"Are you going to show us your ring deployment algorithm?"

"No," said Sam. "I'm going to use Debra's final set of coordinates to replace the ones I've been using in my simulation."

Fisher handed the end of the headset's cable to Sam.

"Have a seat and put on the headsets, guys," said Sam as she plugged a T-junction port into the front of the terminal, and then plugged the ends of each headset into the junction.

Fisher and Dom slid the headsets on and sat in complete darkness.

Fisher could hear the clacking of Sam's keyboard as she pressed the keys. In his display, stars surrounded them.

"Okay, do you see the yellow dot to your left?" asked Sam.

"Yeah," said Fisher.

"No," replied Dom.

"Your other left, Dom," groaned Sam.

"Ah . . . yeah, I see it."

Sam pressed a key on the keyboard, and Fisher watched a blue ribbon grow from the yellow dot across the screen, stopping at a green dot.

"So, is the green dot Uelara?" asked Fisher, pointing up in the air.

"Based on the coordinates I've been working with since I started working in the Tank, yes," replied Sam. She started typing again.

"So, are you saying that's not Uelara?" asked Dom.

The sounds of the clacking keys stopped.

"Ready?" Sam pressed a key on the keyboard, and a red ribbon began to grow from the yellow dot. "This is what I believe is our actual flight path," said Sam.

The red ribbon grew beyond the length of the blue ribbon, floated past the green dot, and continued to make its way across the canvas of stars. After a few seconds the red ribbon eased into a stop. A new green dot appeared at the end of the ribbon.

"See that new green dot?" Sam asked. "*That's* Uelara."

The room fell silent.

"But that's more than twice the distance," said Fisher.

"Exactly," said Sam.

CHAPTER 43

"I've been working with the wrong coordinates all this time," said Sam. "That's why the locations of the rings didn't add up using my algorithm."

"So, what Helena wrote in her journal is true. We aren't going to live to see Uelara," said Dom in a low voice.

"If this data is accurate, which I believe it is, then we'd die long before the Arc reaches Uelara," said Sam grimly.

Fisher lifted the headset away from his eyes and rested it on his forehead. "But why? Why lie to us all these years? Wouldn't it have been easier to simply tell us this when they revealed they wouldn't be making it to Uelara?"

"See? That's what I'm talking about. I mean, how did they think we'd react finding out we'd been lied to our entire lives?" added Dom.

"You heard what Helena wrote. They believed that once we had kids of our own, we'd be locked into the mission. That we'd do it for our kids' sake," said Sam.

Throwing his hands up, Dom exclaimed, "And they believed that would magically stop all of us from losing our shit when we found out?"

"Look, guys, there's no way we can know what they were thinking unless we ask them," said Fisher.

"And you think they'll tell us the truth?" asked Sam.

"I say we go to our parents tomorrow and confront them. Demand the truth," said Fisher.

"Tomorrow? I want to go wake their asses up right now and—"

Fisher raised his hand. "Whoa, slow down! I don't think that's a good idea, Sam."

"Why the hell not?"

"I think we will have much more success if we confront them once we've had time for this to sink in. If we go to them all worked up, it will be easier for them to—"

"No, you're right. I don't want to give them the ability to talk their way out of this," seethed Sam.

"Let's get some rest, meet in the morning, and then the three of us can meet with my parents first," said Fisher.

"Rest? You're going to be able to sleep after what you just found out?" asked Sam.

"Sam, I'm a mess!" yelled Fisher. "I haven't been sleeping, I just discovered my friend killed herself and that I'm going to die on this ship! I just want to close my eyes for a few hours and turn off."

"Sorry, I get it." Sam let out a long sigh. "My mind is spent. Even if I don't sleep I could use the time to take it all in, I guess."

Dom stood up, looking defeated. "I'm going to check on Lance and then head to the galley. I have a few hours before I should be getting up. I'm just going to get a jump on work. It's pointless for me to even try to sleep. Why don't the two of you head to the hive, try and get some rest, and meet me in the galley in the morning."

"Sounds like a plan," said Fisher. "But don't say anything to Lance yet. Let's keep this between us for now, at least until we have discussed it with my parents."

"Yeah, no need to get Lance worked up tonight. There'll be time for that soon enough," added Sam.

"Trust me, I don't want to be the one breaking the news to him," avowed Dom, walking to the exit. Before he left the room, he paused, turning toward Fisher and Sam, and declared, "So, we're never setting foot on Uelara."

"Yeah, we're going to die on the ship," lamented Fisher.

Dom looked down at the floor and said, "This isn't a ship. It's a tomb."

CHAPTER 44

Sam and Fisher left the Tank and walked toward their hive. Sam was crushed by the devastating news about the first gen's deception, and it was taking a tremendous amount of restraint to respect Fisher's wishes and delay confronting her parents. Sam stopped in front of the rec room door just outside of Hive 3 and whispered, "I'm going to check on the Quints and then try my best to get some sleep."

"Want me to come with you?" asked Fisher.

"Nah. You should head to your pod and rest. I won't be too far behind you."

"Okay. I know it won't be easy, but try to get some sleep. You know we have a long day ahead of us tomorrow," reiterated Fisher as he continued toward their hive.

Sam slid the door to the rec room open and quietly stepped inside. She was surprised to see none of the Quints were in their beds. In the center of the room she could see what looked like a fort made from the Quints' blankets. Sam lifted the corner on one of the blankets that was draped over a few chairs and peered inside. Sleeping on a pile of sheets and pillows were her brothers. Sam crawled inside and laid next to them.

As she watched them sleep, it pained her to think they would never get to experience life off the Arc. It wasn't just wrong of her parents. Sam believed it was cruel. She couldn't wait to confront them and demand answers to all the questions that were racing in her mind.

Sam mentally constructed a flowchart of questions, answers, and rebuttals in preparation for what she believed would be an epic battle with her parents. As she played the scenario over in her head multiple times, she slowly fell asleep.

"Sam, wake up!"

Sam opened her eyes and saw Sean sitting next to her. She looked over and could see the other Quints were still sleeping. How long had she slept? Was it already morning?

"Hey, Sean. Is everything okay?" whispered Sam, wiping the sleep from her eyes.

"Where's Mom? She's usually here by now."

Sam pulled one of the blankets over to the side and looked at the digital display on the wall. She was surprised to see that she had slept for almost two hours. "I'm sure she's on her way."

"But she should already be here to help us get ready for the day," explained Sean.

"I tell you what. Why don't you wake your brothers and help get them ready, and I'll go see if I can find her."

Sean rubbed his eyes and nodded in agreement.

Sam left her brothers and began the trip up to her parents' hive. She wasn't going to pretend she was simply fetching her mother for the Quints. Although she promised Fisher she'd wait, Sam now had an excuse to confront her mother.

As she marched up the stairs to the concourse, Sam began to practice what she would say to Fisher.

"I have no idea what happened, Fish. I never planned to confront her. I just went up there to check on my mother, and then out of the blue she just brought it up! I tried to resist her, really, I did. But I never stood a chance. You know my mother. Resistance is futile."

He's never gonna buy it, she thought. She decided she would just have to deal with Fisher later. Grayson's favorite expression came to her mind . . . *better to ask for forgiveness than permission.*

As she approached the concourse, Sam saw a peculiar site. The massive doors to the entrance of the concourse were sealed shut. She had never seen them closed before. Confused, Sam walked to the access terminal on the wall adjacent to the door and could see the words *Concourse Outer Doors Sealed* displayed on the screen.

Sam swiped at the interactive screen, navigating the terminal's menu. Moments later amber lights on the celling lit up and began to spin, and Sam heard intense hissing sounds that increased in pitch coming from behind the concourse doors. Several minutes later the hissing sounds faded, and the door to the concourse slowly began to slide open.

The concourse was pitch black, lit only by the lights that spilled in from the corridor behind her. Sam stepped inside, and the lights hanging from the ceiling began to flicker on in a systematic pattern. The light strips that ran along the center of the interior walls faded on, and a cold chill raced down Sam's back. Something wasn't right.

Sam felt uneasy as she walked through the concourse toward her parents' hive. Although she didn't visit often, she knew that normally there would be some level of activity going on in the concourse with some of the first gen starting their day. She had never seen the large space without lights, and she had never experienced such silence.

As she reached the entrance to the hive, Sam let out a terrified shriek that echoed through the concourse and down the corridor.

CHAPTER 45

Fisher had struggled to sort through all that had just been uncovered. Even with the ocean waves of the white noise machine to calm him, he couldn't stop seeing the new green dot from Sam's simulation. Nothing Fisher and the rest of the second gen could do would change the location of that green dot. They would merely die having never experienced anything other than the confines of the Arc. Fisher tried to look at the situation from his parents' perspective, but nothing he could imagine could justify a lie of this scale. After more than two hours of tossing and turning, he had slowly drifted off to sleep.

Once again, Fisher found himself on the beach. This time, though, he wasn't alone.

In the distance, he could see Helena standing on the beach, calling to him. He started moving closer to her but couldn't quite understand what she was saying. What began as a slow walk turned into a full sprint as Fisher ran toward Helena. The faster he ran, the farther she seemed to get. Then Fisher heard something calling from the ocean.

He could see Echo six meters from shore struggling in the water, splashing violently to stay afloat. *What is Echo doing out there? Clearly, he doesn't know how to swim,* he thought.

As Fisher moved toward the shoreline, he could see more of his friends in the water struggling. Each of them was screaming to Fisher for help. He started running toward the shore to try to save his friends but found it difficult to gain traction in the sand. He looked down and could see that he was sinking.

As Fisher fought to pull his way out of the sand, the screams from the ocean grew louder. Nothing he did to break free worked, and he was slowly pulled beneath the surface of the beach.

Fisher woke, gasping for air, to find himself safe in his pod, drenched in cold sweat. Relieved it was only a dream, his heart rate started to drop. In the distance, the sounds of the screams from his dreams continued. He wondered if he were still dreaming.

He switched off the noise machine, and the sound of waves was quickly replaced by muffled sobs and screams. Fisher opened the door of his pod and looked out to see Sam sobbing uncontrollably.

"What's going on?" asked Fisher.

Sam looked up at him, her eyes red and filled with tears. "They're dead!" yelled Sam. "They're all dead!"

"What are you talking about?" demanded Fisher. "Who's dead?"

"The first gen!" cried Sam. "They're all dead!"

She continued to speak, but her words became fuzzy as Fisher's head spun. He repeated two words over and over as the sound of Sam weeping became white noise. "Wake up, wake up, wake up . . . wake . . . up!"

STAGE TWO

CHAPTER 46

Fisher sat in the front row of the auditorium, staring at the floor, still dazed by the morning's events. Several of the others were having intense conversations around him, but Fisher couldn't focus. He studied the panels that made up the auditorium's floor. He'd never noticed the intricacies of the recessed lines and how each panel interlocked with the adjacent ones.

"Fish. Fish. FISH!"

Fisher looked up, focused his eyes and saw Alec standing in front of him.

"Should we get started?" asked Alec.

Fisher straightened up in his chair, took in a deep breath, and glanced around the room. It looked like the majority of the second gen had arrived, but with a quick scan of the group, he could see not everyone was there. He knew that Sam and Zach were sitting this meeting out while they watched over the Quints and went through the ship's logs to investigate the accident. Avery and a few of the others had opted out of attending as well. They weren't in any condition yet to sit through a meeting and requested time alone. But where was Lance? Fisher realized he hadn't seen him all morning. With all the chaos, Fisher hadn't even thought about him.

"I think we're still missing a few," Fisher replied. "Where's Lance? Does he even know what's going on? Is it possible no one told him?"

"Lance is still locked in the Q, remember? I'm not going to be the one to tell him," said Alec.

Fisher wanted no part of that responsibility, either. It was difficult enough to imagine informing someone that his parents were dead. It was nearly impossible to imagine being the informant when the news recipient was going to be Lance. Fisher had witnessed the damage Lance had inflicted upon Grayson, and he was pretty sure he had little interest in being the one to provoke Lance again.

Reluctantly, Fisher said, "I'll do it. Get a head count, and try to gather the rest of the crew so we can start the meeting when I return with Lance."

"You want someone to go with you?"

"Yeah. But I got this."

Fisher pulled himself out of the seat and began his dreaded trek to the medical bay. He turned the scenario in his mind over, upside down, and sideways. Was there a right way to tell someone his father was dead? That *everyone's* parents were dead? Although Fisher was at a loss for the answer, he was certain of this: Anything was better than how he had discovered it. Was he crazy to volunteer for this task? All he knew was that he couldn't bear to place this burden on one of his friends. And secretly, Fisher wondered if getting pummeled by Lance might ease the emotional pain he was feeling right now.

The Arc felt foreign as Fisher walked toward the Bay. He'd

walked the ship plenty of times during off hours while most of the crew slept, but this felt different. It was as if portions of the ship itself had been removed. Fisher struggled to see how the crew was going to recover from such a devastating loss. How was he going to recover?

Fisher slowed his pace as he approached the Bay. He felt as if a large weight were being placed on each shoulder, and with every new step, an additional larger weight was being added. Was he really going through with this? He could hear Lance shouting as he got closer.

"—anyone. Anyone out there? Come on, guys. This is getting old!"

Fisher quickened his pace and entered the Bay. Lance was standing at the door of his room with his hand on the call box.

"'Bout time! I've been calling out all morning. Where the hell is everyone?"

Fisher started to reply, but the lump in his throat blocked his words.

"Well, Fish? What's going on?"

Fisher swallowed hard, approached Lance, and looked at the floor. "Lance. It's . . . it's our parents."

"What about them?"

"They . . . they're dead."

Fisher winced in anticipation of Lance's response. A look of confusion washed over Lance's face.

"What? What are you talking about?"

"I don't have all the details, but there was a horrible accident last night. Our parents—"

"If this is your idea of a—"

"Lance!" snapped Fisher. "This is serious! The entire first gen is dead!"

As the words left his mouth, it was as if Fisher were hearing it for the first time. He dropped to his knees and began to sob. Choking back the tears, Fisher continued, "I'm sorry, Lance. I don't know how else to explain it. Sam made the discovery this morning. She and Zach are trying to figure out what caused the accident."

Fisher watched as Lance sank to the floor, cradling his head in his hands.

"What accident? What happened to them?"

"I'm still trying to understand it myself," Fisher replied. "But from what I can tell, the master doors to the concourse malfunctioned. They sealed off the entire concourse and connecting hives from the rest of the ship."

"But how could the doors closing cause—?"

"Sam thinks that when the doors malfunctioned, it removed the atmospheric pressure to the area." Fisher looked at the floor and then back at Lance. "They had no oxygen."

Fisher tried to continue, but as these last words escaped him, he couldn't help but visualize his parents fighting for air. He tried to wipe the horrific scene from his thoughts, but it kept clawing its way back into his mind.

"And Sam thinks she can find out how this happened?" asked Lance in an almost whisper.

"I'm sure she will. Between Sam and Zach, the two of them should have answers for us soon." Fisher stood up and unlocked the door to Lance's room. "I'm sorry, Lance. Hate that I was the one to have to tell you."

Lance looked up at Fisher with tears in his eyes. "What are we going to do?"

His question caught Fisher by surprise. When had Lance ever asked Fisher anything except what time the ring deployment celebration was? He must have really been in shock.

"That's why I'm here. I can understand if you're not up for it, but we're all meeting in the auditorium. I think the others could use you there," answered Fisher. "I could use you there."

Fisher reached out his hand to Lance. Lance looked up, grabbed Fisher's hand, and pulled himself up.

"What are we going to do, Fisher?"

CHAPTER 47

The walk from the medical bay to the auditorium was brutal. Lance hadn't said a word since they'd left the Q, and Fisher was struggling just to keep it together. So the two walked the distance in silence.

The expectations Fisher had held concerning Lance's reaction to the news varied from disbelief to rage. Lance was certainly an unpredictable guy, but Fisher realized that the crew could usually count on Lance to have a loud, prolonged outburst about . . . well, just about anything. There couldn't be a more opposing reaction to Fisher's expectations that Lance could have displayed than what Fisher was currently observing.

Lance was completely and utterly silent. Each step taken on this walk echoed louder than Fisher had ever heard. How many times had Fisher wished that someone or something would shut Lance up when he was boasting or taunting or instigating? Now, with the knowledge of their new, grim reality, Fisher would have happily taken any insults Lance could throw. Anything would have been better than this painful silence.

As the pair approached the auditorium, Fisher heard a stew of bickering that became thicker the closer they got. Fisher wasn't prepared for any of this. He was exhausted from his exchange with Lance earlier and simply wanted to retreat to his pod and emerge when all this madness had been washed away.

"They're here. I think we can get started," announced Alec.

Fisher and Lance entered the auditorium and joined the rest of the group. Half of the group was sitting on the edge of the stage, and the remaining crew was sitting in the front few rows. Lance plopped into a seat in the back row behind the others. Fisher joined Dom at the edge of the stage. Dom leaned over to Fisher and whispered, "You gonna tell them about Uelara?"

"I don't think this is the time. Did you tell anyone?"

"No."

"Alec?"

"Not even Alec."

"Okay, good. One tragedy at a time."

Fisher looked out at the crew and wondered how he would ever find the words to break that news to them.

From the front row, Finn asked, "Has anyone figured out what caused the accident?"

"Yeah. Any update about the accident?" added Echo.

"Sam and Zach are looking into it. All we know is that there was a malfunction that triggered the events that killed them," said Alec. "So, how are we going to do this? Lance, you wanna kick this off?"

All eyes targeted Lance. He gave a vacant stare back to everyone. He sunk lower into his seat and in a soft voice replied, "I think we should hear what Fisher has to say."

Color rushed to Fisher's cheeks. His palms started sweating, and for a moment he felt like he was back hiding in the air shaft. What was Lance thinking? The entire reason Fisher had retrieved Lance was to avoid dealing with any of this. He'd assumed Lance would know what to do. Fisher was also afraid that if he started talking, he'd let the news about Uelara slip. There was no way the group could handle that devastating announcement right now.

"Umm, I'm not sure. I'm on board with what the group wants to do," said Fisher, passively rejecting Lance's nomination.

Alec stared at Fisher with a look of surprise. "Fish, come on. It's not that tough. Just pick something. What should we do first?"

A random hot flash streaked through Fisher's chest, catching him off guard. How could Alec sound so smug and condescending? If this were all so easy, why wasn't he up here leading the meeting?

"Fine," Fisher acquiesced. "I think it's clear what needs to happen."

Everyone's attention fell on Fisher.

"I know it's been a tough morning for everyone, but there is no way around it. We have to . . ." Fisher hesitated. He knew what he wanted to say, but he just couldn't believe he had to say it. "We have to deal with our parents."

"Deal with our parents? What do you mean?" asked Bart.

"We can't just leave them in their pods," replied Fisher. *This can't be happening*, he thought.

Kaman slowly raised her hand and quietly added, "I know what we need to do if we are going to follow protocol."

"Protocol?" challenged Kayla. "You're telling me there's protocol for all of our parents dying overnight?"

"Stop it, Kayla," snapped Toby. "Let Kaman speak."

Kaman stood up, cleared her throat and continued. "Dr. Gage had me review the process after Helena was found. Members of the crew are stored in the Hold when they pass away."

"The Hold?" asked Mia.

"Yes. There are huge containers in the Hold designated for the crew."

"I don't understand. Why store them in the Hold?" asked Ashin.

"So that their bodies can be studied by future generations to learn about the effects of long distance space travel on the human body," Kaman explained.

"My parents aren't going to be used for lab experiments!" cried Mia.

"She didn't say that," offered Fisher, trying to soften the blow.

"Screw you. I can read between the lines!"

"Guys, enough! Even if this weren't protocol, it makes sense," exclaimed Alec.

"Putting our parents in storage makes sense to you?" asked Toby.

"What would you have us do?" asked Alec.

The room went silent.

"We can't leave them where they are," continued Fisher. "If we decide on an alternate solution later, we'll deal with it at that time. But for now, we need to remove them from the concourse."

"I'm not going up there!" said Mia.

"I can't go up there either," added a few of the others.

"Listen," Fisher said. "I realize no one wants to do this. I have no desire to go back up there myself, but . . ."

"I'll go," offered Dom.

"Me, too," added Echo.

Fisher had no interest in returning to the concourse. Like many of the others, he had run to the concourse early that morning to confirm what Sam described. The horrific scene that awaited the volunteers was something no one should have to revisit. Despite his reluctance, Fisher knew what was needed and raised his hand. "I'll go, too."

One by one others raised their hands and volunteered.

"Anyone else?" asked Fisher.

Everyone with raised hands looked around at the group. Those without their hands up looked sheepishly at the floor. Lance sat, staring blankly.

"Lance, you joining us?" asked Fisher.

"Sure. No problem," he mumbled.

"Okay," said Fisher, "I count eighteen volunteers. Bart, you and Ashin locate the containers in the Hold and start prepping them."

"I'll head to the medical bay and collect the HRPs and bring them up to the concourse," announced Kaman.

"HRP?" asked Kayla.

"Human remains pouch."

Fisher heard a few cries in the second row. How were they ever going to manage this?

"Finn and Echo, go with Kaman and help her with the pouches. Grab some headlamps from the Center, too. Everyone else, follow me to the concourse," ordered Fisher.

"What should we do?" asked Mia.

Fisher could see that Mia and the others with stationary hands wanted to help—just not in the concourse.

"If you're not helping us, go check on the rest of the crew and make sure everyone is okay. If you change your mind, you know where we'll be," said Fisher.

Everyone in the room started forming into their newly assigned groups. Dom slid off the stage, took in a giant breath, and asked Fisher, "Are you ready for this?"

CHAPTER 48

Alec and the volunteers stood in the center of the concourse, looking at the four entrances to the first gen hives. Everyone gathered around Fisher in silence, waiting to hear what he had to say. Alec found it interesting that Fisher ended up being the one in charge, especially with Lance in the room. Everyone knew Fisher was typically the reserved one in the group, and he rarely enjoyed speaking in front of a crowd.

Alec remembered the time Andrew had asked Fisher to help with a theater performance a few years ago. Fisher said he would have preferred sleeping in the Hold rather than taking center stage. Nope, his comfort zone rested in the background, where he thought he could remain.

What he also found surprising was Lance's waning voice. Lance was always the loud, boisterous guy who, despite his impulsive and arrogant tendencies, often found himself leading his peers. Considering himself a captain-in-waiting, Lance often took it upon himself to make random proclamations and decisions, and for some reason, the rest just followed him. That lethargic, indecisive guy in the back row was definitely not the Lance who Alec grew up with.

"Let's lay down a few ground rules," said Fisher. "I don't think it's a good idea for any of us to go into our own parents' hive. Split up into pairs. Once you place a body in the pouch, let's move it here in the concourse."

The term "body" caused a few of them to shift their weight and look downward.

Fisher continued. "If it gets to be too . . . if anyone has . . . feel free to regroup out in the corridor if you need to take a break."

As the crew began separating, Alec looked over at Dom and asked, "You wanna work together?"

"I've already paired up with Lance."

He didn't realize it, but Alec had been assuming that he and Dom would suffer through this task together. After all, they had a shared loss. And now he felt like a simple afterthought to Dom. Alec wasn't sure if he felt angry, bitter, or jealous. What he did know, however, was his relationship with Dom had shifted, and he could no longer rely on him for support like he once did.

"I'll work with you," said Deuce.

"Sounds good," replied Alec, his eyes still fixed on Dom.

The group stood in nine pairs, waiting for Fisher's next order.

"Remember that the hives no longer have power, so you'll need to manually open the pod doors. Echo, did you guys grab the headlamps?"

"Yeah, Finn and I have them here."

Echo and Finn each held a small case containing lights attached to elastic straps. Everyone in the group pulled one from the case and slid it onto their heads.

"Grab a stack of the pouches and let's get started," Fisher instructed. "The quicker we move with this, the sooner we can be done."

The group split into pairs and made their way toward the hives. Alec, Deuce, Toby, and Kayla entered the hive on the far-right end of the concourse. Their pace slowed as they approached the wall of pods.

Alec stopped as the light from his headlamp lit up the wall. Several of the pod doors were open, allowing him to see some of the parents. Their faces were contorted into ghastly expressions. Alec hadn't anticipated this. In his mind, the parents were going to look like they simply died peacefully in their sleep. Instead, he was looking at the faces of people fighting for their last breath.

"I think I'm going to be—" Deuce barreled over and emptied the contents of his stomach onto the floor.

Alec felt ill. "You okay?" asked Alec, covering his mouth.

After a few more retches, Deuce straightened his posture and wiped his mouth. "Yeah, sorry. Let's get this over with."

Alec dropped the thick, black plastic pouches onto the floor and grabbed the top one. He walked to one of the pods with its door still closed and handed the pouch to Deuce.

"Here, hold this."

Alec climbed to the top pod, flipped back two clips on the door and slid the door open. He turned his head away from the pod's opening, took in a deep breath and peered inside. It was Debra.

Alec quickly looked past her face, but an image had already been scorched into his memory. He reached into the pod, grabbed hold of the front collar of her coveralls, and pulled her toward the opening.

"Get ready, Deuce. I'm going to lower her down." Alec pulled Debra's body to the edge of the pod's entrance and climbed down. "You get her left side, and I'll take the right."

Alec and Deuce reached up and pulled Debra out of the pod. They didn't anticipate the weight of her body, which caught them off balance and knocked them to the ground. Debra's body landed violently on top of Alec.

"Get her off of me! Get her off!" Alec screamed in terror.

Deuce grabbed Debra's collar and pulled her off Alec.

"I thought . . . you had her!" said Alec between gasps of air.

"I did, but—!"

"Never mind. Let's get her in the pouch. We're going to need a better solution for the top pods."

"Let's save those for last," said Deuce. "The lower ones should be easier. It may take four of us working together to do the rest of the top ones."

Alec grabbed the pouch, laid it flat on the floor, and unzipped it. "Grab her shoulders. I'll get her feet."

They placed Debra's body in the pouch. Alec tugged on the zipper pull and started closing the pouch. He stopped just below her chin.

He had never seen anyone who had died. When Alec was a child, his parents had told him about some of the first gen that had passed away, but he'd never actually seen them. He studied Debra's face. She almost didn't look real. Her skin appeared to be made of white stone, and her eyes were lifeless.

"You okay?" asked Deuce.

Ignoring the question, Alec tugged on the zipper pull and closed the pouch.

"Let's move her to the concourse."

As Alec and Deuce carried the pouch to the concourse, the reality of the situation started to sink in. They were thirty years from Uelara, and they had just lost the original crew. Could the second generation handle what was to come? Were they prepared to carry out the *Archean's* mission? There were so many things Alec didn't know about the ship. He'd spent the last few years manufacturing parts for the other departments, and he knew he could run the factory with his eyes closed. That's as far as his confidence could take him. What if the rest of the second gen weren't quite as competent?

"Let's place her here," instructed Alec, setting his end of the pouch down.

Deuce nodded and lowered the other end to the floor. Alec looked up and watched, as several of the others carried pouches out of the hives. He noticed none of the partners were speaking. The silence in the concourse was deafening. Needing a brief escape, Alec bolted from the concourse and sought refuge in the corridor.

None of the training he had received for life on the Arc could have possibly prepared him for this. He crouched down, placing his hands on his knees, and closed his eyes, trying to erase all the dreadful images that were racing through his mind. All he could see was Debra's cold, white face.

Suddenly, an unexplainable calm washed over him. His breathing slowed, and his mind cleared. He felt the panic he had experienced somehow escape his body. Alec straightened his posture and looked back into the concourse. The scene that only a moment ago caused him such distress now evoked no feeling at all.

CHAPTER 49

Sam had been glued to her terminal for hours, desperately seeking the cause of this unthinkable accident. Her penchant for efficient problem-solving was coming in handy today. In addition, Sam was grateful for the distraction. As her younger brothers lay sleeping on the floor, she forced herself to delay the thought that they would never see their mom and dad again. Sam knew no matter how shocked or grief-stricken she was, she at least had the foundation her parents had provided her to carry on with her life in this mission. But those poor babies. Their lives had just begun.

Save it for tomorrow, Sam, she thought.

"I think I found it!" shouted Zach from across the room.

Sam got up from her desk and walked over to Zach's terminal where he sat tapping away at the keys.

Narine was standing behind Zach, watching him scroll through a series of commands.

Narine had joined them in the Tank to help with the Quints and see if she could lend any insight into the door malfunction.

Sam wasn't accustomed to working quite this closely with Zach. Fortunately, Narine was serving as an unwitting yet convenient buffer. Sam was surprised to find that she and Zach were actually working well together. Maybe the seriousness of this task was allowing both of them to set aside their rivalry and work in a more efficient manner.

Narine leaned over Zach's shoulder to get a closer look at the monitor, asking, "So, you're in?"

"Yeah. The information the outriggers supplied earlier helped. According to the ship's log, the outer doors to the concourse were triggered early this morning."

"Can you tell what triggered them?" asked Narine.

"Unfortunately, no," answered Zach. "The log just shows that they were activated. But do you see this?" as he pointed to several commands on the monitor.

Sam's vision was blurred, and she struggled to focus. She'd been up with the Quints since early morning and was both mentally and physically exhausted. "Interesting. It looks like something disabled the alarms that should have activated before the doors started closing. Any idea what caused that?"

"No," Zach answered. "Again, from what I'm able to access in the log, these commands could have been either manually entered or randomly fired off by the ship itself. My guess is that the same glitch in the system caused both events."

"What's this?" asked Narine, pointing to a command.

"It looks like that's when I opened the doors this morning. See the timestamp there?" answered Sam.

"And these? What are these commands further up in the list?" asked Narine, pointing toward the top of the screen.

"Those are all the subroutines of the concourse doors program," Sam responded. "When the doors were activated, it started a sequence of program instructions. See this? That function would normally trigger the alarms. This one here launched the procedure to start shutting off the power to the hives."

"Is that what stopped the flow of oxygen to the pods?" asked Narine, pointing at the screen.

"No. It was this function here. This function removed the oxygen from the concourse and the hives," answered Zach.

Sam looked over to the center of the room. All five of her brothers were still sound asleep. "So, our parents woke up in a vacuum."

"Yes. It would be like waking up in a decompressed airlock. They would have had less than twenty seconds before they lost consciousness." Zach paused for a moment, his eyes tearing up. "Their bodies would have failed shortly after."

Sam had been so caught up in wanting answers that she hadn't considered how all of this might be affecting Zach. They had been so engrossed in programming language and detective work that they hadn't had time to translate the numbers to feelings.

A knot twisted in Sam's side. She wanted to scream or cry, but her desire for answers fought back the pain. "How could this happen?" she asked.

"I don't know. Remember when we were kids and the lift to the Hold was out for over a week? Shit just breaks sometimes," suggested Zach.

"Are there other logs that might contain any additional detail we can access?" asked Narine.

"That might be something operations can look into," considered Sam.

Narine turned to Sam with a look of panic and asked, "Weren't some of the others going to be in the concourse this afternoon?"

"Yeah. Why?"

Narine's face went white. "What if the doors malfunction again?"

"I took the doors offline this morning," explained Sam.

"But, what if—?"

"There's nothing to worry about, Narine. The only way those doors are going to close now is if they are closed manually," said Zach. "Each door weighs over two hundred kilograms. I also turned the power off in the hives."

Narine let out a sigh of relief. "Smart thinking. Last thing we need is anyone else getting hurt."

"None of this is sitting well with me. It just doesn't make sense that a malfunction would happen right after we discovered—" Sam stopped herself.

"Discovered what?" asked Narine.

"That Helena committed suicide," rescued Fisher as he entered the think tank. Sam looked at Fisher, giving him a slight nod.

Perfect timing, she thought. Sam didn't know how she would have recovered from that slipup. The last thing she wanted to do was share the discovery about Uelara the same day everyone lost their parents.

"What are the odds that two tragedies would happen so close together?" added Sam.

"That's a good point," said Fisher.

"I don't know. The two events seem disconnected to me," said Zach. "Helena was depressed and killed herself. Our parents died from an accident due to faulty equipment."

Sam bit her tongue. She hated hearing Helena's suicide simplified to her being depressed. She wanted to change the subject before she said something she would later regret. "How'd things go in the concourse?" she asked.

Fisher looked down at the floor. "I'd rather not talk about it right now."

Fisher's reluctance was unfamiliar to Sam. He and Sam had usually shared just about everything with each other. Fisher was the only person Sam had confided in about her first kiss. It dawned on her that from the minute Helena killed herself, the rules they all lived by had changed. Everything from this point on was uncharted territory. If the concourse was too difficult for Fisher to discuss, Sam was going to have to adjust her expectations and support Fisher however she could.

"I completely understand," said Sam.

"Are you guys any closer to discovering what happened with the concourse?" he asked.

"Zach was able to access the ship's logs, and it sounds like someone manually sealed the—"

"That's not what the logs show, Sam, and that's definitely not what I suggested," interrupted Zach. "Like I told Sam, the system logs indicate that commands were fired that triggered the doors and the sequence of events that followed. Nothing more, nothing less."

"So, what fired the commands?" asked Fisher.

"Or who?" added Sam.

"Let's not jump to conclusions, Sam," Zach cautioned. "This looks like a ship malfunction."

"So, the ship triggered the doors?" asked Fisher.

"It wasn't the ship."

Everyone looked toward the Quints. Sean was sitting up straight.

"What did you say?" asked Sam.

"It wasn't the ship," repeated Sean.

"If it wasn't the ship, then . . ." said Fisher.

Sean looked over at Fisher. "Ships don't close doors. People do."

Fisher looked at Sam and then back at Sean.

"Do you know who closed the doors?" asked Fisher.

"I'm tired. I need to rest." Sean laid back down and closed his eyes.

Fisher and Sam exchanged perplexed looks. She could see that Fisher was deeply disturbed by her little brother's statement. Though she wasn't affected as greatly as Fisher, Sam did think Sean's behavior was a bit odd.

"What the hell was that supposed to mean?!" cried Fisher.

"Shhhh, let him sleep," chided Sam.

"Sorry." Grabbing Sam's arm, Fisher dragged Sam to the other side of the room and lowered his voice. "What the hell was that supposed to mean?"

"I don't know. He's exhausted, Fish. He talks in his sleep all the time."

"No, I have heard people talking in their sleep hundreds of times in the hive. That was no sleep-talking. That right there was the freakiest thing I have ever seen. He knows something, Sam."

Sam could understand why Fisher was losing his composure. It had been the worst few days of their lives, and it didn't take much to push anyone over the edge right now.

"Look," Sam reassured him, "I'll talk to Sean when he wakes up in the morning. I guarantee you he won't remember a thing. Happens all the time. We should let them sleep."

"If it's okay, I'd like to head out and spend time with my hive before turning in," said Narine.

"Do you not see anything bizarre about Sean's statement?" Fisher asked Narine. "Am I the only one whose ears and brain are connected right now?"

A weary yawn escaped Narine's mouth as she placed her hand on Fisher's shoulder. "Fish, he's five. He's been through a pretty big trauma. We all have. Let's get some sleep."

"He's not wrong, you know," offered Sam.

Fisher gave Sam a puzzled look.

"Ships don't close doors. People do," she said grimly.

"Fine," surrendered Fisher. "But promise me you will at least ask him in the morning what the hell he was talking about."

"I will, I will. Narine, I really appreciate all your help with my brothers today," said Sam. "I couldn't have done this without you."

"Yeah. Thanks, Narine. I should probably head back as well," added Zach. Turning to Sam he said, "I'll leave the system log up just in case you want to save it to a file." He and Narine left the Tank as Sam sat down at Zach's station.

"You heading to the hive soon?" asked Fisher.

"I'm going to save the system logs and probably just sleep here in the Tank with the Quints tonight. It doesn't make sense to try and move them."

"Okay. I'm going to head that way." Fisher walked toward the exit and then looked back at Sam. "Are you ready for the meeting tomorrow?"

"As ready as I can be. I really wish someone else could share the news."

"I hear ya. I'm trying to stay positive about it, but I'm struggling to see how tomorrow is going to end well."

"So, are you suggesting that we not tell them?" asked Sam, almost hopefully.

Fisher sighed. "No. I don't think we have a choice. Everyone should know. Plus, there's no way I can carry this secret much longer."

"But is now the time to drop this news on them?"

Fisher looked down and scratched the back of his head. He looked back up with what Sam thought was deep sorrow in his eyes and asked, "Is there ever a good time to deliver a death sentence?"

CHAPTER 50

As Fisher walked to his hive, he was collecting his thoughts about the bizarre events of the day and the new leadership role he found himself in. He had heard himself speak up and begin instructing the others, but it was unclear where this voice originated. What he did find, however, was a sense of purpose in the moment. He was quickly finding that focusing his attention on decision-making and delegating tasks provided comfort in their own, distracting way.

Images from the concourse started attacking his thoughts. He had believed he had years to think about what his life would be like after his parents passed. Nothing could have prepared him for his experience in the concourse.

Fisher tried to nudge the graphic images out of his mind. As his brain made some room, new thoughts entered and settled in. Both of his parents were dead. Fisher didn't want to believe it. He couldn't believe it. How could he? No more chess games, no more unsolicited lectures, no more anything. He let that idea sit for a while as he turned a corner toward his hive.

A new thought arrived, accompanied by unfamiliar feelings of regret. He had never gotten to make things right with his father. Fisher had just assumed that one day, he and his dad would have some enlightening and transformative conversation, and they would somehow become closer. The reality that they were never going to bridge that divide hit Fisher hard in his gut.

A vision of his mother now entered, edging out his dad for a moment. He could imagine his mom's face, smiling as she shared another childhood story of her favorite summer at the beach. Fisher recalled just how much he had learned from her through his own childhood. She had taught him the intangible lessons that created the man Fisher was becoming. And the jokes. Oh, man, all the bad, terrible, horrible jokes she used to tell! What he wouldn't give to hear one of those ridiculous jokes right now.

Did she know? Had Fisher ever let her know just how thankful he was to be her son? How he understood all the extreme sacrifices she had made—both his parents had made—so that he could have a shot at living a healthy life. Fisher knew he would have to come to terms with the new truth of where exactly the rest of his life would take place, but he believed it still beat a shortened, disease-ridden life on Earth.

"Fish!" shouted Dom as he approached Fisher.

Brushing a tear away, Fisher replied, "Hey, Dom. You doing okay?"

"As good as I can be I guess. You?"

Fisher shrugged. "Same."

"I tried to catch you after we left the Hold, but you took the lift up before I got to you. I looked for you in the foundry and then the hive, but you weren't there."

"I was in the Tank. Just left. What's up?"

"Any news from Sam and Zach?" asked Dom.

"Yeah, but to be honest. I'm exhausted. Do you mind waiting to hear the details at the meeting tomorrow? There really isn't much more than what we already heard this morning."

"No worries. But, um . . ." Dom averted his eyes and seemed to be searching for words.

"What is it?"

"I . . . think you should go talk to Lance."

"I talked with him this morning. Like the rest of us, he's a mess over what happened."

"Yeah, but he—" Dom paused. "Look. You just really need to go talk with Lance."

Dom wasn't the type to have trouble speaking his mind. *What is he trying to tell me?* thought Fisher. "What is it, Dom?"

Dom looked down. "It's better if you hear it from him. He's back in the Q."

This doesn't sound good, Fisher thought. "In the Q? Why? Is this about Helena or—?"

"Just go talk with him. I gotta go check on Alec. I haven't really had a chance to talk with him all day, and I want to go see how he's holding up."

"Okay. Are we meeting up in the galley tomorrow before the meeting?" asked Fisher.

"I don't think so. I think I'll work with the others in the galley to bring food to the auditorium. We'll just have everyone eat breakfast at the meeting like we did at the OCP ceremony."

"Good idea. If I don't see you later, I'll catch you in the morning."

"Night, Fish."

"Night."

Fisher turned the corner toward the medical bay. Dom continued down the hallway, turned, and yelled, "Don't forget to go talk with Lance!"

CHAPTER 51

Fisher found Lance on the floor sitting up against the wall in the same quarantine room he had been locked in after the Grayson incident.

What the hell is he doing in there? Fisher wondered. He walked to the door, unlocked it, and stepped inside.

With red and swollen eyes, Lance looked up at Fisher. Lance was obviously struggling with the loss of the first generation and the gruesome experience in the concourse.

"Leave me alone, Fisher," murmured Lance, wiping tears from his eyes.

"I will. But why are you here? You know you're free to go back to the hive. No one's going to—"

"I belong here."

"Lance, if this is about what you did to Grayson . . ."

"This isn't just about Grayson. It's Grayson, Helena, our parents—"

"Lance, Helena took her own life."

"Because I wasn't there for her," spat Lance. "She came to me the night before she killed herself. I could have stopped her. I could have . . ."

Lance began to sob. Fisher had never seen Lance in this state, and it was unsettling. The only emotion Lance showed everyone was rage, usually. What Fisher was witnessing was complete anguish and despair.

Lance continued, "I should have listened to her. None of this would have happened if I had just listened to her."

"You don't know that."

"I fucked up."

"Lance, none of this is your fault. None of us saw this coming. We all could have stopped her, if we—"

"No, Fisher. I fucked up!" growled Lance.

"We all could have—"

Lance jumped to his feet. "I killed the first generation!"

The words jolted Fisher for a moment. He hesitated. With some uncertainty, he continued, "Lance, it was a ship malfunction. Zach and Sam pulled the ship's logs and—"

"The ship did not malfunction. It was me."

Had Lance lost his mind? Was the accident hitting him harder than Fisher realized? "But, Lance, you were locked up in here the whole time. There's no—"

"Not the whole time."

Another jolt. "What are you talking about?"

"I left the Q early that morning. I went—"

"But . . . you were locked in—"

"Dom let me out."

Fisher was terrified of what Lance was about to say. What followed was a wave of cries, sobs, and barely audible words coming from a very broken Lance. Fisher stood in shock, trying to pull together the incoherent story Lance was spewing.

"Dom came by to check—" Lance paused. "I convinced him to let me out. I told him I just needed a break from the room. I promised to be back within the hour! And I was!"

"Why would you want to kill our parents?"

"Fisher, come on! I didn't *want* to kill them! I just wanted to lock them in!"

Fisher was still trying to keep up but was struggling. "Why . . . why lock them up?"

"I was angry! They locked me up! I know what I did to Grayson was wrong. But I wasn't a threat to anybody. They locked me up and wouldn't let me out. I wanted to punish them—even if it were just for a few hours. I wanted them to know what it was like to be trapped, locked up like a prisoner. I triggered the doors! I didn't know that shutting the doors was going to . . . I fucked up, Fisher!"

Before he could register what he was doing, Fisher clinched his right fist and drove it into Lance's face.

A sharp pain ran up Fisher's arm. He had never felt such rage, and his body had reacted before his brain could reason with him. What had he just done? Fisher had never hit anyone before. He had to get a grip. There was no way he was going to be able to process Lance's confession right now. Fisher knew he needed to be in damage control mode. "Sorry. I didn't mean to—"

"No, I deserve it," said Lance, as a small trickle of blood trailed from his nose. "I killed all of our parents. I killed our— your mother. I killed Maggie!"

More sobs echoed through the room. Fisher's head was spinning. "It was an accident, Lance." As angry as Fisher was, he believed this.

"No, it wasn't. It was me. I did this. And don't blame Dom for any of it. He didn't know. He looks up to me, you know that. He just did what I asked him to do."

"Lance, you had no idea this would happen."

"You have to tell the others what I did."

"What?!" *Why is he putting that responsibility on me?* thought Fisher.

"They need to know," insisted Lance.

"This is your truth to tell, not mine."

"I don't think I can bring myself to—"

"Listen. Everyone just discovered that their parents are dead, and tomorrow . . ." Fisher paused. "Tomorrow we have to discuss the future of the mission. The last thing they need to hear is that you were somehow involved in the accident."

"But they need to know that—"

"And *you* can tell them, when the time is right . . . or at least at a better time."

"I don't know what to do, Fisher." Lance slid down the wall and sat in the corner of the Q.

"You don't have to have all the answers now. We'll come up with a plan. Right now, I need you to—"

"What's going on?"

The new, faint voice had come from the other side of the room. Fisher turned to see a still-bandaged Grayson leaning against the door frame.

"Can . . . can someone go get my parents?"

CHAPTER 52

Sam activated the media cube and switched it to projector mode as Mia and Avery wheeled a whiteboard to the center of the stage. Sam removed the cube's remote and placed it in her pocket. She noticed that her hand was trembling and realized she would be less nervous if Fisher were there.

"Is this a good spot for it?" asked Mia.

Sam looked at the whiteboard on the stage.

"Perfect. Thanks, guys," said Sam, giving them a smile.

Sam turned toward the seats in the auditorium, as everyone gathered around the food carts where Dom and the others from the galley passed out breakfast. There wasn't much in the way of conversation, and most people seemed to be pushing the food around on their plates instead of eating. While spirits weren't high and Sam knew it would be weeks before things improved, everyone seemed to be dealing with the accident better today. She cleared her throat to get the attention of the crew.

"We'll get started as soon as Fisher returns with Lance. Please find your seats, and we'll begin shortly." Sam's eyes filled with tears. She just heard her mother's words come from her own mouth.

Several of the group got seated. Sam was happy to see Grayson out of the medical bay and sitting in the front row. She stepped down from the stage and walked over to him. "You doing okay?"

"Yeah. It only hurts when . . . well . . . when I do anything. If it weren't for the pills Kaman gave me, I don't know what I'd do," mumbled Grayson through his swollen jaw.

"Sorry. I'm just happy to see you out of the Bay. If there's anything I can do to help, let me know, okay?"

"Thanks, Sam. How are you holding up with everything that's happened?" asked Grayson.

"Same as everyone else, I guess. Just trying to make it through the day one hour at a time. I'm sorry you had to wake up to all of this."

"Yeah, so am I. So, what do we do now?"

"That's what Fish and I are going to talk about this morning."

"You think we'll be okay?"

Sam really didn't know how to respond. She knew that the remaining crew could continue the mission. Many aspects of the ship had become automated. The second gen already had a few years of experience behind them, and all details about the mission were fully documented and could be found in the archives. So, in Sam's mind, the question wasn't *could* they carry on without the first generation. The real question was *would* they after hearing the truth about the distance to Uelara.

Sam looked at Grayson, smiled and said, "Yes. We'll be okay."

"Sorry I'm late," said Fisher as he approached Sam and Grayson. "How ya doing, Grayson?"

"About the same as last night," he replied.

"I think we should get things started. Where's Lance?" asked Sam.

"He's sitting this one out," replied Fisher.

"What? You explained this was mandatory, right?"

"Yes. Would you like to go try to change his mind?"

While Sam would normally be up for that challenge, she

didn't want to postpone the meeting any longer, and she wasn't sure how Lance was going to react to the news. He'd probably just add fuel to the fire.

"You can fill him in after the meeting," said Sam. She and Fisher climbed up and stood front and center on the stage.

"Dom, could you get the lights?" asked Fisher.

Dom walked to the wall and lowered the brightness of the overhead lights. A screen capture of the ship's log projected onto the whiteboard. She looked at Fisher and nodded.

Fisher took a deep breath and began. "I'd like to first thank everyone for coming this morning. I know it hasn't been easy dealing with the accident, and we'd all rather be somewhere else. As some of you may know, Zach and Sam spent most of yesterday accessing the Arc's logs. Sam is going to share their findings."

Sam cleared her throat and pointed at the code on the screen. "I understand that the system logs are going to look foreign to most of you, but I'll break it down as much as I can. Early yesterday morning, the ship malfunctioned and triggered the master doors to the concourse. This started a series of events that removed the oxygen from the concourse and first gen hives."

"Why would closing the doors remove the oxygen to the hives?" asked Alec.

Sam clicked to the second slide that consisted of additional code from the system's log, and then clicked again to advance to the third slide showing the blueprints of the concourse. "Kayla and the outriggers from Stringer's crew were able to provide details that address your question. That area of the ship was designed as the build site for the exit ring that will be constructed. The concourse is actually a giant airlock where the exit ring will be deployed in Uelara's orbit. When the doors sealed, the area decompressed to equalize the pressure."

Confused expressions looked back at Sam.

"What Sam is saying is that this was an accident," explained Fisher.

"So how do we prevent this from happening in other areas of the ship?" asked Dom.

"Yeah, are we safe?" asked Avery.

"We believe that the concourse is the only area on the *Archean* of its kind. But the plan is to investigate all areas of the ship," said Fisher. "We will add any additional fail-safes needed to ensure the safety of the crew. We feel confident that something like this won't happen again."

"Why weren't fail-safes put into place when they designed the Arc?" asked Grayson.

"What makes you think we can do better than our parents?" asked Bart.

Sam didn't anticipate this question. "We don't have all the answers right now, but we feel confident—"

"I'm sure our parents had that same confidence two days ago!" argued Kayla. "When are you guys going to address what we are going to do about the mission?"

"Yeah. What are we going to do now?" asked Avery.

Sam looked at Fisher. It was obvious that her planned presentation had just gotten derailed, and there was no course correction that would get it back on track.

"Before we move forward, are there any further questions about the accident?" asked Fisher.

"I'd rather hear what our plans are moving forward," said Finn.

"Yeah, what do we do next?" asked Echo.

Fisher took two steps forward, closing the space between himself and the group, and straightened his posture. "We carry on with the mission."

"That's not even possible," objected Deuce.

"Yeah. Have you forgotten how many members of the crew we lost yesterday?" said Kayla, leaning forward in her seat. "There are only sixty of us now. Sixty-five if you plan on putting the Quints to work."

"Fifty-nine," corrected Sam.

"What?"

"Helena."

There was a short moment of silence, and then the room erupted with questions.

Fisher raised his hand to quiet the group. "I understand how all this looks right now."

"It looks like we aren't going to make it to Uelara," declared Alec.

Sam looked over at Fisher. His body was still, and it looked as though he was trying to find the right words to respond. She knew he needed help.

"The Arc *will* make it to Uelara. We *can* continue what our parents started," Sam asserted.

"Empty words. I think you are underestimating what it will take to—"

Sam cut Kayla off. "Look, we know there are many obstacles in our path, but we are ready to deploy the next ring, and that will give us twelve months to be prepared for the next deployment. Don't forget that we have been trained for this. We knew the day would come when we would be crewing the Arc on our own."

"But we thought we had another ten to twenty years before we were on our own!" shouted Bart.

"So, we improvise. Our whole lives have been centered on the mission. If everyone continues to pull his or her weight, the mission can stay on target," said Sam, hoping her words would help focus their energy in a more positive direction.

"Do you really think we can keep the Arc running without the first gen?" asked Avery.

"We don't really have a choice," said Mia.

"Yes, I believe we can," added Fisher. "We just need to pull together and—"

"Where's Lance?" asked Kayla.

"He's not feeling well. He's—"

"Is he going to be the new captain?" asked Deuce, interrupting Fisher.

"We have a lot of things we need to work out, but right now our focus needs to be on releasing the next ring and maintaining the upkeep of the Arc," explained Sam.

"So, you want us to carry on as if nothing happened?" scoffed Alec.

"Alec, we all suffered the same loss. No one is saying to forget about the accident. If you want to honor our parents, you'll continue with the mission," corrected Fisher.

"So tomorrow we just go back to work?" asked Finn.

"We can take a couple of days to regroup. Return to work as soon as you can. We realize everyone is going to process the accident differently," explained Fisher. "Just remember, you're not alone. The next few months won't be easy, but if we help each other, we can all get through this."

Sam looked over at Fisher. She knew it was now or never. Fisher nodded. Sam progressed through the presentation and stopped on a slide with a single button sitting in the center of it that was labeled PLAY. Sam looked back at Fisher, took in a deep breath, and placed her thumb over the play button on the remote. "Before we finish, there is one last thing we need to discuss."

CHAPTER 53

Alec stared at the green dot that glowed at the end of the red ribbon being projected onto the whiteboard. The information that Sam and Fisher had just presented was met with silence from the entire auditorium. Alec sat stewing with his thoughts. The size of this announcement felt as large as space outside the *Archean*, and Alec wasn't sure there was room in his mind for it all. Just as he was coming to terms with their current plan to continue the mission with only a fraction of the crew, Sam and Fisher had attacked him with news in an unexpected blow that knocked the wind out of him. Alec found himself rising from his seat before he realized it was happening.

"I just want to make sure I fully understand what you two are suggesting," said Alec, breaking the room's silence. "Our parents—scratch that. The entire first generation had been lying to all of us our entire lives?"

All eyes in the room were on Alec.

Fisher took a step forward. "I understand this is a lot to take in, but—"

"A lot to take in? You're telling us that everything we know is a lie!" Alec shouted.

"Not everything," responded Sam.

Alec planted his feet and crossed his arms. "Oh, you're right. They just left out the part where we never make it to Uelara, and we die out here in the emptiness of space."

"They were going to tell us. They just—"

Alec couldn't let her finish. "Just what, Sam? They just didn't think we could handle the truth? Or could it be that they knew how much they had screwed us and couldn't bring themselves to come clean? The truth is that they didn't tell us we are going to die long before the Arc makes it to Uelara."

"Why would they lie to us about something like this?" asked Grayson. "It just doesn't make sense."

"This just can't be true. Sam, how confident are you about your calculations? About any of this?" asked Zach.

"My simulation is accurate based on data we obtained from the raw coordinates the first gen were using. I feel very con—"

"How could no one have discovered such a huge discrepancy in the distance to Uelara until now?" demanded Bart.

"Yeah, why now?" asked Deuce.

"We didn't know about any of this until after we discovered Helena's journal," explained Sam.

"What are you talking about?" asked Avery. "What does her journal have to do with any of this?"

"Helena's last entry in her journal was her account of a conversation she overheard between the captain and Debra. It—"

"Is that why she killed herself?" asked Avery.

Sam looked at Avery and the others, closed her eyes, and whispered, "Yes."

Alec struggled to understand how Sam and Fisher could be so accepting of this. Were they not comprehending the grim reality of it all? "How long have you two known about this? Who else knew?" demanded Alec.

Sam looked at Fisher as silence engulfed the room. Everyone waited to hear their response. Fisher looked down at the floor and then back up to the crew. "Sam, Dom, and I put all of this together just before the accident."

A fire ignited in Alec's head. How could his friends keep something this big from him? How could Dom keep this from him? How could Dom look him in the eyes knowing something like this and not say a word? His own brother?

"And you're just now telling us?" yelled Alec, setting his eyes on Dom. Dom sunk lower in his chair.

"When would have been a better time, Alec? The same day everyone lost their parents?" snapped Sam. "We're telling you now! The truth is—"

"The truth is, we're fucked!" screamed Alec.

The room fell silent again.

Alec could see that Sam and Fisher were at a loss for words. Something about this empowered Alec. It was confirmation that he was right.

"I know how devastating this all sounds. But we need to stay focused on the mission," said Sam.

"The mission? Fuck the mission!" spat Alec. "What's the point? We are never going to make it to Uelara. Don't you understand that?" He looked Sam in the eyes and asked, "Why is it that losers are always the last to see the obvious?"

Sam took a step toward Alec, and Fisher gently placed his hand on her arm.

"You're right, Alec. We're not going to make it to Uelara," agreed Fisher. "But we can still play a role in the Arc's mission. We can still save the human race."

Alec was fuming. He found himself stepping out of his row, inching his way toward the aisle. As he spoke, he slowly stepped closer and closer to Fisher and Sam. "The human race? You mean the same human race that decided our disposable lives were a means to an end?"

"That's enough, Alec!" yelled Sam.

"No, I wanna hear what Alec has to say!" shouted Kayla.

Alec continued, "We don't owe any of them a damn thing! They stole our lives from us. We now have a chance to take our lives back and choose our own fate. And you want us to—"

"The Arc's mission was never about us," Fisher interrupted. "It was always bigger than us. We—"

"You can spew your father's bullshit to someone else, Fish. That garbage has been crammed down our throats our whole lives, and I, for one, am over it!"

"Alec, I understand you're upset, but if we don't carry on this mission, everything they sacrificed will all have been for nothing," Fisher reasoned.

Alec looked around the room and realized that this was no longer a group discussion. This had become a debate between the three of them, and he felt like he was winning. "What about *our* sacrifices?"

Clenching his fists, Fisher took another step forward and said, "This is bigger than us. Don't you want to honor your parents? They lost their lives for—"

"And they stole ours!"

Alec could see that Fisher wasn't going to budge, and he had no desire to try to convince him otherwise. "You can preach about the greater good and the bigger picture all you want, Fish. You and the rest of the crew can feel free to blindly follow the first generation to your deaths. I can see right through it."

Fisher joined the rest of the crew in their silence. He was

speechless. Alec had heard enough. He turned around and stormed out of the auditorium.

"Alec, where are you going?" called out Fisher.

Alec didn't respond. As he turned the corner into the corridor, he heard the crew erupt with questions. Alec continued walking.

"Pointless, Fish. Absolutely pointless."

CHAPTER 54

After sleeping late into the day, Avery walked toward the medical bay with thoughts of yesterday's meeting racing through her head. Over the years, she had found life on the Arc to be challenging, and she struggled with the day-to-day monotony of her OCP in the factory. Now that she knew the truth, she couldn't find a reason to move forward with the mission. Avery tried to suppress these thoughts, but the more she tried to block them out, the more they poked at her. The whispers of negativity that frequently nagged her were now constant roars. She tried to follow the advice Dr. Fiona had given her: "Don't suppress, replace."

But what thoughts could she possibly use to replace the fact that she was going to die on the Arc? Years of dreaming of the day she would touch down on Uelara had been stolen from her in an instant. What advice would Dr. Fiona have offered if she were here? If there were ever a time she needed Dr. Fiona, it was now. Avery had loved their counseling sessions, and it was crushing to know that she would never see her again. She missed her parents, but it was Dr. Fiona who had truly listened, who had understood.

Fisher's plea to her and the others after Alec had charged out of the meeting yesterday, while touching, had left Avery feeling hopeless. It was very clear that no one believed they would make it to Uelara. How had Fisher and Sam accepted their new fate so easily? Uelara was the one thing that had kept Avery semi-sane all these years. How would she carry on? Dr. Fiona had always encouraged her to see the bigger picture and to focus on the important role she played in the mission. Perhaps that advice had carried others through the rough times, but for Avery, it just didn't cut it.

As she entered the medical bay, Avery saw Kaman sitting at Dr. Gage's terminal in his office. She looked toward the quarantine rooms and saw Lance sitting on the floor up against the wall. Avery was afraid of Lance. What he had in looks was soured by his callous and unkind treatment of others. Avery scurried into the room across from Lance, hoping she could avoid any and all interaction with him.

"Hey, Avery. What's going on?" asked Grayson. He was sitting in bed, propped up by a few pillows. Avery closed the door and approached the edge of the bed.

"Just wanted to stop by and see how you were doing. You okay?"

"As long as Kaman keeps feeding me pills, yeah," Grayson said with a smile.

"Maybe I should be talking with Kaman. What's your secret?"

He smiled. "Get beaten half to death by the ship's hothead, and everyone aims to please. Grab a seat."

Grayson patted the bed, and Avery walked over and sat next to him.

"How are you handling everything?" he asked.

"To be honest, I'm a wreck."

"You and me both. I still feel dazed from everything that is happening. I keep thinking I'm going to wake up, and this will have just been a bad dream."

She sighed. "More like a nightmare. How do we move on from this?"

"You heard Fish. The remaining crew can handle the workload. We just have to release this next geo-ring, and then we will have time to regroup," he answered.

Avery tucked a loose strand of hair behind her left ear. She was surprised that Grayson seemed so optimistic. "I understand that we can probably continue the work, but why? Why does it matter?"

"What do you mean?"

"We're never going to see Uelara. Why continue the mission if we are just going to die on the Arc?"

"If we don't continue the mission, what would we do? Just sit around and wait to die?" he asked.

"I'm not saying that. I don't know what we should do."

Grayson sighed deeply. "All I know right now is that I miss my parents. It's got me thinking about everything."

"What do you mean, *everything*?"

"The mission. The reason we're here on the Arc, instead of back on the Earth. My parents went into this mission knowing they would die on the Arc."

"But aren't you upset that they lied to us? Grayson, how many years did they watch us play First Things, knowing full well that—"

"You know, I was angry at first. But I have to believe that they chose to keep the truth from us with our best interests in mind."

Avery looked at him like he was crazy. "Exactly how many pills did Kaman give you today?"

Grayson let out his first laugh in days. "Owwww! Don't make me laugh!"

She giggled. "Sorry!"

"No seriously, please hear me out on this," he continued. "Wouldn't it have been easier for our parents to simply live out the rest of their lives on the Earth? They left everything, everyone they knew, for the mission. They sacrificed the last thirty years of their lives. Do you really want them to have done it for nothing?"

"No, but how do we continue, knowing that we—?"

"I almost died, Avery. I could have died and would have never seen Uelara, even if we *were* supposed to make it there. I wasted so many years thinking about the future that I never realized my life was slipping by. I don't want to live for tomorrow anymore. I want to live for today."

This was a point Avery hadn't considered.

Grayson continued. "You know, everyone talks about making a new home on Uelara, but the Arc is my home. It's our home. It's all we've ever known."

"So, you really think the crew will pull together and continue the mission?"

"We have a chance to continue what our parents started. We can forever change the course of the human race."

"But no one will know—"

"I'll know," he asserted. "I'll know that I did everything I could to do right by my parents and what they wanted me to become."

"I just don't know if I'm strong enough, Grayson."

He placed his hand on Avery's. "Of course you are. And if you falter, I'll be there to keep you going."

Avery was startled by the emotions that were stirring inside her. His positive outlook took her by surprise. His willingness to support Avery through dark times comforted her in a way she had never expected. And his touch . . . she didn't even realize how much she needed someone to reach her in that way.

It was hard to believe that this was Grayson sitting in the bed. She had spent her entire life hanging out with him, and not once had she seen this side of him. Was she just blind, or had he really changed? She couldn't be sure, but one thing was evident. Avery liked this Grayson—very, very much.

CHAPTER 55

Fisher awoke eager to return to the foundry. The geodetic ring was in the final stages of testing and would be deployed in less than two weeks. The tragedy still weighed on him, but he used the pain he felt for the loss of his parents and the rest of the first generation as a reminder of how important carrying out the mission was. He refused to allow their selflessness to be in vain.

Fisher had a new, optimistic outlook about the mission and was encouraged by most of the crew's response to the meeting. It had only been two days since he and Sam had revealed the truth, and everyone seemed to be attempting to return to their duties on the ship to prepare for the upcoming ring deployment.

"Okay. Firing stage two," called out Narine from her terminal on the far side of the foundry.

Fisher stood in front of the collapsed geodetic ring, holding on to a thick braided cable. The cable split into four smaller cables that attached to the outer shell of the ring. He heard several latches release and pulled on the cable. The ends of the cable detached from the ring and fell to the floor.

"Cables released," shouted Fisher. "We good?"

Fisher looked over and watched Narine studying the scrolling data on her monitor. A smile crawled across her face.

"Stage two looks good. I think we nailed it."

Fisher clenched his right fist, raised it before his torso, and swiftly pumped it to his body. "Yes! Good work, Narine. Let me survey the latches."

Fisher approached the ring and began inspecting the latches that held the cables in place. When he got to the fourth latch, he noticed that it was slightly misshapen. "We might need to replace the lower right latch. It's probably nothing, but I think it's—"

"Better safe than sorry," Narine said, cutting him off.

Fisher thought back to the time Jeremy had explained the importance of each component that made up the geodetic rings. Jeremy had explained that the structural integrity of every aspect of the ring was vital to support the designed load of the third stage of the deployment. They referred to this stage as the "Bloom."

When the ring bloomed, it would expand four times its size in a matter of seconds, putting massive amounts of stress on all the components that made up the structure. Since they couldn't test the final stage before deployment, there was no way to assess whether the ring was fit to withstand the bloom. The best they could do was put every component through rigorous testing and be ready to improvise on site during the deployment if needed.

Fisher walked to the back wall and pulled one of the cabinet doors open. "We out of latches?"

"Did you look in the cabinet?"

"Not seeing any. I'll call over to the factory and see if they've printed some."

Fisher walked to the call box and pressed 404 followed by the large red call button. No one picked up. "I'm not getting anyone in the factory. They probably can't hear over the sound of the machines. I'll just head over there. Could use a stretch anyway."

"While you're there, can you pick up a few more boxes of cable ties?" asked Narine. "We're almost out."

"On it."

As Fisher left the foundry, a growing concern crept into his mind. He hadn't seen or talked with Alec since the presentation, and Fisher had no idea what state he'd find Alec in when he arrived at the factory. Fisher thought he knew Alec well, but he had never seen him so unhinged. He knew that everyone was handling the truth about the mission differently, but Fisher would never have thought Alec would have reacted the way he did. He hoped that the last two days had given him time to calm down.

Fisher quickly returned his thoughts to the ring. He was excited that the tests today had produced positive results and was convinced they would successfully release the ring on schedule. He hoped that celebrating this year's ring deployment would strengthen the crew's morale and be a strong start to continuing the mission after their tragic loss. It could easily be what any of the crew who were struggling with their newfound reality needed.

As Fisher approached the entrance to the factory, the hairs on the back of his neck stood up. Something didn't feel right. He turned the corner, entered the factory, and was met with silence. None of the machines were running, and there was no crew to be found.

For the first time in the *Archean's* history, the factory was shut down.

CHAPTER 56

Kayla stood in the galley, wadding a ball of protein paste in her hands. Alec, Deuce, and Bart stood behind her in silence as she pulled her arm back and then hurled the paste at the wall. It splattered, leaving clumps of paste clinging to the grooves in the metal surface of the wall panels. The group burst out laughing.

"Nice throw, Kayla," snickered Alec.

"My turn," declared Bart, pulling a glob of paste off the bed of the printer.

The galley was a mess. After gorging themselves on more than their normal rationed breakfast, Alec had led the group in inventing games that involved food and trashing the place.

Kayla was enjoying being able to cut loose and have a little fun after all the recent chaos. It also felt good being included by some people who shared her viewpoint on what Alec was calling the "Uelara deception."

Kayla hadn't felt accepted by the second gen'ers from her hive, and she could never figure out why. She guessed that part of the reason was that they all held such different opinions from her about everything. They never wanted to do anything fun, either. They were content sitting in the hive every night, just reading and talking to each other. Kayla would rather die than live out such a boring existence.

Once she had been assigned to Stringer's outrigger crew, she'd felt overjoyed getting to know Lance and the others. They were all adventurous and kindred spirits of sorts. Landing the outrigger OCP was her lucky break, and she'd gladly followed Lance's guidance as crew shift leader.

After the accident, Kayla had assumed Lance would step up and lead the crew. He'd never shied away from an opportunity to take charge. She would never have guessed he would isolate himself like he had. When Alec stood up at Sam and Fisher's presentation and spoke the words Kayla was already thinking, she'd tracked Alec down. It turned out that a few others did the same. Now here they were, throwing protein paste at the walls and filling their bellies. She saw no purpose in gearing up and working all day when she could enjoy the rest of the years she had on the Arc.

"What the hell?"

Fisher was standing at the entrance to the galley, staring at the mess as if he just watched someone walk out of the Arc without wearing an EMU.

"We're seeing who can leave the biggest mess in one throw. Wanna play?" asked Alec.

"Are you joking? You're wasting food, and the place is a wreck!" shouted Fisher.

"Wreck? I think the room is looking good. Don't you think so, guys?" Alec said, looking at the group for agreement.

"Looks pretty good to me," Bart said with a smile.

Deuce laughed. "I'd say it's definitely an improvement."

"Enough! You're wasting food and more importantly, time!" exclaimed Fisher.

"Have you forgotten already? With fewer mouths to feed, we have all the food we could ever want. And time? Well, we have the rest of our lives with nothing but time," said Alec as he pulled a lump of paste off the printer bed.

"What are you talking about?" Fisher demanded. "We are days away from releasing the next ring and we're—"

"Are you still going on about the mission?" Alec rolled the paste slowly in his hands.

"Yes! We have to—"

"We don't *have* to do anything. There's no point to any of it."

"You're wrong, Alec. Don't you want to continue what your parents—?"

"My parents are dead. They are ghosts on this ship, and so are we. You just haven't accepted it yet."

Kayla watched as Fisher stood speechless.

Fisher seemed so accepting of the huge lie that the first gen had been spinning. Where was his outrage? Kayla began to feel that Fisher's complacency was a giant weakness. He had no fight in him. He was just a gullible fool. Any respect she once had for him was lost. She was enjoying watching Alec put Fisher in his place.

"Let me fill you in on this precious mission of yours, Fish. It's all bullshit. There are so many flaws with the mission that it's obvious we were never meant to complete it."

"What are you talking about?" asked Fisher.

Alec threw the paste to the floor and wiped his hands on the sides of his coveralls. "I'll give you five reasons why you and the rest of the crew are wasting your time."

Alec raised his right fist. Bits of paste still clung to his hand as he extended his index finger and continued, "One. What if humankind becomes extinct before the Arc even reaches Uelara? There has been *zero* communication with the Earth in over twenty-five years."

Alec raised his middle finger. "Two. What if the rings fail? You have no way of knowing if the rings are even still functioning."

Alec raised his ring finger. "Three—"

"You need to—" Fisher tried to interrupt.

"Three. What if Uelara doesn't really exist? And even if it does exist, what if it can't support human life after all?" Alec raised his pinky finger. "Four. The ship is aging. Do you really think you and the crew can keep this thing operational the entire journey?"

Alec raised his thumb. "Five." He paused, and a smile crept onto his face. "Five. Because I don't give a shit."

Fisher stood silent.

"Exactly. Now go run along and play with your fantasy ring."

Fisher turned to leave. A loud crash came from the storage freezer in the far corner, grabbing everyone's attention in the room.

"What was that?" asked Fisher, walking toward the freezer.

"I didn't hear anything, did you guys?" asked Alec with a smile.

"I didn't hear anything, either," added Kayla.

Fisher opened the door and gasped. "What the—?"

Dom emerged from the freezer, shivering and weak.

"Alec, have you lost your mind?" Fisher asked, horrified. "He could have—!"

"He's fine, Fish. He just needed to cool off a little."

Kayla and the others burst out into laughter. Fisher looked at Alec and then back at Dom. He put his arm around Dom, whispered something to him, and the two retreated.

Alec turned to Kayla and the others. "Ready to have some real fun?"

CHAPTER 57

Zach was happy to be back in the think tank. After the long day with Sam and the others rebooting all the machines in the factory, he was ready to return to the comfort of his domain in the Tank. With the geodetic ring deployment coordinates completed and sent to the foundry and operations, he could get back to working his program. He hoped that there wouldn't be any more "call-to-action" requests from Fisher to help in other departments.

For the past few weeks, the software updates for the Arc's power cell memory chips he had been coding had showed significant progress. His time in the Q had already set him back a couple of weeks, and he didn't need any more distractions. He was close to reducing the power consumption by fourteen percent. This reduction would mark the most significant enhancement to the power cells since the Arc had left Earth's orbit. Zach's only regret was that Debra wouldn't get to see his accomplishment. Though Sam and he rarely saw eye to eye, he at least knew that Sam would appreciate the work and effort that went into such a feat. Zach queued up his program and reached for his VR headset. It wasn't there.

He turned in his chair and shouted to Sam, "I really wish you'd stop having people use my terminal every time a stranger comes into the Tank!"

"Huh?" muttered Sam as she stared at her screen.

"Have you seen my headset?"

"No. It's not at your desk?"

"Nope. That's where I left it, so you would think that—"

"Just grab someone else's," huffed Sam.

"Were your brothers playing with my gear again? Where are they, anyway?"

"No, they weren't messing with anything. Grayson took them to the Dome. Face it, you gotta take care of your stuff better, Zach."

Zach let out a long, exaggerated sigh and stood up. He surveyed the desks around him, but his initial scan of the room came up empty. Zach shook his head in frustration.

"Not seeing one, can I use yours?"

"Fine. You can use mine. Just be sure to return it after lunch, I want to run the . . ." Her voice trailed off.

"Run the what?"

Now Sam was scanning the room. "My headset is gone."

"Look, if you don't want me to use your—"

"I'm telling you, it's not here," Sam clipped, as she rose from her seat. She walked around the Tank, searching the desks for headsets. "Are you kidding me? Just yesterday I swear I remember seeing several headsets throughout the room. How could they all go missing?" she muttered.

"Wait. I have an idea," Zach said.

He walked to Debra's office and ran his fingers across the top of the door frame, knocking something metallic to the ground. He reached down, swiped it into his hand, and held it out.

"Bet you didn't know about this!" he beamed.

"You mean the key to the storage cabinets that Debra showed us on the first week we started in the Tank? Yeah, totally didn't know about that."

If you knew, you would have grabbed it yourself, Smarty Pants, Zach thought. He used the key to unlock the cabinets next to Debra's office and retrieved a headset from the top shelf.

"Looks like it's the only one left. Glad I thought to look here." He smiled as he headed back to his terminal. "Best of luck finding another one."

"That's great, but aren't you the least bit concerned that all the other sets are missing?"

Nope, Zach wasn't the least bit concerned that all the other sets were missing. He had snagged the last headset before Sam could get her hands on it, and he was happy. Back to his program to save the day.

CHAPTER 58

Dom held the nail brush under the stream of hot water, wetting the bristles. He squirted soap onto the brush and moved it from side to side under his nails as the soap created a lather. This was Dom's second attempt to remove the remaining white primer from underneath his nails after working in the factory. Fisher's request for everyone to help Avery and the team with the backlog of parts had resulted in a clear reminder of how there were worse OCP assignments than his. The monotony of brushing primer on part after part was torture for Dom's short attention span.

Dom couldn't help but think his time in the factory could have been avoided if Alec had been working the past few days. He was still angry with Alec. Honestly, how could Alec lock him in the freezer? Would he have let him out if Fisher didn't show up? It frightened Dom that he didn't have a clear answer to the question.

Alec hadn't been sleeping in their hive the last few days, and Dom had mixed feelings about it. On one hand, he was happy to avoid further confrontations with his brother. On the other, he was worried for Alec and hated that a divide had formed between the two of them.

Dom tried to shake these thoughts away. He had a busy day ahead of him. The first thing on his list was to drain one of the pools in the protein chamber. With a smaller crew, two pools would produce enough raw material for everyone's daily food rations to be increased with plenty to spare. Having one less pool to maintain would cut down on the workload and allow Dom to assist in other areas on the ship.

He left the scrub room and walked toward the central area of the protein chamber to get suited up. As he approached the dressing station, Dom could see that there were no white chamber suits hanging from the racks. He knew he had seen them there this morning when he arrived. He racked his brain to find a reason for the missing suits.

Dom could not recall a single instance when those racks hadn't been filled with the chamber suits. He even remembered wishing on more than one occasion that they were all somehow destroyed in a mysterious fire, allowing him to skip raking the pools for even one shift. But alas, the dreaded suits were always reliably there, just like an unavoidable "serving of the suck" in the Q.

Maybe Echo had made a pickup without saying anything. He pulled a new suit from the cabinet next to the racks, and noticed there were only two left in there as well. He'd need to have the factory produce more soon.

Dom removed the new suit from the sealed bag and shook it out. The sharp smell of chemicals stung his eyes. Stepping into the suit brought back the memory of the EMU, which quickly led his thoughts to Lance. He understood why Lance was taking the accident so hard. Dom couldn't help but feel partially responsible. If he hadn't let Lance out of the Q, Dom's parents and the others would still be alive. A tear broke free and ran down his face.

What he wouldn't give to have his parents back. It was killing Dom to watch all his friends mourn the loss of their parents. He never imagined Lance would do anything to harm the first gen.

Dom had initially thought the parents were crazy to lock Lance up. Sure, Grayson's mangled body could be an indicator of the damage Lance could inflict. But Dom believed that Lance never really meant any harm to anyone.

Dom's only intention that night was to allow his friend a brief escape from being cooped up in the Q. He had kept his promise to Fisher—he didn't breathe a word about Uelara to Lance. Admittedly, he was tempted to share the news, but when Dom arrived, Lance was so agitated that Dom knew it was better to sit on that information and let someone else handle it. Maybe the parents weren't so crazy after all, keeping Lance "contained."

When Dom and Lance were working together in the concourse after the accident, Lance had confessed everything to Dom. It was difficult to remember that the distressed person in front of him was Lance. Dom always saw him as tough and brash, rarely concerning himself with consequences or others' feelings. Now Lance was crying and confessing and even asking Dom for guidance.

Dom wanted to turn back time and head straight to his pod, rather than running to the Q and unlocking that door. He wanted to run through the ship and scream, "I'm sorry!" at the top of his lungs.

I didn't know! I didn't mean it! Dom kept yelling inside his mind.

Then something floated to the top of his thoughts. It was a memory of Andrew scolding him during the first week of his OCP training in the galley. Dom had left a very sharp knife sitting blade up on the counter. He'd meant to put it away but got distracted and finished his shift without tending to it. Another trainee had ended up with a terrible gash that required seven stitches in his left hand. When Dom had tried to explain that it was a terrible accident and one he'd never repeat, Andrew had explained that the lack of intention was inconsequential. The harm was irreversible.

Tears now freely flowed as Dom took stock of this hard-learned lesson.

The remorse continued as he realized Fisher's confidence in him was probably shattered. Fisher hadn't said a word to Dom about the incident after he'd spoken with Lance, and Dom didn't have the nerve to bring it up. He knew that on some level Fisher blamed Dom for the accident, and at some point, he was going to need to address it with Fisher. He just couldn't bring himself to face him yet. He hoped that in time, Fisher could forgive him.

In the meantime, Dom would do anything he could to make up for his foolish mistake.

CHAPTER 59

Alec stood in front of the mirror wearing the headlamp he'd used days earlier. The light from the lamp reflected back at him, making it difficult to see. It was still a better option, however, than walking blindly in the dark locker room. He clicked the button on the side of the lamp twice, reducing the intensity and allowing him to relax his eyes.

It had been a while since Alec took a real look in the mirror. Over the past few days, he'd felt a change growing inside of him, and he was curious to see if the change was external as well. An older, stronger version of himself stared back.

So many years wasted, he thought.

Alec was enjoying his new freedom and from what he could tell, so were the others who had joined him. For years, he'd known something wasn't right with his life on the Arc, and now he could identify it. Alec smiled as he thought about his encounter with Fisher in the galley yesterday. How foolish were Fisher and the others for believing they were making a difference continuing with the ring deployments?

A new feeling emerged as Alec pictured Fisher standing there, pleading his case. This feeling surprised him, and he closed his eyes to get a true sense of what it was. *Could it be?* Yes, this would explain Alec's ability to humiliate Fisher in front of the rest of the crew. What he was feeling was disgust.

Fisher had always held this pathetic perspective that he kept trying to pawn off on Alec. How many times had Alec tried to enlighten Fisher about what he knew in his heart to be the truth? Sure, he may not have known just how deep the Uelara deception ran, but he had called it; life on the *Archean* was a setup, and the entire, *entire* second generation had all been duped. Alec's stomach turned when he imagined Fisher and his other cronies working in the foundry to launch the next ring.

Alec leaned closer to the mirror. His eyes looked tired. He'd had a full day, and it had been a while since he'd slept. He increased the intensity on the headlamp, turned away from the mirror, and walked toward the pods.

As he approached the wall of empty pods, he thought about Dom's betrayal, and it still left a sting. Alec had tried to talk some sense into him in the galley, but it was evident that Dom's brainwashed loyalty to the mission had blinded him.

This wasn't the first time Dom had betrayed Alec, but it was the most damaging. Alec recalled the heartbreak Dom had suffered when OCPs were assigned and how Dom had had to accept his food prep pathway, rather than the coveted outrigger position. Alec had tried to comfort Dom, and yet it was as though Dom blamed Alec for the disappointment. Alec had always wanted to work in the factory, and *bam!* he got to work in the factory. He knew Dom had had a tough time recovering from that.

The moment the OCPs were assigned, Dom had latched on to Lance. He had seized every opportunity to watch Lance's outrigger work, question Lance's knowledge, and gain Lance's respect. The closer he'd gotten to Lance, the further he'd strayed from Alec. It wasn't too tough for Alec to figure out the dynamics, but it still felt pretty lousy.

Then there was the concourse. Bromance aside, how could Dom *not* work with Alec to remove all those bodies? Didn't he need to hold on to the last bit of family that remained? Clearly, Alec had gotten his answer.

Alec recounted many other brush-offs, dismissals, and cold shoulders, but none of them evoked the level of torment that surfaced in that auditorium. Dom had known they were never making it to Uelara, and he hadn't told Alec. Nothing would ever change this. He had made one final appeal to Dom in the galley, to no avail. Alec was done.

Alec reached up and removed the nameplate above the pod and tucked it into the chest pocket of his coveralls. He removed a new plate from his lower pocket and held it in his left hand. Using his right index finger, he traced the indented grooves of the plate that made up his name: A-L-E-C.

In the past, he had liked his name. His mother had explained that the name Alec had belonged to her grandfather, and she'd wanted to pass it on to her firstborn. She had said that the name meant "defender of men; protector of mankind." Alec guessed that it was no accident or coincidence that his mom had chosen this kind of title for her first son, born on a ship whose mission was to save the world. Again, he thought, *What a joke.* From this point on, the only man he was going to save was himself.

Alec reached up and slid his nameplate into the grooves above the pod and took a step back to admire his work. *Perfect,* he thought as he smiled. He climbed into the pod, laid down, and rolled onto his back. He pulled the headlamp from his head and shut it off. Lying in a blanket of darkness, he let out a heavy sigh. He reached into his pocket and pulled out the old nameplate. Once again, Alec dragged his finger over the letters that scarred the smooth surface of the old plate: D-E-B-R-A. Alec wondered if her name carried any meaning. He slid Debra's nameplate back into his pocket and drifted off to sleep.

STAGE THREE

CHAPTER 60

The reclamation center was quiet today. Most of the crew had gone to help in the Hold with a backlog of deliveries that had piled up over the past few days. Only Echo and Finn remained in the Center. Echo stood at his workstation quickly separating the contents of a bin. Although there was no reason for him to race through the task, Echo tried to maintain his steady workflow.

Echo had felt inspired by Fisher's guiding words for continuing the mission. It was hard to imagine life on the Arc and not envision work as part of the daily routine. Echo heard that some people had ceased performing their OCP duties, and he couldn't understand why anyone would break the rules like that. Fisher instructed everyone that the best way to honor their parents' sacrifices was to carry on with the mission. And that's exactly what Echo intended to do.

The reclamation center felt different to Echo. This was the first day he had worked in the Center without McHail, and Echo was happy that Finn was there to keep him company.

"You doin' okay, Echo?"

Echo looked over at Finn, raised his hand and stuck up his thumb. "Yeah, I'm just about to wrap up this bin. There wasn't much to collect on my run this morning. I even took on some of the other's routes and still came up light."

"You're a good man, Echo. The Arc could use more like you." Finn smiled at Echo, and Echo returned the offering with a smile twice as large. Finn's smile quickly faded. "I'm not sure how I'm going to be able to do all of this."

"What do you mean? You've been handling most of McHail's responsibilities the past few months. You're more than ready to run the Center."

"It's not that I . . . I'm not worried about the added responsibilities of becoming the new director. McHail had been preparing me for that transition for the past year. It's the fact that . . . I'll be running the Center until I die."

The word "die" made Echo shudder a bit. "But I thought you liked working here."

"Oh, I don't mind working in the Center. I accepted my assignment here when it was given to me in the same way I would have accepted any position. With the promise of Uelara, I believed that any OCP was only a short-term work detail. But now . . . now I'll be working in the Center for what, another forty to sixty years? It's just too bleak a future to imagine."

Echo could tell that Finn was "persing." That was Dr. Ben's slang for perseverating. It took Echo a few sessions to fully grasp the word "perseverating," but Dr. Ben worked hard with Echo to help explain the concept. Echo was thankful now for the lesson because he had a feeling that Finn was going to be persing quite a bit today, and Echo was perfectly happy to be a sounding board.

Having the ship's psychologists for parents, Finn seemed to

always over examine every aspect of his life. Right now, Echo knew that Finn needed to talk it out. Perhaps using some of Dr. Ben's favorite phrases and expressions might be just what Finn needed to hear.

"Sounds like you're feeling angry. Want to talk about it?" asked Echo, encouraging Finn to continue.

"I wouldn't say I'm angry. I mean, I understand why my parents volunteered for such an empty life to pass on to a child. I can envision them pre-mission. The Earth was a dangerous planet, and the only future they had known included disease and uncertainty. Suddenly, a once-in-a-lifetime opportunity had presented itself to them, and they embraced it. Maybe they felt that, as dismal as life and death on a ship could be, it still topped either a life ridden with disease and pain or no life at all for their kids. I've come to terms with my parents' choice to board the *Archean*."

Echo didn't know what to say. Was life really dismal on the Arc?

"So I get it. What I'm having trouble grasping, though, is the deceit."

"Deceit?"

"Yeah. My parents were trained clinical psychologists. They must have understood the potential impact a lie as bold as this would have when it was revealed. I know that all the parents had apparently agreed to delay the truth until the second generation had children, but I can't stop one word from circling in my mind."

"Sacrifice?" guessed Echo.

"Cowardice. What a truly cowardly decision our parents made. Throughout my entire life, my father often touted, 'Always choose the hard right over the easy wrong.' I wonder what he'd say to that now!"

None of Dr. Ben's advice or interventions from the past were coming to Echo's mind, and Echo felt helpless. Finn had some very strong feelings, and Echo couldn't relate to any of them.

"Sorry for the rant. I'm sure you didn't need to hear all of that. How about after you finish that bin we go grab—?"

The room suddenly went dark. The lights hadn't dimmed; the whole room appeared to have lost power.

"What's going on?" gasped Echo.

"I think the room's offline."

Echo began to panic. "Is the room getting oxygen? Are we going to—?"

"Stay calm, Echo. The air is on a different system. I can still feel air coming from the vent above me."

"I can't see anything."

"Me neither. Try and find a light."

Echo felt around on the table for the headlamp he used the other day. His hand knocked into a small bin, scattering several brackets onto the floor.

"What was that? Are you okay?" asked Finn.

"I'm okay. I'm looking for my headlamp."

Echo continued to feel around his workstation. He tried to remember where he placed it but was drawing a blank.

"We're coming for you, Echoooo," moaned a voice.

"Who said that?" whimpered Echo.

"Who's there?" asked Finn.

Several moans came from just outside the door, followed by the sound of metal banging on metal. "We're the ghosts of the *Archean*," moaned several voices, "and we want you to join us!"

"Fa-Fa-Finn!" stuttered Echo.

"Whoever it is, this isn't funny! Turn the power back on now!" demanded Finn.

Echo dragged his hands across the desk behind him, and the elastic band of his headlamp snagged onto the middle and ring fingers of his left hand.

"But we like the dark!" the voices moaned.

Echo powered on the headlamp, and an intense beam of light streaked from it. He pointed the light across the room and could see Finn was using his hands to feel around for his own headlamp.

Finn raised his hand to shield his eyes from the light. "Good job, Echo. Shine the light on my workstation so I can find my headlamp as well."

Echo tilted the light down as Finn searched his workstation. "Got it!"

Finn activated his headlamp and charged toward the door, knocking into one of the desks on the way. Bins scattered in all directions, spraying the room with their contents. Echo reluctantly followed. As much as he didn't want to face the frightening ghosts, he also didn't want to be left alone in the Center.

They reached the door, pushed it open, and stepped outside. Laughter roared down the corridor to their left, and they could see several people running away.

"Come back here!" yelled Finn.

Turning back to the door, Echo saw a panel leaned up against the wall and an exposed junction box with several disconnected cables.

"Did you see this?" asked Echo, pointing at the cables.

One by one, Finn reconnected them, and a moment later, Echo could see the reclamation center light up.

"It's okay, Echo. They're gone."

"But what if they come back?"

"We'll be ready if they do."

"I'm scared, Finn."

"There's no reason to be scared. I won't let anything happen to you."

Echo wondered what would have happened if the ghosts had taunted him and Finn had been in the Hold with the rest of the crew rather than here in the Center. He shook off the thought and realized how relieved he felt knowing Finn was so protective.

Finn threw his arm around Echo's shoulder. "I'm a bit shaken by all of this, Echo. Want to join me for a walk? Let's go grab a snack."

CHAPTER 61

Avery sat alone in the factory with only the sounds of the machines to keep her company. She couldn't remember the last time she had worked as hard as she'd been working these past few days. Even with the assistance of the others, she couldn't seem to keep up with the backlog of parts that were needed. Thankfully, all the machines were back online and producing. Although everything needed for the ring deployment had now been completed, Avery still felt pressured to stay busy.

Everything currently being worked on appeared to be standard maintenance and repair parts. That also helped alleviate some of the anxiety plaguing Avery today, but the larger problem was that, without Alec, there weren't enough people to handle the finishing work on all the parts from now on.

"Wow, I don't think I've ever seen you working after dinner before."

Avery turned to see Grayson walking toward her. The bandages that had hidden much of Grayson's face were finally gone, and she could see that he was in good spirits. She noticed that his eyes looked darker than she remembered, and his hair was a bit longer. She didn't think she had ever seen him look this good before Lance's attack.

"Hey, Grayson! Yeah, trying to stay on top of all of this. You're looking better. How are you feeling?"

"Kaman is weaning me off my meds, so I should be able to return to the engine room soon. She and Fisher still want to follow the rules of not operating any of the equipment while medicated. No real complaints, to be honest. While I'm itching to help and do my part, I can't say I'm in a rush to go back in there."

"How have you been keeping busy?" asked Avery, sitting up straighter.

"I've been helping Sam with the Quints." He walked closer to Avery's bench.

"So, is that more or less challenging than the engine room?" she asked with a smile.

Grayson laughed. "Good question. Actually, it's been pretty easy. Of course, it was much easier before the Ghosts took over the Dome."

"Ghosts?" puzzled Avery.

"Oh, you haven't heard? Alec and his gang are calling themselves the *Ghosts* now," he explained, drawing quotation marks in the air.

"Are you serious?" Avery grimaced. "What has gotten into Alec?"

"No idea. He and a few of the others were in the Dome today and wouldn't let us use it. They said it was Ghost territory and started scaring the kids. I thought it was best to just leave."

"Did you tell Fisher?"

"Haven't seen him. He hasn't been in the Bay the last couple of days."

Avery was appalled. "It's bad enough that Alec isn't helping here in the factory, but tormenting the Quints? That's just cruel. Who else was with him?"

Grayson raised his hands in front of his chest and started counting on his fingers. "Kayla and Deuce from Lance's outrigger crew, Ron and Paul from the engine room, Bart from the Hold, and Vlad from the Center. I think that's all of them."

"I just don't get it."

"They're just angry, I would imagine. I'm not saying I agree with them, but I can kind of understand," he reasoned, running his fingers through his hair.

"What do you mean?"

"They're pissed. Think about it. Their parents are dead, and they recently discovered they'll never make it to Uelara. That's some pretty heavy shit to have dumped on you all at once."

"Oh, those poor, poor people," said Avery sarcastically. "Hello?! Did we not just get dumped on with the same heavy shit? But you don't see us running around, tormenting everyone."

"Easy there, kiddo. I'm just saying that everyone deals with this stuff in a different way."

Avery took a deep breath and rose from her bench. She walked over to Alec's station and looked at Grayson. His eyes were fixed on hers, and she was surprised to find herself calming down more quickly than she expected.

"I guess I see your point. I mean, I'm angry one minute, sad the next. Hell, I think I hit every emotion today within the span of two hours."

Grayson smiled. "So where are you now?"

"I'm teetering between apathy and anger at the moment."

"That could be a dangerous combination. What can I do to help?"

"I don't know. Aren't you angry, Grayson?"

"Like I said before, I think I've accepted it. All of it."

"I wasn't sure if that was the drugs talking the other day," she said with a smile.

"I believe every word I said. So, no. I'm not angry."

"I want to be angry," said Avery. "I want to be angry that our parents listened to us go on and on, day after day, about what our lives would be like on Uelara, knowing that it would never happen. I want the opportunity to yell at them for lying all those years. I want to hear them justify their actions. They owe us that much."

"Avery, you know that—"

"But I can't be angry with them. I can't be angry because they're dead. They're dead and I miss them. I miss them so much." Her eyes welled with tears.

"I know you do, Avery. We all do."

Grayson wrapped his arms around Avery and held her tight. She was grateful for the embrace and could feel her heart lift in a way she'd never imagined possible in the midst of such dismay. She felt something brush against her cheek and realized it was Grayson's hand. She looked up and saw that his face was inches from hers. His eyes had a new kindness, and his touch was gentle and soothing. He whispered something, but Avery was too lost in his touch to hear.

"I want to kiss you," he repeated.

Avery thought she responded, but no sound escaped.

Grayson's lips brushed against the corner of her mouth, and Avery's heart jumped. Electric waves danced through her body, and without thinking, she wrapped her arms around his neck. She pressed her lips against Grayson's, and for a long moment, everything—the factory, the accident, the mission—it all drifted away to a beautiful oblivion.

CHAPTER 62

Fisher stood in his hive and could see that almost everyone was asleep in their pods. Sam was staying with the Quints in the converted rec room, Lance was in the Q_2 and Alec . . . well, he had no idea where Alec was. Fisher understood that everyone was dealing with things in his or her own way, but he couldn't understand why Alec was shutting Fisher and the others out. He was also at a loss for how Alec could be so hateful toward Dom. Fisher hoped that in time, Alec would get whatever it was out of his system and return to his friends.

He shifted his thoughts to the mission. Fisher felt good about what he and the crew had been able to accomplish since the accident. Tomorrow they would be moving the finished geodetic ring to the rear airlock in preparation for its deployment, and it appeared that almost everyone else was finding a way to cope with their loss from the accident and the news of Uelara.

Fisher looked up at the nameplate above his pod, halfway hoping it had been vandalized. The nameplate sat in the grooves, glued and unscathed. All those years of fighting with Lance over a simple piece of plastic, and now Fisher would give anything to find it busted. He didn't feel equipped to deal with this new incarnation of Lance and longed for the old one to return.

Fisher climbed into his pod and initiated the white noise machine. His body ached from the long day, and it felt good to get off his feet. His eyes were heavy, and he could feel himself start to sink into the shadows of his pod.

A few hours later, Fisher jolted from his sleep, awakened by the wailing sounds of sirens. Startled, he crawled out and could see others emerging from their pods.

"What's going on?" shouted Dom over the screams of the alarm.

"No idea. We should go check and—"

Fisher went silent as the alarm stopped. Everyone stood outside their pods, dazed. Loud, uproarious laughter came from outside the hive entrance.

"It's the Ghosts," quavered Echo, as he slid a headlamp onto his head.

Fisher looked at Echo, confused. "Ghosts? What are you talking about?"

"Grayson told me . . ." Avery's voice trailed off as Alec and Kayla entered the room. They were each wearing white suits from the protein chambers, and their faces were crudely painted white. Fisher rubbed his eyes and attempted to make sense of the strange scene playing out before him.

"I see that all of the children are awake," rasped Alec.

Fisher stared at Alec with a hardened face. "What do you want, Alec? And what's with the—"

"It's not what I want," interrupted Alec.

"What are you talking about?"

Alec grinned. "The Ghosts of the ship are inviting all of you to play in a new game."

"We don't have time to—"

"Oh, but we created this game specifically for you. And I think you'll definitely be up for playing," said Alec, staring at Fisher. Alec then scanned the room, making eye contact with each member of the hive. "I think you'll all want to play this game."

"You look ridiculous. What's with the paint?" asked Avery.

"Alec, just leave us alone. It's bad enough that you aren't helping us. Do you really have to keep us from getting rest?" spat Dom.

"You're right, Dom. I really should let you get some sleep. You're all going to need it."

"Just leave us alone," asserted Zach, taking a few steps toward Alec and Kayla.

Alec looked at Zach and laughed. "Come on, Kayla, the children need their sleep if they're going to be ready to play in the morning."

"We're not playing your stupid game!" shouted Dom.

Alec smirked. "We'll see about that." He exited the hive before anyone could protest. "Nighty-night."

Everyone listened to Alec and Kayla's laughter as it faded down the corridor.

Fisher looked down and saw that both of his hands were clenched, and he realized that his entire body was tense. His tolerance for Alec's rebellion was diminishing.

"I'm scared," whimpered Echo.

Avery slid a comforting arm around Echo and pulled him close. "There's no reason to be afraid. Alec and the others are just acting out."

"Avery's right, Echo. Don't worry," confirmed Grayson.

Fisher was baffled that Alec had chosen this route, but he knew that his friends needed to be reassured that they could continue with the immediate plans for the mission.

"Listen up. I don't know why Alec and the others are doing any of this, but don't let them get to you. Just stay focused on the mission and let them do whatever they want. We can't let them distract us. They're harmless. They just want to get a rise out of us," advised Fisher.

Avery cleared her throat and took a step forward. "It's not just this, you know. Grayson said they have been hogging the Dome. They even scared the Quints."

"When was this?" asked Fisher.

"Today," replied Grayson. "I was going to tell you tomorrow if you were in the Bay."

"I think they may have stolen all the VR headsets from the Tank this week, too" added Zach. "They all went missing, and we haven't been able to find them."

"They shut the power off in the reclamation center earlier today," added Echo in a soft voice.

"They obviously took the suits from the Chamber. Do you know how long we have to wait for new ones to be made?" said Dom, furrowing his brow. "And did you forget what they did to the galley? I swear, Alec seems happier than he's ever been. How messed up is that?"

"Look, I get it. They're out of control," agreed Fisher. "Let's just get the ring deployed. We are so close now and will have plenty of time to sort through the rest of this mess soon enough."

Avery shrugged. "Maybe they'll get bored and—"

Dom interrupted Avery. "And if they don't get bored?"

"Yeah. They appear to be getting worse. Did you see their faces? What was with the paint?" added Zach.

Fisher raised his hand, motioning to silence the group. "We're giving them exactly what they want right now—attention. They just want attention. Do your best to work around their nonsense, and I promise, I'll talk with Alec soon. Right now, I think we should get some rest. You've all been working really hard, and I just want you to know I appreciate it. Your parents would be proud of what you are doing."

"Thanks, Fish," said Avery.

"Yeah, thanks, Fish," added Echo.

"See you guys at breakfast?" asked Dom as he crawled into his pod.

"Yeah," nodded Zach.

Fisher entered his pod and collapsed on his back. He fell into a deep sleep quickly, but it was far from a restful slumber. His dreams were filled with dried-out beaches and floating white faces.

CHAPTER 63

Echo could not have named a single item he placed on his food tray. His mind was so preoccupied that his hand grabbed the nearest food choices and just dropped them onto his tray. He was still rattled by the Ghosts' visit last night. Echo couldn't believe how much life on the Arc had changed in such a short time.

It was as if one minute Echo were playing Ghosts in the Graveyard, and the next minute he was afraid all the oxygen was going to be sucked out of the room. He heard some of his friends vent angrily about things like "deception" and "betrayal" and "purpose," and yet all Echo felt was sadness. He missed his mom and dad. And the worst part was that any time he went through something stressful, his parents had been the ones who could coax him into finding a happier perspective.

His dad, Andrew, had had this incredible ability to sense the minute Echo was feeling the least bit "off." Echo recollected the time when his dad had walked him down to the galley in the middle of the night. Echo had been feeling rejected because he hadn't been included in a little Dome party thrown by a group from his hive. His dad had created this special meal for just the two of them in the galley while weaving this huge, hilarious tale about Echo's mom rejecting his dad five times before she'd succumbed to his insistent attempts to impress her.

Echo knew he would have to find a new way to cope with his overwhelming sadness. Staying busy was the only means of distraction he could entertain. Hopefully the other departments would allow him to assist them. Maybe through the extra work, Echo could find some peace of mind.

"Finn told me I can assist one of the other departments if you guys need help today," said Echo, placing his tray on the table in the galley.

"Not much for you to do in the foundry or the Tank," said Fisher, scooping the last bits of scrambled protein into his spoon. "You need any help over in the Chamber, Dom?"

"Nah. Unless Echo can help us figure out what we're going to do with all the excess protein we're going to have for the next couple months."

"I could use you in the factory," mumbled Avery with a mouth full of food.

Zach laughed. "Chew much?"

"Sounds fun!" said Echo.

"Sam coming this morning?" asked Grayson.

"She said she'd be coming later with the Quints," said Fisher.

"We should probably offer to relieve her of Quint duty sometime today," suggested Avery. "You're all caught up in the foundry, right, Fish?"

"Some of us are going to be moving the ring to the airlock today. How about you, Zach?" asked Fisher.

"What? Are you suggesting I babysit the Quints?" scoffed Zach.

"Why not? I'm sure Sam would—"

"I've got plenty to keep me busy. Plus, I wouldn't even know where to begin with those five. It's like trying to patch a hull breach, and when you finally get it sealed, four more pop up!" said Zach.

"You're so dramatic," sighed Avery, rolling her eyes. "Not to spoil the mood, but have any of you seen the Ghosts today?"

"Can you not call them that, please?" begged Dom. "It's only going to encourage Alec and the others."

"Dom's right. The last thing we need to do is feed into Alec and his band of buffoons," agreed Zach.

"To answer your question, I haven't seen any of them in the commissary this morning," said Dom.

"Good. Let's hope they just hang out in the Dome or somewhere far away from all of us," said Grayson. "Anyway, I'll see if Sam needs some help with the Quints."

"Thanks," said Fisher, rising to his feet. "Thanks for the grub, Dom. I'm off to go—"

The lights in the room dimmed, as small amber lights started to flash on the ceiling.

"You gotta be kidding me!" seethed Fisher. "What now?"

"It's the Ghosts," quavered Echo.

"Will you stop calling them that?" insisted Dom.

"Guys, I don't think this is the Ghosts," announced Grayson. Dom let out a disgusted grunt.

Fisher looked at Grayson. "What do you—?"

Grayson interrupted, "When was the last time someone surveyed the engine room?"

CHAPTER 64

All eyes were on Grayson as they raced into the engine room. He looked along the east and west walls of the facility and surveyed the power cell compartments. In the far-right corner of the west wall, he could see three of the power banks were not lit up and were no longer being powered, causing their associated pistons to sit stationary.

"See anything, Grayson?" asked Fisher.

Grayson stood dormant, fixated on the inactive pistons. He'd worked in the engine room for a few years and had never seen a single piston at a standstill.

Dom shoved Grayson. "Grayson!"

Grayson took a step forward to maintain his balance, but his eyes remained focused on the pistons. "Give me a minute!"

"Do we have a minute?" argued Zach.

Grayson ran over to a terminal in the center of the room and began swiping through a series of menus. He pulled up the resource monitor and received confirmation for what he'd suspected. Three of the power banks were offline and running on the reserve power clusters. The remaining west power banks were compensating for these inactive units, causing their power to drain rapidly.

He pulled up the reserve diagnostics and could see that the reserves had dropped to unsafe levels. He knew that if the reserves ran out, it could cause system failures throughout the ship. Grayson recalled Thomas explaining that the reserves were only intended to be used while the drained cells were being swapped for fresh ones. From what he could ascertain, this set of clusters had been running for more than a few hours. He couldn't believe that Ron and Paul had let it get to this point while he was away.

"Fish, Avery, Dom, Echo!" Grayson called out. "Get suited up. I'm going to need you to replace the spent power cells in those compartments." He pointed at the back wall.

"What can I do?" asked Zach.

Grayson pointed to a collection of power cells docked in their charging stations.

"Go check the readings on those live cells over there, and let me know what they read."

Zach ran toward the power cells. "Got it!"

The engine room came alive with activity as the team frantically worked to restore power under Grayson's direction. It felt like only yesterday that Grayson had been finding ways to cut corners and avoid work altogether. Now he stood in the center of the engine room, orchestrating a team.

"Fish, pull that cell out of compartment twelve and drop it in the cooling bath. Lower your face shield and be careful of the backsplash," instructed Grayson, pointing toward the opened hatch.

"I'm on it," affirmed Fisher.

Grayson strapped the swing arm around a power cell, called out to Dom and pointed. "Dom, fire up that deployment lift. This cell is ready to be loaded."

Dom ran to the lift and powered it on.

Grayson looked over to the power cell. "Zach, is that power cell charged?"

"Almost, it's at ninety-two percent."

"Good enough. Seal it up and let's get it over to compartment fourteen."

"What's the code to raise the lift?" called out Avery, standing in front of compartment seventeen with her hand over the lift's keypad.

"Seven eight nine!" shouted Grayson.

"Thanks!"

"Fish, wheel that bath off to the side there. I'll break it down tomorrow when I return," said Grayson, pointing at his workstation.

"No problem."

Grayson returned to the terminal. As he did, he heard footsteps approaching. He turned toward the entrance to the room and saw Narine and Ashin sprinting in with panicked expressions.

"Everything okay here?" asked Narine.

"We're wrapping things up. Should be all set in a few minutes," replied Grayson.

"Ashin and I just left operations once we determined the problem was coming from the engine room. Do you know what caused the power drain?"

"How could they let it get this bad? The engine room has been unattended for days. We're lucky the alarms warned us before we experienced fatal system shutdowns," explained Grayson.

"Compartment fourteen is loaded and back online!" yelled Zach.

"Same with seventeen!" added Avery.

"How are we looking, Grayson?" asked Fisher.

"Readings look good. I think we're in the clear. Great job, everyone!"

"Excellent work, Grayson. You really saved the day," said Fisher.

"We *all* did it," corrected Grayson.

"So, what do we need to do to prevent this from happening again?" asked Narine.

"It's really not that difficult," answered Grayson. "We just need to continue monitoring the cells and swapping them out when they get low. If Fisher and Kaman can clear me for work, I can stay on top of this. I'll also need some assistance if Ron and Paul continue with their little Ghost escapades and dodge their duties."

"If you can get me up to speed, I can help," offered Ashin. "I can split my time between here and the Hold until we have more options."

"I appreciate the offer and will definitely take you up on it," said Grayson.

"If Finn is okay with it, I can help as well," added Echo.

"Sounds like we have a temporary solution. Thanks, everyone," said Fisher.

"Fish, are you free to head to the foundry and package the ring for transport?" asked Narine.

"Grayson, we good to go?" asked Fisher.

"Sure. I'm going to stick around and do a second pass on all the units. If anything major arises, I'll buzz you," replied Grayson. "Thanks again, everyone."

"You were amazing, Grayson," bubbled Avery. "It was great seeing you take charge."

Grayson tucked a strand of Avery's hair behind her left ear and smiled.

As everyone started to leave, Grayson stood and surveyed the room. He felt proud of what he and the group had accomplished. He thought of what Thomas would have said if he were still alive. Thomas had always talked about pride in ownership, about being accountable and trusted to do the right thing, even when no one was watching. For the first time, Grayson truly felt like he understood what Thomas had been talking about all those years.

CHAPTER 65

Fisher was excited to join Narine in packaging up the latest geodetic ring. They had been working toward the deployment for several months, and now it was merely days away. The relocation of the ring to the airlock marked a significant step in the long process. With the recent tragedies that had crushed everyone's spirits, Fisher was excited to have an uplifting event for a change.

"I can't express how impressed I am that you guys turned the engine room crisis around so quickly!" exclaimed Narine as she and Fisher walked toward the foundry.

"Grayson is the one to thank. He really came through for all of us today. I'm not sure what we would have done without him," he said.

"It'll be nice once the ring is deployed and we can have a day or two without some form of calamity sideswiping us."

"I hear ya!" agreed Fisher. "I think the universe should pick on someone else for a while. If Alec and his Ghosts can just stay out of the way for a few more days, we should be in good shape."

"What's with this whole Ghosts thing, anyway?" asked Narine. "Bart and Vlad woke up my hive last night wearing the protein chamber suits and had white paint all over their faces.

And I heard this morning they've been causing trouble all over the ship."

Fisher shook his head. "I don't know what's gotten into Alec and the others, but they aren't making things any easier for us right now."

Narine slowed her pace and looked at Fisher. "You know, most of us weren't really that surprised when we found out Alec was the ringleader of the group."

"Really? How well do you know Alec? This is so unlike him."

"Well, it's not so much that it was Alec as much as it was someone from your hive. You guys have a bit of a reputation. I mean, come on. You guys are still playing Graveyard, which obviously has inspired this whole Ghost theme, and don't get me started on the drama that flows out of your hive."

"Have you been talking with Kaman?"

"No, why?"

"No reason."

"Sorry if this is a touchy topic for you, but most of us thought that at some point your hive would get their shit together."

"What are you talking about?"

"You guys are a collective mess on so many levels."

Fisher had never considered that the other hives would spend so much time talking about his friends. He wasn't sure he liked it.

"Ouch. Are we really that bad?"

"Let's see. You have Lance, the loose cannon. Alec . . . do I need to go into detail about Alec at this point? And let's not forget Echo. I mean—"

Fisher had heard enough. "Now you're just being mean. Yes, some of the members of our hive have extreme personalities, but Echo is a good guy. He's loyal and a hard worker. I'm not going to stand by while you—"

"No, you're right. I'm sorry."

"Remind me again which members of the hive discovered the fact that we won't be making it to Uelara? And which hive prevented irreparable damage to the Arc this morning?" snapped Fisher.

"Fish, I said—"

"And my hive doesn't have to own the actions of Alec and his lackeys. Everyone is dealing with the accident in different ways. Can you really fault them for their behavior right now?"

Narine looked straight ahead as they continued walking and said nothing for almost a full minute. "It was unfair of me to say those things. I'm sorry."

It was Fisher's turn with the silent walking now. After a few minutes he said, "Sorry for snapping at you. I'm just under a lot of pressure with the ring deployment and—"

"No apology needed. And not everything is your responsibility. Let's just get through this deployment and see where we are when the dust settles."

"Agreed. Plus, don't worry about Alec and the others. They're harmless. Sure, they are being annoying, but they're just looking for attention."

Narine and Fisher entered the foundry, ready to package up and transport the ring. After taking a few steps, they stopped and stared. In the corner were empty straps and anchor points. The ring was gone.

Looking at Fisher, Narine whispered, "I think they have our attention now."

CHAPTER 66

Sam watched as her five brothers scurried around the oxygen farm in search of the missing ring. Although she hadn't visited this area in ages, Sam imagined it was one of the few rooms in the Arc that could possibly house the hidden ring.

The enormous room was lit by recessed lights in both the floor and ceiling. A series of cables, pipes and hoses snaked in all directions and reminded Sam of the magnolia tree branches. A spiral staircase led to a catwalk that ran along the walls of the room high above, giving the engineers access to the upper portions of the oxygen tanks. A collection of rechargeable nitrogen canisters was plugged into the ship's air supply network between the oxygen tanks along the walls, but the rest of the Farm was large and spacious.

Within minutes of entering the cavernous room, Sam could see that the ring wasn't there. She knew she would be able to cover more ground if the Quints were not involved with the search, but she believed it was important for them to participate.

Sam wanted her brothers to experience working with the rest of the crew toward a common goal, even if their efforts were preventing her ability to aid her friends. Sam had always done her part to help her parents with the Quints, but now that her responsibility for them shifted to full time, she was overwhelmed.

Even with the aid of her friends, she struggled with the thought of raising them over the coming years.

Sam watched as her brothers put forth their very best five-year-old efforts to search for the ring. Their search locations were comical, but Sam was just grateful that the boys had a distraction from their recent loss. She also enjoyed a brief respite from her pain listening to the Quints' string of innocent banter.

Sam called out, "See anything, guys?"

"Nothin' over here."

"I think I . . . oh, never mind!"

"Is this it?"

"No, that's a square, dummy. We're looking for a circle!"

"What about this?"

"No, silly, that's a center-future compressor just like before."

"Centrifugal."

"That's what I said!"

Sam wished she could enjoy this entertainment all day, but they didn't have that kind of time.

"Ten more minutes, guys. Then we move on to a new location."

"Any luck in here?"

Sam looked up to see Fisher standing on the catwalk above her. "Nothing so far. How are you and the rest faring?"

Fisher descended the stairs toward Sam. "We're all coming up empty-handed. It just doesn't make sense. It's not like there are a lot of places they could have stashed it."

"Have you checked the cargo hold?" asked Sam as she surveyed the room to check on the Quints.

"Ashin and Toby have been down there, and a few of us will be joining them soon. To be honest, I've kinda been avoiding it."

"I don't blame you! It's freezing down there, but it makes sense that it could be in the Hold."

"Yeah. Lots of open spaces."

Sam shrugged. "I think we're going to head to the upper observation decks. Not an ideal place to hide a ring, but it will be easier to manage these guys there."

"Hello, Fisher."

Fisher turned around to see Sean standing right in front of him. "Hu . . . Hi Sean," Fisher stuttered.

"Will you be joining us in our search for the geodetic ring?"

"Uh . . . actually, I'm just about to head down to the Hold to help some of the others look there."

"You know I can help you find the ring, right?"

Fisher looked at Sam, who was busy watching her other brothers. He looked back at Sean and said, "Do you know where the ring is right now, Sean?"

"Nope. But I can help you look. Want me to go to the Hold with you?"

Fisher laughed. "Sean, it's way too cold for you down there! But thanks for offering. Stay warm with your brothers and just help your sister, okay?"

"Okay."

"Sean, can you go round up the others for me? We should go look in some other places on the ship," said Sam.

"Okay. Bye, Fisher."

Sean looked up at Fisher, smiled and then walked away.

"What's with that kid?" whispered Fisher.

"What do you mean?" asked Sam, watching Sean walking toward his brothers.

"He doesn't creep you out?"

Sam turned to face Fisher. *Look at that poor, stressed-out face,* she thought. With all the recent chaos, she had forgotten about this little crisis Fisher was dealing with. Sam kept pressing.

"What?" she asked innocently. "Of course not. What are you talking about?"

Fisher looked bewildered. "Why is he always staring at me with that creepy smile? It's like he's judging me or something. And he just . . . knows stuff. When I was teaching your brothers the history of the mission, the other four were goofy and silly and acting like, well, like five-year-olds. Sean was like this forty-year-old man in a kid's body, I swear!"

Sam smiled. How long was it possible to prolong his confusion for her own amusement? A giggle was brewing inside Sam's stomach that was quickly morphing into the heartiest roar of her life. She tried to stifle it as long as possible.

"Wow," said Sam, covering her mouth. "Do you think the experiment went too far?"

"Ex . . . exper . . . iment?" whispered Fisher.

"You know, the one Dr. Gage—" Sam was weaker than she thought, and her smothered laughter erupted as she sat down on the bottom of the stairs and wiped tears from her eyes.

"What the hell? Sam, I'm serious here!"

"I know! That's why it's so funny!"

"Uh, a little clarification, please?" he asked.

"Man, I got you good this time!"

Fisher looked confused. "Got me? What are you talking about?"

"Fish, I put Sean up to this! I told him it would be fun if anytime he saw you, he pretended he was an alien. I thought you would have seen through it weeks ago! I coached him for days, helping him memorize that mission speech. And did he love it!

Honestly, I didn't expect him to have such a blast, but he just loved staring you down."

Fisher rubbed his eyes, and Sam thought she spied a slight blush rise in his cheeks.

"W-w-wait," Fisher stammered, "so you're telling me all the staring, all the freaky robot talk, that was all . . . you?"

Sam's smile grew wide. "One of my best pranks, thank you very much."

Fisher sat down next to Sam as her laugh continued. He asked, "But what about the whole door comment?"

"Door comment?"

"Ships don't close doors, people do?"

"Oh, that one was completely random! Perfect timing, though."

Sam threw her arm around Fisher's side and gave him a light squeeze. She was so grateful for the lighthearted moment. Never did she think that in the middle of all the heartbreak and trauma of the week that she would be capable of a belly laugh, even if it were at Fisher's expense.

"You know, I want to be mad at you right now. But as usual, that was brilliant," Fisher said with a smile. He stood up and stretched. "I should head down to the Hold."

"Yeah. I'll gather up the boys and head to the upper decks. Best of luck, Fish."

"Thanks. I'm getting nervous. We need that ring soon if we're going to deploy it on time."

"Have you thought about trying to convince Alec to simply tell you where it is?"

"That's my fallback plan. Not excited about that conversation. Would love to avoid it if possible."

"That's understandable."

Sam envisioned Alec all painted up running through the darkened ship. She asked, "Do you think we'll ever see the old Alec again?"

"I'm not sure it's possible to return to the way things were . . . for any of us. The accident, Helena, the news about Uelara . . . I think it's changed us all."

Hearing Helena's name was still painful for Sam. Fisher was right; their lives were forever changed. "I hope Alec finds his way back through all of this," she said.

"So do I."

"Well, in the meantime, I'm going to activate Sean's mind-control mechanism to locate the ring. I'll give you a status report ASAP."

"I'm never going to hear the end of this, am I?"

CHAPTER 67

Fisher stood at the entrance to the concourse attempting to collect his thoughts. This was the last place he wanted to be, but he had run out of alternatives. He and the crew had spent the past twelve hours searching every square inch of the Arc and hadn't come up with a single trace of the missing ring. His bones still ached from the three hours spent in the Hold, and he felt defeated. When they began the search, he was convinced the crew would find it within an hour. After all, there were only so many places you could hide a giant, four-meter ring.

What made the search even more intolerable was the fact that Alec and his Ghosts had spent the entire time taunting the rest of the crew while they searched. Fisher found himself with no other option but to try and reason with Alec. This was something Fisher wasn't feeling very optimistic about, but he knew he was running out of time. He took in a deep breath and began walking through the concourse toward the hive where he could hear Alec and the others laughing.

Fisher was expecting to find the same surroundings he had experienced when they'd removed their parents' bodies. As he surveyed the hive, he was surprised to find more cozy accommodations. Rather than complete darkness, the room was dimly lit.

The Ghosts had dragged two power generators and a lighting rig up to the hive and were apparently feeling quite comfortable. Fisher noticed various items the rest of the crew was claiming to be missing scattered around the floor. He saw VR headsets, protein chamber suits, headlamps, and even food that had been taken from the galley. Alec was standing in the center of a circle of seated, painted Ghosts and appeared to be impersonating some of Fisher's friends hopelessly searching for the ring.

Fisher had an uneasy feeling being back in the first generation hives after the accident. A coldness spread over his body that sent shivers down his arms and legs. As Fisher entered the hive, everyone's gaze focused upon him.

"Well, well. If it isn't Fish, the treasure hunter himself," rasped Alec. "So, I take it you and your pathetic group of mission fanatics have come up empty-handed."

"Alec was right. You guys really do suck at this game. I mean. How hard could it possibly be to find a giant piece of junk on this ship?" prattled Kayla as she tore the other sleeve off the chamber suit she was wearing, creating a symmetrical look.

Fisher could barely recognize the Ghost's leader who had once been his close friend. What stood before Fisher was someone transformed into a malicious person who took great pleasure in watching him squirm. Fisher was enraged.

"Enough!" seethed Fisher, trying to bite back his anger. "You win. We give up."

"So soon," grinned Alec, cocking his head to the side. "I have to say I'm quite disappointed in you, Fish. I thought you were better than this."

"Just tell me where it is, Alec. We're running out of time."

"Time? All we have is time. What's your rush?"

"You know that's not true. If we don't release—"

"Then what? You're fantasy mission will fail? I've already explained to you that your mission is bullshit. Why can't you accept it? You know what? Let's pretend for a minute that the mission can be successful. They don't deserve it."

"Who?"

"People. Humanity. They had their chance, and they blew it. Everything they ever needed on a beautiful, perfect planet, and they pissed it all away. Oh, if they only had a warning! Wait, they *did* have a warning—years and years of warnings. But did they listen? Nope. Why change your behaviors and make sure your kids can actually remain on the same planet as you? Hey, here's a great idea! Let's pile everyone into spaceships, sail across the stars, and take over another planet. How long can we consume Uelara before we deplete the shit out of it? The human race is nothing but one giant virus. Selfish, all of them. Damn, selfish behaviors. They don't deserve a second chance."

"You're preaching about selfishness? I can't think of anything more selfish than refusing to continue this mission!" Fisher was dumbfounded that Alec believed his own argument.

"Like I said, this mission is a giant waste of time."

"If the mission is a waste of time, then why stop us? Why is it so important to you how we choose to spend our time? If you want to sit out the mission, fine. But why stop us?"

"I'm not stopping you," said Alec. "Find the ring, and release it. I won't stand in your way."

"By hiding the ring from us you are preventing us from—"

"Fish, Fish. We aren't preventing you from anything. Your lack of creativity is blinding you from the obvious location of the ring. Why don't you come spend the day with us tomorrow in the Dome? I fear that you are working yourself too hard."

"Just tell me what you want, Alec."

Alec laughed. "What *we* want?" Kayla and the others joined in with laughter as Alec continued, "We have everything we need. You're the one who wants something."

"Just tell me what I need to do, and I'll do it."

Alec slowly stepped outside of his doting circle, moved closer to Fisher, and said, "I can see you're not going to drop this."

Alec tapped his fingers together and looked around the room slowly. Fisher felt his fists tighten, and he had to consciously relax them.

"We're reasonable," Alec said slowly. "I'll give you until tomorrow morning to come up with a fair trade. If you come up with something good, we'll give up the location of the ring. If not, well . . . I think you know what that means."

Fisher's mouth went dry and his mind raced. He realized he had no other options. "Fine. We meet tomorrow morning and trade," yielded Fisher.

"If . . . we like what you're offering, sure. Where are we meeting?"

Fisher had to think quickly. "We can meet in the Dome."

"Nice. Can't wait. Now run along, little Fish. You have your work cut out for you."

As Fisher turned his back on his former friend, he felt like he was summoning every ounce of strength and willpower to continue walking out the door and not turn on his heels, charge at Alec, and smash him into a million tiny ghost pieces.

Who the hell did Alec think he was? How dare he reduce a decades-long mission into a casual challenge? In the distance he could hear Alec and the others break into laughter. Every audible sound from the Ghosts slashed at Fisher like a knife in his back.

He searched for some inspiration that would placate Alec and persuade him to unveil the location of the ring. Fisher slowed his hurried pace, and a warm feeling of excitement began to bubble inside him, spreading throughout his body. A wry smile crept across his face as Fisher came to a halt in the corridor. Little did he know, Alec had just given Fisher a brilliant idea.

CHAPTER 68

"I need you guys to just trust me on this," said Fisher as he stood in front of the west observation deck window while the others sat on the benches and listened. He had just given them a rundown of his conversation with Alec and explained that he had come up with a way to get Alec and the Ghosts to reveal the location of the ring. He went on to explain that his plan could only involve two others.

"So, we need to trust you, but you don't trust us?" argued Ashin, rising from the bench.

"I didn't say that," defended Fisher.

"You might as well have," retorted Narine, standing to join Ashin.

"So why just you, Zach, and Kaman?" asked Grayson.

"Yeah, why them?" added Echo.

Fisher took a step closer to the crew.

"I understand how this all sounds. Really, I do. But if this plan is going to work, the fewer people that have to be involved, the better."

"And this plan of yours . . . you think Alec is going to give up the location of the ring?" asked Avery.

"Yes. I feel extremely confident this will work, but only if everyone follows my directions."

"And if it doesn't work?" interjected Ashin.

"I know you're tired of hearing me say it, but trust me. This will work."

"I trust you, Fish!" said Dom. "Just let me know how I can help."

"Thanks, Dom. I need you to get with Avery, collect some food, and deliver it to the Dome before tomorrow morning. I need Zach and Kaman to come with me, so we can prepare for the meeting."

"What about the rest of us?" asked Narine.

"If everyone else can continue looking for the ring, it will—"

Ashin let out a sigh. "But we've—"

"I know we've looked everywhere," interrupted Fisher. "But the ring is somewhere on this ship. We are just overlooking something. I'd rather avoid what I have planned, if possible. If we find the ring before tomorrow morning, then the plan can be aborted."

"I'd feel a whole lot more comfortable with all of this if I knew what you were going to do," Narine said as she sat down.

"I'm sorry. I really am. But I promise you will understand when it's all over," said Fisher. "I need all of you to avoid the Dome tomorrow morning. I don't know how messy it's going to get down there, and I don't want any of you getting hurt."

Fisher knew his plan was risky. He didn't love the idea of putting Alec through this. If someone had told him a month ago that he would be plotting something so damaging and sinister, he would have laughed. But Alec had boxed him into a corner. Too much was at stake. The mission had come too far to throw it away without utilizing every last effort. The very survival of humankind was riding on this.

"I hope you know what you're doing," said Zach.

So do I, thought Fisher, looking at his friends. *So do I.*

CHAPTER 69

Zach nervously sat on the edge of a table he and Fisher had placed in the center of the Dome. Zach had been anxious this morning and had skipped breakfast, something he was regretting now. He looked over his shoulder and surveyed the crates of food that Dom and Avery had delivered the night before and wondered if he had time to grab something to eat before Alec and the others arrived.

Zach started to question the plan. The longer he waited, the more his concerns grew. What if something went wrong? What if all the Ghosts didn't show up? Zach jumped to his feet as the door to the Dome opened. His pulse quickened as Alec and his gang of Ghosts entered the room, spreading out around the circumference of the Dome.

"We're either early or your fearless leader is backing out of our agreement," snorted Alec.

"Maybe he got scared and decided not to show," jested Kayla.

"He's on his way," said Zach, interlacing his fingers and squeezing them together.

Alec grinned as he closed the door behind him. "Good, good. Looks like you'll just have to keep us company until he arrives."

Zach started to sweat. He hadn't really thought about how he'd be stuck in a room by himself with all the Ghosts. He sat back down on the edge of the table, trying to look relaxed.

"Why are you guys doing this?"

Alec looked around the room at the Ghosts and laughed. "Doing what? Living our lives?"

"You know what I mean!"

"Simple, simple Zachary. Fish still has you guys believing you're going to all be heroes. That you'll save humanity from their demise. You're no different than the rest of the fools trying to carry on with the Arc's hopeless mission. You're no hero. You're just a replacement part."

"Replacement part?"

"Well, that is what you are, am I right? You're no different than the parts grown in the factory. And once you're used up, you'll be replaced by your offspring and forgotten."

"Don't you care that you'll be killing billions of people on the Earth by not—?"

"There you go again, regurgitating the fairytale you've been told your whole life. Can't you see through those lies? Can't you see that you have a chance to be free from—"

Zach stood up curling his hands into fists. "You've lost it, Alec. You and your pathetic Ghosts."

The Dome erupted with laughter. Alec turned his back to Zach to address the Ghosts.

"Did you hear that? Zach thinks we're the ones who are pathetic." Alec turned and pointed at Zach, his smile quickly vanishing and his eyes narrowing. "Let me make something perfectly clear to you," Alec snarled. "It's you and your crew who are the pathetic ones. All of you, chasing after your parents' fallacy that the human race can be saved. If you need a reminder of how well that worked out for your parents, I'd be happy to escort you down to the Hold and show you."

Zach felt like Alec had just thrown a right hook directly into his gut. He had never had such a physical reaction to spoken words. Each interaction with Alec was more baffling than the last. Had Alec not lost his parents as well? Was he somehow immune to the grief Zach and the rest of his friends were experiencing? How could Alec be so callous, so indifferent, to the loss? Zach was so livid that all the clever responses he had thought of during his walk to the Dome escaped his mind. He just stood there, dumbfounded.

"No comeback? Just as I thought. Now, where is your cowardly leader? I don't want to spend all day attempting to educate you," scoffed Alec.

Zach opened his mouth to speak but was interrupted by Fisher's voice coming over the Dome's intercom system. "Alec, are you there?"

"Everyone's here but you. What's the hold up?" said Alec, looking up at the speaker in the ceiling.

"Just wrapping things up. Zach, can you come help me with the case?"

"Oh, a case. This sounds promising," chortled Alec.

"On my way." Zach glared daggers at Alec as he walked past him and exited the Dome.

"Don't leave us waiting too long, now!" yelled Alec. "You know how we Ghosts don't like waiting!"

Moments later, Zach reentered the room carrying a small silver case. He placed it gently on the table in the center of the room, turned to Alec, and smiled. Everyone's eyes were on the case. Zach started leaving the Dome as Alec and the Ghosts approached the table.

"What do you think it is?" asked Bart.

"Think it's something we want, Alec?" asked Kayla.

"It better be," added Paul.

Zach peered into the Dome past the edge of the door. As Alec reached for the case, the others crept closer to the table. Zach couldn't believe the plan was working. He smiled as he quietly closed the door to the Dome.

CHAPTER 70

Alec was having the time of his life. He and the Ghosts had the others right where they wanted them, and he knew that nothing Fisher offered would persuade them to give up the ring's location.

Alec thought he had made it perfectly clear that the human race didn't deserve a second chance. Did Fisher actually believe anything in this case could convince him otherwise? He couldn't wait to see the looks on their faces when he rejected the trade. He wondered just how long he could lead them on.

Alec popped the final latch on the case and looked toward Kayla. "Any guess what it could be?"

"No idea. Just open it already!" Kayla grinned with anticipation.

The case let out a breath as Alec raised the lid, and it separated from the base. Everyone leaned in closer for a better look at what treasure they would find inside. Alec's eyes widened as he looked inside.

"Empty? Are you serious?" scoffed Kayla.

"Wait. There's nothing inside?" added Vlad.

Alec winced. He looked at Ron. "Go check the door."

Ron ran to the door and attempted to open it. "Locked."

Alec looked up to the ceiling of the Dome and smiled. "You

think locking us in here is going to get you any closer to your precious ring, Fish?"

"What if they cut the oxygen to the room?" stammered Ron.

Alec looked around the room and sneered. "Let them try. This room can't be sealed off. They'd have to cut the air to the entire section of the ship."

"Alec's right," Kayla confirmed.

Alec was losing more respect for Fisher by the minute. It was strange how effortless controlling him could be. Was Fisher really so devoid of creativity, of resourcefulness, as to believe Alec could be duped by an empty container or a locked door? Fisher was about to discover what a strong, independent thinker really looked like.

"You're only postponing the inevitable, Fish. And to think, I was ready to make a trade with you."

"I think you will still be making that trade," replied Fisher over the Dome's speaker.

"Is this your big plan, Fish? Lock us up until we get hungry or need to take a leak?"

"Not my style, Alec. I've ensured that you have plenty to eat. Have a look in the crates next to the table. They're loaded with enough food for all of you. And if you feel the need to relieve yourselves, I've left a couple of empty storage containers under the table for you and your Ghosts."

"What's with the empty case?" snapped Alec, swatting at the case and knocking it to the floor.

"Empty? Oh, that case wasn't empty," said Fisher in a calm, even tone.

"Then your boy Zach brought us the wrong case, because the one I'm staring at is empty." Alec kicked the case, sending it sliding across the floor.

"Well, let me rephrase my last response. That case wasn't empty, but it is now. You see, you have just released a virus into the room. If my understanding is correct, by now you've all been exposed to it."

"Bullshit. I don't believe you," snarled Alec.

"Whether you believe me or not, right now the virus is making its way into each of your systems," explained Fisher. "According to Kaman, this particular bug should start kicking in and showing signs of infection within several hours."

"What virus did you expose us to?" asked Kayla.

"Oh, it's a nasty little thing. I asked Kaman for the deadliest one she could locate in the Q. And boy did she deliver."

"If you think I'm going to believe you would infect us with a deadly virus, you really must think I'm an idiot, Fish. There is no way you would knowingly kill anyone."

"Oh, I won't be killing anyone, Alec. Your death, and the death of all your frightening little Ghosts can easily be avoided if we get the proper antiviral drugs into your system in time. So, your lives are truly in your hands at this point."

"You want me to believe that if we don't give up the location of the ring, you'll let us die?"

"What choice have you given me, Alec?" yelled Fisher. "You've put me in a position where I have to choose between the lives of seven on the Arc or billions back on the Earth."

"I'm calling your bluff, Fish. The case was empty. You're not getting anything from us. Enjoy looking for the ring."

"I thought you might not change your mind. So be it. But before I go, I'd like to share some details of what the next twenty-four hours are going to look like for you and your Ghosts."

"Save your breath, Fish. We're not buying it."

"Humor me, then. I'd like to say that the symptoms are going to start gradually, but unfortunately, this beastly virus hits strong and fast."

Wow, thought Alec, *Fisher is upping his game with this little charade. Was that emotion I just detected? He's going full force. Perhaps this match can keep me entertained a bit longer than I expected. Let's see what he's got.*

Fisher continued, "First, your body will begin to ache all over and you'll start feeling feverish. That'll let you know that the virus has spread throughout your body and has really dug itself in nice and snug. Then, as the virus makes its way into your respiratory system, your throat will start to burn and constrict. The good news is, at this point there is still time to introduce the antiviral drugs to combat the virus."

"You're wasting your time, Fish!" yelled Alec, staring up at the ceiling.

"Time? Oh, I've got all the time in the world. Isn't that right, Alec? But you guys . . . once you start vomiting and experience diarrhea? Well, that's a clear sign that time won't be on your side."

"So, what are you going to do when none of us are showing any of these symptoms? Better yet, what are you going to do when we're all still alive, relaxing, while your precious deployment window passes you by?"

"Oh, don't worry. Kaman told me that the case held the full batch of the virus that was intended to be used on every crew member of the Arc over the course of the entire mission. I am quite confident that you'll be experiencing something very soon. I'd love to stay and chat, but I have a ring to find. Unless you are still interested in that trade."

"Dream on, Fish. You're full of it, and we all know it."

"Fair enough. But just to show that I'm not unsympathetic to your current situation, I'll try to make it as relaxing for you in there as I can."

The overhead lights dimmed as the Ghosts were suddenly surrounded by a gray, desolate sky and frozen tundra.

"I'll check back later to see if any of you change your mind."

"Don't bother."

Alec heard a click through the speaker, and the silence in the room was replaced with the sounds of wind blowing through the frozen landscape that engulfed them.

"I don't know about this," said Ron with a worried look. "Fish doesn't sound like he's fooling around."

"Yeah. I think you might have pushed him too far, Alec," added Paul.

"Guys! I've known Fish his whole life. He doesn't have it in him to carry this out. I'm telling you. That case was empty. There's no way—"

"I don't know, man. I'm not feeling so good right now," whimpered Vlad.

"Is anyone else getting warm? I'm starting to sweat," added Kayla.

"It's all in your head," said Alec.

"But what if it's not? I didn't sign up for this shit," quavered Paul.

"Yeah, it was fun watching their scared faces for a while, but I'm thinking that dying here in the Dome isn't exactly the way I want to go," added Deuce.

"You guys sound like them! Stop worrying, my friends. Kick back and relax. They'll come crawling to us, begging us to tell them where the ring is. We'll be back in the hive by the end of the day."

CHAPTER 71

Dom felt defeated, having just left the concourse without a single clue as to where the ring could be. He had hoped that he would discover something, anything that would point him in the right direction. His stress had increased as the day wore on and the ring was still nowhere to be found. Part of what had him so worried was not knowing what Fisher's end game was with Alec and the Ghosts. He trusted Fisher but couldn't help thinking that Alec might have the upper hand.

Dom was out of ideas and ready to check in with the others. Maybe someone had found the ring, or Fisher had convinced Alec to reveal the location. As he headed toward the observation deck, he saw Mia approaching.

"Find anything in the concourse?" she asked.

"Nope. I got nothin'. I take it you had as much luck as I did," he replied.

"I've been all over the ship, and the more empty-handed I become, the more I am questioning the obvious."

Dom waited for her to complete her statement, and Mia gave him a weird look.

"What?" he asked.

"Tell me you know what the obvious is."

"Well, yeah, of course . . . I just want to hear you say it."

Mia sighed and shook her head. "How sure are you that they didn't release the ring into space?"

Dom closed his eyes and felt the air escape his lungs. Obvious? This was the last thing he would have imagined Alec would do. "No way."

"Kayla and Deuce are outriggers," Mia pointed out. "They were trained right alongside of me. They have the knowledge and experience to do it."

"I mean, there is no way Alec would do that. He's not going to launch the ring into space. He just wouldn't go that far."

Mia looked at Dom and softly asked, "Did you ever think he'd be running around the Arc with a painted face?"

Dom stared at the floor, feeling somewhat ashamed that he was related to the person wreaking all this havoc on so many people. He refused to believe Mia's theory and searched for proof that it just wasn't possible. "Narine checked all the logs earlier today. She would have noticed if any airlocks were accessed recently."

Mia crossed her arms and said, "Maybe they changed the logs."

"I don't think any of them would know where to begin," he replied. "I know that Alec wouldn't know how, and I doubt that Ron or Paul from the engine room, or Vlad from the Center, would have a clue how to access that information."

"What about Kayla or Deuce?" she asked.

"From everything I have learned from Lance over the years, the outriggers never had access to system logs or data of that kind. That was all fed to them from the crew in operations. Were you ever trained on the system logs?"

"No, you're right, that was never part of our training. What about Bart from the Hold? Doesn't he spend most of his time on a computer in the office down there?"

"I can't say for sure, but I doubt he'd know how, either. I

think it's safe to say the ring is somewhere on the Arc," explained Dom. He was feeling a bit more relieved now that he had been able to counter Mia's scenarios. His arguments also seemed to shift her theory away from the unthinkable—at least for now.

"What happens if we don't find the ring?" asked Mia.

"I really don't know. To my knowledge, rings have always been deployed on time, without fail," recalled Dom.

Mia looked at the floor for a moment and then looked up at Dom and smiled.

"What is it?" asked Dom.

"This might sound crazy, but I may have an idea of where they could have hidden it."

Dom felt a surge of energy. "Crazy might just be what we've been missing from our search. Whatcha thinking?"

"Follow me to the protein chamber," she instructed as she started walking toward the stairs at the end of the corridor.

Dom followed her. "Mia, we've looked everywhere in the chamber that the ring could possibly fit. You've seen the size of the ring, there is no—"

"How tall would you say the ring is if it were laid down on the floor? Two meters maybe?" she asked as her pace quickened.

"I don't know. Maybe two meters, no more than two and a half. Why?"

"And the ring is about four meters in diameter pre-bloom, correct?"

Dom struggled to see where she was going with all of this. "Yeah, but—"

"When was the last time someone raked the protein pools?"

Dom's eyes widened, and a large grin swept across his face. "Oh, shit! Brilliant thinking, Mia!"

The two charged down the corridor in a full sprint.

CHAPTER 72

Fisher sat anxiously tapping his fingers on the desk in the Dome's control room. Each of the crew searching for the ring had checked in with the same bleak report, and there was still no word from Alec and the Ghosts. Fisher was beginning to worry. He replayed the morning's events in his mind, looking for anything he might have missed. Surely, they'd be experiencing even the beginning stages of symptoms by now.

"Fish! Enough with the tapping. You're driving me nuts," complained Sam.

"Sorry. Didn't realize I was—" Fisher jolted in his chair as Dom entered the room. "Tell me you got something, Dom!"

Dom looked at the floor and then back at Fisher. "Mia and I really thought we found it. But it was another dead end."

"Crap! You two were the only ones who hadn't checked in recently. I really hoped you found it."

"Sorry to be the bearer of bad news," lamented Dom. "I take it you guys haven't had any luck with Alec and his crew."

"Not a word," replied Sam.

Fisher sunk back into his chair. "Any minute now they'll—"

"Am I the only one starting to think Fish's plan may be a bust?" asked Dom. "Why don't we just go in there and beat the location out of him."

"We just need to remain patient," explained Fisher. "One of them has got to cave soon."

"And if they don't?" asked Sam. "Will you let them die?"

"It's not going to come to that, I promise," said Fisher, looking at the call box on the wall next to him.

Sam shrugged her shoulders. "It's been more than twelve hours, Fish. I thought you said—"

"Give me a second," interrupted Fisher as he muted the audio for the Dome, reached over to the call box and pressed the intercom button. "How are you Ghosts holding up in there?"

"You're not getting anything"—Alec coughed—"from us, Fish. You're wasting your time."

"You sure? That cough doesn't sound so good. How are the rest of you holding up? You know all it takes is one of you giving us the location of the ring, and you'll all get the drugs you need."

"Not going to happen, Fish."

"So you say. I'll be sticking around for another few minutes if you change your mind, but then I'm off to bed and won't be back until later. Come morning, well, I can't promise there will be time for the drugs to take effect."

"Ramble all you want, Fish. You're wasting your time."

"If you say so, Alec."

Fisher released the intercom button and leaned back into his chair. "Five more minutes."

"You keep saying that," said Sam, rising from her seat. "I'm starting to like the sound of Dom's plan."

"Do you really want to try to take on Alec and the others?" asked Fisher. "Have you seen the size of Ron and Paul? I mean, they've lifted power cells all day for the past two years."

"Maybe we can rush them when they're asleep. Catch them off guard," said Dom.

Sam looked at Fisher and pleaded, "All I'm saying is that the deployment window closes tomorrow. If we don't find the ring soon—"

"If they don't give in soon, we go with Dom's idea," interrupted Fisher.

Although Fisher was attempting to maintain a strong front, his resolve was beginning to waver. Perhaps his scheme wasn't as foolproof as he had hoped. It was difficult to remain patient when a huge deadline was looming. The ring needed to be deployed—tomorrow. Would they really have to resort to violence? All Fisher knew was that it was critical that the ring was found, by whatever means were most effective.

The call box speaker crackled, interrupting Fisher's thoughts. "Fish."

Everyone in the room jumped and looked at the call box. Fisher looked at Dom and Sam. "Did you guys here tha—?"

"Fisher"—Kayla let out a series of raspy coughs—"are you there?"

"I'm wrapping things up," replied Fisher. "Was just about to head out."

Kayla released a wet cough. "We're ready to talk!"

CHAPTER 73

Fisher, Narine, Sam, and Dom stepped out of the lift into the midsection of the cargo hold, donning their warm gear and hard hats. The chilled air nipped at Sam's face, making her wince. Even though the Hold was an uncomfortable place to be, she was happy to be involved with the rest of the crew while Grayson and Avery managed the Quints. While she loved her brothers, she had been feeling useless to the mission lately.

Shaking her head, Narine asked, "Of all the places to hide the ring, am I the only one who doesn't understand how Alec could choose this part of the Hold?"

"Right? Clearly Alec has snapped. I mean, this is just sick," rasped Sam.

"They must have known that none of us would think to look in there," said Fisher, looking back at Sam.

"That's because none of us are crazy like them," Dom reasoned. "It's actions like this one that make me question if Alec and I are really related."

"How much farther? I'm freezing," moaned Narine.

"It's just up ahead," replied Fisher.

"What if the ring isn't there?" asked Sam.

"Did you hear Kayla, Deuce, and Bart?" asked Fisher. "They were ready to do anything for the drugs."

"Ron and Paul didn't seem like they were putting up much of a fight, either," added Dom.

"Who would have guessed Alec would have been so stubborn? Does he really have that much of a death wish?" asked Sam.

"He would have come around eventually," replied Fisher.

Sam still couldn't believe that Fisher had concocted such a dangerous strategy. She understood the importance of releasing the ring, but this was a side of him that she never would have suspected existed.

"Let's just hope the ring is there," said Sam.

"Once we get the ring to the airlock, what's left to do?" asked Dom.

"As long as the Ghosts didn't damage anything when they moved it, the ring should be ready to go," replied Narine through chattering teeth.

"She's right. We should be able to release the ring midday tomorrow, giving us time to spare," added Fisher.

Sam couldn't believe how close they were to releasing the ring. She was eager for the week of upheaval to come to its conclusion. The stress of relentless ordeals had taken a harsh toll, and a successful ring deployment was sure to raise everyone's spirits.

"We're here," said Fisher, stopping in front of a set of double doors. "Remember, we just need to get in and out. Let's make this quick."

"No arguments here," said Dom.

Sam and Narine nodded in agreement.

Fisher paused, looking at the others. Sam had trouble maintaining eye contact with him. She couldn't believe what they were about to enter.

Looking at Sam and Narine, Fisher said, "Dom and I have already been here. I know how difficult this is going to be. Do you want me to describe what you're about to see? Will it make it any easier for you?"

Sam could only shake her head.

"Let's just get this over with, Fish," said Narine.

"Okay, but just know . . . in and out. We'll deal with it afterward."

Fisher lifted two large latches that held the doors closed and motioned to Dom.

"Dom, grab the other door." Fisher and Dom swung the doors open and stepped inside the mouth of the giant container.

"Activate the lights on your hard hats," instructed Fisher. "This container doesn't have any internal lights."

Sam turned her light on and took in a deep breath of the cold air. It stung the back of her throat. *You can do this,* she thought, as she took a step into the container. The groups' lights illuminated the interior of the container, revealing racks of HRPs that lined the walls from floor to ceiling. A thin layer of ice crystals coated the pouches, causing them to shimmer as light traveled across their surfaces. Sam did her best to not think about what lay inside the pouches, but her mind failed her, and she began to think about Helena and her parents.

"I'm sorry, guys," apologized Sam. "I don't know if I can do this." She choked back a sudden sob.

"It's okay, Sam. We're almost done. I can see the ring toward the back of the container," said Fisher.

Narine walked back to Sam and put her arm around her. "It's okay. Just a couple more minutes, and this will all be over."

Sam wiped her eyes and continued forward. Helena was in one of those awful bags. Her mom and dad were lying here, frozen.

The ring. Think about the ring. You can do this, she repeated to herself. Her stomach was beginning to turn.

She and Narine caught up with Fisher and Dom, who stood in front of the transport cart to which the ring was strapped.

"Looks like it's intact. I see no signs of tampering or damage," said Fisher.

"Let's just get this thing out of here and inspect it later," suggested Narine, looking at Sam.

The four of them grabbed hold of the cart, powered it up, and guided it out of the container. As Sam made her way through the container, she kept her eyes focused toward the floor, trying not to look to the sides. Alec-directed rage grew with each step she took inside the container. *How could he do this?* she thought. *How could he be so heartless?*

Moments later, the ring sat outside the mouth of the container. Fisher and Dom closed the doors and secured the latches back in place.

"You guys need to take a break before we head to the lift?" asked Fisher.

"No, we should keep moving," said Sam.

"Yeah, let's get the ring up to the airlock," agreed Narine.

"Great work, everyone," praised Fisher. "I'm proud of you. I think I can speak for all of us when I say I hope we don't have to revisit that container for a very, very long time."

"I can guarantee there'll be no do-over for me," said Sam.

Fisher walked over to Sam, hugged her, and whispered, "You are the strongest person I know."

Sam squeezed Fisher tight. He always knew the perfect words she needed to hear.

"So, does this mean you'll be delivering the antiviral drugs to the Ghosts now?" asked Dom.

"I'll have Kaman and Zach deliver some acetaminophen, and maybe you could make some hot soup as well."

"Acetaminophen?" questioned Narine.

"Wait. Isn't that what Dr. Gage used to prescribe for my headaches?" added Sam.

"How are hot soup and acetaminophen going to counteract a deadly virus?" asked Dom.

A mischievous smile appeared on Fisher's face. "No clue, but it does wonders for the common flu."

BLOOM

CHAPTER 74

A newfound energy propelled Fisher down the corridor. The geodetic ring was primed and parked in the airlock. Alec and his Ghosts were contained in the Dome, suffering their way through a heavy serving of the suck, and everyone was in place to aid in the deployment of the ring.

Just one final piece to the puzzle, and we're good to go, thought Fisher.

He entered the medical bay and saw Grayson and Lance engaged in what looked like a serious conversation. As Fisher walked closer, Grayson turned toward him.

"Hey, Fish. How are the preparations for deployment coming along?"

"Everything's all set. Sorry to interrupt," said Fisher, realizing he probably should have waited out in the corridor. He looked at Lance who was sitting against the wall, but Fisher couldn't read what state he was in.

Grayson smiled. "No worries. Lance and I were just finishing. I have to head over to the factory and grab Avery anyway. The two of us are going to be watching over the Quints in the observation deck. Since Sam cross-trained in operations, she's going to head there to help you guys today." Grayson looked back at Lance and gave him a nod. "Catch you after the deployment?"

"Yeah. I'd like that," said Lance, with a small nod back.

"Well, off to test my patience," Grayson said with a grin. "Wish me luck."

Fisher chuckled. "I don't envy you. Who knows? Maybe Sam will pay you back by taking some shifts in the engine room for you."

"Seems like a fair trade!" Grayson laughed as he left the room.

Fisher turned toward Lance, sensing that he might have come at a good time after all. Lance appeared to be in better spirits now. "How you holding up, Lance?"

"Good. I'm good."

"Looking forward to seeing you out of the Q. I was starting to think you might like it in there."

A corner of Lance's mouth raised, producing the first grin Fisher had seen from Lance in a while.

"Everything okay with you and Grayson?"

Lance looked at Fisher but didn't respond.

"Sorry. That's none of my bus—"

"I don't mind. I think things are okay. We talked about it, and he forgives me. I can't say I understand why, but he does."

"That's good to hear," said Fisher. "I'm sure he recognizes what you must have been going through when you discovered the news. It hit us all hard."

"But all of you kept it together. I—"

Kept it together? Fisher thought Lance needed a new definition of the word "together." "Are you kidding me? Have you seen Alec lately?"

Again, no response from Lance.

Changing the subject, Fisher said, "I've come to ask for a big favor."

"What's that?"

"I'm sure you're aware that we're deploying the ring later today."

"Yeah, Grayson filled me in on the nightmare you guys have been dealing with trying to locate it. I was happy to hear you found it. That was a pretty messed-up plan you concocted, Fisher."

"Yeah. I kind of surprised myself with that one," he said and smiled.

"What if Alec and the others had already been exposed to that strain of flu like Zach? How did you know they'd get sick?"

"Kaman."

"What do you mean?"

"I had Kaman access their files," Fisher answered proudly.

"Wow. You really thought it all through, didn't you?"

"Amazing what stress does for problem-solving. Anyway. Everything is in place. We just really need . . ." Fisher paused. "We really need you, Lance."

"Why? Toby can easily lead you guys during the deployment. He has just as many hours under his—"

"Toby is getting cold feet. He said he'd feel more confident if—"

"I don't know, Fisher. Do you know how hard it is for me to look at the rest of the crew? Every time I look at them, I think about what I took away from . . . Do you think Grayson would have forgiven me just now if he knew what I—"

"Lance, it's going to take time, but I honestly believe the crew is going to—"

340

"Fisher, even if the crew can somehow come to terms with all of this, I just don't think I can."

Fisher's voice softened. "We don't have to solve all of this today. We'll have plenty of time to address how to move forward. I'll support you any way I can. You know that, right?"

"I appreciate it. I don't get it. But I appreciate it."

"This could be your opportunity to make things right, Lance. Look, what you did ended up being a terrible accident, and I just know everyone will understand someday. But if you feel like you don't deserve their forgiveness, then maybe deploying this ring will somehow bring you some peace of mind. You could help everyone—the remaining crew and generations to come. You could guarantee that this mission does not fail. And that, my friend, would mean that our parents' legacy and honor would endure."

Fisher stood over Lance and extended his hand. "So, what do you say? You up for leading the most untrained group of outriggers on their first ring deployment?"

Lance stared at the ground for a long, hard minute. Fisher could see that he was contemplating something, but it was unclear what his answer would be. Glancing up at Fisher, a look of resolve settled on Lance's face.

"I'm in." Lance reached out and grabbed Fisher's hand, pressing it tight. "I'm in on one condition."

CHAPTER 75

"**T**HIS IS AWESOME!"

Dom's view was awash with stars. He thought about how each one of those stars was really a sun, and that each sun could potentially have planets orbiting them. His heart raced as he stared out at a luminous red star that looked so close he believed he might be able to reach out and touch it. He'd spent years peering out into the vastness of space, dreaming of the opportunity to experience a real spacewalk. He had finally come to terms with the fact that this dream would never become a reality. And yet, here he was, all thanks to Lance.

"Dom, this is Sam in operations. Do you read me?"

"Operations, this is Dom! I read you loud and clear!" he responded enthusiastically.

"Dom, looks like your heart rate is climbing and your oxygen consumption is increasing. I need you to try and relax," cautioned Sam.

"Roger that!"

"Oh, and Dom, please refrain from relieving yourself while you're out there."

"No promises, Operations."

Dom turned back toward the geodetic ring they had just moved outside the airlock. Lance and Toby detached the upper straps from the ring while Fisher connected the release cables to the outer shell.

"Operations, this is Fisher. How are we looking on time?"

"You guys are looking great. We have a solid two-hour window, so take your time."

"You guys ready to do this?" asked Lance.

"Ready!"

"Okay, just like we discussed. Dom, you and I will detach the lower straps," instructed Lance. "Toby, you and Fisher hold the release cable. Let's keep chatter to a minimum, guys. We need to keep this line clear."

Lance motioned to Dom, and Dom moved to the left side of the geodetic ring. Toby reached down and confirmed that the cable was tethered to the hull of the ship, grabbed the cable, and motioned to Fisher to stand in front of him. Fisher clasped the cable with both hands and widened his stance.

"Okay, when Dom and I release the ring, you guys need to be ready. We go on three." Lance looked over at Dom. "You wanna do the honors?"

Dom's eyes widened, and a giant smile engulfed his face. "Absolutely! You serious?"

"It's all you," Lance said with a smile.

Dom was relieved to find Lance back to normal and seemingly overnight, too. It gave Dom hope that maybe even a fraction of their former lives could resume once the deployment was complete.

"Okay, guys"—Dom reached down and placed his hand on the straps' latch—"we release in ONE . . . TWO . . . THREE!"

Dom and Lance pulled up on their latches, and the ring broke free from the straps. The geodetic ring moved slowly out of the docking station and away from the crew.

"Operations, the ring is on the move. Prepare to detach the umbilical," instructed Lance.

"Ready for detachment on your mark," replied Sam.

Dom and Lance joined Toby and Fisher and grabbed on to the cable. As the ring drifted farther from the crew, the cable straightened.

"Get ready, guys," announced Lance.

The cable pulled taut, and the crew lurched forward as the geodetic ring reached the end of it. The ring shifted from side to side as the outriggers held onto the cable. Minutes later the ring appeared to sit stationary.

"Operations, we have clearance," said Lance.

"Copy that, Lance. Detaching umbilical now."

Dom watched as the four smaller cables broke free from the ring, and the larger cable he was holding grew slack.

"Operations, I've got visual on cable separation. You are good to go," informed Lance.

"Firing stage two," said Sam.

Dom held his breath. The ring continued to drift farther away from the crew, clearing the back of the ship. Dom watched as the geodetic ring violently expanded, growing multiple times its size. The force of the expansion made the ring's components rock and sway for a moment before settling into place. Dom had watched this process for many years, but seeing it this close was astonishing. Everyone exploded with excitement.

The ring appeared to hover in front of the crew, and Dom was breathless for a moment. He had seen the ring in its collapsed state for years. Viewing it now, in all its expanded glory, created a sense of pride and pure awe that Dom had never experienced.

"Operations, we have visual. The ring has bloomed!" shouted Lance. "Good job, everyone."

"Operations here. Activating the motion drives."

"Copy that," confirmed Lance. "Will report back with visual confirmation."

Dom and the others stared out at the ring, taking in their accomplishment. Once the ring began to slowly spin, the deployment would be a success, and they could truly celebrate.

Lance placed his hand on Dom's shoulder. "Great work, Dom. I couldn't have asked for a better partner today."

"Thanks. I still feel like I'm dreaming. Remind me that—"

Fisher interrupted. "Guys . . . we might have a problem."

CHAPTER 76

"What do you mean problem?" asked Toby.

"The ring should have already started spinning," replied Fisher.

"He's right," agreed Lance, eyeing the ring. He went through a mental checklist of scenarios that would prevent the ring from spinning. "Operations, this is Lance. Can you confirm that the motion drives are live?"

"All systems read as live. Do you guys have visual confirmation?"

Lance looked back at the ring as it continued to drift away from them. "That's a negative."

"What happens if the ring doesn't spin?" asked Dom.

"Then eventually it will lose power and go offline," explained Lance.

"If the ring goes offline, it can't communicate with the other rings," added Fisher.

"That's correct," affirmed Lance. "It also means that the system that repositions the rings to keep them aligned wouldn't be functioning, which could change the transport ships' trajectories."

Dom looked at Lance. "What are we going to do?"

"Don't worry, Dom. We trained for this," assured Lance. "Operations, looks like the ring is going to need a manual kick start."

"Copy that, Lance."

As Lance walked to the payload bay near the airlock, he said, "Fisher, you up for navigating me to the motion drive's master propulsion system?"

"You're going out there?" gasped Fisher.

Lance stopped, turned back to Fisher and asked, "Do you know of an alternate way to manually activate the propulsion system?"

"No, I know. I just . . . you feel safe going out there on your own?"

Lance smiled. "I won't be alone. You're gonna be guiding me the whole way."

"Great . . . no pressure, huh?"

"You got this, Fisher. I trust you."

Lance backed into the manned maneuvering unit on the wall in the payload bay and snapped the life-support system into place. He unfolded the controller arms and adjusted their length.

"Operations, this is Lance. I'm detaching the MMU from the wall and switching to a private line with Fisher."

"Copy that."

"Fisher, switch to comm-line three," instructed Lance.

"Operations, this is Fisher. Switching to comm-line three."

"Copy that."

Lance exited the payload bay and disengaged the magnets in his boots. As he started to drift away from the outer hull of the Arc, he used his fingertips to manipulate the hand controllers at the ends of the MMU's two arms. Small amounts of gaseous nitrogen escaped from the nozzle thrusters placed at different locations on the MMU, allowing Lance to travel toward the geodetic ring. The distance from the ring continued to increase, but Lance felt confident he could reach it.

"Fisher, this is Lance. Do you copy?"

"Fisher here."

Lance continued to use the MMU's nozzle thrusters to close the gap between him and the ring.

"Don't worry, Fisher. I've practiced this many times. I just need you to point me to the right spot on the ring and walk me through it."

"Alright. See the four copper discs on the outer plating of the shell?"

"I see them."

"Okay, head to the lower right disc."

"On my way," affirmed Lance. He released a few small bursts of nitrogen from the forward-facing thrusters to decrease his speed as he approached the ring.

"Looking good, Lance," confirmed Fisher. "You're almost there."

Lance performed minute movements with his fingertips, sending bursts of nitrogen in multiple directions, allowing him to ease into contact with the ring. Lance reached out and grabbed the edge of the ring's outer shell with his right hand. Using his left, he connected a strap from his suit to an anchor point on the geodetic ring.

"Okay, Fisher, I'm good to go."

"Look for three nozzles in a triangular formation."

Lance surveyed the outer plating of the ring and quickly spotted the nozzles. "Got it."

"Perfect. If you look to the left of the nozzles, you should see a circular dial recessed into the panel."

"The one with the small red arrow pointing?"

"That's the one," confirmed Fisher. "Okay. Where's the arrow pointing?"

"Looks like it's pointing at a black solid dot."

"You need to turn the dial to the right so that the arrow is pointing at the empty red circle. That should open the pressure valve. Before you do, you'll need to detach yourself from the ring. You don't want to be connected when the propulsion system kicks in."

"Copy that."

Lance unhooked the strap from the ring, placed his hand on the dial and closed his eyes. All the past events that had brought him to this moment rushed his mind.

"Everything okay out there, Lance?"

"Here we go!" Lance opened his eyes, turned the dial and let go of the ring. Using the MMU, he increased the distance from himself and the ring and waited.

"How long should it take?" asked Lance.

"It should kick in any second now," Fisher answered.

Lance's eyes were locked onto the nozzles. Moments later, a small burst of gas sprayed out of the nozzles, and the ring slowly started to roll.

"You guys seeing this?" asked Lance as he watched the ring continue to spin.

"YES!" effused Fisher. "Excellent work, Lance!"

Lance looked down at Fisher and the others and could see them celebrating. A smile grew across his face. He was proud of what he and the team had just accomplished and knew it would bring much-needed hope to the rest of the crew. Lance's eyes began to fill with tears and his smile vanished.

"You're a real leader, Fisher. You should be proud."

"What are you talking about, Lance? You just saved the day!"

"I've always known you would make a great captain. I want you to know that," Lance said, his voice catching.

"Lance, head on back and let's celebrate. We can argue about who would make a better captain over a warm meal."

Lance continued watching the overjoyed crew, and his resolved expression returned.

"I'm not coming back, Fisher."

"What are you talking—?"

"I can't come back. I can't face the rest of the crew."

"Lance, of course you can. You'll get past this. We'll all get past this."

The ship continued to move farther away from him. Lance reached down, detached the MMU from his suit and pushed it away. He knew there was no return from the terrible acts he had committed. When Fisher enlisted his help, Lance had seen the opportunity to find a sense of redemption. Looking out at his friends now, he realized that no amount of grace from them could allow him to forgive himself.

"LANCE! What are you doing? You have to come back to the ship," pleaded Fisher.

"Tell everyone I'm sorry. Tell them—"

"It's not too late, Lance! Grab the MMU before it gets—!"

"Make sure Helena and our parents get a proper memorial. They deserve to be honored for their sacrifices and commitment to the mission. And make sure you all stay true to the mission. The Arc must reach Uelara."

Lance could hear Fisher screaming through the CCA. "LANCE! YOU CAN'T DO THIS! YOU HAVE TO—!"

Lance silenced his communication carrier as he drifted farther and farther away from the *Archean*. A sense of peace overcame him. He looked at the stars surrounding him and thought of Helena as he twisted his helmet to the side and removed it.

The coldness of space stung Lance's skin as images of Dom, Fisher, and the Arc flashed through his mind. *What the hell am I doing? I don't want to die!* he thought. Lance instantly realized that everything in his life that he thought was unfixable could be salvaged—everything except what he just did.

It was nearly impossible to breathe as he reached for his helmet, trying to secure it back onto the EMU. His muscles wouldn't cooperate, and as he struggled, everything went black.

CHAPTER 77

Dom, Fisher, and Toby sat in the locker room with the components of their EMUs scattered across the floor. Several minutes had passed without a word being spoken between the three of them.

"Help me one more time, Fish," said Dom, breaking the silence. "What the hell happened out there?"

Do I tell them? Fisher wondered. He had been grappling with the shock of hearing Lance surrender to the battle with his guilt, the trauma of watching him remove his helmet, and the confusion of how to explain both of these to his friends. Would Lance be remembered as a coward for not owning his actions, or would he go down in *Archean* history as a hero who sacrificed himself for the success of the mission? Fisher hated knowing that he held the key to determining the outcome of Lance's legacy.

His eyes traveled from Dom to Toby and then to the floor. "He said something was malfunctioning with his EMU. I tried to calm him down, but he—"

"I bet he panicked," interrupted Toby in a soft voice. "Stringer warned us that even the most seasoned outriggers have been known to panic while outside the ship. Hell, I freaked out on my fourth walk, and it took both Lance and Deuce to physically stop me from trying to remove my kit."

"What do you think he panicked about?" asked Dom.

"Anything. Lack of oxygen, possible leak, improper seal, itchy nose—you name it. Must have been something sudden and pretty bad to remove his helmet like that. He knows better," said Toby.

"I thought my eyes were playing tricks on me. What the hell? I can't believe we have to go through this again," said Dom.

"Again?" asked Toby.

"We just lost another friend! First Helena, then all our parents. Now Lance? Shit, shit, shit. I can't believe he did that. Shit! How the hell are we supposed to tell everyone that he just ended it out there?"

Fisher could see that Dom was struggling. He raised his hand. "All anyone needs to know is that Lance died while ensuring the mission continued."

After a brief silence Toby added, "You're right. Without Lance, the deployment would have failed. The crew should know that."

Dom looked down at the floor and murmured, "Man, I'm going to miss him."

"We're all going to miss him," echoed Toby. "I think what would—"

The door to the locker room swung open. Ashin was standing in the threshold. "Sorry to interrupt."

"Hey, Ashin. Everything okay?" asked Fisher.

"Kaman asked for help moving Alec and his crew to the Q, and we could use one more set of hands," he explained. "They're in pretty bad shape, and Kaman feels like the Dome isn't the ideal place for them at this point. I know you guys are probably wiped out, but—"

"I'll help," offered Toby. Fisher guessed that Toby was eager to find an escape from the reality that yet another crew member was gone.

"You sure?" asked Ashin.

"Yeah. I have a pretty good rapport with Deuce, and I was going to head over to see Kaman anyway."

"I hate to rush you, but do you have time now to head back with me?" asked Ashin.

Toby rose from the bench and walked toward the door. Looking back at Dom and Fisher, he said, "Impressive work today, guys. Let's make sure we celebrate the success of the deployment soon."

"I don't really feel that much like celebrating," replied Dom.

Toby looked at Dom and said, "I understand, but Lance would want us to. We should celebrate in his honor."

Fisher agreed, "Yup. In his honor."

"I'll catch up with you guys later," Toby said with a nod.

"What do you mean, in Lance's honor?" asked Ashin, looking confused.

Toby gave Ashin a pat on the back and sighed. "Fill you in on the way,"

Fisher sat across from Dom and struggled to find words to break the newfound silence that hung between them.

"I'm sorry," mumbled Dom under his breath, staring at the floor.

"Huh?"

"I'm so sorry, Fish."

"It's not your fault, Dom. None of us could have known that Lance's EMU—"

"No. I'm sorry I let Lance out that morning. If I hadn't—"

"What Lance did is not your fault."

"But if I hadn't let him out, none of this would have happened. The first gen would still be alive, and Lance would still be here."

Fisher hadn't considered that Dom could have been carrying a tremendous amount of guilt. So much chaos had consumed their lives during the past two weeks that Fisher overlooked Dom's involvement with any of it. What a heavy burden for anyone to carry. He knew he needed to set Dom straight.

Fisher walked over to Dom, sat next to him and slid his arm around Dom's shoulder.

"We'll never know what would have happened. But what I do know"—Fisher pulled him closer—"is that you can't own Lance's actions. None of us can."

"Can you forgive me?" asked Dom as a tear rolled down his face.

"There's nothing to forgive. You have a big heart, and you wanted to help a friend. I can't say I wouldn't have done the same."

"I'm really going to miss him, Fish."

"I know," lamented Fisher, as he ran his hand under his nose. "Lance and I had our issues, but I never forgot the friendship we had growing up."

Dom looked at Fisher. "What do we tell the others?"

Fisher straightened his back and declared, "We tell them that Lance's EMU malfunctioned, and he died a hero."

"But what about what he did to our par—?"

"You and I are the only ones who know the truth about what Lance did. I see no reason the others need to know about that. It won't change where we are today."

"Wouldn't you want to know the truth?"

"You know, I've been asking myself that question. Would I want to know the truth? It's hard to answer knowing what I know now. Am I better off than the rest of the crew because I know what really happened to our parents? Who's to say? What I do know is that all of us need to stay focused on this mission. Really, nothing is more important than that. I've never been more sure of anything in my life. And you know what else? I think I get it now. I understand why our parents waited to tell us about Uelara. Did their plan backfire in the worst way possible? You bet. But their intention was to make sure this mission is completed above all else. My father always said that this mission is not about you or me or anyone on the *Archean*. We never waver from the mission. I think I finally understand."

"Dude, I feel like I should be standing up and saluting you or something right now!"

Fisher laughed. "I'm serious!"

"So, what do we do now?" Dom asked.

"We celebrate," said Fisher. "We celebrate the release of the ring and the heroic efforts of our good friend."

"I like the sound of that."

CHAPTER 78

Fisher sat at the edge of the stage in the auditorium and stared out at the faces of the crew gathered before him. It felt like months since the last time all of the second gen had assembled like this, which reminded him just how much had happened in such a short period of time. A tinge of guilt tickled his mind as he reflected upon the lie he had fabricated. He hated keeping anything from his friends but believed he had made the right decision. Unveiling the truth of Lance's reasons for removing that helmet would only lead down a path Fisher had no interest in following. The truth would help no one at this point. The crew had been through enough. It was time to move on.

Grayson, Avery, and Mia entered the room and joined the rest of the crew. Fisher slid off the stage and stood on the floor, preparing to address the group. He cleared his throat and took a step closer to the front row where Sam and the Quints sat. "Everyone ready to get started?"

"Get on with it, Fisher, some of us have lunch to prepare," yelled Dom with a chuckle.

Several of the crew laughed. Fisher was happy to see that spirits were up and there was a new, positive energy that moved through the group. Fisher looked at Dom and smiled.

"If it's anything like breakfast," Fisher said, "I don't think anyone is in that much of a rush."

The crew laughed again. Fisher clasped his hands behind his back, looked at the floor, and took in a deep breath. He slowly exhaled, raised his head, and looked out at his friends.

"I'd like to start off by thanking each of you for your hard work over the past week. Without your efforts, we'd never have been able to keep the ship online and deploy the ring. We've had several close calls recently, and it feels good to have all that behind us. The first generation would be very proud of our accomplishments."

"Speaking of our parents, are we going to honor their . . . passing in some way?" asked Narine.

"Excellent question, Narine," replied Fisher. "Of course, we all want the opportunity to acknowledge the passing of our parents, as well as Lance and Helena, and to remember them as we knew them in life. This is something that would normally be arranged by the council. Until we've had time to form a new council, I think we should put a small group together to plan the details of the event. Would anyone like to volunteer?"

Avery slowly raised her hand. "I'd like to volunteer," she said in a soft voice.

"Me, too," added Mia, raising her hand.

"Ashin and I will help as well," added Narine.

Fisher looked out at the crew, waiting to see if anyone else wanted to volunteer. After a few moments, he continued. "Thanks for heading this up. If the four of you need anything, please reach out. I'm sure everyone here will be willing to assist with anything you need."

"What are we going to do about the Ghosts?" asked Toby.

"The first thing everyone needs to do is to stop referring to them as the Ghosts," replied Fisher.

"We can't keep them in the Q forever," said Finn.

"They still need to be held in the Q until they recover from the flu," explained Kaman. "My guess is that will be for at least another week."

"But what happens after that?" asked Toby.

"That's something we need to be thinking about," responded Fisher. "It's my hope that we can reintegrate them into the hives."

"I'm sure they were just acting out of frustration and grief," added Kaman. "Just like us, they have some healing ahead of them. Remember, these are our friends."

"Our friends who have been a pain in the ass and almost kept us from releasing the ring," huffed Ashin.

Fisher took in a deep breath and released it while collecting his thoughts. "I understand your concerns. I'm right there with you, but there is something I want all of you to consider. If they really wanted to prevent us from deploying the ring and sabotage the mission, they could have."

"What do you mean? If you hadn't tricked them into giving up the location, then we wouldn't have been able to release the ring in time," countered Ashin. "It might still be sitting down in the Hold."

"Kayla and Deuce could have released it into space," suggested Mia.

"If they really wanted to stop us, couldn't they have destroyed it?" questioned Dom.

"Dom and Mia are right," agreed Fisher. "Look, I'm not going to try to defend their actions. But I must believe that, given time, they'll—"

"They lost their parents just like the rest of us did," said Grayson, rising from his seat. "Who are we to dictate how something like that is going to affect someone?"

Fisher looked at Grayson and nodded. "We just need to work together to help them through this. I believe they will come out the other side of this and help us continue the mission."

"And if they don't?" asked Toby.

Echo slid to the end of his seat and raised his hand. "What if they continue to—?"

"Then we solve that problem when it arises," answered Fisher. "We have enough to deal with now. Let's not borrow trouble."

"Are you the new captain?" asked Sean, staring up at Fisher.

Fisher's thoughts drifted to Lance's final words. Was Fisher to become the new captain? Could he handle the responsibility of leading the crew of the Arc? He recalled some of his advice to Lance in the Q. He didn't have to have all the answers right now. Fisher looked down at Sean and smiled.

"Once we have a new council in place, they will decide things like that. I'm sure whoever they appoint to the position will make a fine captain."

"So where do we go from here?" asked Avery.

"We keep moving forward. We continue the mission," declared Fisher. "But right now, let's celebrate our victory. With the latest geodetic ring deployed, we have time to regroup, mourn the loss of our parents and friends, and work together to continue what they started."

"Do you think we are ready to continue on our own . . . without the first generation?" asked Avery.

"I believe so," stated Fisher. "I have to believe our parents prepared us for this. I'd like to think if my parents were here today, they would say the same. We just need to have faith in our training and in what our parents instilled in us. Most importantly, remember that none of you are alone in this mission."

As Fisher scanned the group sitting before him, he noticed a change. Was the crew talking differently? Was it a new energy in the air? As he considered this new dynamic, he caught a glimpse of Avery in his periphery. She was whispering to Grayson. Fisher thought she looked taller, somehow, and more at ease. Grayson, too, had a different, more resolute look.

Interesting, Fisher mused.

Fisher continued to search his friends' expressions as the crew had begun chatting among themselves. Zach was standing in the back row listening to Dom and Mia discuss something. It was the first time Fisher could recall Zach listening to a discussion without trying to hijack the conversation. He looked . . . mature.

Was it possible that there could ever be some positive outcome from such tragic, unthinkable events that they had all endured? Earlier, Fisher would have answered with a resounding no. And yet, he sensed a deep, impactful change had occurred with all his friends. Maybe surviving the worst forces people to become their best.

Fisher dismissed the crew and watched them slowly disperse. As dismayed as he had felt just days ago, a new kind of clarity was growing inside of him. Perhaps it was possible to move forward and continue life on the *Archean* with the purpose of the mission solidly planted in their vision.

Something tugged at his sleeve. Fisher turned to find Sam attempting to capture his attention.

"Got something I think you want to see," she said. "Meet me in the observation deck in an hour."

And things were going so well, he thought. "Sam, I swear I cannot take another surprise or drama or revelation or shock or anything else. That quota is officially filled for the next twenty years."

"Trust me. One hour."

CHAPTER 79

Sam's Log, Y20 D175

People of the Earth,

My name is Sam, and I will be the new author of these journal entries. The past two weeks have been filled with both tragedy and triumph. I'm not going to attempt to describe everything that has occurred in one piece of writing, but I'll sum things up as well as I can.

I am heartbroken to report that our dear Helena, original author of these entries, has died. The details of her death . . . I will share them in a later entry. I still need time to come to terms with it all. But know this: Helena believed in the light and hope of humanity more than anyone I know. We will all miss her terribly.

It is also devastating to report that due to a tragic accident, the entire first generation has died. It's nearly impossible to describe the painful impact this loss has had on the second generation. We all reacted to the news in different ways.

Perhaps the largest shocker of all is the fact that the *Archean* will not be reaching Uelara in thirty years. The second generation will live and die on the Arc. I'm guessing it will be common knowledge by the time this is read, but it was certainly news to us. Strange how writing these words makes this reality more straightforward somehow. I'm sure it's not difficult to imagine how tormented some could feel, learning everything they've been told was a lie. What's worse is that we never even got a chance to confront our parents or hear for ourselves their rationale for why they believed this deception was necessary. However, bitterness and resentment won't help accomplish the mission, and we are going to need to come together, overcome our sense of betrayal, and move forward—which brings me to my final update.

Lance led a crew in our most recent successful ring deployment. It would take me more pages than what remain in this journal to discuss the details leading up to and involving this event. What's important to note is that Lance's suit malfunctioned, and he didn't make it. It was pretty shocking. I think it's safe to say that Lance and I were less than amicable (and I'm guessing Helena may have shared that tidbit in prior entries), but I'll forever be grateful for his ultimate sacrifice and for saving the mission.

Fisher just held a meeting to discuss details of how we all should proceed. It's hard to say, but something has changed in him. Maybe we've all grown up a bit these past two weeks. I can think of easier ways to mature than what we've all endured, that's for sure! But what I also know is that we need to continue to hold the purpose of this mission in the forefront of our minds. I can say that I am proud of the crew of the *Archean*. Ultimately, we have put the fate of humanity ahead of our own interests.

Well, I think I'll end this journal entry on that note. Hopefully I can continue recording our travels as well as Helena did. It would be a wonderful way of honoring her memory. I'm meeting Fisher in a few minutes—I found something that will no doubt be a game changer for our crew. I'll share his reaction soon.

CHAPTER 80

Fisher stood in the west observation deck next to Sam, looking out at the borderless landscape of stars. It had been a while since he'd felt at peace, and he welcomed the wave of optimism that washed over him. He looked at Sam and noticed that she was looking at him in a strange way, almost as if she were studying him.

"You know what, Fisher?" she said with a smile. "I think I just might have you figured out."

"What do you mean?"

"You're a leader. I think it took everything we've experienced lately for me to see it, but you always have been."

His right eyebrow raised high on his forehead. "I think you may be spending too much time at your terminal."

"I'm serious. I'm proud of you," she said, looking at him.

"For what?"

"For everything. You did great today."

"Really? It's funny, because I think my anxiety took over, and now I'm struggling to remember what happened."

Sam turned to face her friend. "You were strong, and I think the crew really took in what you said. I think we're going to be okay."

"I think we're going to be okay, too."

Sam returned her sights back to the stars. The two stood in silence, each waiting for the other to speak.

"So, are you sure you want to go through with this?"

Fisher looked at Sam and asked, "Are you serious? Nothing in me wants to go through with this. But—"

"Do you think the others will be on board with it?"

"No idea. No one's talking about it. We could just pretend we didn't find the files, and I'm sure no one will notice."

"Fisher! No one's talking, but everyone's thinking about it."

Sam turned toward the bench behind her and picked up a sealed file folder.

"Have you opened it yet?" asked Fisher.

"No. I thought we'd open it together."

Fisher nodded.

Sam held the file up and ran her fingers across the embossed letters on the front of the folder. She turned the folder over, grabbed hold of the string, and unwound it from the button closure. She reached in, took in a deep breath, and removed the Pairing assignments.

AFTERWORD

When I first met William, he shared his story about a generation ship and its crew. He talked for hours about it. And he just kept talking and talking and talking. I had little choice but to absorb the story and became mesmerized by its characters and plotline. Soon enough, I was encouraging him to create more of this futuristic world.

The story became a part of our little family. We lived with these characters, and we took them everywhere we went—on long runs, on cross-country trips, to birthday parties, weddings and funerals, and even to dentist appointments. Our friends and family members were the patient, unfortunate souls who heard all about these characters, whether they wanted to or not.

After about five years, I began urging William on a weekly basis to write the story. He would launch into another, "You know what would be cool? If Lance suddenly . . ." And I would slap him on the shoulder and say, "Stop telling me and write it down!"

One night over a bottle of wine we made a pact that *2nd Gen* would be written. We had no clue how, but it was going to get done. Our problem was that neither of us had written fiction before. William had written or contributed to eighteen books, but they were all technical in nature. I had written a whopping one book, but it was a very *non*-fiction memoir.

367

I gave William the push, and he began to write. He quickly found that telling a story was much easier than writing it. He asked me to give it a go, so I gave it my all—all one night of an attempt. I was tasked with writing the description of a room on the *Archean*. Really? My knowledge of sci-fi was limited to 1.21 gigawatts for the flux capacitor.

We discovered that we were going to have to find a way to write this thing together. After several frustration-filled weeks, we finally crafted a method of cooperative writing that worked for us.

We found our groove writing the manuscript and were feeling optimistic about its completion. And then, editing time arrived. We were so fortunate to work with Gary and Carol Rosenberg, aka The Book Couple. They had helped me with my book, *Invisible Target*, and it was the most valuable contribution I received. We were eager to receive their feedback for *2nd Gen*. And then it hit us—William and I had to agree on all of our changes. Two strong-minded people agreeing on chapter, character, and even plot changes was brutal and not the least bit enjoyable. But we powered through it and emerged wiser.

Although we would love for at least one person (besides my mother) to read and enjoy *2nd Gen*, our true victories with this book rest in the completion of it and the fact that we have grown, both as individuals and as spouses.

So many people cared about Fisher and his friends along this writing journey. We want to thank all our colleagues, friends, and family who trudged through the trenches with us. I'm guessing they are more excited than we are about the book's release. They can finally stop hearing about it. Thank you all for your patience, feedback, and constructive and non-constructive criticism. It made the book better.

A very special thank-you goes to my son (and William's stepson) Zach. No one listened more to our incessant discussions than he did. Zach provided valid questions, strong opinions, useful input and a constant ear. We'll always reminisce about the writing of *2nd Gen* with Zach clearly in view.

And finally, William and I thank you for taking a chance and reading *2nd Gen*. Whether it becomes one of your favorite books or your favorite doorstop, we appreciate your support. We're going to miss this creative outlet. It feels like a sad good-bye in some ways. Who knows? Perhaps we will revisit the Arc and its crew at some point in the future.

ABOUT THE AUTHORS

Andrea moved to Southern California with her mother but quickly found herself the target of a group of bullies who studied karate at the Cobra Kai dojo. Fortunately, Andrea befriended William, an unassuming repairman who just so happened to be a martial arts master himself. He took Andrea under his wing, training her in a more compassionate form of karate and prepared her to compete against the brutal Cobra Kai. Andrea won the tournament with a crane technique that allowed her to deliver a disabling blow to her opponent's head using only one leg.

Oh, wait. That's the synopsis for *The Karate Kid.*

2nd Gen is the product of Andrea and William Vaughan's first attempt at writing fiction as well as writing together. Against all odds, the two completed this book and remain happily married anyway. Follow them at www.Uelara.com.